Every Tear a Memory

Other books by Myra Johnson

One Imperfect Christmas

Till We Meet Again Series
When the Clouds Roll By
Whisper Goodbye
Every Tear a Memory

Autumn Rains
Romance by the Book
Where the Dogwoods Bloom
Gateway Weddings (anthology of above 3)
A Horseman's Heart
A Horseman's Gift
A Horseman's Hope
Pearl of Great Price

Every Tear a Memory

Myra Johnson

Abingdon fiction™
a novel approach to faith

Nashville

Every Tear a Memory

Copyright © 2014 by Myra Johnson

ISBN: 978-14267-5372-5

Published by Abingdon Press, P.O. Box 801, Nashville, TN 37202

www.abingdonpress.com

Published in association with the Natasha Kern Literary Agency, Inc.

Macro Editor: Teri Wilhelms

Library of Congress Cataloging-in-Publication Data

Johnson, Myra, 1951-
  Every tear a memory / Myra Johnson.
    pages cm. — (Till we meet again ; 3)
  ISBN 978-1-4267-5372-5 (binding: soft back,trade pbk. : alk. paper) 1. Telephone
operators—Fiction. 2. Brothers—Fiction. 3. Disabled veterans—Fiction. 4. Triangles
(Interpersonal relations)—Fiction. 5. Hot Springs (Ark.)—Fiction. 6. Arkansas—History—
20th century—Fiction. 7. Domestic fiction. I. Title.
  PS3610.O3666E94 2014
  813'.6—dc23
                                                                          2014008452

Printed in the United States of America

1 2 3 4 5 6 7 8 9 10 / 19 18 17 16 15 14

For Johanna and Julena, my brave and beautiful daughters. I am inspired daily by your resilience, your courage, and your faith.

And for Miss Rose Hart Dale, my ninth-grade English teacher. I hope you know how dearly I cherish the encouragement you gave me.

Acknowledgments

On the office wall opposite my desk is a collage of photographs from my childhood. In one photo, I see my loving grandparents cradling my tiny, blanket-wrapped form. In another, I'm a little girl in white gloves, bonnet, and frilly pinafore. My favorite shows me at about two years old, on the lap of my grinning daddy. He's sitting on what looks like a wall or fence with his arm around my chest as if he's trying to keep me from leaping off into the unknown. The photos remind me of hope and innocence, of a time when life was sweet and the future full of possibilities.

My father died before my fourth birthday, so he never knew my love of story or my dream of writing books. Sadder still, my mother, who never remarried, slowly succumbed to failing health and depression, much like Joanna Trapp's mother in my story.

But life and faith have taught me that God is able to bless—more importantly, to *use*—every experience He sends our way. During those growing-up years, when I missed having a father and didn't understand my mother's bouts of sadness, imagination became my friend. In the stories I read and the stories I wrote, I found not just escape but catharsis.

More than thirty years would pass before my stories reached beyond family and close friends. Then I wrote and hoped and prayed through twenty-five more years before I saw my first novel in print. Ten published novels later, it still seems surreal.

Those books would never have come into existence if not for the people along the way who believed in, helped, and encouraged me. I know I'll forget someone important when I start naming names, but here goes.

To all my English teachers, especially Miss Dale, thank you for making good writing an important part of the curriculum.

Thanks to the friends and relatives who at least pretended to look forward to the creative (and sometimes crazy-weird) annual

Christmas letters I used to write. (My letters are a little tamer and a lot shorter these days, for which I'm sure you're grateful.)

Thanks to my husband, Jack, for hardly blinking when I asked for the money to enroll in the Institute of Children's Literature course back in the '80s. Though for many years your career kept you too busy to pay much attention to my writing life, thank you for never scoffing at my dream. I appreciate so much how in retirement you've stepped into the role as my first reader and unofficial PR guy!

To my daughters, Johanna and Julena, thanks for not begrudging (too much) the time Mom spent writing while you were growing up. Thanks also for not cringing when I used you and your friends as story fodder for those children's stories that kept hope alive until my first novel sold.

I can't forget my ICL instructor, Kristi Holl. Your patient teaching in the basics established a firm foundation of writing skills. Who knew I'd start out writing short stories for children and end up an inspirational romance novelist?

Thanks to Michael Dixon, the first editor to purchase one of my short stories, an ICL course assignment ("My Time, Your Time," *Alive! for Young Teens*, 1985). You gave me my first heady taste of writing success.

Thanks to all the writer's groups and critique partners I've learned from over the years, most recently the Tulsa and Charlotte chapters of American Christian Fiction Writers. It's such a blessing to share the writing journey with likeminded friends.

A big group hug and eternal gratitude to my ever-lovin' Seeker sisters: Audra Harders, Cara Lynn James, Debby Giusti, Glynna Kaye, Janet Dean, Julie Lessman, Mary Connealy, Missy Tippens, Pam Hillman, Ruth Logan Herne, Sandra Leesmith, and Tina Radcliffe. Find us anytime at www.seekerville.net. Ladies, you make every day fun and the writing gig less lonely!

Heartfelt thanks to all the editors I've worked with over the past six years. I learned so much from each of you about how to make a good book even better. I truly appreciate the opportunity to work with Abingdon Press fiction editor Ramona Richards and her staff. It has been a pleasure!

Huge thanks and a warm hug to my amazing agent, Natasha Kern, 2013 ACFW Agent of the Year. I don't know where I'd be without you, my dear friend! Through all the ups and downs of this business, your optimism and encouragement remain constant. I treasure your wisdom, guidance, industry knowledge, and (most especially) your unwavering belief that my stories matter. I thank God every day to be counted among your clients.

Finally, to my readers, thank you once again for allowing my stories into your lives and hearts. I love hearing from you, so please contact me anytime through my website, www.MyraJohnson.com.

And whatever you do, whether in word or deed, do it all in the name of the Lord Jesus, giving thanks to God the Father through him.—Colossians 3:17 (NIV)

Till We Meet Again

There's a song in the land of the lily,
Each sweetheart has heard with a sigh.
Over high garden walls this sweet echo falls
As a soldier boy whispers goodbye:

Smile the while you kiss me sad adieu
When the clouds roll by I'll come to you.
Then the skies will seem more blue,
Down in Lover's Lane, my dearie.

Wedding bells will ring so merrily
Ev'ry tear will be a memory.
So wait and pray each night for me
Till we meet again.

Tho' goodbye means the birth of a tear drop,
Hello means the birth of a smile.
And the smile will erase the tear blighting trace,
When we meet in the after awhile.

Smile the while you kiss me sad adieu
When the clouds roll by I'll come to you
Then the skies will seem more blue
Down in Lover's Lane, my dearie,

Wedding bells will ring so merrily
Ev'ry tear will be a memory
So wait and pray each night for me
Till we meet again.

Music by Richard A. Whiting,
lyrics by Raymond B. Egan

1

*J*ack's letter, still unopened, accused her from atop the dresser. Hard to ignore her name pressed deeply into the vellum in her brother's precise cursive, but Joanna Trapp wasn't in the mood for more depressing news from the home front. Not today.

After securing unruly straw-yellow curls off her face with tortoise-shell combs, she turned from the mirror and glanced at her friend Véronique, snuggled in a narrow bed beneath a faded quilt. No reason to wake the sleepyhead. Joanna had planned all along to face this day alone.

Pulling on a thick wool sweater, she slipped out of the tiny bedroom they'd rented at a local *pension* and crept down the narrow stairway. Aromas of baking bread, sizzling ham, and buttery eggs wafted from the kitchen, but Joanna had no taste for food. As she stepped through the front door, a brisk breeze whipped strands of hair across her cheeks. She tugged the sweater tighter around her and picked up her pace. Not for the first time she wondered if coming here had been a mistake.

She hadn't been out of the house five minutes before footsteps thumped the hard-packed dirt road behind her.

"You did not wait for me, *ma chère*."

Véronique's breathless reprimand halted Joanna's steps. She turned with a guilty smile. "You were sleeping so peacefully. I hated to wake you."

Catching up, Véronique linked her arm through Joanna's. "I told you I would be with you today. We go together, *oui?*"

"*Oui. Et merci.*" Utterly useless to argue with a friend as determined as Véronique. Drawing a bolstering breath, Joanna resumed her purposeful march.

The rolling expanse of the Champagne, pockmarked by grenades and artillery shells, stretched in all directions. Pale sprigs of sprouting winter grass barely concealed the scorched earth. The ruins of stone barns and farmhouses stood like tilting obelisks marking this place of death and devastation.

Joanna and Véronique kept to the road, avoiding the detritus of battle—shell casings, rusting mess kits, rotting boot leathers, sad reminders of the lives lost here. Ahead, the land sloped gently toward Blanc Mont Ridge, where a ragged copse of trees reached skyward. A dusting of autumn-hued leaves adorned skeletal branches but failed to disguise the blackened, disfigured trunks. How long would it take for time and nature to erase the ugliness of war?

Joanna's gaze followed the arcing tree line until she spied the remains of a trench. She stopped suddenly and pressed a hand to her stomach. With her other hand she gripped Véronique's. Three tiny words nearly choked her: "There it is."

Véronique pressed her temple to Joanna's and released a mournful sigh. Together they stood in the road, silence shrouding them, while Joanna envisioned the battle that had raged here one year ago—the cannon fire, machine guns, grenades, and flamethrowers. The screams of the wounded. The pain, the sacrifice, the unflinching patriotism in the face of certain death.

A former "Hello Girl" with the Army Signal Corps, Joanna had come to France seeking adventure. She never expected to fall in love with a soldier, much less envisioned standing only meters away from the spot where he'd died.

Véronique tucked Joanna beneath her arm. "Now you have seen it. We should go back."

"I can't. Not yet." Joanna edged away, the gaping wound of the trench beckoning her.

"You must not leave the road," Véronique warned. "There could still be explosives—"

"I don't care." A fatalistic sense of bravado heated Joanna's chest. Striding toward the trench, she pictured Walter vaulting over the lip in what would be his final charge at the enemy. Did he hear the whistle of the artillery shell rushing toward him? Did he know the moment of impact, count his last breaths, feel his lifeblood draining into the earth?

"Joanna. You must stop." Firm hands clamped her wrists, and Véronique's pleading gaze pinned her to the spot.

The effect was like a cold slap to the face, wrenching Joanna back to the present. She blinked several times and forced her paralyzed lungs to take in air. A tremor snaked down her limbs, but she refused to cry. Tears wouldn't bring Walter back.

Clarity returning, she straightened and attempted a reassuring smile. "I'm all right now. It's just . . . harder than I expected."

"And why?" Véronique's eyes held both sympathy and reproach. "Because your sweetheart was killed here. You have never allowed yourself to fully grieve."

"I had a job to do." Once again, Joanna's glance drifted toward the ridge. She stifled a moan. "We all did."

Gently but firmly, Véronique nudged Joanna toward the road. "Perhaps, but one day you will pay the price for holding your grief inside."

Their return to the village of Saint-Étienne seemed endless. By the time they reached the *pension*, Joanna's steps had grown leaden, her chin drooping ever closer to her chest.

"Ah, you have returned!" Speaking in French, Monsieur Leveque, their rotund innkeeper, met them at the door. "Rather early for long walks, is it not? You must be perishing from hunger. Madame has kept breakfast warm for you, though I daresay the eggs will be hard as stones."

Out of politeness, Joanna followed Véronique to their seats at the rustic trestle table in the dining room and allowed Madame Leveque to serve her an ample portion of eggs and ham. Monsieur had exaggerated, though, for the eggs melted in her mouth like rich cream. No doubt the couple had taken extra pains to treat their only guests well. Not only had the war decimated France's economy, but many villages near the front had been reduced to rubble and now struggled to rebuild. Damage to the Leveques' *pension* had been significant, evidenced by plaster patches in the ceilings and walls as well as the cracked, mismatched pottery on which Madame Leveque served her delicious meals. When Joanna paid her bill upon their departure, she intended to add a sizable gratuity.

Two cups of coffee later, and with her plate mopped clean with a thick slab of Madame Leveque's crusty bread, Joanna felt a measure of optimism return. She was a survivor, after all—an adventurer—the qualities Walter had admired most. Tears were a waste of time. To continue living life to the fullest would be the best way to honor his memory.

She patted her abdomen as she eased her chair away from the table. "*Merci beaucoup*, Madame. *C'était délicieux*—better than the best restaurants in Paris."

The gray-haired matron clapped her hands together. "You will tell your friends, *oui*? Send them to Saint-Étienne for a lovely stay in the countryside?"

"But of course!" Véronique crumpled her napkin and rose. "Your hospitality is unsurpassed."

On their way upstairs to freshen up, Joanna whispered, "You don't think all those compliments will go to their heads, do you?"

"What of it? We have spread a little joy into their lives." In their room, Véronique plopped onto the bed, her feet dangling over the side. Her mouth stretched open in a gaping yawn. "A long walk, a big breakfast, and I am ready to sleep again!"

Joanna chuckled as she shrugged out of her sweater. "Shall I wake you in time for lunch?"

"Please do." Véronique kicked off her shoes. "Pull the shades, will you?"

"My, but you're bossy." And the best friend Joanna had ever known. She couldn't help being thankful her companion had insisted on coming along on this pilgrimage. Véronique's pragmatism provided the perfect balance of strength and good cheer, exactly what Joanna had needed to survive the past year.

Smiling over her shoulder, she went to the dresser to brush her windblown hair—only to be drawn up short at the sight of her brother's letter. She should never have brought it along, and certainly wouldn't have if the postman had not arrived with the mail at the same moment she and Véronique walked out the door of their Paris flat two days ago. Joanna had stuffed the letter in her handbag, intending to read it once they'd settled into a room at the *pension*, but then she'd talked herself out of it.

More than once.

Now she'd run out of excuses. A glance at Véronique revealed she'd drifted off to dreamland. Honestly, the girl could sleep hanging from her toes in a rainstorm with a locomotive thundering past. Joanna wished she could nod off half so easily. Unfortunately, she'd been cursed with a brain that didn't know when to shut itself down at the end of a busy day.

And now she knew her mind wouldn't rest until she'd opened Jack's letter and filled herself in on the latest doings back in Hot Springs, Arkansas. Bracing herself for another onslaught of her brother's pleas for her to come home, she sank onto the bed by the window and tore open the envelope.

Hot Springs, Arkansas

"Of course I'm happy for you, Clare." Thomas Ballard willed his mouth into what he hoped passed for a congratulatory smile and fought to ignore the twinge between his shoulder blades. "You and Elliott have been wanting to start a family ever since the war ended. It's just—"

"I know, sir." The Arlington Hotel's blushing switchboard operator leaned forward and rested one hand on Thomas's desk. "I hate leaving you in a bind just when the busy winter season begins, but I simply wouldn't feel right about continuing to work after I'm . . . you know . . ." If her plump cheeks turned any redder, she could pass them off as ripe tomatoes.

Thomas suspected his own face had taken on a crimson hue. All this talk of babies and delivery dates made him extremely uncomfortable.

Not to mention envious. Happily married couples surrounded Thomas these days—radiant sweethearts who would probably soon be starting families of their own.

He cleared his throat and forced his attention to the matter at hand. Consulting a calendar, he counted off weeks. "Would you be amenable to staying on through Thanksgiving? I don't see how I can find and train a replacement much before then."

Clare pursed her lips. "I'll be nearly five months along."

"Perhaps you could . . ." With flicking fingers, Thomas motioned vaguely toward her attire.

"Wear something loose?" An acquiescent sigh hissed between her clenched teeth. "I suppose, so long as morning sickness doesn't do me in first." As if to prove her point, she covered her mouth to suppress a tiny burp.

Thomas shoved the calendar aside, his own stomach feeling none too steady at the moment. "Let's see how it goes, shall we? I'll place an ad in the paper and hope for a quick response."

Clare thanked him and stood. "I'd best get back to the switchboard before Austin gets too many lines crossed."

As she exited the office, Thomas's telephone rang. Grateful for anything to get his mind off this conversation, he snatched up the earpiece. "Thomas Ballard."

"Oops. Sorry, sir, I meant to ring housekeeping."

At the sound of the desk clerk's flustered tone, Thomas suppressed a chuckle. "It's all right, Austin. Clare's on her way."

"Thank goodness! By the way, your mother telephoned. I told her you were in a meeting."

"Good thinking." No time was a good time to take a call from Evelyn Ballard. "Did she leave a message?"

"She asked me to remind you of your dinner engagement this evening at your brother's."

"Thank you, Austin." Hanging up, Thomas checked his watch. Still another hour before quitting time, but he dare not be late getting home. This dinner engagement was all his mother had talked about for several days. With Gilbert's new bride, Mary, nursing him back to health after he'd been trampled by a horse, Mother had been sending meals out to the farm several times a week. This evening, however, they would deliver dinner in person, complete with Mother's best china, silver, and stemware—a belated wedding celebration since the couple had married in the hospital and had yet to enjoy a proper honeymoon.

The humor in all this was that Thomas's mother rarely set foot in her own kitchen other than to instruct Marguerite concerning the daily menu requests. Still, Mother's display of goodwill toward Gilbert's new bride boded well. Evelyn Ballard had resisted Gilbert's relationship with army nurse Mary McClarney with every ounce of her society-minded, blue-blooded bias.

Nor had Mother been especially kind to Gilbert's German-born housekeeper. After rescuing the widowed and destitute Katrina Frederick from near-starvation, Gilbert had purchased her farm and then graciously provided the woman with permanent living quarters in exchange for both her farming expertise and household management skills. Mrs. Frederick, as Thomas well knew from boyhood days playing with the Frederick children, was an excellent cook and more than capable of tending to Gilbert and Mary's needs. Thus, Thomas could only hope his mother's recent benevolence was in truth an act of atonement.

Thomas's telephone jangled again. Startled out of his thoughts, he lifted the earpiece and muttered a gruff greeting.

"Sorry to bother you again, sir," Austin, the front desk clerk, said. "Jack Trapp is here delivering the order from Kendall Pottery, and he'd like a moment if you're free."

"Certainly. Send him in." Clicking off, Thomas shuffled papers around his desk until he found the Kendall Pottery purchase order. Jack surely wouldn't be expecting a check already. Usually Mr. Kendall billed the hotel at the end of the month.

The office door creaked open and Jack stepped in, smoothing an unruly blond curl off his forehead. "Hope this isn't a bad time."

"Not at all." Thomas stood and reached across the desk to shake Jack's hand. "We aren't late with a payment, are we?"

Puzzlement flickered in Jack's eyes. "No, it's just . . ." He released a slow sigh. "I know my grandmother sent a note right after the funeral, but I've been meaning to thank you in person for sending the flowers. Mama would have loved them."

"I wish I could have done more." Remorse formed a knot in Thomas's stomach. Here he'd been worried about staffing issues and invoices while Jack and his little sister grieved the loss of their mother. "How is Lily holding up?"

"Not so good, I'm afraid. Grandmother is at her wit's end." Collapsing into the nearest chair, Jack knotted his hands between his knees and drew a ragged breath. "We knew Mama was tired and despondent—even more so after Dad died last year—but I never thought her health would decline so rapidly." His voice broke, and he looked away with a sniff.

Thomas swallowed hard to see such agony in his friend's face. Coming around the desk, he took the chair next to Jack's and wordlessly patted his shoulder. How did you comfort someone over such a difficult and unanticipated loss? Mrs. Trapp's obituary had tactfully alluded to what her family and closest friends believed: *The grieving widow and beloved mother of three has at last escaped the bonds of this earth and found the peace she sought, joining her recently departed husband in the heavenly choir.*

Giving Jack a few moments to compose himself, Thomas filled one of the water glasses on the corner of his desk and pressed it into Jack's hands. "Any word from Joanna?"

"Nothing yet, but hard telling when my letter would have reached her."

Thomas furrowed his brow. "You didn't send a telegram?"

"I should have, I know, but how could I tell her in a few short words that our mother died of a broken heart?" Jack's mouth twisted into a grimace, and he blew out a noisy sigh. "Joanna would never have made it home in time for the funeral anyway, and writing it all out in a letter made it easier to break the news."

"But still . . . don't you think she'd have wanted to know?"

"You obviously don't know Joanna."

Thomas had to admit he didn't know her well. Joanna had been a year behind him in school, and not particularly sociable. He did remember she'd had a rebellious streak. "So Joanna and your mother didn't get along?"

"They were always at odds." Jack took a sip of water then set the glass on the desk. He rubbed his palms up and down his pant legs. "Mama never could understand why Joanna wanted to go away to college. Then to choose career over family—and this whole business of enlisting with the Signal Corps."

"It had to be hard on your mother, having both you and your sister over in France with the war raging."

"Equally hard on Lily, especially after Dad died. At least I made it home soon after. Lily was only fourteen then, not an age when a girl needs to be burdened with her mother's . . ."

The unspoken reference to Mrs. Trapp's emotional instability hung between them. Thomas sat straighter, nervous fingers gripping the chair arms while he tried to think of something helpful to say. People simply didn't speak of psychiatric disorders in polite society, although the term *shell shock* had certainly come into common usage as soldiers fighting in the Great War came face-to-face with battlefield carnage. Thomas had seen such mental anguish firsthand while his brother, Gilbert, recovered from war wounds. Gilbert's friend Samuel, an army chaplain, had barely survived his own emotional trauma.

But a young girl losing her mother to mental illness? And not just in death but one painful day at a time through worsening bouts of depression. No wonder Lily Trapp was so troubled. Rumors abounded among their congregants at Ouachita Fellowship—Lily caught smoking behind the school building, filching the latest issue of *Harper's Bazaar* off the Schneck's Drugstore magazine rack, locking lips with the star of the high school football team.

Jack rose abruptly, clearing his throat. "Look at the time, will you? Mr. Kendall will wonder if I got lost en route."

Following Jack to the door, Thomas halted him with a touch on the elbow. "If there's anything I can do . . ."

"Just pray Joanna comes to her senses and gets herself home where she belongs."

"Three weeks. She's been dead three weeks and I didn't know!" The wind in Joanna's face whipped the words from her mouth even as she spoke them. Why hadn't Jack wired her immediately?

Véronique shrieked a French curse when the motorcycle bounced over a pothole and nearly tossed her out of the sidecar.

"Slow down at once, or your mother will be greeting the two of us at Saint Peter's gates before this day ends!"

Reluctantly, Joanna eased back on the Indian's throttle. She'd been battling an unholy mix of anger and grief since reading Jack's letter yesterday. She could forgive him for wanting to explain everything in a lengthy letter, but how could their mother have simply given up like this—on her children, on *herself*? Such weakness, such utter self-absorption, made Joanna want to scream.

The bottom line is I can't raise Lily alone, Jack had written. *Please come home, Joanna. If not for me, then for your little sister. She needs you.*

Their grandmother had come to stay temporarily, but she was getting up in years, and Joanna couldn't imagine her coping with a difficult adolescent without risking her own health.

So now, going against every conviction she held, every plan she'd made for life on her terms, Joanna had no choice but to return to Paris, pack her things, and book passage on the next ship bound for the States.

Véronique tapped her arm, then pointed up ahead. "A village—let's stop for lunch. I'm starved."

Tasting grit between her teeth, Joanna realized her thirst. Why she was in such a hurry to begin the dreaded journey home, she had no idea—except she couldn't help worrying about Lily. Jack was a wonderful brother and a hard worker, but how could he know anything about the needs of a fifteen-year-old?

Shutting off the engine in front of a roadside café, Joanna climbed from the motorcycle seat. Her body still thrummed from road vibrations as she offered a hand to Véronique in the sidecar. She avoided her friend's annoyed glare as they both tugged off their goggles. "We should wash up before we eat. I'm sure I look as awful as you."

"I am certain you look much, much worse." Using the tail of her scarf, Véronique scrubbed at the road dust coating her cheeks and forehead. With a huff, she marched into the café. "I cannot wait to get home and take a long, hot bath."

By the time they'd freshened up in the *toilettes* and had eaten their fill of ratatouille and brown bread, tempers had eased. Seated at a small table on the veranda, Joanna waved away cigarette smoke drifting toward them from nearby diners. She gazed up the narrow village street at buildings scarred by bullets and shellfire. Again she wondered if France would ever recover.

"So sad," Véronique said as if reading her thoughts. "You Americans are lucky. You can go home to things as they were. The French must live with war's reminders every day."

Joanna slid her eyes shut. An image of Walter vaulting out of the trench at Blanc Mont Ridge wavered behind her lids. "Over a hundred thousand Americans dead, twice as many wounded, and we're *lucky?*"

"Forgive me, I know full well what the Americans sacrificed for us. But remember, the French were fighting for almost three years before your President Wilson brought the United States into the war." Heaving a shaky breath, Véronique brushed wetness from her cheek. "France lost over a million of her sons, brothers, husbands, fathers."

"I know. . . . I know." Joanna reached for her friend's hand. "Let's not argue, okay?"

"*Mais non*—of course not. You are leaving soon, and it breaks my heart!"

Joanna's throat shifted as she swallowed unshed tears. "You could come with me."

Véronique shook her head. "I could never leave France. This is my home."

"Mine, too, now." Blinking rapidly, Joanna looked away.

"No, *ma chère*, your home is with your family. They need you far more than you are needed here."

2

"Why should I go with you?" Lily Trapp stomped across the kitchen, feeling every jolt from her soles to her eyebrows. She dropped her schoolbooks onto the table with a thud. "I hardly even know Joanna. I was just a little kid when she went off to college."

"You're *still* just a little kid," her brother snapped. "Or at least you act like one. And you're going with me to meet the train whether you like it or not. Now get yourself out to the car this second before I toss you over my shoulder and wallop you good."

"I'd like to see you try!" Even so, Lily didn't trust the look blazing in Jack's eyes. She flounced out the back door with just enough sass in her step to let him know he couldn't boss her around so easily.

It was the second time in a week they'd made the trip to the depot. Too bad Grandmother couldn't stay longer, or maybe Jack wouldn't have been so anxious for Joanna to come home. For goodness' sake, Lily was fifteen years old. She did *not* need a babysitter. Much less both her older brother *and* their sister running her life.

Just as she yanked open the passenger door, someone called Jack's name. She looked up to see their neighbor Mrs. Kendall crossing the street.

The dark-haired woman smiled sweetly as she approached. "So today's the day?"

Jack turned, standing in the open driver's-side door. "Sure is, Mrs. K. We're just leaving to meet Joanna's train."

"You'll have your hands full getting your sister settled after her long trip, not to mention she'll be exhausted." Mrs. Kendall stepped up next to Lily and tucked her arm around her waist. "Why don't you all come over for supper later? I baked a cherry pie this morning, and I have a savory pot roast in the oven."

"Very kind of you." Over the roof of the car, Jack offered a relieved smile. "We should be home in an hour or so, provided the train's on time."

"Perfect. And I wonder . . ." Mrs. Kendall smoothed one of Lily's curls off her shoulder. "Maybe you'd leave Lily here with me. I could use her help setting the table and such, and I imagine Lily has school assignments she should finish for tomorrow. We could have it all wrapped up before you return with Joanna."

Lily shot Jack a hopeful glance. "That's a great idea, don't you think? And you'll have more room in the car for Joanna's stuff. I bet she's bringing *tons* of luggage."

Jack's jaw worked. He glared at Lily through narrowed eyes. Finally, he said, "Okay, but you mind your manners. And no dallying with your homework."

Muting a grateful sigh, Lily slammed the car door. "I'll get my schoolbooks and be right there," she told Mrs. Kendall before darting into the house. By the time she'd gathered her books and pulled the kitchen door shut behind her, Jack had backed out of the driveway. He cast her another warning glare through the windscreen before turning up the street.

Catching up with Mrs. Kendall on her front porch, Lily heaved a groan. "Thanks for saving me, Mrs. K. I did *not* want to go with Jack to the depot."

The woman gave her a peculiar frown. "I didn't do this for you, dear. I did it for Joanna. The last thing your sister needs after her long journey is to deal with you and Jack arguing like rabid cats and dogs." When Lily's mouth dropped open, Mrs. Kendall continued, "Don't look so surprised. Why, the entire neighborhood can surely hear the bickering when you leave for school each morning."

"But Jack is so—"

"Jack is doing his best to take care of you." Mrs. Kendall ushered Lily through the front door. "Now sit yourself down at the kitchen table and start on your schoolwork while I finish with supper."

"But I—"

Lifting one eyebrow, Mrs. Kendall silently pointed toward the kitchen.

Lily lowered her gaze and hugged her books to her chest as she trudged past the staircase. Even before she entered the Kendalls' warm, welcoming kitchen, the tantalizing aroma of pot roast and potatoes teased her nostrils. Mama had never been much of a cook, and since Grandmother left, Lily and Jack had been subsisting on leftovers. It would be wonderful to taste a hot, home-cooked meal again.

Even more wonderful would have been having a mother like Mrs. Kendall. Now the best Lily could hope for was that Joanna would stay only long enough to help dispose of their mother's things and then go back to France where she belonged.

Because a bossy big sister was the *last* thing Lily Trapp needed in her life.

"No, Austin, this is still Thomas Ballard, *not* the maintenance department."

"Sorry, sir. I keep getting these blasted lines crossed." With a frustrated groan, the desk clerk clicked off.

Frustrated, too, Thomas slammed down his telephone earpiece. Clare had been out with morning sickness more days than she'd reported to work the past couple of weeks. Unfortunately, Thomas's only part-time switchboard operator wasn't interested in increasing her hours, and his employment ads hadn't brought in many promising applicants for the full-time position. Either they didn't have the necessary experience, or they weren't willing to work the late shift. Thomas had already promised the day shift to Lillian Zongrone, next in line in seniority.

He shoved his chair away from the desk and raked stiff fingers along his temples. Maybe he'd been too quick to wean himself off the Camels his mother detested, because he sure could use a smoke right now. Before he bit someone else's head off, maybe he should get out of the office and walk off some of his annoyance. Donning his gray suit coat, he strode to the outer office and informed his secretary he'd be back in an hour.

Five minutes later, he strolled the magnolia-lined walkway along Bathhouse Row. Rolling stiff shoulders, he found himself sorely tempted to stop in at the Fordyce and ask for a massage appointment. Except afterward he'd never convince himself to return to the office, and, like it or not, he still had plenty to do.

Across the street, a shopper exited Annemarie Vickary's ceramics shop. Bearing a carefully wrapped vase-shaped package, the gentleman wore a triumphant grin. Another satisfied customer, no doubt. The daughter of pottery factory owner Joseph Kendall, Annemarie had quite the reputation around town for her artistic creations.

Annemarie also would have been Thomas's sister-in-law if his brother hadn't gone half-mad after the war and broken things off with her. Now she was happily married to U.S. Army chaplain Samuel Vickary, but Thomas still thought of her as the sister he never had. Maybe he'd pop in and say hello.

Dodging traffic, he darted across Central Avenue and leapt to the sidewalk in time to avoid a passing trolley. As he pushed open the shop door, a tiny brass bell tinkled.

Annemarie looked up from wrapping a package, her smile spreading wide. "Thomas, what a nice surprise!"

He glanced around the shop, noticing several vacant spaces on the display shelves. "Business must be good."

"It seems some of my customers have started their Christmas shopping early. I also have a number of special orders to fill." Annemarie nestled the wrapped piece in a small wooden crate and set it behind the counter. "Sam won't be happy I've accepted all this extra work . . . especially now." Her smile softened into a blushing sigh.

"Oh, no. Don't tell me—"

"It's true. We'll have a new addition to our family in about six months."

"Annemarie, how wonderful." Thomas edged around the counter to wrap her in a brotherly hug. "If I didn't know better, I'd think there was something in the water."

Leaning away, Annemarie cast him a curious look. "Not Gilbert and Mary . . ."

"Not that I know of, anyway. Besides, Gil's still healing. I don't think they—I mean—" Heat suffused his face. Giving a nervous chuckle, he shoved his hands in his pockets. "Actually, I was talking about Clare, my switchboard operator at the hotel. She gave notice a couple of weeks ago." He described his difficulties finding a suitable replacement.

Touching one finger to her chin, Annemarie pressed her lips together. "You know Joanna Trapp put herself through college working as a telephone operator. It's one reason she was accepted so quickly into the Army Signal Corps."

"I hadn't thought of Joanna." A spark of hope ignited in Thomas's chest. "Do you suppose she'll be looking for work while she's in town?"

Annemarie snatched up a feather duster then marched to the display in the front window. Arching a brow, she paused and turned toward Thomas. "I suspect Joanna's the kind of woman who wouldn't be satisfied to *not* be working."

Hot Springs, Arkansas. A cosmopolitan city, to be sure, but it wasn't Paris.

Reeling with exhaustion, Joanna tugged her valise from the overhead rack and worked her way down the aisle. Nearly two weeks aboard ship for the Atlantic crossing had allowed her body to adjust to the time difference, but lazing about the ocean liner had proved a boring waste of time and intellect. It hadn't taken her long to miss the challenges she'd left behind as part of the effort to improve conditions in postwar France.

Now, all she had to look forward to was riding herd over a balky teen—a daunting challenge in itself.

Just not the kind Joanna felt remotely qualified to take on.

Stepping to the platform, she scanned the area in search of her brother's blond head. Had he changed much since his war service? The last time she'd seen Jack was the summer of 1917 when his unit, among the first to be deployed, passed through New York on their way overseas. Though Joanna had joined the Army Signal Corps less than a year later and shipped off to France as well, their paths never crossed. Their only contact had been through letters and the one time they happened to connect by telephone when Jack placed a call from his commanding officer to General Pershing.

Hearing her little brother's voice had brought a lump to her throat, and for a moment it was as if she'd forgotten how to work a switchboard—until her supervisor stepped up behind her with a firm but quiet reprimand.

"Joanna! Over here!"

She snapped out of her reverie to see Jack striding across the platform. Offering a tentative wave, she firmed her grip on the valise and started toward him. "Hey, little brother!"

A second later, she struggled for breath in Jack's stranglehold of a hug. "I've missed you, sis! Good to have you home at last."

The valise slipped from her grasp, and she wrapped both arms around her brother's neck. After so many months of knowing him only through letters, she couldn't stifle her amazement at how wonderfully solid and real he felt. An unexpected knot formed in her chest. While her heart shouted with joy to know they'd both survived the war, all she could force from her trembling lips was, "I've missed you, too."

Reluctantly, she eased from Jack's embrace. Straightening the jacket of her traveling suit with one hand and smoothing her hair into place with the other, she stepped back for a better look at her brother. She tilted her head and smiled appraisingly. "You look . . . good. Definitely more mature."

Jack's lips twisted. "I'd be surprised if I wasn't sporting a gray hair or two, the way things have been going lately. If you hadn't come home—"

She silenced him with an upraised palm. "Hot Springs is *your* home, not mine."

"Don't say that, Joanna. Dad's gone, and now Mama, too. You, me, and Lily—we're all that's left. We need each other."

The desperation in his eyes pierced Joanna's heart. How could she tell him she intended to return to France at the earliest possible opportunity?

Instead, she squared her shoulders and reached for her valise. "Well, I'm here now, so shouldn't we be on our way? And where is our little sister? Didn't she come along?"

"Long story." Jack reached for Joanna's valise. "Here, let me put this in the car while we wait for the rest of your luggage."

"Um, that's all I brought."

He narrowed one eye. "You aren't serious."

"You were expecting a frivolous female with scads of trunks and travel cases? Please!" Then, remembering, Joanna glanced over her shoulder toward the rear of the train. "I did bring my Indian, however."

"Your . . . Indian." Jack cocked his head. "I'm sure you can't mean an actual *Indian*, as in a gentleman from Bombay."

"No, silly! I'm talking about my motorcycle."

Drawing a hand down his face, Jack uttered a weak laugh. "I should have known."

"I wasn't about to leave it in France. Besides, I'll need my own transportation while I'm here." Joanna marched off in search of a porter while Jack stumbled to keep up. "We'll have to come back for it after we pick up some gasoline. I had to empty the tank for transport."

After tipping the porter with instructions to keep an eye on her motorcycle until they returned, Joanna followed Jack to the street. A moment of nostalgia hit her when she recognized the 1915 Dodge Touring Car her father had boasted about in his letters. It felt strange to see the car for the first time, knowing both her parents were gone.

When Jack held the door for her, she shook off her gloomy thoughts and cast him a disparaging glance. "I'm not helpless, you know."

"Independent as ever, aren't you?"

"More so." She climbed into the passenger seat and yanked the door out of his grip.

Once Jack started the engine and aimed the car toward downtown, Joanna succumbed to the fatigue she'd been fighting all day. The padded leather seat seemed to mold to her body, inviting her to slide lower and rest her head. She hardly noticed when Jack pulled into a filling station, then barely opened her eyes as he asked the attendant to fill a gasoline can.

After setting the can on the floor behind the seat, Jack nudged her arm. "You're in no shape to be driving anywhere. What do you say we leave your motorcycle at the depot until tomorrow?"

"Mmm, good idea." Joanna shifted, her nose wrinkling at the acrid fuel smell filling the car. She curled her hands beneath her cheek and didn't know another thing until Jack woke her in their driveway.

"We're here, Jo. Time to put on your 'big sister' hat."

She sat up, groaned, and wished she could board the next train back to New York.

⁂

Yawning, Joanna trudged to the stove to refill her coffee mug. Sleeping in her old room last night had felt strange, while also strangely . . . comfortable. She'd never expected to find the room still unchanged since she'd left for New York eight years ago to begin her college education at Barnard. Had Mama been so sentimental?

More likely, she simply hadn't put forth the effort.

In fact, everything about the Trapp family home seemed frozen in time. Same cabbage rose wallpaper in the kitchen, same faded upholstery in the parlor, same gouge in the wall going up the stairs where in a fit of temper Joanna had hurled Mama's favorite blue Delft vase and smashed it into a thousand pieces.

She closed her eyes, remembering the ugly scene as if it were yesterday.

"You couldn't be bothered, could you? Couldn't drag yourself out of bed long enough to see me receive my medal. I'm the smartest math student in my class, and you don't even care!"

"I'm sorry, Jo, truly I am." Face blotchy and swollen, Mama clutched her robe with a knotted fist. *"Next time, I promise—"*

"That's what you always say, and nothing changes! I hate you, Mama!"

Wincing, Joanna heard all over again the shatter of porcelain and wished she could take back her spiteful response. As a girl, she hadn't understood how sick her mother was. As a young woman striving to make her own way in the world, she hadn't wanted to care.

Now, she had no choice. Somehow she had to make things right for Lily, because she couldn't bear the thought of her little sister growing up bitter and angry over their mother's final act of betrayal. Because, intentional or not, that's what it was. For her children's sake, if for no other reason, why couldn't Stella Trapp have resisted despondency and fought harder to live?

The scuff of shoe leather across the floor drew Joanna's attention to the kitchen door. Gripping her coffee mug, she propped a hip against the counter. "Good morning, Lily. Sleep well?"

"Not especially. Hard to sleep with strangers in the house." The girl slogged to the icebox and pulled out the milk jug. "Where's Jack?"

Swallowing a sharp retort along with a much needed gulp of hot coffee, Joanna reminded herself she hadn't been much more congenial at age fifteen. "He already left for the factory. He walked, though, so I have the car to drive you to school."

"Fine, but we have to leave in ten minutes. What's for breakfast?"

"How about toast and eggs? It won't take long—"

"I don't like eggs."

"Then what do you usually eat?"

"Kellogg's Corn Flakes. But we ran out yesterday. You need to go to the market."

Joanna drew a long, slow breath. She set her mug on the counter and locked her arms across her abdomen. "I shall be glad to do the marketing, just as soon as I figure out what we need. In case you've forgotten, I only arrived yesterday."

Lily muttered something unintelligible as she poured herself a glass of milk, which she slurped noisily while gathering up the schoolbooks and papers she'd left scattered across the kitchen table. At supper last evening, Mrs. Kendall had warned Jack and Joanna that Lily still had assignments to complete. From the looks of things, a lesson or two might still remain unfinished.

Well, Rome wasn't built in a day, as the old saying went. Clearly, Joanna had a long, hard road ahead with her little sister. The mere thought of the struggle she faced was enough to drive her to her knees in prayer.

Almost, anyway. Joanna and God weren't exactly on speaking terms.

Leaving Lily to clean up after herself, Joanna hurried upstairs to dress. Her beige traveling suit was a wrinkled mess, despite her draping it across a chair overnight. She tugged the skirt on anyway, along with a clean white blouse from her valise. It would have to do until she could wash out a few things.

Afterward, she ushered Lily out to the car, but the moment she opened her door, the biting odor of gasoline assaulted her.

"Ewww!" Lily peered into the backseat. "What's *that* doing in here?"

"It's for my motorcycle. I have to pick it up at the depot later."

Lily's brows shot up. "You have a motorcycle?"

At her sister's awestruck tone, Joanna resisted a smug smile. "I bought it from an army sergeant in France after the war ended."

"Will you teach me to drive it?"

"We'll see." Joanna slanted Lily a wry glance. "*If* you can keep your grades up and show me you can be responsible."

Lily's mouth flattened as she slammed her door and faced forward in the passenger seat. Behind those troubled brown eyes, Joanna glimpsed a flicker of adventure and knew she'd taken the first step toward building a bond with her sister.

Maybe . . . somehow . . . it would help to make amends for the mistakes she'd made in France.

3

On Sunday morning, Thomas almost talked himself out of getting up for church. With Clare's frequent absences, keeping the hotel switchboard covered had nudged him to the edge of exhaustion. Last night, he'd taken it upon himself to work the late shift to give his other two operators what relief he could. He'd have to hire someone soon, or both those ladies would quit on him as well.

Annemarie's suggestion about Joanna Trapp had certainly played on his mind, but he didn't want to seem pushy. She'd been home only a few days and needed time with her family during this period of mourning.

However, the Trapps would most likely be at worship today, which might present the ideal opportunity to personally express his condolences to Joanna . . . and perhaps inquire whether she had any interest in securing employment.

Showered, shaved, and dressed, Thomas arrived downstairs in time to gulp a quick cup of coffee before rushing out the door—but not before Marguerite snagged him long enough to straighten his tie and plaster the cowlick at his temple with a dampened fingertip.

"Bad enough you slept through breakfast, but I'll be switched if I'll send you off to church lookin' like you just tumbled out of bed—even if it's the truth!"

With a roll of his eyes, Thomas planted a kiss on the housekeeper's brown cheek. "Say a prayer for me, Marguerite. If things go the way I'm hoping, by next weekend I'll be all caught up on my sleep."

He stepped through the doors at Ouachita Fellowship as the congregation sang the opening hymn. Squeezing in next to his mother, he tugged a hymnal from the rack while joining in with the final lines of the third stanza: "Nor doubt our inmost wants are known/To Him who chose us for His own."

In fact, every verse of the hymn "Leave God to Order All Thy Ways" spoke a reminder to Thomas's heart that all this anxiety over hotel staffing issues was best laid at the feet of the Lord. Even if it turned out Joanna Trapp wasn't interested in coming to work for him, he wouldn't regret making the effort to get himself to church. He may not be the most faithful or pious among his peers, but he had only to look as far as at his own brother to witness God's amazing power to change lives.

As the last chord faded and the congregation took their seats for the reading of the epistle lesson, Thomas released a calming breath and allowed his glance to roam the sanctuary. Across the aisle and two rows up, Jack Trapp sat at the end of the pew, one arm draped behind the slim shoulders of his younger sister, Lily. She sat stiff and straight, eyes downcast as if she'd rather be anywhere than seated next to her brother in church.

Looking past Lily, Thomas found his gaze riveted by a woman with hair the color of Marguerite's homemade lemon butter. Stray tendrils escaped a haphazard bun and tickled her neck. But even with the awkward crease ironed into the collar of her beige suit, instead of appearing careless, the effect was somehow charming.

When the woman turned her head to glance at Lily, Thomas immediately recognized Joanna, and his heart somersaulted.

Stunned and embarrassed by the unexpected reaction, he shifted. His hymnal slid to the wood floor with a thunderous clap.

Everyone around him flinched, and for the space of three long seconds the sanctuary went utterly silent. Then from the pulpit, Pastor Yarborough fixed Thomas with a crooked grin before proclaiming, "Thus spake the Lord!"

While the titters died down, Thomas hid his burning face behind a Sunday bulletin, but he couldn't resist another peek in Joanna's direction. When he caught her looking his way with a tiny smirk skewing her lips, he wished he could crawl beneath the pew and hide—and possibly would have if his mother hadn't elbowed him in the ribs.

"Whatever are you doing, son?" Her raspy whisper hissed in his ear. "Not only are you late for worship, but you're fidgeting like a two-year-old. Do sit still and pay attention."

"Sorry, Mother." Thomas lowered the bulletin and faced forward. He rose with the rest of the congregation as Pastor Yarborough announced the reading of the gospel.

"Ah, I see the problem," his mother murmured with a tug on his coat sleeve. She tipped her head toward Joanna Trapp. "You'd best steer clear of her, young man. I hear she's another of those suffragists. Women fighting for the vote, then going off to war to do what only men were meant to do—"

The gentleman seated in front of them turned with a glower and a finger to his lips. "Madam, if you please!"

Laying a hand on his mother's arm, Thomas cast the man an apologetic smile. So much for those moments of peace. And he wasn't about to engage his mother in an argument over women's rights—in church or anywhere else. She may have mellowed slightly in her attitude toward Gilbert's new bride, but Thomas doubted his mother would ever change her opinion of women in the workplace.

When the service ended—an eternity later, so it seemed— Thomas escorted his mother from the pew and sent her off to greet her bevy of society friends. He hung back to shake the hand of a business acquaintance or two while discreetly watching for the Trapps to come his way.

Distracted by a friend asking about Gilbert and Mary, Thomas swung around in surprise when someone tapped his shoulder. The luminous brown eyes smiling up at him made him choke on the friendly hello he couldn't seem to get past his lips.

"Thomas Ballard. I'd recognize you anywhere." Joanna Trapp tilted her head appreciatively. "Taller than I remembered, but you've filled out nicely from the skinny kid I recall from high school. Apparently you recovered from your run-in with the backboard."

Self-consciously Thomas reached up to massage the tiny scar in his left eyebrow. "You remember, do you?"

"How could I forget? Only seconds to go in the game, and you miraculously stole the ball and made a mad dash for the basket. You were totally in the clear, and all you had to do was shoot. But no—"

"Please, spare me." Thomas waved his hand, a chuckle dying in his throat. "I'd just as soon forget my unfortunate attempt at a jump shot. I wish you would, too."

"It must have been something to see!" Jack gave Joanna a playful slug in the arm. "But, of course, my snooty sister would never have thought of taking her little brother to a basketball game."

Joanna leaned closer, peering up at Thomas's eyebrow. "How many stitches did you end up getting?"

He caught a whiff of coconut-scented shampoo. "Just three. But it bled like crazy."

Behind Jack, Lily folded her arms and breathed an annoyed sigh. "Can we go home now? I'm hungry."

Eyes darkening, Joanna whirled to face her sister. Her voice dropped to a whispered warning. "What have I told you about your attitude? Rudeness will not be tolerated."

Lily took a minuscule step backward and Thomas wanted to do the same. Clearly, Joanna's time spent in service to her country had only sharpened her assertiveness.

"Excuse us, will you?" With a disgusted frown, Jack hooked an arm around Lily's shoulder and ushered her firmly toward the narthex.

Joanna gave her head a small shake. "I suppose you've heard all about the troubles we've had with Lily since . . ." Her glance fell to the faded maroon carpet, and she exhaled tiredly.

"It's good you came back to help. I'm so sorry about your mother."

"Yes, it's a shame." Her eyes hardened.

Thomas decided to let the subject drop. He tucked his hands into his pants pockets while framing the question he'd been itching to ask. "Listen, I realize it may be a bit soon to be thinking about such things, but if you should find yourself in need of employment while you're in town . . ."

Her head snapped up. "What did you have in mind?"

Joanna held her breath while she waited for Thomas to elaborate. A paying job doing *anything* had to be better than wandering about their drafty old house day after day while waiting for Lily to get home from school so they could have another argument. Joanna could be cleaning and cooking, of course. Not to mention laundry and mending and all those other domestic chores designated women's work.

She'd rather eat dirt.

"I understand you have extensive switchboard experience," Thomas began. "You see, one of my operators is expecting and can't work much longer, so—"

"Sounds perfect. When can I start?"

Thomas flinched as if she'd slapped him. "Don't you want to hear the details?"

"You have a switchboard, right?"

He nodded.

"You'll pay me in American dollars?"

"Well, naturally."

"Then what more is there to discuss?" Joanna thrust out her hand, holding it steady until he slowly withdrew his from his pocket and accepted her handshake. "As I said, when do I start?"

Thomas stared at their locked hands. "See, here's my problem. My other girls have seniority, so I owe them first choice of shifts. I need someone who's willing to work nights."

"I can do it." Chin raised, she released her grip. "You can't imagine the crazy hours we worked in France. Besides, if I take the late shift, I can still be around for Lily during the day."

Eyes lighting, Thomas rubbed his jaw as if he couldn't quite believe his good fortune. "I can't thank you enough, Joanna. You're a lifesaver."

"Actually, you just saved *my* life." Joanna's lids fluttered closed as a relieved sigh rippled through her. If she believed in answered prayer, Thomas's offer would certainly qualify. "Just let me know when you need me. I can start any time."

Thomas cast her a nervous grin. "Uh, how about tonight at eight o'clock?"

"Absolutely." She started to shake Thomas's hand again, but before she could reach for it, his mother interrupted them.

"Thomas, dear." The well-dressed matron laid a gloved hand on her son's arm while casting Joanna a brief but condescending smile. "Are you planning to stand here chatting all day, or may we please hurry along to our luncheon?"

"Don't let me keep you." Joanna had forgotten Mrs. Ballard's reputation for bossiness. She offered a deferential nod, then returned her attention to Thomas. "You can telephone me at home later with more details."

"Or you could join us for lunch." His mouth turned up in a hopeful smile. "Mother and I often dine at the Arlington after church."

Joanna couldn't miss the startled hike of Mrs. Ballard's brow— enough reason right there to accept this spur-of-the-moment invitation. Nothing Joanna liked better than causing uppity rich ladies to squirm in their silk bloomers. And possibly by applying the right amount of pressure, she could coerce the woman into making a sizable donation to the French war orphans fund. She owed Véronique a letter anyway, and it would be nice to enclose a hefty check.

Her heart clenched at the thought. She missed her friend. She missed France.

"Joanna?" A look of concern narrowed Thomas's eyes.

Rousing from her brief and utterly annoying descent into self-pity, she drew a sharp breath and pasted on a smile. "Actually, I'd love to join you for lunch. Let me tell Jack and Lily and I'll meet you at the Arlington in . . . say, fifteen minutes?"

Their plans arranged, the Ballards left by a side door and Joanna hurried out front to find her brother. He stood on the sidewalk in deep conversation with Pastor Yarborough, while Lily paced near their car, her face twisted in a scowl. The girl's scathing glances could have gouged trenches deep enough to swallow a house.

Torn between giving her sister a piece of her mind and simply ignoring such childish behavior, Joanna opted for the latter. Lily would be forced to grow up eventually, and no amount of lecturing would speed things along. Unfortunately, like Joanna, the girl would probably have to learn her lessons the hard way.

Joanna sidled next to her brother. "Sorry to interrupt, Pastor, but I need a word with Jack."

"Of course, my dear." The minister offered a polite nod. "May I say, though, how nice it is to have you home again. I only wish your return had been under happier circumstances."

Joanna offered a wordless smile of gratitude. When Pastor Yarborough stepped away, she opened her mouth to tell Jack of her lunch plans only to stop short at the troubled look clouding his expression. She wrapped her fingers around his wrist. "What's wrong?"

Jack's jaw muscles bunched. He shot a glare toward Lily. "Pastor Yarborough just informed me an usher caught Lily slipping into the church office a few minutes ago. She was about to help herself to some of the cash in the offering plate."

"She *what?*" Mouth falling open, Joanna jerked her head around to stare at her little sister.

"Keep it down, will you?" Jack hooked her elbow and guided her farther along the sidewalk. "I'd rather the whole congregation didn't know our business."

Loath to believe her sister capable of such an act, Joanna palmed her forehead. "But you two walked out of church together. When did she have time to visit the office?"

"It must have been when Mr. Kendall pulled me aside. He needed to remind me he has business in Little Rock tomorrow and won't be in until—"

Joanna dismissed Jack's explanation with a flick of her hand. "But are they certain Lily was taking money? Maybe she went to the office for some other reason."

"What other reason could there be?"

"I don't know—to borrow a book, perhaps?" Joanna lifted her eyes heavenward at the absurdity of her own suggestion. Gathering up laundry off Lily's bedroom floor yesterday, Joanna had discovered her sister's penchant for tawdry romance novels, the type of which one would *never* find on the bookshelves of a respected cleric.

Hands braced on his hips, Jack kicked at a piece of gravel. "I'm at my wit's end, Jo. You have to do something."

"*I* have to—" Joanna clamped her teeth together, before she let fly a few of the handy French curse words she'd learned. She could understand Jack's frustration, even sympathize. But she'd been home only a few days. How could he expect her to step blindly into a difficult situation and miraculously have all the answers?

She glanced at her wristwatch. Obviously they wouldn't solve anything standing in the church parking lot, and soon Thomas would wonder why she hadn't arrived for lunch. She inhaled a calming breath. "May we please continue this discussion later? I need some time to sort things out. Besides, I . . . I've been invited to lunch with the Ballards."

Jack's brows pinched. "Thomas and his mother?"

Joanna nodded. She dropped her gaze, knowing full well Jack wouldn't be happy to know she'd accepted Thomas's job offer—more accurately, practically begged him to hire her on the spot. "I'll explain later, all right?" She edged away, hating the worry shrouding her brother's gaze. "I have to go. I'm sorry."

Thomas waved away the waiter's third pass with the coffee carafe while ignoring his mother's disgruntled frown. The five-minute drive from the church to the hotel had been filled with her incessant badgering about why in heaven's name he'd invited "that radical-minded Trapp girl" to lunch.

The questions had ceased once he'd stated Joanna would be stepping into the vacant switchboard operator's position, thereby relieving Thomas of his current management woes. But once they'd been shown to their usual window table in the Arlington's opulent dining room, Mother had resorted to silent martyrdom. Dining with the working class? How utterly outré.

Unfortunately, their guest had yet to arrive, which in Thomas's mind didn't bode well for a successful working relationship. If Joanna Trapp couldn't be on time for a luncheon engagement, how could he rely upon her promptness on the job? Considering everything Jack had told him about Joanna's loyal service with the Army Signal Corps, Thomas had expected much better.

He'd almost decided she wasn't coming and was about to call their waiter over to take their order when he looked up to see the maître d' escorting Joanna through the restaurant. Rising as she approached, he read apology . . . and something else . . . etched in her hesitant smile.

"I was afraid you'd changed your mind," he said as he held a chair for her. "Is everything all right?"

"Family problems. I'm sorry you had to wait." Slanting an uneasy glance toward Thomas's mother, Joanna pulled her lower lip between her teeth.

Thomas's mother lifted one hand, wiggling her fingers to get the waiter's attention. "Yes, we've heard tales about your naughty little sister. A good spanking—"

"Mother, please. It's none of our affair." Thomas snapped open a menu. He passed it to Joanna, his tone mellowing. "Order anything you like. It's on the house."

"I can pay my own way, thanks." Then, after a few moments perusing the entrées, she sat back with a wry grin. "Perhaps before I order, we should discuss the salary you're offering?"

Thomas laughed out loud. "Not nearly enough, believe me!" He reached for her menu. "I'd be honored if the lady would permit me to choose for her from the Arlington's most popular luncheon selections."

Joanna's lips creased, and Thomas worried he'd offended her. Stupid of him to forget how independent she'd always been.

Then a sparkle came into her eyes. "I shall consider this meal a down payment on what you *should* be paying me based on my excellent skills and extensive experience."

A pleasant warmth spread in Thomas's chest, and he decided he liked the grown-up Joanna Trapp very much indeed. She was certainly an enigma, presenting an air of steely self-confidence but with the tiniest glimmers of vulnerability peeking through.

He'd glimpsed a crack in her façade at least twice today—once as they'd spoken at church, and again upon her arrival in the restaurant. He couldn't begin to imagine what she must be going through at home, what with the family in the throes of grief over Mrs. Trapp's untimely death and the ever-increasing problems with Lily.

He'd like to know, though, why Joanna had stayed away so long. He could count on one hand the number of times he'd seen her back in Hot Springs after she finished high school and left for Barnard. Even when her father passed away, she hadn't made the trip home. True, the war was still raging at the time, but even after the Armistice she'd chosen to remain in France. Apparently Joanna favored the excitement of a big city like New York or Paris over a mundane existence in the boring Midwest.

Conversation ebbed while they dined on tenderloin of beef with mushrooms, creamed spinach, and baked mashed potatoes. Joanna ate with what could only be called reverence, savoring each bite as though tasting it for the first time. Only then did Thomas consider Joanna's life in France this past year and a half may have involved more sacrifice than adventure.

When the waiter served them each a huge slab of Black Forest cake for dessert, Joanna groaned in ecstasy. "I may be stuffed already, but I intend to force down every last crumb if it's the last thing I do."

Thomas chuckled and moved his own plate to the far edge of the table. "Come near mine and you risk being impaled with a fork."

Their eyes met, hers almost as chocolaty-brown as the cake and equally intoxicating. Something zinged through Thomas's chest, and for a frightening fraction of a second he couldn't breathe. Then with a nervous cough he tore his gaze away and filled his mouth with a huge bite of dessert, hoping he could chew and swallow without choking.

Had she felt it, too—whatever *it* was that had just passed between them? He slid a glance her way, only to find her facing forward with eyes closed as she relished a bite of cake.

Apparently not. Disappointment left him drained, and not at all pleased with himself for reading something into the moment that clearly wasn't there.

Fork poised daintily above her plate, his mother narrowed her gaze at him, one brow lifted in curiosity. Then she smiled knowingly and gave her head an imperceptible shake before tasting her dessert. Dabbing her mouth with the corner of a linen napkin, she tipped her head toward Joanna, who had by now scraped up every last dab of frosting, cake, and cherry filling. "You poor dear, one would think you hadn't had a decent meal in months." Her expression filled with pity. "How terribly hard it must have been to be a working girl in France."

"We ate rather well, actually." Grinning, Joanna licked her fork clean. "But nothing as fancy or decadent as this." With a quick gulp of coffee, she slid her chair back. "Thomas, I can't thank you enough for the delicious lunch—or the job offer. But if I'm going to make it back this evening to start work, I must go."

"I understand." Thomas laid aside his napkin and stood. He started to help Joanna from her chair and then thought better of it. Instead, he pushed his own chair in to make room for her to pass. "See you at eight?"

She turned with a questioning glance. "Oh. I assumed one of your other switchboard operators would be showing me the routine."

Once again, a peculiar sensation tied knots in Thomas's throat. Maybe he should forego returning to the hotel this evening. Lillian Zongrone could certainly handle Joanna's training with no help from Thomas. Yet already he found himself counting the hours until he'd see her again.

Cocking a hip, he strove for a casual stance with one hand on the back of his chair. "You'll be in good hands, of course, but I might drop in for a bit and see how it's going."

Joanna shrugged. "Don't change your plans on my account. I'm sure you have better things to do on a Sunday evening."

Oh, yes, can't miss my weekly cribbage game with Mother. "We'll see, then. May I drive you home?"

"No, thanks. Actually, I'm in need of a brisk walk."

"Good for the digestion, of course." Thomas patted his belly.

Her expression hardened as she looked away. "Right. That, too."

The sudden shift in her mood reminded Thomas of the problems with Lily she'd alluded to. "If there's anything I can do . . ."

Fatigue glazed her eyes, and she smiled weakly. "You already did, remember?"

"Ah, the job."

"Best thing to happen since I got back to town." Joanna thrust out her hand. "Thanks again—for lunch, and for hiring me."

Accepting her handshake, Thomas nodded. "The pleasure is all mine."

4

*W*hat good did it do to tell the truth if no one believed you, anyway?

Arms locked across her ribcage, Lily slouched against the settee cushions. Jack had finally given up questioning her, which was fine since he'd already made up his mind she was guilty. Now she could hear him rattling dishes in the kitchen and tossing out the occasional curse while searching for something to throw together for lunch.

Lily had already told him fifty times she wasn't hungry. Who could eat after being verbally flogged for an hour—and over something not even her fault?

A tear slid down her cheek, and she whipped it away with the back of her hand. Just see if she'd wait around for Joanna to get home so they could start the interrogation all over again! Shoving up from the settee, she marched into the front hall and yanked a sweater from the coat tree. Without bothering to tell Jack where she was going—and knowing she'd catch you-know-what for it later—she barged out the front door.

Ten minutes later and gasping for breath, she leaned into the buzzer at her friend Abby Wright's house. Abby swung open the door and tugged Lily inside before she could mutter a quick hello.

"Oh, Lily! I heard what happened," Abby gushed as she prodded Lily upstairs to her room. She whisked the door shut and then plopped onto the purple quilt covering her bed, pulling Lily down beside her. "Tell me you weren't *really* going to steal from the church offering plate."

"Of course not." Lily rolled her eyes. Abby's family didn't even attend Ouachita Fellowship. Leave it to the gossips around town to spread the news.

"Then why would they accuse you of such an awful thing?"

Biting her lip, Lily smoothed a hand across the neatly made bed and wished she were more like her friend. Smart. Sensible. Popular.

And pretty. Abby's hair was the same lustrous pale blonde as Joanna's.

Thinking about her sister made Lily's stomach hurt. She wanted to cry all over again.

"Lily. Talk to me." Abby squeezed her hand.

Jerking away, Lily stormed across the room. "Why does everyone else have to be so perfect? Why am I such a mess?"

Her own reflection in Abby's dresser mirror mocked her. Drab, mousy hair hanging in limp curls. Skinny as a fence post with not a curve in sight. A mouth that drooped at the corners just like her mother's.

And Mama was the *last* person on earth Lily ever wanted to resemble. In any way whatsoever.

Sidling up next to her, Abby encircled her with a warm hug and smiled through the mirror. "I think you're perfect just the way you are, Lily Trapp. You're my very best friend, and I love you."

A noisy sigh raked Lily's chest. "You may be the only one who does."

"Nonsense. Your brother loves you, too, or he wouldn't care so much when you—" Abby pressed her lips together.

"You can say it. When I get myself into trouble." Lily harrumphed. "I should say, when I get myself into *more* trouble."

Softly, Abby asked, "Are you going to tell me what really happened this morning?"

"Does it matter?"

"It matters to you. I can tell by how upset you are." Linking her arm through Lily's, Abby turned back to the bed. "So come sit down and let's talk about it. *Please.*"

Suddenly Lily's stomach heaved. Hand to her mouth, she lunged toward the door. "I think I'm going to throw up!"

✒❤

"What do you mean, she's not here?" Joanna tossed her handbag onto the kitchen table, nearly knocking over her brother's glass of milk. She loomed over him, hands on hips. "How could you let her walk out before we get this matter cleared up?"

"*We?*" Jack tossed a half-eaten ham sandwich onto his plate and shifted sideways in his chair. "As I recall, it was just *me* left here to clear things up. *You* conveniently went out to lunch with the Ballards."

Guilt pummeling her, Joanna edged back a step. "I didn't feel I should turn down an invitation from my new employer."

"Your new—" Jack gaped, then shook his head. "I don't believe this. You've already finagled a job at the Arlington? I thought you came home to help look after Lily."

"I did. I *will.*" Joanna sank into the chair opposite Jack's. She reached across to peel a strip of crust from his sandwich and tucked it into her mouth. Amazing she could still be hungry after such a delicious meal. Must have been the long walk home.

However, her walk had failed to bring any more perspective about Lily than she had before she started.

Jack slapped her hand before she could steal more of his sandwich. "When were you planning to tell me about this job?"

"Thomas made the offer while we were chatting after church. Then you hit me with the news about Lily's latest transgression.

It didn't exactly seem an appropriate moment to say, 'Oh, too bad about Lily, and by the way, I'm going to work at the Arlington tonight.'"

"*Tonight?*" Jack's open palm smacked the table. "This just gets better and better." He bolted from his chair and paced the kitchen. "I don't understand you, Joanna. We just lost our mother, in case you've forgotten. How can you even think of working—tonight, next week, or next year—when you're needed right here at home?"

Teeth pressed together, Joanna inhaled long and deep. "Of course, I haven't forgotten. And you're right—you *don't* understand me. No one in this family ever has. It's why I got as far away from Hot Springs as I possibly could. Why I never wanted to return."

"Then maybe you should have stayed in France." Jack stalked to the table, scooped up his sandwich plate, and tossed the remains of his lunch in the waste bin. Then, hands braced along the edge of the kitchen sink, he stared out the window toward the street and heaved a tired sigh.

Slowly, Joanna rose and went to his side. She tucked her arm around his slim waist and rested her head on his shoulder. "I'm sorry, Jack. I want to help—truly I do. Please, let's not fight."

He uttered a humorless laugh. "We sure fought plenty as kids, didn't we?"

"But we always made up. You're my favorite little brother, you know."

"And you're my favorite bossy big sister." He slid his arm around her and kissed the top of her head. "So what's the lowdown on this job of yours?"

"It's going to turn out for the best all around, I promise. I'll be working the late shift as a hotel switchboard operator, so I'll always be around when Lily's home from school." Giving her brother a final squeeze, Joanna slipped out of her suit jacket and rolled up the sleeves of her blouse. "And it'll be good for me, too," she said as she filled the sink with water and dish suds, "because I thrive on work, and I'll make myself crazy if all I do is ramble around the house all day."

Taking the hint, Jack reached for a dry towel while Joanna scrubbed the dishes from breakfast and Jack's lunch. He wiped a bowl and set it in the cupboard. "We still need to talk about Lily and what happened this morning."

Joanna rinsed another bowl and handed it to her brother. "Did she ever explain?"

Jack snorted. "She kept saying I wouldn't believe her side of the story, anyway."

"Do you think her side is any different from what the usher told you?"

"I'd like to hope so, but it's hard when she won't even defend herself."

With a swish of suds to make sure she hadn't missed a fork or spoon in the bottom of the sink, Joanna released the stopper. As dishwater circled the drain, she propped a hip against the counter while she dried her hands. "If it *were* true, though . . . what in heaven's name would prompt Lily to steal?"

"To get attention? To embarrass the family?" Jack put away the last plate and then tossed the damp towel over a hook. His next words came out on a world-weary sigh. "Or maybe it's her way of getting back at Mama for deserting us."

A rock-hard lump of bitterness settled in Joanna's abdomen. "It's true, you know. Mama did desert us. She may have been here physically, but when it counted—when we needed her—"

"Don't say it, Jo. She couldn't help how she was."

Joanna had no defense against the stark emotion behind Jack's stare. He'd always loved their mother best, always took Mama's side when she and Joanna clashed—which was often. And loud. And heated. Joanna had assumed it was because boys were naturally loyal to their mothers, while girls, especially as they reached the teen years, were naturally rebellious.

But this was different, more than simply a son's devotion to his mother. Jack obviously understood something about Mama that had eluded Joanna. Something that had enabled him to empathize, even forgive.

Something that made him a better person than Joanna could ever hope to be.

Her eyes stung, and longing filled her for the one person who'd loved her for herself, who'd never asked her to change, at least not until—

Walter, my darling, forgive me! I miss you so much!

Before the tears fell, she swung around and marched across the kitchen. "Goodness, it's almost three o'clock," she stated with feigned surprise. "If I'm going in to work tonight, I'll need a nap." Then, pausing in the doorway, she glanced over her shoulder with a penitent smile. "But do wake me when Lily comes home. I—I'll do my best to talk some sense into her."

Following lunch, Thomas's mother suggested a drive out to Gilbert's farm. The place had undergone quite a change since Gilbert purchased it last summer and began restorations. Fields that only months ago had lain fallow now glistened with green in the afternoon sunshine as sprigs of wheat poked through the plowed earth.

Of course, Gilbert's pride and joy was his retired racehorse, Mac, along with the two mares carrying the stallion's foals. Gilbert might be missing a leg, but it didn't stop him from maneuvering about his property in a wheelchair.

Although the chair would soon require replacing if Gilbert were much rougher on it.

Glancing down on their way out to see the horses, Thomas kicked one of Gilbert's dirt-encrusted wheels. "You realize those things weren't intended for gallivanting around a farm, right?"

Gilbert looked askance at Thomas's pristine suit pants and shiny leather shoes. "You've got a lot of room to talk."

"Mother didn't want to take time to go home and change."

They reached Mac's paddock, where he munched lazily on tufts of grass. The horse had been retired because of lameness, but Gilbert had seen something special in the old boy . . . or maybe dollar signs, seeing as how Mac was descended from the famed thoroughbred Bonnie Scotland. Even with Prohibition putting an end to racing, Gilbert had reasoned there'd always be a market for horses of quality.

At any rate, the farm and the horses had given Gilbert a renewed sense of purpose, and Thomas couldn't fault his brother for dreaming big, especially after the war had robbed him of so much. His leg. His dignity. The woman he'd always planned to wed.

But army nurse Mary McClarney was hands down the best thing that to ever happened to Gilbert. The love that had grown between them over the past year had been tumultuous, fraught with obstacles, and yet pure and powerful and enduring. What Gilbert had shared with Annemarie hadn't come close to such passion.

A familiar ache rose in Thomas's chest. Despite everything his brother had been through—the war, the injuries, the pain, the heartbreak—Thomas envied him. He'd almost be willing to cut off his own leg if it would guarantee him the kind of happiness Gilbert knew with Mary.

"Hey, brother." Gilbert backhanded him on the thigh. "Why so glum? After you said you'd hired Jack's sister for the switchboard, I thought all your worries would be behind you."

The mention of Joanna brought back memories of lunch earlier . . . and the anticipation of seeing her tonight. For a moment his heart lightened, only to sink again when he recalled the utter lack of mutual interest he'd seen in her expression. He was her employer, nothing more. He hunched his shoulders against the chilly November breeze. "You know me, always thinking about work. If it isn't the switchboard, it'll be something else."

Gilbert's arched brow spoke his skepticism. "You need to get out of the office more. Have a little fun, add some adventure to your life. You know what they say about all work and no play."

"Adventure—*me?* I'm the boring brother, remember?"

Across the paddock, Mac lifted his head, nostrils quivering as if he caught the scent of something on the wind. Giving a snort, he pawed the earth and then cantered to the far side of the field. Though he clearly favored his lame left foreleg, the horse carried himself with spirit and confidence, every muscle taut with anticipation.

"See?" Gilbert said, pointing. "Even ol' Mac is up for an adventure. New experiences are good for the soul."

Light, feminine laughter sounded behind them. "And what sort of adventures, dear husband, are you and Thomas cooking up?"

"Don't panic, Mary." Gilbert scooped an arm around the waist of his red-haired Irish bride. "I'm just trying to convince my stick-in-the-mud little brother he spends far too much time behind his desk."

"And you don't spend enough behind yours," Mary chided. "Our creditors will be hammering at the front door if you don't tend to those bills piling up."

"I'll get to them, sweetheart, I promise. But on a gorgeous day like today"—Gilbert stretched his free arm wide—"how can you fault me for wanting to be outdoors enjoying my farm?"

"And I've enjoyed the afternoon as well," Thomas said with a glance at his watch. "But it's time Mother and I head back to town."

"Ah, yes, mustn't be late to train your new switchboard operator." Seizing the wheel grips, Gilbert turned his chair toward the house. "Though I bet Joanna Trapp could teach you a thing or two," he added with a wink. "Now there's a girl who knows the meaning of adventure."

Thomas couldn't argue the point. Little wonder a woman like her would never give Thomas a second glance. Obviously, Joanna saw him exactly as he was—and as Gilbert had so succinctly described him: a stick-in-the-mud.

Could he help it if he preferred life to be predictable, safe, ordinary? All he'd ever wanted was to find a quiet, gentle woman with whom to settle down and raise three or four happily compliant children. They'd live in a stately Victorian behind a white picket fence, and Thomas would leave for the hotel each morning knowing his patient wife would see the children off to school and then cheerfully go about her daily chores at home.

A fantasy, to be sure. And one that belied Thomas's nagging remorse because his brother and so many friends had sailed off to France to fight the Germans, while he had been declared unfit for military service. He could thank—or despise—a heart weakened by a childhood bout of rheumatic fever. Either way, no matter how sorely he both envied and respected the men who served their country so valiantly, he couldn't deny his "service" behind a desk at the Arlington suited his personality much better than battlefield heroics.

5

"One moment, please, and thank you for calling the Arlington."
Joanna connected the caller to the guest room he'd requested.

"You're a fast learner." Lillian Zongrone, a quick-witted woman
with silver hair, rolled her chair away from the switchboard and
reached for a coffee cup on the table behind them.

Joanna already liked the friendly telephone operator who
shared her little sister's name—although Lily hadn't been called
Lillian since grade school. Too common, she'd insisted, claiming "Lily" sounded much flirtier. A sign of problems to come, no
doubt.

This was no time to be dwelling on the situation at home.
Whooshing out a sigh, Joanna removed her headset. "Compared
to the boards I manned in France, working here will be a snap."

"Then maybe *you* should be training me," Lillian said with a
laugh. "If I'd been twenty years younger and single, I might have
enlisted in the Signal Corps myself."

"You have a family?" Rising to stretch her shoulders, Joanna
stepped over to the hotplate and poured coffee for herself.

"Married for thirty-two years, one fine daughter and four
strapping sons." Lillian's glance slid to one side as sadness veiled

her expression. "Well, three sons now. The Spanish flu took our youngest not long after he reported for duty at Camp Pike."

"I'm sorry. The flu was rampant in Europe as well. I felt fortunate not to catch it." Taking a cautious sip of the steamy brew, Joanna eased into her chair. She'd just as soon not dwell on the many friends and acquaintances who'd succumbed. Véronique had suffered terribly, taking weeks to recover.

And yet . . . if not for Véronique's illness, Joanna might never have met Walter. She'd literally run into him as she exited the pharmacy where she'd picked up medicine for Véronique.

Another call came through. Setting her coffee aside, Joanna whipped on the headset, plugged in a line, and greeted the caller. With practiced efficiency, she redirected the call to the proper extension.

"Wow, I'm impressed."

Joanna spun in her chair to see Thomas Ballard leaning in the doorway. She beamed him a smug smile. "You had doubts?"

"None at all." Thomas sauntered into the room, tie loosened and hands tucked casually into his pants pockets. "Good evening, Lillian. Thanks for staying late to get Joanna settled in."

"She hasn't needed much 'settling.' This gal's a keeper, Mr. B." Lillian downed the last sips of her coffee then rose and collected her handbag and sweater. "If you don't mind, I'll be on my way. Joanna, you can telephone me at home if you have any questions later." She patted Joanna's shoulder. "But I know you'll do fine."

"Good night, Lillian, and thank you." Turning back to the switchboard, Joanna checked the status of the calls in progress. When one of them disconnected, she slid the plug from the jack.

Thomas sank into the chair Lillian had vacated. Jaw twitching, he toed a scrap of paper on the floor. "Guess I didn't need to drop by. Looks like you have everything under control."

There was something odd about his tone, and Joanna slanted him a curious glance. She had the awkward feeling she should say something encouraging but couldn't think what or why.

Then the board rang with a call from one of the guest rooms. Joanna forced a smile into her voice. "Good evening, this is the operator. How may I help you?"

"My room is stuffy, and the window's stuck," an elderly male voice growled. "I need you to send someone up immediately."

"Of course, sir. I'll see to it right away." Disconnecting, Joanna started to ring the maintenance department as Lillian had instructed for such calls, but a twinge in her chest made her stop. With a quiet cough, she swiveled toward Thomas. "My first disgruntled guest. Could you make sure I handle this right?"

Thomas perked up at once. "What's the problem?"

The light in his eyes convinced Joanna she hadn't misread her instincts. She explained about the stuck window. "I was just going to ring up maintenance, but the man sounded quite upset." A *slight* exaggeration. "I'm afraid it may take more than a repairman to placate him."

"I'll take care of it personally. What's his room number?" Thomas stood and adjusted his tie.

Joanna jotted the number on a message pad, tore off the top sheet, and handed it to him. "Thanks. I wouldn't want to alienate a hotel guest my first night on the job."

"I'm sure it'll be fine. Glad I was here to help." Looking the picture of the competent manager, Thomas exited the switchboard room.

Returning her attention to the board, Joanna laughed softly and shook her head. What a change from a few moments ago! Thomas had seemed almost disappointed at how smoothly things were going. She certainly hadn't required his assistance with the grumpy guest in the third-floor suite, but clearly Thomas had needed to be needed.

What *was* it with men, thinking they always had to come to a woman's rescue?

And what was it with women who would feign helplessness just to feed a man's ego?

At least Walter had never treated her like a helpless female. Whenever he'd get a few days' leave they could spend together, he'd teach her how to work on a car engine or load and fire a pistol. "An American woman alone in France needs to know these things," he'd tell her, "especially when I can't be around to take care of you."

All right, so Walter may have had a few heroic tendencies of his own. But it was different somehow. She could let Walter take care of her because she knew he also respected her. Her independent nature wasn't a threat to him.

A huge bubble of grief surged in her chest, and for a moment she couldn't breathe. Walter's face swam before her, exactly as he'd looked on the last day they spent together. She could hear his chiding tone as if it were yesterday. *"If things go bad, no regrets, you hear? And I don't want you crying buckets over me. When I look down from heaven, I want to see you going on, finding new adventures, living the best life ever."*

Giving a hearty sniff, she flicked away the single tear that had escaped down her cheek. With what strength of will she could muster, she mentally boxed up the memories and stored them away. This might not be the "best life," but she'd make the best of it for Walter's sake.

The switchboard remained quiet for the next few minutes, and Joanna was glad she'd had the foresight to bring along a magazine. Véronique had made sure to stuff Joanna's suitcase with several back issues of *Lectures pour Tous*, and tonight Joanna turned again to the article about Sir Arthur Conan Doyle. She'd grown quite fond of the "Sherlock Holmes" mysteries. The stories never failed to transport her vicariously to new and ever more fascinating adventures.

So engrossed was she in her reading that she didn't realize Thomas had returned until he spoke. "Our guest is now quite mollified," he said, sinking into the chair. "His window's open, and his bill has been credited with a complimentary night and dinner for two in the restaurant."

"Certainly more than his complaints deserved." Using one finger to mark her page, Joanna closed the magazine. "I hope it's all right to bring something to read between calls."

"Of course. Once things quiet down for the night, there isn't much to keep you busy." Thomas angled his head for a better look at the magazine cover. He grimaced. "Is that French?"

Joanna chuckled softly. "*Oui, monsieur. Parlez-vous français?*"

"Er, no. At least not much. What are you reading?"

"It's a piece about Arthur Conan Doyle. Very interesting."

"Then I should let you get back to it." Again, the unsettling tone in his voice. Thomas rose stiffly. "Pamela Clement should arrive for the morning shift by the time you leave at three. If not, let the night desk clerk know, and he'll watch the switchboard until she gets here."

Joanna followed him to the door. "Thanks again for taking care of Mr. Grumpy."

"My pleasure." Thomas paused in the passageway and smiled over his shoulder.

"And for lunch today, too. And for hiring me." Heat rose in Joanna's face. Why was she babbling on like this? "In case I haven't thanked you enough," she added, dipping her chin.

"I repeat, the pleasure is all mine. And the gratitude." His grin widened. "In case I haven't mentioned it, you're an answer to my prayers."

The switchboard buzzed with a call, and Joanna wasn't sorry to put an end to the awkwardness between them. With a quick farewell wave, she hurried over and tugged on her headset. "Good evening, Arlington Hotel. How may I help you?"

"'Mornin', young sir." Marguerite plopped a heaping scoop of scrambled eggs on Thomas's plate. "I must say you're looking a sight more rested than I've seen you for quite some time."

"A decent night's sleep makes all the difference." With a friendly wink, Thomas reached for the pepper mill. "Mother isn't up yet?"

Marguerite filled Thomas's coffee cup. "Oh, she done ate breakfast and left for some charity meeting. I swan, the woman's busier'n a whole hive of bees."

The mention of bees reminded Thomas of his brother's recent accident. A vindictive acquaintance—at least so everyone suspected—had chased the horses out of Gilbert's barn, then knocked over Mrs. Frederick's hives. Terrified by the angry bees, one of the horses had trampled Gilbert, crushing what remained of the leg he'd lost during the war. Now it was doubtful Gilbert could wear a prosthesis again. Was there no end to the suffering he had to endure?

Yet to see Gilbert yesterday, reveling in the life of a gentleman farmer and happily married to his charming Irish bride, no one would suspect the depths to which he'd sunk during those first months home from France. Gambling, depression, morphine addiction—desperate times when Thomas feared he'd lose his brother to a different kind of war.

Given the same set of circumstances, Thomas wondered if he'd have found it within himself to overcome such adversity. Certainly the hand of the Lord had moved powerfully in Gilbert's life, even when his faith had faltered and the prayers of others carried him through. But Thomas's faith—much less his courage—had never been tested to such an extent. He hoped it never would be.

"Mister Thomas, eat up. Them eggs is getting cold." Marguerite flicked her fingers at him as she swept up crumbs beneath his mother's empty chair.

Snapping to his senses, Thomas polished off his breakfast and slurped down his coffee. It wouldn't hurt to get to the hotel a little early and catch the night clerk before his shift ended. Stanley Fessler could fill him in on how the rest of Joanna's evening went.

By seven-twenty Thomas had parked his Jeffery Touring Car in his reserved spot near the Arlington's rear entrance. A bite to the early-November air sped his steps as he hurried inside. Reaching the front desk, he found Stanley in serious conversation with the same gentleman who'd complained last night about his window sticking.

"Excuse me, may I be of assistance?" Thomas edged up next to the man.

The jowly man harrumphed, glaring at Thomas from beneath bushy white eyebrows. "What kind of hotel are you running? Your man Fessler here tells me he can't get an extra sofa moved into our suite by this evening. We're entertaining several friends, and we absolutely *must* have extra seating."

Barely able to maintain a placid expression, Thomas slid a glance toward Stanley while inhaling a calming breath. "Sir, you occupy one of our largest suites, which is already furnished to capacity."

The man looked aghast. "Perhaps I should take my business to the Eastman. I'm sure *they* would be more than delighted to accommodate my needs."

"Now, sir, if you'll give me a moment to see what can be arranged . . ." Thomas closed his eyes briefly. They might all rest easier if "Mr. Grumpy," as Joanna had dubbed him, took his patronage elsewhere. However, he and his wife had reserved their suite for a full month. If Thomas's boss found out the couple had checked out three weeks early—even worse, took up residence at a competing hotel—suffice it to say Thomas couldn't expect another "distinguished hotel service" plaque to pair with the one he'd been awarded last year.

Which was insignificant, of course, when compared with his brother's Distinguished Service Medal awarded by President

Wilson for courage under fire. How much courage did it take to face down a nettlesome hotel guest?

Enough. More than enough. Thomas drew himself up and marched around to the other side of the desk. "Stanley, has our second-floor salon been reserved for this evening?"

Shifting sideways and lowering his voice, Stanley replied, "I believe it's available, sir. But the room is sized for larger meetings and receptions. I doubt this gentleman will want to pay the standard rate."

"I doubt he'll want to pay anything at all," Thomas muttered. "Mark it reserved, no charge. I'll deal with the repercussions later."

Steeling himself, Thomas faced Mr. Grumpy. Easier to fake a smile with that honorific in mind. *Thank you, Joanna.* "Sir, I'm pleased to offer you and your visiting guests the complimentary use of our well-appointed salon on the second floor. I think you'll find it more than spacious enough to meet your needs, with ample comfortable seating as well."

Those grizzled brows reached toward the ceiling, while the man's mouth stretched into a self-satisfied grin. "I'm delighted to know I can continue to rely upon the Arlington's excellent service."

"Always, sir, always." Watching their gloating guest stride toward the elevator, Thomas sagged against the desk with a groan. Why did he have the feeling he'd just been thoroughly manipulated? Lifting tired eyes to Stanley, he murmured, "Next time the gentleman contacts us for hotel reservations, make a note to tell him we're completely booked."

Stanley smirked. "Even if it means he'll take his business to the Eastman?"

"I wouldn't have it any other way." Thomas drew a hand down his face and straightened. "So, how did things go last night?"

"Swimmingly." Stanley tipped his head toward the switchboard room. "The new operator, Joanna—she's a card! Had me in stitches with her stories about working for the Signal Corps. Did you know she once connected a call between President Wilson and General Pershing, only she got flustered and accidentally called the president 'Woody'?"

Thomas snorted a laugh. "Bet that went over well." Although he couldn't imagine the confident Joanna Trapp getting flustered about anything.

"Good morning, Mr. Ballard." Austin Lindsey marched up behind the desk. "Fessler, what are you still doing here?" He nudged his counterpart aside. "Go home and get some sleep."

"Just leaving." With a nod to Thomas, Stanley unclipped his name badge and tucked it into a drawer. "Thanks for arriving in the nick of time to handle the . . . situation."

"Wish I could say the pleasure was all mine." With a roll of his eyes, Thomas excused himself.

Before heading to his office, Thomas slipped around the desk and peeked in on Pamela Clement at the switchboard. "Everything all right with you this morning?"

"Oh, hello, Mr. Ballard." The petite brunette swiveled in her chair and beamed a welcoming smile. "I'll never be able to thank you enough for moving me to the early-morning shift."

"Glad it's working out for you. Lillian seems happy with her new hours as well."

"I met the new girl when I arrived. Stanley says she's a dilly of a telephone operator." An incoming call interrupted Pamela. "Gotta catch this."

Leaving her to her duties, Thomas continued on to his office. For once, he could spend the day on projects of importance, rather than agonizing over how he'd keep the switchboard covered. By noon, he'd made a sizable dent in his inbox and tidied up his desk to where he could actually find things again. When his stomach growled, he decided he'd earned himself a hearty lunch in the hotel dining room and then a leisurely walk down Central Avenue.

He hadn't gone far when he remembered he'd soon run out of shaving lather. Sorrell's Drug Company carried the Colgate's he preferred, so he picked up his pace and continued down the block. Entering the store, he took a moment to get his bearings before finding the men's toiletries. The store was abuzz with noontime shoppers, along with several customers sipping drinks at the soda fountain counter.

Thomas's mouth started watering for a Sorrell's peach flip. Unable to resist, he took the first available seat at the counter and placed his order.

"Hello, boss."

He spun around to find Joanna Trapp scooting onto the stool next to his. Beneath a manly-looking cable-knit sweater—Jack's, perhaps?—she wore a pale blue pinstripe blouse and the same beige skirt she'd had on last night. And, if he recalled correctly, the same one she'd worn to church Sunday morning. No one could ever accuse Joanna of being a slave to modern fashion.

Even so, the sheer effortlessness of her attire, the apparent indifference to what others might think, appealed to Thomas in a manner no overdressed society girl ever could. He caught himself gazing at her with slack-jawed fascination.

Only when the server plopped a tall, frothy peach flip in front of him did he snap to attention. Blinking several times, he uttered an embarrassed chuckle. "Sorry, I wasn't expecting to see you again so soon."

Traces of fatigue shadowed her easy smile. "I needed a few things from the market and remembered how much I used to love Sorrell's. They make the best sodas, don't they?"

"Can't be beat." Thomas poked a straw into his glass and savored a long sip of the peachy concoction. "What's your favorite?"

Joanna perused the menu. "I used to always get the vanilla cream flip."

"Plain vanilla, huh? I'd have pegged you for more of a 'lime flip' or 'admiral frappé' kind of girl."

"Oh, so you've figured out I'm a bit of a daredevil." Laughing out loud, Joanna shrugged out of her sweater and laid it across her lap. "Well, then, I wouldn't want to disappoint you." Signaling the freckle-faced boy behind the counter, she ordered the admiral frappé. "And an extra straw for my friend here, if you please."

"Coming right up, miss."

A chill raced up the back of Thomas's neck, and he couldn't blame the shiver on the icy drink he sipped. "I'm enjoying my peach flip just fine, thank you."

"Now, Thomas, sometimes you have to leave behind the familiar and try something different. A little adventure never hurt anyone."

He shot her a sidelong glance. "Have you been talking to my brother?"

"Gilbert? No, I haven't seen him since I've been back." She sobered, offering Thomas a concerned smile. "How is your brother? Jack told me what happened during the war, and then the horrible accident with the horse."

"He's doing amazingly well. I've never been prouder of him." Growing pensive, Thomas stirred his drink. He noticed Joanna had turned quiet as well, her gaze fixed on the glass lampshade hanging above the soda fountain. Serving in France, she must have witnessed firsthand the gruesomeness of war. For a woman who'd always valued her independence, those experiences could only have amplified her determination to present a tough-as-nails exterior.

Yet just as he'd observed yesterday after church, Thomas detected minute cracks in the façade. Those deep brown eyes held hints of sadness that evoked a longing to hold her, comfort her, tell her everything would be all right. Instead, he clamped both hands around his soda glass and waited for the icy chill to cool his futile impulses.

He glanced up when the counter attendant set Joanna's admiral frappé in front of her. "And two straws, like you asked," the boy added with a wink in Thomas's direction. "Enjoy."

All smiles again, Joanna handed Thomas one of the straws. She nodded toward the tempting strawberry concoction. "Are you ready for some adventure?"

Suddenly, Thomas could think of nothing else he wanted more.

"I'm sorry to have called you away from your work, Mr. Trapp, but I felt I had no choice." Miss Maynard sat primly behind her desk in the empty classroom and tapped the end of a red grading pencil atop a stack of papers. "Lily simply isn't doing the work I know she's capable of, and I'm worried about her."

Jack ground his teeth, avoiding the teacher's concerned frown. Surrounded by the smells of chalk dust and musty textbooks, he felt awkward enough having to pry his lanky frame into a front-row student desk. But now, to endure another inquisition about his obstreperous little sister—and at the hands of an attractive woman whom, under any other circumstances, he might seriously consider asking out—was more than his manly pride could stomach.

Besides, weren't these dreaded conferences exactly why he'd been so anxious for Joanna to come home? Where was she this afternoon? Gallivanting across the county on her motorcycle, no doubt.

"Mr. Trapp? Are you listening?" Ice-blue eyes bored into him. Did she have to look so ravishing with the pink-and-orange flowered scarf holding back her riot of blonde curls? What happened to all those gray-haired draconian schoolmasters from Jack's days at Hot Springs High? Not even the school was familiar anymore since a fire in 1913 leveled nearly sixty city blocks . . . a day Jack would just as soon forget.

Straightening, he folded his hands upon the desktop and cleared his throat. "Miss Maynard, we've recently lost our mother. Surely you can understand what a troubling time this has been for Lily—for all of us."

"I do understand." Miss Maynard rose and came around to the front of her desk. Leaning against it, she crossed her dainty ankles just inches away from Jack's toes, and he self-consciously pulled his feet deeper under the desk. "However, Lily's education is at stake, as is her reputation, if I may be so blunt. If she's caught once more in a . . ." A crimson blush worked its way up her cheeks, and she glanced away. "In a *compromising position* with a certain member of the football team, the principal will have no choice but to suspend her."

"You can't—" Jerking out of his seat, Jack nearly toppled the desk. He grabbed the front edge with both hands and carefully settled it back into position. Then, inhaling slowly through his nostrils, he faced Lily's teacher. "You can't kick her out of school," he stated with quiet insistence. "My older sister's home now. I'm hopeful she'll provide the stable maternal influence Lily needs." *If only she'll stick around long enough.* "Please, give us some time to work this out."

Miss Maynard's sad-eyed gaze drilled a hole in Jack's heart. "Time is precisely what I cannot offer, Mr. Trapp. Midterm exams are only a few weeks away. If Lily doesn't buckle down and focus on her lessons, she will most certainly fail—*if* she isn't expelled first."

Jack nodded grimly. "We'll do our best."

"I'm sure I can count on you." With a nod of dismissal, Miss Maynard returned to her chair and picked up her red pencil.

In the corridor, Jack found Lily seated on the floor, knees drawn up beneath her plaid skirt. She looked up at him with resignation in her eyes. "How much trouble am I in *this* time?"

At his wit's end, Jack swept a hand through his hair. He could do little more than shake his head and motion Lily to follow him to the exit. "We'll talk about it at home, okay?" *When I corral Joanna, that is. And wring her mutinous neck.*

6

Joanna should have known she was in trouble the moment she turned into the driveway and saw Jack's car. Shutting off the motorcycle, she swung her leg over the seat and adjusted her skirt. As she tugged off her goggles, she glimpsed Jack standing on the back porch steps, arms crossed and jaw rigid.

"Where have you been?" he demanded.

"Out for a drive." Joanna smiled weakly and tried to keep her tone light. "You're home early."

"And you're not." Glaring, Jack marched down the steps and met her in the middle of the driveway. "I thought I could count on you, Jo. How could you just take off?"

Stunned by the venom in her brother's tone, Joanna bristled. "I didn't realize I had to request *your* permission to leave the house. Besides, it isn't even—" She glanced at her watch, only to have her stomach plummet to her toes. How did it get to be nearly five o'clock? "Jack, I'm sorry. I had no idea it had gotten so late. Is Lily still at school? I can—"

Jack drew air between his teeth. "We've been home for more than an hour."

"I see." Joanna rolled the strap of her goggles between her thumbs and fingertips. She took a tentative step toward the house. "I should get inside and clean up—"

"I don't think you do see." Jack encircled her upper arm with his claw-like grip, and she had no choice but to stop and face him. His accusing glare bored into her for a full second before he released her arm with a huff. "How many ways do I have to say it? Lily needs you. *I* need you. If we can't rely on you, then you may as well go back to France."

For the space of half a breath, she was ready to seize the opportunity. Then she glanced up and saw Lily watching them from the other side of the screen door. The girl's chin lifted defiantly, yet the haunted look in her eyes shredded Joanna's heart like cat's claws through a gauze curtain.

She turned away and forced herself to look up at her brother. "You *can* rely on me, Jack. I just need some time to get used to being . . ." She had to push the next word out. "Home."

Jack's mouth flattened in a stubborn scowl. "You've been here nearly a week already. Exactly how much time do you need?"

"I admit it—I didn't want to come. I've resented nearly every minute since I left France." Joanna kept her voice low, hoping Lily wouldn't overhear. "But don't judge me, Jack. I'm here now, and I'm trying, whether you believe me or not."

His shoulders softened, and he exhaled long and slow. "I'm not oblivious to how hard you had it growing up in this house." His tone dropped another notch as his gaze flicked toward Lily. "Which is why your sister needs you now more than ever. You can make a difference in her life. This is your chance to be the mother to her you both should have had."

"Oh, Jack, you don't know what you're asking." One hand stifling a sudden lurch deep in her belly, Joanna shook her head. Images filled her mind—French orphanages filled beyond capacity with children who might never again know a parent's love. Caregivers stretched so thin that even the effort of a kind word sometimes seemed too much. As often as they could spare the time, Joanna and Véronique had volunteered at an orphanage near their Paris flat.

And always returned home wishing they could have done more. Joanna had never felt more helpless or inadequate.

Until now.

She looked toward the back door again, but Lily had disappeared. With a muted groan she reached for her brother's hand. "I mean it, Jack—I'm sorry. I'll try to do better."

He pulled her into a hug, nearly crushing her beneath his arm as he buried his chin in the top of her head. "And I'll try to be more understanding about what an adjustment this is for you."

"It's an adjustment for all of us. I've been selfish, thinking only of myself while you've borne the burden of keeping the family together."

"I figured you had things to finish up over in France, but I'd hoped—" Jack's whole body spasmed before he bellowed with a gigantic sneeze. "Your hair—you smell like—" Letting her go, he took a step backward and sneezed again.

"Bless you!" Joanna found a handkerchief in her pocket and offered it to him.

He pressed it to his nose and then immediately flung it back at her. "For heaven's sake, Jo, this thing's as coated with dust as"—another sneeze—"you are!"

Glancing down at her clothes, she realized he was right. Evidence of her motorcycle jaunt through the countryside clung to every inch of her. "Let me clean up and then I'll find something to fix for supper." She cast her brother a timid smile. "And afterward, I promise we'll sit down together and talk about Lily."

Drying off from her shower twenty minutes later, Joanna regretted she'd packed so poorly for this trip. Her wardrobe was not anything she could call extensive—until the Signal Corps released her, she'd needed little more than the standard dark blue wool uniform—but a plain and serviceable dress or two would be nice to have. She'd worn her beige traveling suit so often since leaving France, the hem and cuffs were beginning to fray.

Wrapped in her faded chenille robe, she scurried along the upstairs hall to her bedroom, but hushed sobs drew her to a halt outside Lily's closed door. She leaned close to listen, wondering if she should knock, or barge right in, or simply keep walking and pretend she hadn't heard.

Her sisterly instincts won out. "Lily? May I come in?"

"Go away," came the muffled response.

Hand on the knob, Joanna eased open the door. Her heart twisted at the sight of her little sister sprawled across the bed, face buried in the pillow, her entire body trembling with the force of her tears.

"Oh, honey." Joanna hurried to the bed and crawled up next to Lily. She tucked the girl's damp curls away from her face and then massaged those thin, fragile shoulders. "Won't you talk to me? Maybe I can help."

"Nobody can help. Nobody cares anyway."

"I care. Very much."

Lily flopped onto her back, sniffling loudly as she mopped her wet cheeks with the sleeve of her blouse. "Don't pretend. You'd never have come home if Jack hadn't begged."

The hard truth made Joanna wince. Straightening, she traced the diamond-shaped pattern of Lily's quilt with the tip of her index finger. "You're right, I didn't want to return to Hot Springs. And believe me, I wouldn't have, except for the fact that I *do* care about you."

Lily's face contorted. She skewered Joanna with a look so full of hurt and bewilderment Joanna had to look away for a moment. "Then why did you go away? Why did you *stay* away?"

Unable to answer immediately, Joanna rose and paced to the dresser. She picked up Lily's hairbrush and ran her thumb across the bristles. With a resigned sigh she returned to the bed. "Here, sit up and let me brush your hair."

Obeying silently, Lily sat on the edge of the mattress and presented her back to Joanna. As Joanna drew the brush through the long, silky, dishwater-blonde curls, Lily's breathing slowed and her shoulders relaxed. A contented moan escaped her lips.

"Feels good, doesn't it? When I was little, Mama used to brush my hair like this."

"Mine, too," Lily murmured. "Then . . ."

"I know. Then things changed." Laying the brush aside, Joanna encircled her sister in the shelter of her arms and pressed a kiss to her temple. "I'm sorry I wasn't here for you."

Once again, Lily's tears fell. "Why couldn't she fight harder? Why didn't she love us enough to try?"

"Oh, she loved us, Lily. In spite of everything, I must believe she did." Perhaps someday Joanna would understand . . . and forgive.

✍♥

For what felt like the hundredth time since returning from lunch, Thomas checked his watch. Only half past six? Surely the thing was broken! He couldn't recall when an afternoon had passed with such dreadful slowness. He didn't usually pay much attention to the time—what did he have to look forward to after work besides another dull evening at home with Mother?—but after sharing the "adventurous" admiral frappé with Joanna earlier, he'd been counting the hours until her shift started at eight.

Ridiculous. And what excuse could he possibly offer for staying well past his usual quitting time? Certainly not any hint of concern over Joanna's work skills. Telephoning his mother to explain why he wouldn't be home for dinner, he'd made up a lame story about a last-minute staff meeting. Not exactly an untruth since he definitely planned to meet with a certain charming new staff member, but—yes—utterly ridiculous to allow his hopes to climb so high.

When he'd stretched his paperwork to the limits of credibility, he rang up the kitchen to order a light supper brought to his office. The meal dispensed with another half-hour, and now it was almost eight. Joanna would arrive at any moment. Straightening his tie and slipping on his suit coat, Thomas turned off the lights and strolled out to the lobby. The shiny marble floors, elegant furnishings, and polished wood smelling of lemon oil never failed to fill his chest with a bubble of pride. No doubt about it, he loved the Arlington and he loved his job.

"Evening, Mr. Ballard." Austin, manning the front desk, plucked a wilted leaf from a potted plant. "Didn't expect to see you here this late."

"Had some work to finish up." Thomas tried to look nonchalant as he propped an elbow on the counter. "Everything all right with you?"

"Things got pretty quiet after most of the weekend guests checked out. I'm just killing time till Stanley gets here."

Thomas could relate. "Lillian is on the switchboard now, I take it?"

"Yes, sir." Retrieving a dust cloth, Austin polished an oily fingerprint off the edge of the counter. "And the new girl, Miss Trapp—she got here about ten minutes ago."

A thrill zinged through Thomas's abdomen, making it hard to keep his voice even. "Maybe I'll say hello before I leave."

He forced himself to inhale a discreet calming breath before circling the front desk, and again before he stepped through the doorway into the switchboard room. "Ladies . . ."

"Oh, Mr. Ballard, good evening." Giving a light laugh, Lillian Zongrone handed Joanna the headset. "Just in time for the changing of the guard."

"Hi, Thomas." Joanna smiled nervously as she took the chair at the switchboard. "Or maybe I should call you Mr. Ballard while I'm on duty."

"First names are fine," Thomas answered quickly. "We're friends, after all." She had a vulnerable look about her again. Though she tried so hard to keep it hidden, it worried him.

After slipping on her sweater, Lillian turned to give Joanna's shoulder a quick squeeze. "Remember, honey, you can call me anytime."

Joanna offered a grateful nod, then looked away self-consciously when Thomas caught her eye. She flicked something off her cheek.

Thomas waited until Lillian had left before rolling the extra chair closer. He sat down, hands clasped between his knees. "Joanna, forgive me for prying, but . . . is everything all right?"

She tried to laugh, but the sound was harsh. "Oh, everything's peachy—except for the fact that I'm an utter failure as a big sister."

"I don't believe it for a second."

"Well, you should. If I hadn't selfishly stayed away for so long, maybe Lily wouldn't be having such a difficult time now."

"Serving your country isn't selfish." Across the small room, the coffeepot burbled on the hotplate. Thomas rose and poured them each a cup. "Cream or sugar?"

"Black, please. I got out of the habit of using sugar during the war."

"Same here, but in the evenings I like a dollop of cream." After adding the cream and stirring his coffee, Thomas handed Joanna her cup and then sat back down.

"Thank you." She blew across the surface of the brew before taking a cautious sip. "And for the record, I was an absent sister long before the war began. I doubt either Jack or Lily will ever fully forgive me."

"I'm sure they will in time. You did what you felt you must."

"It's kind of you to say . . . even if you don't believe it."

A telephone call interrupted them, and while Joanna connected the caller to Room Service, Thomas sat back to admire her skill and efficiency. At least, so he told himself. In truth, he couldn't take his eyes off the curve of her throat, the messy tilt to her bun, the way she lifted her nose and smiled ever so slightly as she spoke into the headset.

"Thomas?"

He blinked several times and nearly spilled his coffee. "Sorry, was I staring?"

"As a matter of fact." Joanna's forehead creased. "Surely, you don't find the switchboard *that* fascinating."

Not the switchboard, just the operator. "What were we talking about before the call came in?"

Joanna laughed suddenly, fluttering her hand. "Can't we find a more cheerful topic?"

"That's a habit of yours, you know."

"I beg your pardon?"

His coffee now cold, Thomas crossed to the table and set the cup on a tray. "Whenever you get too close to revealing yourself, you change the subject."

"How absurd. You don't know me well enough to make such an assumption."

Before he could reason out why he shouldn't simply agree, say good night, and be on his way, he blurted, "Then maybe we could change things, because I'd like very much to get to know you better."

She should have said no. Without hesitation, without remorse, without so much as a moment's consideration. Because the *last* thing Joanna wanted or needed was the interest of a man.

Not when, with every beat of her heart, she still grieved for Walter.

And certainly not while she had so much to atone for with Lily and Jack.

Still, she couldn't deny something about Thomas drew her. Maybe it was his natural friendliness. Or perhaps his simplicity. He seemed quite comfortable in his hotel management position, perfectly suited to the unchanging daily routine.

The problem was, Joanna couldn't decide whether her interest in Thomas stemmed from a compelling desire to help him break from routine and introduce some excitement into his life . . . or from envy. Because there was no denying she'd have avoided a mountain of heartache if only she'd been content to stay in Hot Springs as the dutiful daughter and eldest child her parents expected her to be.

At any rate, when Saturday rolled around, she found herself primping—if that's what you called dressing in a borrowed frock, repinning her bun, and dabbing on a touch of lipstick—for an evening out with Thomas. Hard to say no when her own boss had given her the night off and she couldn't use work as an excuse.

"How do I look?" she asked as Lily peeked into the bedroom. Things between them were still tentative, but at least they'd been talking more since Monday.

Lily propped her shoulder against the doorframe. "Where on God's green earth did you get this dress? It's hideously out of style."

"Oh, dear." Joanna drooped as she studied her reflection. "Mrs. Kendall lent it to me. She found it among Annemarie's old things."

"I can see why Annemarie left it behind." Lily marched over and tugged loose the green satin sash. "For starters, this thing *has* to go. It's limp as wilted lettuce. And about the same drab color, too."

Joanna had to admit the dress looked slightly better without the sash. "The hem's a little long, but there's nothing I can do about it now."

"Maybe you could . . ." Chewing her lip, Lily tried tucking the skirt higher beneath the overlapping drop-waist bodice. "There. We just need a few safety pins and no one will ever know."

Ten minutes later, the dress looked entirely different. If not stylish, at least passable. Joanna squeezed her sister's hand. "What would I have done without you, Lily?"

Immediately, the girl closed off. "Exactly what I've done without *you* all this time."

"Lily—"

Too late. She barged from the room and slammed the door.

So much for improved sisterly relations. Tossing on a musty-smelling wool shawl she'd scavenged from the bottom drawer of the wardrobe, Joanna marched downstairs in search of Jack. She found him sprawled on the sofa, eyes closed as he listened to the Victrola.

Tweaking the toe of his sock, she stated, "You and Lily are on your own for supper, brother dear. I'm going out."

"So you said." Jack crossed his arms over his chest. "Have a nice date."

"It isn't a *date*."

"Dinner. A show. That's a date."

Joanna thrust out her chin. "It isn't a date if I pay my own way. Which I fully intend to do."

"Mmm-hmm. Change the record for me, will you? I've heard enough Caruso for one afternoon."

"Change it yourself. I'm not the hired help." Plopping into a chair, Joanna smoothed the shimmery green fabric of her dress and hoped Lily's safety pins held. "Anyway, I should think you'd be the one making plans for a Saturday-night date. Home almost a year and you still don't have a steady girlfriend."

Jack bolted upright, thrusting his feet to the floor and searing Joanna with his glare. "I've been a little busy, in case you need reminding."

Stung, and duly chastised, Joanna heaved a repentant sigh. "How many times must I apologize, Jack? I don't have to go out tonight. I'll cancel my plans with Thomas right now." She stood and started for the telephone in the entry hall.

"No, stop." With a groan, Jack pushed up from the sofa. "Go out and have a good time. You've earned it, as hard as you've been working." He plucked a piece of lint from her shawl. "And I don't just mean at the hotel. I've seen a difference in Lily these past few days."

"Have you?" Joanna cast him a hopeful look. "I've tried, Jack. Tried my best."

A motor sounded in the driveway, and Jack glanced toward the front door. "I think your beau's here."

"Thomas is *not* my beau." She gave her brother's arm a good, hard slap. "And so help me, if you start spreading tales, I'll blister your sorry hide like I did when you were a runny-nosed little boy."

Laughing, Jack brushed past her to answer the door. "Hello, Thomas. Nice to see you. Joanna's all ready for her da—I mean, your evening out together."

Joanna pasted on a cheery smile to divert Thomas's attention from the subtle bump she gave Jack with her hip. She snatched up her handbag from the hall table. "Shall we go?"

Five minutes later she sank into the plush passenger seat of Thomas's yellow Jeffery Touring Car and breathed a sigh of relief to have escaped her brother's teasing. "So where are we dining? The Arlington again?"

"Oh, no." Thomas slanted her a grin as he steered the car toward downtown. "I figured we'd try something a little more . . . adventurous."

"Adventurous? In tame little Hot Springs?" Joanna hiked a brow.

"You *have* been away too long." Thomas's mouth hardened briefly. "In case you haven't noticed, we've grown into a bustling municipality—complete with all the accompanying problems. Prohibition has only exacerbated the situation."

"I'd have thought closing down the bars and racetrack would've had a positive effect."

"People will find a way to indulge their vices one way or another, even if it means breaking the law."

Joanna fell silent for a moment. "When you said we'd try something more adventurous, surely you didn't mean . . ."

Slowing at an intersection, he gaped at her. "What? No! I just meant—" His expression turned smug as he continued north along Park Avenue, heading out of town. "Never mind. I'd rather you be surprised."

She couldn't have been more surprised when Thomas turned off the main road and wound up a steep mountain lane. The sun had already set behind the forest, casting long shadows across the hood of the car. Through the trees, Joanna glimpsed a doe and her fawn grazing along a ridge. "Are you sure there's a restaurant out this way?"

Thomas chuckled. "Did I ever actually use the word *restaurant?*"

"You suggested dinner and a show. I naturally assumed—"

"I promise you, we *will* have dinner and a show." He winked. "In an adventurous sort of way."

"You're making me nervous, Thomas."

"Why? Because you don't think I'm capable—" He tapped the brake. "Ah, we've arrived."

7

The look on Joanna's face was priceless—and worth every moment of trepidation Thomas had experienced as he'd planned this excursion. Wanting to prove both to himself and to Joanna he wasn't the stick-in-the-mud the rest of the world assumed him to be, he'd pulled Zachary aside yesterday to ask for suggestions. If anyone knew where to find tasty food and lively entertainment off the beaten path, it was the Ballard family chauffeur.

"Yessiree, I know just the place," Zachary had said, eyes bright against his dark complexion. "You head up north about six miles or so and you'll find my cousin's fishing shack. Every Saturday night it's a regular feast up there. He'll be frying up a mess of catfish with all the trimmings. 'Course half the county'll be there, too. But the more, the merrier, right? You and your lady friend will have a grand old time, I guarantee."

Judging from the number of automobiles parked at odd angles all around the cabin, Thomas figured Zachary's estimate of "half the county" wasn't too far off. As he stepped from the car, the tantalizing aroma of fried catfish brought a spontaneous growl from his stomach. Laughter, raucous singing, and banjo music wafted from somewhere behind the building.

As he should have expected, Joanna didn't wait for him to help her from the car. Before he'd rounded the front bumper, she stood beside her open door taking in the sights, smells, and sounds. She beamed an appreciative smile. "Thomas Ballard, you are full of surprises."

A short, round fellow with graying sideburns tromped down the porch steps. "Hey, there, folks. You must be Zachary's acquaintances. Welcome. I'm Zach's cousin Isaac."

"Thanks for allowing us to join the festivities." Thomas extended his right arm, careful not to wince at the man's enthusiastic handshake.

"Y'all come on around back for some food. We got more catfish and cornbread cookin' than you can shake a stick at. Purple hull peas and collard greens, too."

As Isaac led them along a well-worn path skirting the cabin, it seemed only natural Thomas should tuck his hand around Joanna's elbow. Just to steady her, of course. Any gentleman would do the same. At his touch, she glanced over her shoulder, lips turning up slightly. Feeling brave, Thomas firmed his grip and moved closer to her side.

The music grew louder and the aromas more intense as they reached the backyard. Kerosene lanterns hung from the trees, casting an amber glow across rows of pine picnic tables spread with gingham cloths. Most every seat was taken, while other guests milled about the food tables filling their plates from the heaping platters and bowls. From the back porch the musicians belted out a spirited tune about Jonah and the whale, and in the open space at the foot of the steps several couples twirled and stomped in an exuberant circle dance.

One couple, spying Thomas and Joanna, split off from the group. The man hooked arms with Joanna, while the woman did the same with Thomas, and before he could claim he didn't know the steps, he found himself whirling and twisting and kicking up his feet in his best imitation of the other dancers.

"Whoo-eee," someone yelled. "You folks sure can cut a rug!"

Joanna had long since lost her shawl, but she laughed so hard she appeared not to notice. The next spin brought her face-to-face with Thomas, and she collapsed against him, holding on to his neck for all she was worth. Breathless, she shouted in his ear, "If you don't get me off this dance floor right now, I'm afraid my carefully pinned skirt is going to fall down around my ankles and trip me!"

Thomas glanced down, only then noticing her hem dipped lower on one side. "We can't have that." Waving off the woman who'd first ushered him into the dance, he tucked his arm around Joanna's waist and escorted her a safe distance away. Finding an empty split-log bench at the end of the porch, they both sank down with sighs of relief.

Joanna immediately went to work on her dress. "I worried Lily's pins wouldn't hold. If we'd been seated in a quiet restaurant, perhaps, but kicking up my heels in a country reel? Not in a thousand years!"

If not for the grin lighting her eyes, Thomas would fear he'd ruined their evening completely. The lantern light brought out a shimmer of perspiration on her forehead and cheeks, giving her a dewy radiance that would have sent other women rushing to the ladies' room to powder their faces.

Isaac found them and held out Joanna's shawl. "Believe this is yours, miss. Once you catch your breath and cool down some, you'll be needing it. Y'all come on over and fill a couple of plates. I got seats waiting for ya at the table right yonder with me and my missus."

"Thank you, Isaac. We'll be right along." Rising, Thomas helped Joanna to her feet and draped the shawl around her shoulders. "Ready for some catfish?"

"Can't wait!"

An hour later, their bellies full and a mound of fish bones piled between them, Thomas decided it was the best meal he'd ever eaten. True, Marguerite had served fried catfish any number of times at the Ballard table—but usually when only the boys were at home while their mother dined with society friends. Evelyn Ballard was *not* a catfish-and-cornbread kind of person.

No doubt about it, tonight was something special. Maybe it was the picnic atmosphere, or the crisp autumn nip in the air. Maybe the music, or maybe . . .

From the corner of his eye he watched Joanna savor her last forkful of pecan pie. Turning the fork upside down, she drew it between her lips. Her eyelids drifted shut in sensual delight.

Thomas noticed a crumb at the corner of her mouth. "You have a . . . little something . . ." He raised his hand, and she held perfectly still as he flicked away the crumb with the edge of his thumb.

"Thank you," she murmured, reaching for her napkin. In the pale glow of the lamplight he thought he detected a shiver. The smile had disappeared. "It's getting late. Perhaps you should take me home."

"I'm not going to church, and you can't make me." Lily hunched over her bowl of corn flakes, determined not to even look at her brother. He didn't understand and never would.

"Come on, Lily, don't be this way." Jack pulled out the chair across from her, spun it around, and straddled it. Hands folded, he rested his arms on the back of the chair. "Whatever happened last Sunday, you need to face up to it. Apologize to Pastor Yarborough and promise you'll never do it again."

She ground her teeth together. As if the fusty old pastor mattered a whit.

"Lillian Matilda Trapp!" Jack's hand landed on the table with a resounding slap. "I'm sick to death of this attitude of yours. It has to stop."

"Or what?" Lily filled her tone with all the ferocity she could manage, considering the tremors churning her belly. Jack had been angry with her before, plenty of times, but the mix of fire and fatigue in his eyes suggested he'd lost his last remnants of patience.

Shoving up from the chair, Jack stormed across the kitchen. "For Pete's sake, Lily," he said, whirling to face her, "I have no idea what to do with you anymore. All I know is—"

Joanna swept into the room. "What's going on? I could hear you all the way upstairs."

"Ask *her*," Jack said, aiming his index finger at Lily. "I've got no time for this. I need to dress for church." Growling, he whipped past Joanna, every step echoing through the house as he stomped upstairs.

Standing at Lily's shoulder, Joanna methodically tied the sash of her robe. "All right, I'm asking," she stated quietly. "Will you please tell me why Jack is so upset?"

Lily shrugged and kept her eyes on her cereal bowl. "He wants me to go to church. I told him no. Simple as that."

"I'm certain there's nothing *simple* about it. Jack has never been one to lose his temper without provocation, and it's clear you've provoked him mightily—again."

"Oh, sure, blame me. Whatever's wrong around here is *always* my fault." Lily scooped up a spoonful of corn flakes, only to stifle a gag when she tried to swallow. With all the lectures and arguing, her breakfast had grown soggy.

Joanna sank into the chair next to Lily's. Resting both elbows on the table, she massaged her temples. Then, straightening, she turned to Lily. "Don't you think it's time you take responsibility for your own actions and attitudes?"

"Why? Because *you're* so good at it? You ran away first chance you got, so don't think you can show up all of a sudden and start running my life!" Thrusting back her chair, Lily burst up from the table. "And Jack's no better, acting all tough and bossy and strutting around like he's the man of the house since Daddy died. You're both a couple of hypocrites!"

"Lily—"

She fled, refusing to listen to one more word. If not for the fact that Abby would be at church with her own family, Lily would have rushed straight to her friend's house. Besides, she still wore her nightgown and robe, so there'd be no "rushing" anywhere except straight to her bedroom. She gave the door an extra-hard slam to make sure both Jack and Joanna understood how angry she was.

Angry. Pretty much the only emotion she felt these days. She was angry with Daddy for dying, angry with Mama for being so sad and withdrawn for so many years and then dying, too. She was angry with Jack for going off to war and making Lily worry about him every second he was away. And—perhaps most of all—she was angry with Joanna for having the courage, the smarts, and the wherewithal to break away and live her own life.

I'd do it, too. Do it in a heartbeat if I could.

Flopping onto her bed, she pounded the mattress with both fists. How horrible to be fifteen and trapped in a life she despised. So her brother and sister thought the worst of her. Why even bother trying to prove them wrong, when it was so much easier living up—or should she say, living *down*—to their expectations?

A certain boy on the football team would be more than happy to help her meet those expectations. She knew for a fact Rudy Hegney avoided church. And she had a good idea where she might find him on a Sunday morning.

Joanna might be physically present at Ouachita Fellowship's Sunday morning worship service, but her thoughts remained elsewhere. How could she fault Lily for not wanting to attend, when Joanna herself wasn't sure why she'd come? She had yet to forgive

God for taking Walter, but his untimely death was only one of many reasons her faith had faltered.

Truth be told, she'd been drifting spiritually for years, and the war had only increased her doubts. Her stomach clenched as she pictured those waif-thin orphans who approached so shyly when she and Véronique would visit. One little girl in particular had captured Joanna's heart. As Joanna sat reading from a storybook, the dark-eyed child would creep up beside her and twine her tiny, dirt-stained fingers through Joanna's hair.

"*Très jolie*," the girl would murmur with a smile of longing.

Then Joanna would lay the book aside, pull the child onto her lap, and use her own brush to gently work the snarls from the girl's thin, matted hair.

Sadly, she'd been more of a big sister to this one orphaned child than she'd ever been to Lily.

"Hey." Jack elbowed her arm. "You planning to sit in church for the rest of the day?"

She looked up with a start to realize the organist already pounded out the postlude as congregants made their way down the aisle. Rising, she tugged at the hem of her jacket—the same tired beige traveling suit she'd worn almost every day since leaving France—and joined her brother at the end of the pew.

Jack greeted an acquaintance across the aisle before murmuring, "You've been in a daze all morning, Jo. Too much partying last night?"

"You know I was home before nine." Joanna smiled across the way at Mr. and Mrs. Kendall. "I've just been thinking what to do about Lily."

"About time." Though Jack kept his expression pleasant, Joanna couldn't miss the accusation in his tone.

Noticing Thomas headed their way, she bit back a spiteful retort and pasted on a friendly smile instead. Besides, though the truth continued to chafe, Jack wasn't far wrong in his assessment.

"Good morning, Joanna." The hesitation in Thomas's tone reminded her she hadn't been very courteous last night when he'd brought her home.

"Thomas, I don't think I thanked you properly for the . . . *adventurous* evening." She hoped her expression conveyed sincerity, because she truly had enjoyed their time together. But going out with him as if they were courting had ignited the most awful sense of betrayal.

Thomas's eyes brightened. "It was an adventure, wasn't it?"

"Where'd you take my sister, anyway?" Jack asked with a grin. "She's been awfully tight-lipped about your date."

Joanna cringed but kept her smile in place, keeping silent as Thomas described their evening at Isaac's fishing cabin.

Mrs. Ballard, mouth agape, stepped up beside her son. "You took this young lady *where?*"

"Now, Mother, it was all in fun." Thomas shot Joanna an apologetic frown. "And Zachary's family couldn't have been more hospitable."

Joanna winked. "He's right, Mrs. Ballard. I haven't had such a grand time since returning to Hot Springs."

"How unfortunate for you, my dear." Nose in the air, Mrs. Ballard excused herself. "I shall wait for you at the car, Thomas. Don't tarry."

"Guess I should be on my way." Thomas toed the carpet, then looked up hopefully. "I don't suppose you'd care to join us for lunch again?"

Joanna's heart gave a thud. She hated disappointing him, but the invitation was too fraught with meaning. And the consequences of accepting too uncertain. "Thanks for asking, but Jack and I have a . . . situation at home we must deal with."

"Lily, I presume?"

"She's quite the handful lately," Jack stated. "Wouldn't even come to church this morning."

"Fifteen's a difficult age under the best of circumstances." Thomas's gaze held sympathy. "Well, I mustn't keep Mother waiting. You'll be at the hotel tonight, Joanna?"

"Of course." She felt obliged to add, "See you there, perhaps?"

Thomas glanced away. "You have the job well in hand. No need for me to hover."

The tinge of regret in his voice stirred something in Joanna. He was attracted to her, she could tell. How could she make him understand she wasn't anywhere close to being ready for a new relationship?

ℐ♥

When the telephone rang shortly after eight Monday morning, Joanna had just crawled back under the covers after seeing Lily and Jack out the door. She'd promised Jack she wouldn't let her work at the Arlington interfere with helping to prod Lily out of bed in time for school, but rousing herself after only a few hours of sleep was proving more difficult than she'd expected.

Dragging herself downstairs to the foyer, she didn't even bother tying the sash of her robe but stumbled straight to the telephone. "Hello?"

"Miss Trapp, this is Madison Maynard. I'm Lily's history teacher and academic advisor."

This couldn't be good. Grasping the candlestick-style telephone, Joanna lowered herself onto a velveteen-upholstered chair. "Good morning, Mrs. Maynard. How may I help you?" For heaven's sake, she was using her operator voice!

"It's *Miss* Maynard, actually. I'm calling about Lily."

Naturally. Joanna decided a businesslike tone might be the best approach after all. "Is there a problem?" A *new* problem, or just more of the same? She and Jack had spent most of Sunday afternoon hashing out what do to about their rebellious younger sister and coming to no satisfactory conclusions. Lily's refusal to explain her actions, much less defend them, didn't help.

"Yes, Miss Trapp, I'm afraid we definitely have a problem. Has Lily mentioned a young man named Rudy Hegney?"

Joanna scoured her brain. "Sorry, no. Is he one of Lily's classmates?"

"An upperclassman." Miss Maynard softly cleared her throat. When she spoke again, she sounded almost embarrassed. "This is rather awkward to explain over the telephone. Could you possibly come to the school right away?"

So much for catching another hour or two of sleep. *Oh, Lily, what have you done this time?*

Twenty minutes later, once again clad in the traveling suit that hung more limply every day, Joanna marched out to her motor-cycle. Hiking her skirt, she climbed onto the seat and turned the ignition.

Nothing.

Popping open the engine cover, she fiddled with the spark plug then tried the ignition again. This time the motor growled but still refused to start.

With a groan, Joanna stepped to the driveway, hands on hips. She considered giving one of the tires a swift kick but decided not to risk breaking a toe. Calling Jack at the pottery factory was out of the question. He'd made it plenty clear yesterday he'd all but exhausted Mr. Kendall's good graces with the many times he'd already taken off work to deal with Lily.

Joanna glanced across the street. Perhaps Mrs. Kendall could help. Marching up to the neighbor's front door, she pressed the bell.

Moments later Mrs. Kendall answered. "Joanna, dear. Come in, won't you? I've just brewed a fresh pot of tea."

"Sounds lovely, but I can't. I wondered if you could drive me somewhere."

Chagrin creased Mrs. Kendall's lips. "Joseph took the car to the factory today. Normally he walks, but he had some light deliveries to make."

Inhaling long and slow, Joanna shifted her gaze toward the street. "I'll just walk, myself, I suppose."

"Do you have far to go?"

"The high school."

Mrs. Kendall's eyes crinkled in a knowing look. She lowered her voice. "Lily?"

Joanna nodded.

"Then you'll need some moral support. *And* a ride, because you'll wear clean through the soles of your shoes before you get there on foot."

"But how—"

Mrs. Kendall grasped Joanna's wrist and drew her inside. "Go pour yourself a cup of tea. I'll be back in two shakes."

It was pointless to argue. While Mrs. Kendall marched around the corner to the study, Joanna went to the kitchen as ordered. Behind the third cupboard door she tried, she found the cups and saucers, then filled a cup from the steaming china teapot sitting on the counter. The soothing aroma of orange pekoe filled her nostrils as she carried the cup to the table.

Seconds later, Mrs. Kendall returned. As she poured tea for herself, she announced, "It's all arranged. Annemarie will be right over to drive you to the high school."

"I hope you didn't call her away from anything. Doesn't she need to be at her shop?"

"On Mondays she doesn't open until noon." Beaming, Mrs. Kendall took the chair across from Joanna's. "Now, while we're waiting, you can tell me all about your lovely evening out with Thomas."

8

I simply cannot abide that woman! I have tried, Thomas. Truly, I have. But I'm at my wit's end!"

Holding the telephone receiver a good two inches from his ear, Thomas forced himself to listen to his mother's rant. As soon as she permitted him a word in edgewise, he said, "Now, Mother, Mary's simply doing what she thinks is best for Gil."

"Yes, but really, would it tire him so much to attend his own mother's dinner party? We've been friends with the Hegneys for years, and they will be so disappointed if Gilbert doesn't come."

"He's still healing. I think the Hegneys will understand."

His mother harrumphed. "Naturally, you'd take that tyrannical army nurse's side over mine."

"I'm not taking anyone's side. I'm just—" Thomas heaved a breath and rubbed his eyes. Drat it all, why did he always get stuck being the mediator? "Please don't be this way, Mother. Do you want to drive both Gilbert and Mary away?"

"I wouldn't mind being rid of the latter at all. You and Gilbert both, taking up with riffraff instead of one of the fine girls more suited to your social standing—how on earth have I failed to raise my sons with any sense of propriety?"

And just when Thomas had dared to believe his mother had climbed down from her high horse and become more accepting. Teeth clenched, he muttered, "Mary is not riffraff, and neither is Joanna Trapp. Say one more word against either of them, and I'm hanging up on you."

A wheedling tone entered her voice. "Do forgive me. I was just so put out by Mary's adamant refusal of my dinner party invitation. Gilbert seems so much stronger, and I thought surely he'd be ready for a pleasant evening away from his dreary farm."

"He loves the farm, and you know it. Now enough of this nonsense, Mother, and let me get to work. I'll see you this evening." Without waiting for her to say good-bye, Thomas ended the call.

No sooner had he hung up than his secretary tapped on the door. "Pardon me, Mr. Ballard, but you have a visitor. It's your sister-in-law."

Mary, here—*now*? Thomas sat straighter and adjusted his tie. "Send her right in."

Moments later, Gilbert's new bride edged into the office. "Please forgive me for bothering you at work, but I didn't know what else to do."

Worry gnawed Thomas's belly. "Gil—is he all right?"

"Oh, he's much improved. We just came from seeing his surgeon. I left him at the hospital to visit with the chaplain for a bit—said I needed to run some errands." Gaze averted, Mary fidgeted with the clasp of her handbag. "Truth be told, I need your perspective about . . ."

Thomas groaned. "Our mother." When Mary lifted her eyes and gave a quick nod, he continued, "I'm sorry she's pressuring you about the dinner party. If you don't think Gilbert's up to it, she'll simply have to accept the fact."

"Actually, I'm the one who isn't up to it." Mary pursed her lips. "I'm afraid I've only been using Gilbert's recovery as an excuse."

Puckering his brows, Thomas waited for her to explain.

A kaleidoscope of emotions flitted across Mary's face. Her shoulders heaved with an anxious breath. "After you and your mum visited yesterday, Gilbert told me more about this family she's inviting to dinner."

"The Hegneys."

"Yes, and . . . well . . . it's clear I'm not their kind of folk, and I'd just end up making a fool of myself and embarrassing your mother worse than she already is about having me for a daughter-in-law."

"Now, Mary, you mustn't feel that way." Although her words came closer to the truth than Thomas cared to acknowledge. Gilbert's sweet wife should never have to worry about making a fool of herself, but the Hegneys were among the most class-conscious families in Hot Springs. He eyed Mary thoughtfully. "Did Gilbert want to accept Mother's invitation?"

"I think perhaps he did—he mentioned Colonel Hegney had kindly written a letter of nomination to West Point—and now I'm feeling awful for insisting Gilbert should stay home."

Caught in the middle again. Thomas picked up his fountain pen and idly drew circles on a scrap of paper. "Mary, you know perfectly well Gilbert would do anything to make you happy. And you also know how quickly he's come around since the accident, even with being confined to a wheelchair. So whether you accept Mother's invitation or not, do it for the right reasons. Don't let her or anyone else intimidate you."

"You're right, I know. I knew I could count on your good sense." Mary took a deep breath and stood. "And now I know what I must do."

Thomas followed her to the door. "What's that, Mary?"

"Be honest with my husband about my feelings and then let him decide what he is or isn't ready for."

"You're a wise woman, Mary. My brother's a lucky man."

"I'm the lucky one. Blessed, to be sure." She smiled over her shoulder as she stepped into the corridor. Then, chewing her lip, she asked hopefully, "If by chance we do accept, you'd be there, too, wouldn't you?"

"Most certainly. You can count on me."

Relief flooded her expression. "Your kindness means everything, Thomas. Thank you."

He waved goodbye as she scurried toward the lobby. Then, alone in the corridor, he collapsed against the wall. Was he to spend the rest of his days solving everyone else's problems? Just for a while he'd like to let someone else take the reins, or at least give others the space to work out their own issues.

Perhaps it was partly why he found Joanna so appealing. Self-assured and independent, she didn't seem to *need* anything from him. Even better, she wasn't the type who'd ever cower beneath his mother's social bias—which gave him an idea. If anyone could enliven one of Mother's tediously formal dinner parties, Joanna certainly could. And perhaps Joanna's presence would help bolster Mary's confidence.

Yes. Yes, indeed. He'd invite her right away.

Pivoting on his heel, he marched back to his desk and picked up the telephone. "Pamela, ring up Joanna Trapp's number, will you?"

Only after he heard the first ring did it occur to him Joanna might still be abed after working her shift last night. He checked his watch—half past ten—and almost hung up before she answered.

Then her breathy "Hello?" whispered in his ear.

"I'm sorry if I woke you. It's Thomas."

"No, no, I've been up for hours. Sorry if I sound distracted. What did you need?"

Something in her tone brought a twinge to Thomas's chest. "It can wait. You obviously have other things—"

"Actually, I'm desperate for an objective listener. Are you free for lunch?"

How was it possible to be both elated and crushed in the same moment? More than anything in the world, he wanted to spend time with Joanna—but *not* in the context of problem-solving. He had no doubt this had something to do with Lily, and what did he know about dealing with an intractable schoolgirl? Still, he couldn't say no, not when the mere thought of being with Joanna sent his pulse racing. "I can arrange it. What time?"

A thoughtful pause. "How about eleven-thirty? You'll have to come here, though. My motorcycle isn't running. How do you feel about ham sandwiches?"

"One of my favorite meals." Right up there with fried catfish and dancing under the stars.

"Ow!" Jack kicked the filing cabinet where he'd just slammed his fingers in a drawer. Muttering a spate of curses, he gave his hand a hard shake and drew back his foot for another swift kick.

"Jack Trapp!"

He spun around to see Annemarie Vickary standing in the workroom doorway. She must have come in through the rear entrance.

She folded her arms, one eyebrow arched accusingly. "I'm going to pretend I didn't hear such foul language coming out of your mouth."

Grimacing, he tucked his throbbing fingers beneath the opposite armpit. "Sorry for the trench talk. It only comes out when I get really, really mad."

"And filing cabinets can be so obstinate. Shame on this naughty drawer for biting your fingers." Laying her handbag on Jack's desk, Annemarie walked over to the drawer he'd been filing in and gently pushed it closed. "See? That wasn't so hard, was it?"

Jack blew air between his teeth. "Guess I've been a little pre-occupied lately."

She turned with a concerned frown. "Lily?"

He nodded.

"I'm so sorry, Jack. I could see how upset Joanna was when I drove her to the school this morning."

Jack's throat clenched. He swallowed with difficulty and tried to keep his voice even. "Why did you have to drive Joanna to the high school?"

"Her motorcycle wouldn't start, and my mother didn't have the car today, so she—" Annemarie cocked her head. "You don't know anything about this yet, do you?"

Another sharp breath gusted from Jack's nostrils. "Lily's gotten herself into more trouble, obviously. Do you know what happened?"

"All I know is Joanna had an appointment with Lily's advisor to discuss the issue. She wouldn't even let me wait for her but said she'd find another way home."

If there was any consolation, at least Miss Maynard had called the house and Joanna had been there to answer. He palmed his forehead, only to wince at the pressure on his bruised fingers. "I suppose I'll hear all about it tonight."

"I'm sure this is just a stage Lily's going through, her way of coping with the losses your family has experienced."

"I hope you're right." Jack almost couldn't bear the sympathy in Annemarie's tone. Clenching his jaw, he moved to his desk and neatened a stack of purchase orders. "Can I help you with something? Need some pottery supplies?"

"Papa's already carrying a few things to my car."

Forcing a smile he didn't feel, Jack leaned against the desk. "Your father told me you finally talked the chaplain into buying an automobile. I hear it's the latest thing from Ford—electric starter and everything."

"Sam still would rather walk whenever he can, but with the ceramics shop, I needed *something* for picking up supplies and making deliveries." Uttering a light laugh, Annemarie lowered her eyes as she rested a hand on her abdomen. "Anyway, in a few months an automobile will be an absolute necessity."

Heat rose behind Jack's ears. "I didn't know. Congratulations to both you and Sam."

"Thank you. We're still getting used to the idea of an addition to our family."

"You'll be wonderful parents." Returning his attention to the purchase orders, Jack feigned rapt attention to the first one in the stack. He couldn't even parent his own sister. How could he ever hope to marry and have a family of his own someday?

❧

Joanna tore a crusty edge from her sandwich and nibbled without tasting. She'd drawn Thomas away from the hotel so she could pour out her problems with Lily, and now she couldn't find the words—much less the strength—to relate what Miss Maynard had told her this morning.

Thomas's gentle voice nudged her from her thoughts. "You've scarcely said three words since I arrived. It can't be so bad, can it?"

"Believe me, it can." Dropping the remains of the bread crust beside her barely touched sandwich, Joanna shot Thomas a forlorn glance. "I admit I was equally rebellious at Lily's age, but I still had my pride. I'd never—" She clamped her lips together and looked away, heat suffusing her face.

"Talk to me, Joanna. Tell me how I can help." Her chagrin only deepened when Thomas reached across the table to take her hand. The warmth of his touch shouldn't feel so comforting, shouldn't conjure up thoughts of melting into his embrace and willing the world away.

Giving a sniff, she jerked her hand into her lap and sat straighter. And what *was* this wetness sliding down her cheek? She snapped up her napkin and pretended to dab crumbs from her lips.

"Joanna?" Thomas's eyes spoke his concern.

"I'm afraid I've allowed myself to become ridiculously unstrung by the whole ugly business." She tried to laugh. "Why should I be surprised Lily has a boyfriend? She's almost sixteen, after all."

"A boyfriend—so *that's* what this is all about?"

"It isn't just the boyfriend." Joanna closed her eyes briefly then forced out the words. "It's the compromising position the two of them were found in."

Thomas sat silent for a moment. "So they were . . . ?"

If Joanna's face grew any hotter, her skin would sizzle. She couldn't even look at Thomas when she replied, "Miss Maynard assured me things had not . . . progressed that far. However, Lily and the boy were discovered in the backseat of an automobile in a shamefully advanced state of undress."

Shifting sideways, and clearly as uncomfortable with this discussion as Joanna, Thomas drummed his fingertips on the table. "Where and when did this happen?"

"One of their classmates happened upon them near Whittington Park. It was yesterday, while decent people were attending worship." Or, in Joanna's case, sitting in church pretending to worship. Again, she felt the sting of her anger at God, only intensified by these added worries over Lily. How could a loving God allow so much heartache in one family? The mixed aromas of buttered bread and sliced ham suddenly nauseated her, and she pushed her plate to the other end of the table.

Thomas folded his arms. "I hope the school administration has called the boy to account. He must take *some* responsibility."

"Apparently, the boy's parents are insisting Lily led him on." Rising tiredly, Joanna trudged to the sink and filled a water glass. She cooled her aching throat with several swallows and then poured the rest down the drain. "She's too young for this, Thomas. She has no idea the risks she's taking, the trouble she could get herself into."

Nor did you at her age . . . or later.

When Thomas appeared at her side, she stifled a shiver and prayed he wouldn't offer a hug, because if he did, she'd surely make a fool of herself. This was not a time for weakness, not when both Jack and Lily depended on her.

And certainly not when she saw her sister starting down the same perilous path of defiance Joanna herself had traveled.

Thomas rested his hand unsettlingly near hers on the lip of the sink. He stood close enough for her to notice the sandalwood scent from his shaving cream. "I wish I knew how to help," he murmured. "But I'm afraid my perspective is based solely on having once been a sixteen-year-old boy. And I *don't* think it would give you any encouragement."

Joanna couldn't help but laugh, though the sound was painfully thin. "You're right, it wouldn't."

"Have you talked to Lily about this yet?"

"No, she's still at school. Besides, I feel I should discuss the situation with Jack first so we can agree on how best to handle things."

"Good reasoning. You two should present a united front." His little finger—the one nearest hers—twitched almost imperceptibly. He cleared his throat. "Would you prefer not to come in to work tonight?"

Joanna glanced up in surprise. "No! I mean, of course I'll be there. Why would you suggest otherwise?"

"I just thought you could use the time at home . . . all things considered."

Shifting to face him, Joanna locked her arms across her abdomen. "I don't require special consideration. I have a job to do, and I'll do it."

"I didn't mean to offend you." Thomas took a half-step back.

"You didn't." Shoulders slumping, Joanna returned her gaze to the window over the sink. "I guess I'm not handling any of my responsibilities very well lately."

"Don't be so hard on yourself. You've had a lot to deal with. Your whole family has."

She fought an overwhelming urge to leave it all behind and rush back to Paris. At least there her life made some crazy kind of sense. At least there she could hope to make a difference. Her strong-willed independence was no asset here. With a brother she kept knocking heads with and a sister careening out of control, she'd never felt so ineffectual, so utterly powerless.

"I don't know what I'm doing here."

She didn't realize she'd spoken aloud until Thomas clamped both hands around her upper arms, compelling her to look him in the eye. "What you're doing here is taking care of your family. Jack was falling apart before you came home. And Lily needs you desperately, whether she's ready to admit it or not. I don't know what you left behind in France, but I'm certain it can't be more important than this."

A shudder raked her from head to toe, and with trembling lips she allowed Thomas to pull her into his embrace. Though she fought with every ounce of strength to hold back the tears, moments later his lapel grew wet beneath her cheek.

"It's all right, Joanna. I promise it'll be all right." Thomas's arms tightened around her, and she hated herself for how reassuring, how comfortable, it felt to be held this way.

Walter . . . oh, Walter, I'm sorry.

Abruptly she pushed away. Sniffing loudly, she swiped her blouse sleeve across her eyes. "This is embarrassing—look what I've done to your suit." Snatching a dishtowel off the hook, she dabbed at Thomas's coat front. "I'm not usually like this. It was just—"

"Joanna." He stilled her fluttering hand. "You don't have to pretend to be strong. You're worried, scared, frustrated. There's nothing wrong with borrowing a friendly shoulder to cry on."

Swiveling aside, Joanna used the corner of the dishtowel to finish mopping her tear-streaked face. She drew a steadying breath before facing Thomas again with what she hoped was a reassuring smile. "Of course, and I'm grateful. But it was wrong of me to involve you in my personal problems. You're my employer, after all. I owe you more professional respect than to drench your shoulder with my self-indulgent tears."

"Your employer—" Thomas's eyelids closed, and two rock-hard knots appeared on either side of his jaw. One fist opened and closed in a slow, tense rhythm. As he exhaled long and slow, Joanna's stomach twisted with the disturbing sense that she'd hurt him . . . hurt him deeply.

How could she be so callous? All the special attention he'd give her, from the shy smiles and lingering glances to their not-a-real-date at Isaac's fishing shack—she'd purposely ignored what was happening between them, at least from Thomas's perspective. She couldn't let this continue a moment longer.

He read in her expression the moment understanding dawned, and he wished he could turn back time and just be her friend again. Her *employer*. Because the look in her eyes—regret, chagrin, bewilderment—scalded his soul like a blast of Hot Springs water straight from the source.

One hand palming the back of his neck, the other shoved into his pants pocket, he forced a dry chuckle. "Don't think any more about this, okay? You may work for me, but it doesn't mean we can't also be"—he nearly choked on the word—"friends. I hope you'll always feel comfortable talking to me. If you ever needed to, of course. Because I'd understand if you—"

"Oh, Thomas, there's so much you *don't* understand about me." Joanna pulled her lower lip between her teeth. "Believe me, I'd never have asked you to come over, much less confided in you, if I didn't think of you as a friend. You've been more than kind, and if I've led you on, I apologize."

"Don't, please. And you haven't. Led me on, I mean." Far from it, in fact. Thomas looked longingly toward the back door. All he wanted now was to escape to the sanctuary of his office. Only a couple of hours ago he'd thought the worst that could happen was being drawn into Joanna's problems with Lily. "I should go . . ."

But then he foolishly glanced her way and found his gaze riveted to her soft, pink mouth. His breath caught somewhere just above his heart.

"Thank you for coming over." Joanna's words jolted a measure of clarity into his muddled brain. "You may not think you helped, but you did, just by listening. And by—" Brusquely she looked away, mouth tight, as if she couldn't bring herself to acknowledge that only moments ago he'd been holding her in his arms.

"Clearly, I've made you uncomfortable." He sighed audibly and moved closer to the door. "I promise, nothing like this will happen again."

"Wait, please." Before he could turn the knob, he felt her hand on his arm. She looked up at him with a plea in her eyes and a teasing smile skewing her lips. "We're both being silly, don't you think?"

He didn't think there was *anything* silly about the situation. In fact, it was downright heartbreaking. But if agreeing meant an easing of the tension between them—at least on her part—he could accept it.

With a nervous laugh, he released the doorknob and turned toward her. "You're right. Guess we both overreacted."

"Exactly. We were caught up in the emotion of discussing this thing with Lily." Joanna whooshed out a noisy breath. "I feel better already. So glad we cleared the air."

"Me, too." Thomas shuffled backward, one hand fumbling for the door. "I should be on my way, though—a lot to catch up on at the office."

She pushed a stray lock of straw-colored hair off her forehead. "Thanks again for listening."

"Anytime." He knew he was stalling but suddenly couldn't make himself open the door and leave. "You know, I was thinking . . ."

"Yes?"

"My mother is having friends over for dinner Thursday evening. Would you come?"

Joanna hesitated and glanced away. "I'm not sure I should."

Thinking quickly, Thomas blurted, "I'm only asking because Gilbert and his new bride are expected. I think you'd enjoy getting to know Mary. You two have a lot in common."

"I'd love to meet Mary, but . . . what about your mother? Her opinion of me is blatantly obvious."

A snort of stifled laughter burst from Thomas's chest. "Believe me, your presence would be a breath of fresh air. Not to mention Mary would greatly appreciate having someone besides herself in Mother's crosshairs."

Arms folded, Joanna tapped her fingers against her elbows. "So I'm to serve as a distraction, deflecting your mother's attention from Gilbert's wife."

"It certainly isn't the only reason I invited you, but . . ." Thomas grinned. "It certainly would be fun watching the fireworks."

"In that case, count me in. Madness and mayhem are my specialty."

9

Abby Wright leaned across the lunch table, her tone a rasping whisper—as if anyone could overhear them in the noisy lunchroom. "All right, Lily, tell me the truth. How much trouble are you in?"

"A lot." Shifting her gaze toward the table where Rudy Hegney sat with his loud-mouthed cohorts, Lily scrunched up her mouth. "I doubt *he* even cares."

"Why should he? He's a spoiled brat whose parents think he can do no wrong." Abby took a bite of her sandwich and chewed thoughtfully. "Honestly, how can you let yourself be taken in by him? Rudy's no good for you, and you know it."

Maybe not, but being Rudy's girl made Lily feel special. Wanted. Important. Which was more than she could say for her overbearing brother and sister. They'd both raked her over the coals last night after supper, accusing her of all sorts of sordid things. And Jack was still harping on the incident at church a couple of Sundays ago.

If he only knew why she'd really shut herself in the pastor's office Sunday morning.

Well . . . if he knew, he'd probably go after Rudy Hegney and his friends with a horsewhip.

Right after he locked Lily in her room and threw away the key.

Abby kicked her under the table. "Lily, are you listening to me?"

"What? Of course." She peeled a strip of crust from her sandwich and recalled the despairing look Joanna had given her this morning as she prepared Lily's school lunch.

"Then promise me you'll stay away from Rudy from now on. You know he only wants one thing. You're better than this. I know you are."

"You don't know any such thing." A knot grew in Lily's throat until she could barely swallow. She stole another glance at Rudy just as he looked her way. When he murmured something to the guy next to him and then broke out laughing, she stiffened and faced forward. "Anyway, don't worry about me. I know how to take care of myself."

Finishing her sandwich, Abby folded and creased her purple cotton napkin with painstaking attention and then tucked it into her lunchbox. She snapped the latch with a sharp click. "You aren't fooling anyone, Lillian Matilda Trapp. You're feeling alone and scared. You're angry because your parents died, and you think this is the only way to get attention."

"Don't be ridiculous. I don't want or need anyone's attention." Giving her friend a withering look, Lily gathered her things and pushed up from the table. "Least of all yours."

She pretended not to notice the hurt in Abby's eyes. Instead, she flounced over to a vacant table and ripped a sheet of paper from her notebook. Selecting a sharpened pencil from her pencil case, she jotted a quick note.

While folding the page and tucking away the pencil, she let her gaze travel around the room. Miss Maynard sat in the far corner with three other faculty members. The principal stood in deep conversation with one of the mathematics teachers. Though Miss Maynard had strictly admonished Lily against any further association with Rudy, at school or elsewhere, could Lily help it if she had to pass right behind his chair on her way out of the lunchroom?

And such an easy thing to "accidentally" bump his chair, drop one of her books, and then allow him to hand it to her while she oh-so-casually slipped him the note. Palming the note, he wiggled one eyebrow suggestively. She gave an imperceptible nod and hurried on her way.

Just let anyone try to stop her and Rudy from being together. If Joanna and Jack could run their own lives, so could Lily. And the snooty Miss Maynard had better keep her nose out of it.

"Are you sure you don't mind, Lillian?" Telephone receiver pressed to her ear, Joanna paced the entryway.

"Not at all. I'm perfectly fine with staying an extra hour or two until you can get here."

"I should have asked you right away after Thomas invited me, but things were rather unsettled then."

"I could see how upset you were when you came in to work Monday night." Lillian sighed. "Are things any better?"

"Not really. We've restricted Lily's privileges and expect her to come straight home from school every day." Joanna peered out the narrow window beside the front door. At the far end of the porch, Lily sat in a wicker rocker, history book open on her lap. She was supposedly studying, but judging from the faraway look in her narrowed eyes, Joanna imagined the girl was plotting how to take revenge on her cruelly unreasonable brother and sister.

"Having raised a daughter of my own, I certainly sympathize," Lillian said. "But try to remember how you were at her age. Kids in their teens tend to blow everything out of proportion. Five years from now, she'll have forgotten all about the boy—*and* how strict you were with her."

"I hope you're right." In truth, Joanna would rather forget what she'd been like at Lily's age. She squeezed her eyes shut at the memory of her mother's tear-streaked face the day Joanna had broken the vase. "Thanks again for filling in for me. I'll try to be there by ten at the latest."

"If the party goes longer, don't worry about it. Enjoy yourself." A bantering smile came into Lillian's voice. "You and Thomas Ballard make quite the charming couple, you know."

"Oh, please! He's just a friend." Joanna certainly didn't need to be reminded of his interest—or her own confused feelings about him.

Lillian gave a low chuckle. "I could name more than one happy couple in town who started out as friends."

"I've heard all about Annemarie Kendall and Chaplain Vickary. Believe me, it isn't happening with Thomas and me." Seeing Lily close her history book and start for the door, Joanna decided she'd better hang up and finish dressing for dinner before she risked another sisterly confrontation. Thanking Lillian once more for agreeing to stay late at the switchboard, Joanna ended the call and hurried upstairs moments before Lily slammed the front door.

"Spying on me?" Lily shouted up the stairs. "I saw you looking out the window. Maybe you'd rather handcuff me to the drainpipe and be done with it."

Pausing on the landing, Joanna clenched her fists and counted to ten. She couldn't allow herself to be goaded by a fifteen-year-old. When she felt she could speak calmly, she leaned over the banister. "I've put a meatloaf in the oven, and there are fresh snap peas in the icebox ready to cook. Jack should be home at the usual time."

"I know, I know. I'm not a baby." Lily tossed her schoolbooks onto the hall table and slogged into the kitchen.

Gazing after her, Joanna shook her head and hoped Jack got home from the factory before Thomas arrived. Lily's surly attitude didn't inspire trust, and Joanna worried about leaving her to her own devices for even a few minutes.

Fortunately, having sought fashion advice from Annemarie during a shopping excursion yesterday, Joanna wasn't nearly as worried about dressing for dinner at the Ballard house. In her room, she paused at the open wardrobe door to admire her new rose-pink tiered skirt with matching shawl-collared blouse. Annemarie had insisted the color was especially flattering to Joanna's fair complexion—not something Joanna was accustomed to thinking about, but she did appreciate the assurance of looking her best tonight.

Now, if only her unruly hair would cooperate!

Or maybe it would provide a window of opportunity.

After slipping into the skirt and blouse then running a brush through her hair, she steeled her nerves and went out to the landing. "Lily?" she called in her gentlest tone. "I wonder if you'd come upstairs for a minute."

Lily appeared at the foot of the stairs, a scowl marring her delicate, heart-shaped face. "Now what did I do?"

Joanna winced. Considering how she and Jack had been riding Lily, why shouldn't the girl assume she was in trouble again? Raising the brush, Joanna heaved an exaggerated shrug. "I can't seem to do anything with my hair. Would you help?"

"Oh, all right." With a roll of her eyes, Lily plodded up the steps, but Joanna felt certain she'd glimpsed a spark of interest, well-disguised though it was.

Joanna handed Lily the hairbrush and then sat in front of her dressing table mirror. "I thought dinner with the Ballards deserved better than my usual messy bun, but I'm just no good at this."

"You could always cut it short. I read in a magazine that bobs are the latest trend." Lily frowned into the mirror as she combed her fingers through Joanna's thick mass of hair. "But I wouldn't if I were you. It's too pretty."

The last words were spoken so softly that Joanna wondered if she'd actually heard them. "How do you keep your hair so soft and manageable?"

Glancing away shyly, Lily appeared surprised by the compliment. "Abby taught me about using a lemon-juice rinse after I shampoo." She gave Joanna's hair a twist, pushing it one way and another while studying the effects in the mirror. "Hand me some pins and one of those tortoise-shell combs."

Ten minutes later, Lily had styled Joanna's hair in a quite passable pompadour. "There. Now all you need are some earrings. And maybe a brooch. Your blouse is nice, but the neckline is rather plain."

Joanna turned her head from side to side, admiring the hairstyle she'd never have achieved on her own. "I don't have much jewelry—never had any use for it."

"Wait right here." Lily scurried from the room and soon returned with small cherrywood keepsake box. She set it on the dressing table and opened the lid to reveal three rows of compartments lined with red velvet. Selecting a pair of dainty pearl earrings, she dropped them into Joanna's palm. "Here, try these."

Joanna lifted one and held it to the light. "They're lovely. Are you sure you don't mind?"

"Just don't lose them. Abby gave them to me for my birthday." From another compartment Lily chose a gold filigree brooch, the center of which was a glass-encased miniature rose. "This will look pretty with your dress."

By the time Joanna had donned the jewelry and slipped into the stylish brown pumps she'd borrowed from Annemarie, she felt quite elegant. She turned in a small circle in front of her full-length mirror. "Will I pass inspection with the Ballards?"

Lily smiled her approval. Only the barest glimmer of a smile, true, but a welcome sight nonetheless. "You should dress up more often."

A car rumbled in the driveway, and shortly afterward the kitchen door banged. "Jack must be home," Joanna said as she gathered her shawl and handbag.

Immediately, Lily's expression soured. "The changing of the guards."

"Oh, honey, don't think of us that way." Joanna went to her sister and cradled her cheek with one hand. "Believe me, everything we do is only because we love you."

Arms crossed, Lily pursed her lips. "You'd better hurry downstairs. Your beau will be here any minute."

"Thomas isn't—" Oh, why did she even argue the point? Bristling, Joanna started for the door. She had much more important things to be concerned with than how others perceived her friendship with Thomas Ballard.

✐❧

Thomas paused on his way past the dining room and peeked in to find his mother making minute adjustments to a floral centerpiece. "I'm just leaving to pick up Joanna. We should be back before everyone else arrives."

"Good, because it might be wise to instruct Miss Trapp in the finer points of table etiquette. I've observed her social skills are rather lacking."

"Whatever you say, Mother." Giving his head a tiny shake, Thomas continued down the hall, only to be stopped by his mother's continued discourse.

"I do hope you are not entertaining ideas about courting the young lady."

Taking three giant steps back, Thomas swiveled to glare at his mother. "And if I were?"

Evelyn Ballard folded her bejeweled hands at her waist. "Then I would once again strongly urge you to consider the repercussions of such an ill-favored relationship."

"And I would once again urge *you* to cease judging people by your ridiculous societal standards and accept your sons' right to fall in love with whomever they choose."

She had the decency to look duly chastised as she stepped toward him with one hand outstretched. "Surely, you know I always and only have your best interests at heart. As for dear Mary, who can deny she's been an absolute angel in her devotion to Gilbert?"

"You, apparently. You criticize her at every turn." Thomas couldn't believe he'd let himself be drawn into another of these pointless discussions.

Neither could he believe he'd actually used the words *falling in love*. This attraction he felt for Joanna—was it growing into love?

His mother's muffled sob dispelled such thoughts. She pressed a fist to her mouth. "Do I? Do I *really*?"

He dredged up his last words, already nearly forgotten. "Yes, Mother, you are highly critical of Mary. And what's worse, instead of confronting her directly, you go behind her back and complain to me. This behavior has to stop."

"Am I so horrid?" His mother retrieved the monogrammed lace handkerchief tucked at her waist and dabbed her eyes.

With a pained sigh, Thomas strode into the dining room and wrapped his mother in a hug. "No, no, you're not a horrid person," he murmured, patting her back. "I know you've tried to make peace with Mary, but you can't do it halfway. Your acceptance of her must be without reservation." Shifting to look her in the eye, he added sternly, "And it goes for Joanna, too. I don't know where things are headed, but she has become very special to me."

His mother nodded, as acquiescent as he'd ever seen her. "I'll try. Truly I will."

Rather than question her sincerity, Thomas decided to simply send up a prayer of thanks and hope Mother's attitude lasted. "All right, then. You finish getting ready for dinner while I fetch Joanna. I'll be back soon."

On the drive over to Joanna's, Thomas allowed his thoughts to carry him back to Monday and those magical moments when he'd held her in his arms. She may not be ready to see him as anything other than a friend, but time could change things. Maybe another prayer was in order . . . and the faith to believe that if God could work in his mother's heart, He could change Joanna's heart as well.

Arriving in her driveway, he took a moment to collect himself before striding up the front walk and ringing the bell. When she opened the door, her lips curving upward in a shy smile, he almost couldn't breathe. "Wow. You look stunning."

Pink crept up her already glowing cheeks. She handed him her shawl and then turned so he could drape it around her shoulders. "Lily helped me with my hair. I hope the dress is appropriate for the occasion."

"Absolutely." Thomas waited while she called goodbye to Jack and Lily.

"I admit I'm rather nervous about this evening," Joanna said as they started out to the car.

"There's no reason to be." He wished he could give her hand a reassuring squeeze. "Just be yourself, and I promise you'll get along famously with everyone."

"Even with your mother?"

"If she gives you any trouble, she'll answer to me—and she knows it."

"All right, then." Joanna lifted her chin. "I'll simply pretend tonight is another kind of adventure."

Thomas laughed. "Good strategy. I may do the same, myself."

When they arrived at the Ballard house, Mary had just steered Gilbert's Cole Eight into the driveway. She'd only recently learned to drive and hadn't done a good job of parking.

"Mother won't be happy about her azalea bush," Thomas said with a groan. Shutting off the engine, he glimpsed Joanna reaching for her door handle. Then, just as quickly, she drew her hand into her lap. He didn't know whether to feel honored or concerned.

Either way, he intended to take full advantage. Rounding the car, he opened her door and offered his hand. She accepted it graciously, extending one lovely brown slipper to the ground.

As he closed the door behind her, she nodded toward Gilbert's roadster, where Mary struggled to drag his wheelchair from the backseat. "Should we help?"

"Give her a minute." Thomas couldn't keep the smirk from his face as he stated, "Mary's as independent as you are."

Even in the gathering dusk, he caught the spark in Joanna's eyes. "I sincerely hope you meant that as a compliment."

He grinned. "Most definitely."

As soon as Mary had assisted Gilbert out of the car and into his wheelchair, Thomas led Joanna over to say hello.

"Joanna Trapp," Gilbert said with his typical charm. "Last time I saw you, you were a skinny schoolgirl with a pigtail down your back."

She narrowed one eye. "And last time I saw *you*, you were a shaggy-haired, stuffed-shirt eighteen-year-old who couldn't wait to get to West Point." Then her tone softened. "I'm sorry for what happened to you in the war . . . and afterward."

Gilbert took Mary's hand and gazed up at her with adoring eyes. "If not for the war, and what's happened since, this beautiful lady would never have come into my life. Joanna, may I introduce the love of my life, Mary McClarney Ballard."

The two women shook hands. "It's my honor, Mary," Joanna said. "Thomas has already told me so much about you."

"And I've heard a wee bit about you as well. It's clear Thomas is quite—"

Standing behind Joanna, Thomas shook his head violently. "We should go inside, don't you think? Mother may need some last-minute help before the Hegneys arrive."

Joanna spun around, a strange look on her face. "I'm sorry, who else is coming?"

"Colonel Ira Hegney and his wife, Fannie." An uneasy feeling churned in Thomas's belly. "They're old family friends. Didn't I mention them before?"

"If you'd mentioned the name Hegney, I would certainly have remembered."

"Why? Do you know them?"

"I sincerely hope not, or this could prove to be a most provocative evening." Her lips flattened. "They don't happen to have a son at Hot Springs High, do they?"

Thomas's mouth went dry. "You don't mean—"

"I do."

10

*I*f he thought for an instant he could convince Joanna to get back in the car and let him take her home, he'd do so immediately. But the determined look in her eyes promised he'd have a huge fight on his hands if he so much as suggested the idea.

"Pardon us," he said to Gilbert and Mary before drawing Joanna aside. Keeping a stiff smile in place, he whispered, "Please, Joanna, don't say anything to embarrass my family or the Hegneys. The colonel is a respected member of Hot Springs society, and I'm sure he will be most willing to address the situation. Just not"— nodding toward the house, he muted a groan—"here."

Joanna's gaze followed Mary and Gilbert's progress up a recently constructed ramp at one end of the front porch. "Don't worry, Thomas. I have no intention of causing a scene."

"Thank you." Thomas offered his arm as they started for the porch steps.

"However, I plan to take full advantage of this opportunity to gauge what kind of people the Hegneys *really* are."

Glimpsing the scheming look in her eyes, Thomas wondered exactly how worried he should be.

They reached the front door as Marguerite opened it for Mary and Gilbert. "My two favorite boys and their young ladies! Y'all get yourselves in here right now. Your mama's in the parlor, so go on in whilst I hang up your wraps."

Thomas slid Joanna's shawl from her shoulders and handed it to Marguerite. "Are the Hegneys here?"

"No, sir, not yet." Marguerite cast Joanna an appreciative glance before scurrying down the hall to the coat closet.

By the time Thomas showed Joanna into the parlor, his mother had risen to greet Gilbert with a hug and a kiss on the cheek. Then, to Thomas's amazement, she took both Mary's hands and smiled affectionately. "My dear, you look lovely this evening. I'm so glad I persuaded you to come."

"Why, thank you, Mrs.— I mean, Mother Ballard." Mary's throat shifted with a nervous swallow. "It's so . . . nice . . . to be here."

"And Joanna." Thomas's mother laid a hand to her bosom and sighed as if greeting a long-lost friend. "You are a vision in pink. And your coiffure—you *must* tell me who styles it for you."

Sharing a disbelieving glance with Thomas, Joanna lightly patted her coiffure. "My sister did my hair. She's much more adept than I am."

The pleasantries aside, Thomas led Joanna to the sofa, seating her next to Mary. While the two of them got better acquainted and his mother went to check on dinner preparations, Thomas drew a striped satin side chair closer to Gilbert's wheelchair. "You look stronger every day, Gil."

"I'm coming along." Gilbert absently massaged the stump of his left thigh.

"Mary said you saw your surgeon recently. Any hope at all you might get another prosthesis?"

Gilbert's jaw tensed. "The doctor doubts what's left of my leg could support an artificial limb."

"I'm sorry, Gil. I hoped . . ." Grimacing, Thomas looked away.

"Don't feel sorry for me. I'm happier than I've ever been in my life." His gaze shifting to Mary, Gilbert's eyes lit up.

A spasm of envy twisted through Thomas's gut. "You amaze me, brother. I pray I'd have even half your courage under similar circumstances."

"It's God who's amazing. Look at how He's blessed me." With a knowing grin, Gilbert gestured toward Joanna. "Looks like you're getting a blessing of your own."

"Joanna's not interested in anything but friendship." Still, Thomas found his gaze drawn to the way she tilted her head just so, a crooked smile quirking her lips as she listened to Mary talk about life on the farm.

"Maybe you two just need to spend more time together, share a few more 'adventures.'" When Thomas looked at him askance, Gilbert went on, "I heard about the catfish fry. Also heard my stodgy little brother really cut loose on the dance floor."

Stifling a snicker, Thomas felt heat climb into his cheeks. "Most fun I've had in a long time."

"See? I told you to get out from behind your desk more often."

"Maybe so, but—"

The doorbell rang, followed by a commotion in the entry hall as Marguerite admitted the Hegneys and Mother hurried from the dining room to greet them. Rising, Thomas shared a look with Joanna and hoped she caught his silent plea for tact.

Jack used half a biscuit to mop up the last traces of meatloaf gravy and then carried his dishes to the sink. As he rinsed his plate, he scowled over his shoulder at Lily. "You shouldn't have taken so much food if you had no intention of eating it. It's downright wasteful."

"So add it to my growing list of sins." She scowled back, one arm hooked around her barely touched plate of food. Then, heaving a pained sigh, she rose and carried her plate to the icebox.

"Don't worry, I'll eat it tomorrow. I promise not to squander your hard-earned provisions."

Teeth clenched, Jack recalled Joanna's words to him before she'd left this evening: *"You know the old saying about catching more flies with honey than with vinegar? Try it with Lily. You might be surprised."*

Before she could round the table and escape upstairs, Jack blocked her path. "I'm sorry for snapping at you. If you're not feeling well, I understand."

Without meeting his gaze, Lily folded her arms across her abdomen. "I'm just not as hungry as I thought. Can I go to my room now?"

"Yeah, sure." Jack stepped out of the way.

When she'd disappeared through the kitchen door, Jack sank into his chair with a groan. He wanted to be angry with Joanna for leaving him to deal with Lily alone—again—but how could he fault her for enjoying an evening out with friends? Joanna had really tried the last few days to handle things on the home front, and there were definite signs she was making headway with Lily.

But this latest problem—if Jack ever got his hands on that Hegney boy, he'd throttle him good!

As he reached for his water glass, his elbow brushed the stack of mail he'd carried in earlier. Leaning back, he thumbed through the envelopes. Not much of interest other than a couple of bills and a Kress's Dime Store advertisement.

At the bottom of the pile he came across a thin envelope addressed to Joanna. The letter bore a French postmark, and somewhere en route the flap had been torn, allowing one of the onionskin pages to work its way through the opening. Jack didn't intend to snoop, but his eye was drawn to the looping, feminine signature—*Véronique.*

Curiosity won over his better judgment. Jack slid a finger beneath the tattered envelope flap, tore it the rest of the way, and unfolded the letter. He'd hoped only to get a glimpse of the life Joanna had left behind and perhaps understand her a little better—until he saw the entire letter was written in French. He'd learned enough to get by while serving in France, but the contents of this letter far outpaced his translation skills. Only a few phrases were immediately recognizable:

La jeune fille—the little girl.

Morte—dead.

The name Walter.

And finally, just above the signature, *Retourne-toi bientôt, s'il te plait*—please return soon.

A twinge in his gut, Jack stuffed the letter back into the envelope and smoothed the torn flap as best he could. Who was the little girl this woman wrote about? Who was Walter? Was one of them ill or dying?

Thudding footsteps alerted him to Lily's approach. He buried the envelope beneath the rest of the mail and then strode to the sink, hoping to look busy doing dishes. After some rustling sounds in the foyer, he heard her start upstairs again.

Breathing out a sigh, Jack shut off the water faucet and collapsed against the counter. Guilt gnawed at him for prying into Joanna's private correspondence—though he hadn't learned much. Even so, it was what he *didn't* know that concerned him. How many times did he have to remind himself his sister had left a whole other life behind in France? She must have friends there, perhaps even people she loved like family.

A little girl. Someone named Walter. Would whatever news Véronique had shared entice Joanna to return?

But we're her family, Lord. Lily and I need her here. Please don't let her leave us again.

Hard as Joanna tried not to like Colonel Hegney and his wife, she found them quite cordial. As it turned out, the colonel insisted he recognized Joanna's voice from her service with the Army Signal Corps.

"You 'Hello Girls' did an outstanding job over there," he said, raising his glass to her during dinner. "I daresay you were invaluable in helping us win the war."

"I was proud to serve. It's an experience I will never forget." Joanna sliced off a bite of poached salmon. Seasoned with lemon and dill, the fish was quite flavorful, yet somehow not nearly as enjoyable as Isaac's fried catfish. Remembering that night— another experience Joanna would never forget—she smiled to herself. She still could hardly believe Thomas had arranged such an "adventure."

Mrs. Hegney tilted her head to peer around the candelabra standing between her and Joanna. "You must have found it unnerving, being a woman and so close to the front. Ira tried to spare me the distressing details in his letters, but I read between the lines." She sent her husband a loving glance. "I worried myself sick the whole time he was gone."

"How well I know, Fannie." Mrs. Ballard's eyes glistened as she looked toward Gilbert at the opposite end of the table. "We are all so blessed our loved ones came home alive."

Gilbert reached across the corner of the table to take his wife's hand. "How about we change the subject? Colonel, I heard you might have some political aspirations after you retire. Any chance of throwing your hat in the next mayoral race?"

"Oh, no! At least not until Rudy graduates." Colonel Hegney clicked his tongue. "Our youngest son has become quite full of himself."

Thomas's hand found Joanna's beneath the edge of the tablecloth. At his meaningful squeeze, she slanted him a subtle glance of reassurance. Catching the colonel's eye, she said casually, "He must be in his teens."

Mrs. Hegney released a withering sigh. "How did you know?"

"Just a guess." Joanna smiled knowingly as she buttered a roll.

"Rudy will settle down once he graduates." Colonel Hegney pursed his lips. "He'll have to, if he expects to succeed at West Point."

From there, the conversation veered to military life as Gilbert and the colonel traded West Point stories. Reassured the Hegneys had at least attempted to raise their son well, Joanna allowed herself to relax and enjoy the rest of the evening. Tomorrow she would call on the Hegneys at home, introduce herself as Lily's sister, and speak with them privately about the teens' involvement.

After the dessert plates were cleared away, Mrs. Ballard invited her guests to the parlor for coffee. When they passed the grandfather clock in the hall, Joanna sucked in a breath. "Oh, dear, it's later than I thought. I told Lillian I'd relieve her by ten."

Thomas apologized. "Mother's dinners do go on and on. It's only a little past nine. How about one cup of coffee and then I'll drive you straight to the hotel?"

"How am I supposed to get home after my shift?"

"We'll have Jack meet us there with your car, and I'll drop him back at home."

The plan would prevent her from keeping Lillian waiting any longer than necessary. "All right, but just one cup and then we leave."

"Agreed."

After telephoning Jack with the plan, she joined Thomas on the sofa, almost wishing she'd insisted he take her home at once. It was hard enough sitting next to him at dinner, sensing how his family and friends interpreted their being together. She liked Thomas very much, but she'd already been in love, and never again did she want to risk the agony of loss.

Besides, love was a fickle thing. Parents said they loved you but then let you down when you most needed them. Friends betrayed. Lovers died. And God? If God's love were trustworthy, He'd have long ago quashed the evil running rampant in this world.

"Cream or sugar, miss?"

She looked up with a start to find Marguerite standing before her with a silver coffee service. "No, thank you. I take it black." She lifted one of the delicate china cups from the tray.

"You looked a million miles away just then." Thomas stirred a dollop of cream into his cup.

Joanna offered a weak smile. "Just thinking about . . . family problems."

As soon as politeness would allow, she made her excuses to Mrs. Ballard and company, expressed her gratitude for the lovely evening, and asked Thomas to drive her to the Arlington.

"You seemed rather withdrawn after dinner," Thomas said as he helped her into the passenger seat. "I hope you aren't sorry I convinced you to stay."

"Not at all." She gave a short laugh, hoping to lighten the mood. "It was lovely getting to know Gilbert's wife. The Hegneys turned out to be quite pleasant as well."

"I told you it would be an interesting evening." With a satisfied smile, Thomas closed her door and hurried around to the driver's side.

As he started the motor, Joanna shifted to face him. "And I daresay your mother was on her best behavior."

"Wasn't she, though?" Chuckling over his shoulder, Thomas backed the Jeffery into the street. "We had a little chat earlier. I'm rather proud of the way she comported herself."

They continued in silence until Thomas parked in his space behind the Arlington and shut off the engine. When he reached for his door handle, Joanna looked over at him in surprise. "I can see myself inside."

"Nonsense. I wouldn't think of leaving my dinner date at the curb."

"Thomas, I'm not—"

He held up one hand. "Poor choice of words—sorry. Look, Joanna, the truth is I enjoy spending time with you, but I know better than to expect anything to come of our . . . friendship." His glance danced sideways before he looked back at her with barely concealed longing in his eyes. "I'd like to ask you out again soon. Say you won't turn me down, okay?"

Throat constricting, she tore her gaze away. To agree to continue seeing him risked giving him false hope she'd eventually soften her heart toward him. But it was impossible. Her true heart, along with everything she held most dear, had died on the battlefield at Blanc Mont Ridge.

Before a tear escaped—and before common sense prevailed—she blurted out, "Of course I won't turn you down, Thomas. Who knows what the future holds? Let's just have fun together for as long as we have."

He gave her an odd look. "All right, if that's what you want." Breaking eye contact, he shoved open his door and stepped from the car.

Not this time. Joanna had her door open and was standing on the pavement before he rounded the hood. "You're not obligated to see me to the hotel door. Besides, Jack should be here any minute."

"Who said anything about seeing you to the door? I forgot I left some notes on my desk I need to look over before a meeting tomorrow." Leaving her standing beside the car, he started up the walkway, then paused with a nonchalant glance over his shoulder. "Aren't you coming? It's nearly ten. You don't want to keep Lillian waiting."

11

Saturday, blessed Saturday! With no reason to drag herself from bed to see Lily off to school, Joanna relished another two hours of uninterrupted sleep.

Uninterrupted? Maybe. Sleep? Debatable. As usual, Joanna tossed and turned more than she actually slept. Cursed with a brain that resisted repose, she'd already lost too much sleep over Monday's visit with Miss Maynard concerning Lily's latest problems. Then the last two nights had been given over to reliving the Ballard dinner party, and its aftermath, ad infinitum.

Did she truly believe she could pursue friendship with Thomas and not lead him on, even unintentionally? Was it fair to either of them to try?

Rolling over, she pulled the sheet over her eyes to block the sunlight slicing through flimsy linen curtains. Maybe today would be a good day to shop for heavier drapes. If she continued working the night shift, she must start sleeping better. Or longer. Preferably both.

After sending Lily off to school yesterday, she'd walked around in a stupor most of the day, finally choosing to postpone the visit with Mrs. Hegney. It wouldn't do to tackle the issue without a clear head. Perhaps today would be better.

The clatter of pots and pans echoed from the kitchen. Jack must be making breakfast, and he didn't know how to do so quietly. Throwing off the covers with a moan, Joanna heaved herself out of bed and dragged on her chenille robe. She flung open the bedroom door and trudged to the landing as another crash shook the house. "Jack. Jack! What on earth are you doing down there—remodeling the entire kitchen?"

"Dropped a skillet," he shouted back. "Sorry if I woke you."

Just then Lily's bedroom door opened. Scraping a hand through her mop of sleep-mussed hair, she yawned. "What's going on? Did we have an earthquake?"

"Next thing to it. Grab your robe and slippers. We'd better go rescue what's left of the kitchen, if Jack hasn't destroyed it already."

A glimmer of a smile lit Lily's face, but only for a split second—and enough to give Joanna hope. Before Lily could balk and retreat to her room, Joanna swooped past her, grabbed Lily's robe off the foot of the bed, and kicked her slippers into the hall. "I mean it," she said, shaking out the robe and holding it open for Lily. "Let's go help before he sets the house afire."

"Oh, all right." Grudgingly, Lily slipped on her robe and slippers and followed Joanna downstairs. "Although I can't say you're much better at cooking. I'm getting sick and tired of your lumpy oatmeal."

"You know where we keep the corn flakes." Joanna grinned at her sister.

Lily flounced past Joanna and into the kitchen. "Jack, I hope you're not making pancakes again. Last time, they were tough as shoe leather."

Pausing in the doorway, Joanna held her breath as she waited for Jack's response. Touchy as he'd been lately, one rashly spoken word could easily destroy what meager progress they'd made with Lily.

Facing the counter, he inhaled slowly and then turned with a plastered-on smile, a batter-coated wooden spoon held aloft and dripping down his arm. "If either of my dear, sweet sisters thinks she can do better, I shall gladly allow you to take over."

When Joanna glimpsed the dusting of flour coating his shirt and trousers, she had to suppress a giggle.

Lily wasn't so kind and doubled over in a fit of laughter. "Oh, Jack, you're a mess!"

"Now, Lily, we can't fault a man for trying." Joanna hooked her arm through her sister's. "What do you say we let him off the hook? Help me make breakfast?"

Lily rolled her eyes. "Fine. It may be the only way I get anything decent to eat around here." She trudged across the room, snatched the spoon from Jack's hand, and inspected the array of ingredients he'd been mixing. Sniffing the batter, she wrinkled her nose and then flushed the whole thing down the drain.

"Now wait a minute!" Jack raised his hands in disbelief.

"Believe me, this would *not* have been edible. Jack obviously doesn't know there's a difference between baking *soda* and baking *powder*."

Eyes widening, Joanna asked meekly, "There's a difference?" When Lily's mouth dropped open, Joanna flicked a hand and started for the pantry. "Just teasing. I knew that. Really, Jack, how ignorant can you be?"

"I'm not ignorant. I just—" At Joanna's pointed stare and brisk nod toward Lily, he snapped his mouth shut. A second later, he lightened his tone. "Well, maybe I can learn a thing or two from you . . . experts."

Before long, the three of them sat at the table devouring Lily's fluffy, perfectly browned pancakes and laughing over the mess Jack had made of the kitchen. Listening to her brother and sister in playful banter took Joanna back to the happier days of her childhood, before their mother's deepening melancholia cast a pall over the entire family. This was the way a family should be. Laughing together. Helping each other. Sharing the good times and bad.

What happened to you, Mother? Or perhaps the real question was, when did Joanna give up trying to understand?

Finishing breakfast, Joanna rose to clear the dishes. As she stacked plates and silverware, she noticed the growing stack of mail at the other end of the table. "How long has this been piling up?"

Gaze shifting nervously, Jack drained his coffee cup. "A few days, maybe."

Joanna dropped the dishes in the sink and then returned to her chair. She pulled the stack of envelopes and advertisements to the middle of the table and began sorting through them. "I've been so preoccupied this week, I haven't even thought about checking the mail. I hope we don't have any overdue bills. "

"I glanced at it once or twice." Jack rose and marched to the stove for more coffee.

Lily's chair scraped the floor as she stood in a huff. "You wouldn't be so preoccupied if you weren't watching my every move twenty-four hours a day."

Her sister's sudden mood change reminded Joanna of the problems they still needed to resolve. Hoping to restore the pleasant atmosphere they'd enjoyed over breakfast, she reached for Lily's hand and smiled up at her. "Honey, I know how hard you've worked all week to follow house rules and keep your grades up. I thought you might like to invite a friend over later."

Lily glanced down, fingers twisted together until her knuckles turned white. She shook her head firmly. "I don't think so. I'd like to go to my room now." Without waiting to be excused, she darted from the kitchen.

Sharing a look with Jack, Joanna chewed her lip. "Things were going so well. I thought she'd be happy about a little more freedom."

"I've given up trying to understand the girl." He plunked his coffee cup on the counter and set to washing dishes.

"Neither of us has the luxury of giving up on her. I may be late in accepting my responsibility, but I'm here now, and I'm determined we'll keep what's left of our family intact." With a resolute sigh, Joanna resumed her perusal of the mail.

The sound of running water ceased. "Joanna, there's something I should tell you."

"Yes?" Coming to the bottom of the stack, she found a thin, stained envelope and recognized Véronique's handwriting. Then she noticed the torn flap. "Jack, did you open this?"

"I was going to tell you." He took the chair at the end of the table. "It was already coming open. I couldn't help myself. I'm sorry."

"You read my letter? My private correspondence?" Staring at her brother in dismay, Joanna slid the pages from the envelope.

"Not exactly. I don't know much French." Jack palmed the back of his head. "It was wrong, I know. I just thought if I knew more about your life in France, it would help me understand you better."

Joanna was already skimming the letter, and what she read clutched at her heart. "Oh, God, no—not Yvette!"

"What happened? Who's Yvette?"

Tears streaming down her face, Joanna crushed the pages against her chest. "She's a little girl I'd grown attached to at the orphanage where I volunteered. Oh, Jack, she's dead!"

"I'm sorry, Jo." He pulled her to her feet and held her close while she sobbed against his shoulder.

"It isn't fair," she mourned. "I'll never understand how men of reason can justify going to war and slaughtering one another in the name of patriotism. What do they gain but widows and orphans and whole countries brought to ruin?"

"I've got no answers for you. I wish I did."

With a shudder, Joanna freed herself and found a napkin to dry her eyes. "I can't help thinking if I'd been there, I could have done something. Yvette was an innocent little girl. She shouldn't have died."

Jack retrieved the letter Joanna had dropped and carefully smoothed the wrinkled pages. "I'm sure your friend—what's her name, Véronique?—must have done whatever she could. And this guy Walter—is he connected with the orphanage?"

At the mention of Walter's name, another wave of grief flooded Joanna. Staggering, she sank into a chair before her knees collapsed. Rather than succumb to more tears, she focused her anger on Jack. "Don't you ever, ever, *ever* open my letters again!"

Thomas couldn't stifle his disappointment at not seeing Joanna in church Sunday morning. Jack and Lily sat in their usual pew, and, as usual, Lily looked quite unhappy to be there. Jack didn't look particularly attentive, himself.

When worship ended, Thomas sent his mother on ahead and timed his exit from the pew to coincide with Jack's. "No Joanna today?" he asked casually.

Jack shook his head. "She hasn't been sleeping well and wanted to catch up on her rest."

Thomas knew she'd started her shift early last night in exchange for Lillian's covering for her last Thursday. She had Sunday off this week, though, and he'd hoped to plan another of their so-called friendship outings. "Do you think she'd mind if I telephoned later?"

"I honestly can't say." One hand on Lily's shoulder, Jack pointed her toward the narthex doors. "We'd best be getting home. Nice to see you, Thomas."

A brush-off if he'd ever experienced one. More trouble with Lily, most likely. Following a few paces behind, Thomas wondered if Joanna had spoken yet with the Hegneys.

"There you are, Thomas, dawdling as usual." His mother stood on the front walk chatting with friends. "The O'Neals have invited us to join them for lunch at the Eastman. Tell me you won't feel like a traitor if we accept."

He wasn't sure which was worse, the risk of being recognized while dining at a rival hotel, or allowing his mother to play matchmaker again with the O'Neals' twin daughters. Doing some quick thinking, he replied, "Didn't I tell you, Mother? I made other plans for lunch."

He didn't mention he'd made them only this instant.

"It was so *thoughtful* of you to let me know." Puckering her lips, his mother turned to Mrs. O'Neal. "Honestly, today's young people. What can be done with them?"

Or their mothers, he didn't say aloud. Leaving her with her friends, Thomas went on to his car. A quiet meal at his desk seemed exactly the ticket, considering his current mood. It may be the Sabbath, but if he couldn't spend time with Joanna, he may as well catch up on paperwork.

At the Arlington, he stopped in the kitchen to order a salad and bowl of soup, then went to his office and shrugged out of his coat and tie. While waiting for lunch, he attacked his inbox, which lately seemed to fill up twice as fast as he could empty it. As he sorted invoices, staff schedules, and various items of correspondence, he came upon a plea for donations to a European war orphans fund. Folded within the letter was a magazine picture of a doughboy offering a candy bar to a waif-thin boy in tattered clothing. The letter also referenced a *Life Magazine* article where one could view more photographs of orphaned children.

"Poor kid." Staring at the picture, Thomas sat back with a muted groan. When a waiter delivered vegetable beef soup and endive salad a few moments later, he barely glanced up. Hard to imagine devouring a delicious meal when he'd just been made aware of thousands of homeless and hungry children.

Regrettably, he couldn't authorize a donation on behalf of the Arlington without approval from higher up. However, a check from his personal account was another matter. After stuffing the pages back into the envelope, he tucked it into his inside coat pocket. He'd be sure to show the letter to his mother and Gilbert as well. Family money had to be good for something besides expensive clothing, lavish dinner parties, and the newest automobiles.

Though seeing the picture of the little boy had dulled Thomas's appetite, he decided leaving his lunch uneaten would do nothing to help a hungry orphan. Eating with one hand and riffling through paperwork with the other, he emptied his soup bowl about the same time he reached the bottom of his inbox—fortunately, without leaving too many broth stains for his secretary to find when she filed.

By two o'clock he'd cleared his desk and could find no more excuses to avoid going home. He could always drive out and see Gilbert, but did he need another reminder his war-hero brother was happily married, while Thomas remained a perennial bachelor with no prospects?

He stared at the telephone. Would he risk so much to ring the Trapp house and simply ask if Joanna cared to step out for a bit? Though it was mid-November, the day had turned beautiful and sunny. They could drive up Hot Springs Mountain and climb the observation tower, or perhaps wander through Happy Hollow and have silly pictures made at one of those touristy photograph galleries.

Before he could second-guess himself, he picked up the receiver and asked Lillian at the switchboard to call Joanna's number.

She answered on the third ring. "Thomas, I'm just on my way out the door. Is this about anything urgent?"

He didn't care for the tension in her tone. "Is everything all right? Jack said you haven't been sleeping well."

"I never sleep well. And it's none of Jack's business anyway," she added under her breath.

He braced a hip against his desk. "You're upset about something. I can hear it in your voice."

A soft sigh whispered through the telephone line. "Between the problems with Lily and now Jack meddling in my private life, I'm about ready to give up and return to France."

Thomas winced at the sudden twinge in his gut. "Please tell me you're not serious."

"About which part?"

"Joanna . . ." As if he had to spell it out. "Look, why don't I pick you up and we can go somewhere to talk?"

"I can't. I told you, I'm on my way out. The Heg—" She cleared her throat, and it sounded as if she covered the mouthpiece. "No, Lily, I haven't seen your literature book. Have you looked in the parlor?" Another few seconds went by before she came back on the line. "Sorry, I didn't want Lily to overhear."

"I think I got the gist of it. You're seeing the Hegneys this afternoon?"

"I am. Lily doesn't know."

"Is Jack going with you?"

Her tone bristled. "I prefer to handle this without his involvement."

Something was definitely going on between Joanna and her brother. "Then how about I tag along? Since the Hegneys are family friends, maybe I can help smooth the way."

Thomas could hear her measured breathing. "You have a point. I can pick you up on my way. Are you at home?"

"No, I'm at the hotel."

"Fine. Meet me out front in ten minutes."

Joanna driving? This should prove interesting. Snatching up his coat and tie, he ducked into his private lavatory to straighten his clothes, rinse his teeth, and run a comb through his hair.

Then, waiting under the Arlington portico, he watched Joanna drive up on her Indian motorcycle with sidecar and decided any efforts toward personal grooming had been utterly wasted.

"Hop in," she said, tossing him a pair of goggles. Once again dressed in the beige traveling suit he'd seen her wear countless times already, she also wore goggles along with a filmy white scarf tied around her head.

Thomas circled the sidecar, eying it uneasily. "Is it . . . safe?"

With a skewed grin, she revved the motor. "Come on, Tommy-boy, just think of it as another adventure."

The look on Thomas's face was priceless. Joanna watched over her shoulder as he settled clumsily into the sidecar. She tried not to laugh at how clownish he looked in the goggles. She doubted she looked much better.

"Mrs. Hegney gave me directions," she called over the engine roar as they started north on Central Avenue, "but if you know a shorter way from here, shout it out."

"Just stay to the right when we merge with Park Avenue, then turn onto Arbor."

A few more turns, and they arrived at a stately white Victorian set back from the street and surrounded by a wrought-iron fence. Joanna steered the Indian through the gates and coasted to a stop in the circle drive. After shutting off the motor, she loosened her scarf and removed her goggles. "Still with me, Ballard?"

"I'm . . . here." He sounded shaky and out of breath. The motorcycle bounced as he climbed from the sidecar. Ripping off the goggles and brushing at his suit pants, he said, "Do you always drive like a maniac? Or only when attempting to terrify unsuspecting passengers out of several years of their lives?"

Laughing, Joanna stepped to the driveway and adjusted her skirt. "You look like you survived just fine. Stop complaining and tell me if I pass inspection." While shoving loose pins back into her bun, she turned in a small circle.

When she faced him again, she wished she'd never asked, for the look in his eyes said more than words ever could. He lifted a hand to her temple. "Just let me . . ." His fingers grazed her cheek as he tucked a strand of hair behind her ear.

"Right. Thanks." With a hesitant smile, Joanna stepped around him and started up the broad porch steps. She pressed the doorbell and rocked on her heels.

Moments later a silver-haired housekeeper ushered them inside. "The colonel and his wife will see you in the drawing room."

Drawing room? The term sounded infinitely more formal than *parlor* and only added to Joanna's discomfort about this visit. Passing a gilt-framed mirror in the foyer, she stole a glance at her windblown reflection and wished she'd taken the family car.

Walking along beside her, Thomas discreetly reached up to smooth the collar of her jacket. "You look fine," he whispered. "And the Hegneys already like you, so there's no reason to be nervous."

"Right, except for the fact that I'm about to disabuse them of any illusions concerning their son's moral character."

The housekeeper entered the drawing room ahead of them. "Your guests have arrived."

Colonel Hegney rose. "Miss Trapp, I see you've brought Thomas along. Nice to see you both again." Though his tone remained polite, the tension in his jaw revealed his puzzlement about the reason for Joanna's visit.

"Do come in and sit down." Mrs. Hegney patted the sofa cushion next to her. "Would you care for coffee, tea, or perhaps a glass of water?"

Easing onto the sofa, Joanna swallowed, already wondering where she'd find the necessary words. "Water would be most appreciated."

Thomas took a chair opposite the colonel's, and for the next few minutes they exchanged small talk about Mrs. Ballard's dinner party, the lovely November weather, and recent news shared by the Hegneys' married daughter in Birmingham.

Then, after the housekeeper returned with a glass of water for Joanna and coffee for Thomas and the colonel, Mrs. Hegney turned to Joanna. "When you telephoned earlier, you suggested you had an important matter to discuss. May we know what this is about, please?"

Joanna set her glass on an end table, then folded her hands in her lap. Meeting Mrs. Hegney's gaze, she replied, "It has to do with your son Rudy and my younger sister, Lily."

The woman uttered an affronted gasp. "Your *sister* is the flirt who's been chasing our son?"

Arching a brow, Joanna replied, "Their relationship is hardly one-sided, from what I gather."

Colonel Hegney sat forward, one hand gripping the chair arm. "Why didn't you tell us Lily was your sister when we met you the other evening?"

"I didn't want to put a damper on Mrs. Ballard's dinner party." Joanna glanced at Thomas, welcoming his supportive nod. "More importantly, I needed to be convinced you wouldn't rush to your son's defense and simply sweep all this under the rug."

"What kind of people do you think we are?" Clearly distraught, Mrs. Hegney rose and stood beside her husband's chair. "After Miss Maynard informed us of the nasty rumor, we told our son plainly that we will not abide such unseemly behavior."

"I wish it were only a rumor," Joanna began. "Unfortunately, we're not talking about an isolated incident. According to Miss Maynard, Lily has been late to several of her classes this week."

Patting his wife's hand, the colonel said, "Are you implying her tardiness involves Rudy?"

Throat dry, Joanna took another sip of water. "Please believe me, I have no wish to put all the blame on you or your son. I only hope we can come to some agreement about where we go from here."

Mrs. Hegney returned to the sofa but kept her distance. "Other than forbidding the children to see each other, what can we do? We certainly can't watch them twenty-four hours a day."

"Obviously not." Glancing at Thomas, Joanna pressed her lips together. This meeting wasn't going as well as she'd hoped. She heaved a tired sigh and shifted to face the Hegneys. "We've tried talking to Lily. We've tried taking away privileges, all to no avail. I was hoping with your years of parenting experience, you could supply the insights I lack. I'm afraid I'm completely out of my depth."

Mrs. Hegney's posture relaxed, and she cast Joanna a condescending smile. "It never gets easier, dear, no matter how many children we've raised. It must be especially hard for you, having to step into a parental role when you have no experience."

"Very hard. But I'm trying my best to accept this huge responsibility and do what's right for my sister." Joanna locked her fingers together and lowered her voice. "The *last* thing I want is for Lily to repeat my mistakes."

12

Concealed behind a hedge, Lily peered toward the high school. Where was Rudy? He'd promised to meet her here as soon as his literature class ended, and she couldn't wait much longer or risk Miss Maynard's wrath again by being tardy for history.

Finally she glimpsed him slipping out through a side door. He headed straight for the hedge, and within seconds he smothered Lily with a rough kiss. His books hit the ground with a thud as he pawed her hair, his breath hot against her neck.

"Stop . . . stop!" Her throaty laugh stole the force from her protests. She liked Rudy's kisses. She liked them very much.

"You can't have it both ways, girl. Make up your mind." Leaning away from her but keeping one hand looped around her waist, Rudy ran his index finger down her nose, pausing to toy with her parted lips.

"It's just . . . we don't have much time." Lily kissed his finger-tip. It tasted of pencil shavings. "And we're in so much trouble already."

Rudy grimaced. "Yeah, I got the talking-to from my parents. Again. Why'd your bossy big sister have to go sticking her nose into our business? Wish she'd go back to France and stay there."

His sharp tone made Lily wince. A secret part of her had grown to admire her sister's courage and independence, not to mention her beauty. Joanna Trapp was everything Lily longed to be.

And honestly, since coming home hadn't Joanna done everything possible to be both a good sister and a friend?

"Why the pout?" Rudy lifted Lily's head with a finger beneath her chin. "Come on, sugar, you're the one who said we don't have much time. Let's make the most of it." His mouth came down hard on hers.

She gasped for air and pushed him away. "I said stop!" This time he couldn't mistake the seriousness of her tone. Straightening her dress, she shifted sideways and just out of reach.

"You're a tease, you know it?" Grumbling, Rudy snatched up his books. "If you're gonna be this way, I'm heading back to class."

"Rudy, wait!" Lily hated herself for the fickleness of her feelings—the crushing need for his attention when they were apart, the shame and guilt when they were together.

He swung around and glared. "Let me know when you're ready to quit being such a baby. Until then, I'm not wasting any more time with you."

Hugging herself against the threatening tears, Lily watched him march back to the school building. It took every ounce of restraint to keep from chasing after him and promising him everything he asked for. Why not, after all? Didn't half the school already believe the worst of her? The two guys who'd cornered her in the church corridor two weeks ago certainly hadn't expected she'd slam the pastor's door in their faces.

Recalling that horrible Sunday morning made Lily want to run straight home, climb into the bathtub, and scrub away the memory of their groping hands. She'd rather everyone believe she *had* slipped into the pastor's office to steal from the collection plate. Better to be thought a thief than a—

"Lily Trapp, come out of there this instant." Miss Maynard's stern command left no room for refusal.

With a quick swipe of her cheeks, Lily pushed through the hedge and stood before her teacher. "I'm sorry, ma'am. I just came out for a little air and—"

"Don't make excuses. I know exactly what is going on here." Miss Maynard stood with her hands on her hips. "You do realize I could have you expelled for this latest infraction?"

"Please don't! It'll never happen again, I promise!" Lily would have fallen prostrate and kissed Miss Maynard's shoes if she thought it would help.

"Your promises no longer carry much weight with me." With a hand to Lily's spine, Miss Maynard propelled her toward the school building. "Perhaps a three-day suspension will encourage you to rethink your actions. Your sister is already on her way to pick you up."

* * *

Thomas was thankful he'd come in yesterday to work on his inbox, because in only a matter of hours Monday morning, the blasted thing had filled up again. By noon, he had a pounding headache, at least three paper cuts, and an intense desire to catch the next train to . . . anywhere.

This isn't like you, Ballard. Groaning, he palmed his eye sockets. What happened to the conscientious hotel manager? The man who thrived on challenges, who regularly arrived early and stayed late?

Today, all he could think of was escape.

Maybe he needed a vacation. He hadn't taken one since before America entered the war. Hard to imagine where he'd get away to, however. And what fun would it be to travel alone? Or, worse yet, with his mother?

"Excuse me, Mr. Ballard." His secretary stepped into the room. "There's a big to-do going on among the kitchen help. Someone needs to step in."

Someone, meaning Thomas, naturally. He rose and shrugged into his suit coat. "Thank you. I'll see to it immediately."

Twenty minutes later, having barely averted an all-out brawl between the pastry chef and a clumsy waiter, Thomas stormed through the hotel lobby. He ignored the stares earned by the powdered sugar dusting his dark suit, not to mention the pink frosting smeared across his lapel. Before he reached his office door, he made a sudden detour. With only a brief word to his secretary about stepping out for a bit, he took the rear exit and climbed into his automobile.

For the next hour, he drove around and fumed. No, this wasn't like him at all, and he'd like to know what had spawned such insanity. With only a bit of thought, he came up with a sizable list of probable causes, beginning with one name: Joanna Trapp. He could pin down the first subtle shift in his attitude almost to the day and hour he'd seen her back in town.

That wasn't entirely true. Life had changed for Thomas when war broke out in Europe and he'd been informed his health prevented him from serving. Nothing quite compared to the awkwardness of explaining why a seemingly able-bodied male such as himself had not enlisted and gone off to fight for his country with other men his age.

Even so, he'd survived the embarrassment and learned to deal tactfully with the questions. He'd even grown to take pride in his hotel managerial skills and relish the responsibilities given him.

But Joanna . . . Joanna had him questioning everything again. His work. His wealth. His hopes for the future.

And she had no interest in him whatsoever beyond friendship.

When the cloying scent of sugar and frosting became unbearable, Thomas steered the car toward home. He certainly couldn't return to work looking like someone's unfinished birthday cake. After parking in front of the garage, he hurried inside through the kitchen door.

Marguerite halted him with a gasp. "Lands' sakes, Mister Thomas, what have you gone and done to yourself?"

"Kitchen accident. I came home to change."

"Give me your suit coat right now. I'll get to work on the mess whilst you head upstairs. I got no desire to see you in your altogether, so you can bring me your pants when you're done."

Obediently, Thomas slipped out of his coat and handed it over. Up in his room, he opened the wardrobe and selected the suit he'd worn to church yesterday. In minutes he'd changed clothes, including a fresh shirt and tie. Standing before the wardrobe mirror, he adjusted his tie and slid his arms into the coat sleeves.

As he straightened the lapels, he noticed something stiff in the inside breast pocket and pulled out the envelope he'd tucked away while at the office yesterday. After the wild ride in Joanna's sidecar and the difficult afternoon at the Hegneys', he'd all but forgotten the letter asking for a donation to the European war orphans fund.

Thoughts spinning, he tapped the edge of the envelope against his palm. He'd intended only to write a generous check. Now, something inside him cried out to do more. Surely, this urgency came straight from God as a call to action, to make a difference in the world with more than just his money.

Then, almost as quickly, the feelings ebbed. He was only one man, not to mention he hadn't the slightest idea how to help. Maybe, after all, sending money was the best he could offer. But he couldn't shake the disappointment. For one fleeting moment, he'd actually felt empowered, excited, inspired.

With a tired shake of his head, he scooped up the soiled pair of suit pants and carried them downstairs to Marguerite. "These aren't as bad as the coat, anyway," he said.

"Ain't *that* a blessing in disguise." Giving a snort, she held the pants up to the light and brushed at them with the back of her hand. "You best be more careful around your kitchen staff from now on, is all I can say."

"Yes, ma'am." With a mock salute, Thomas marched out to his car.

Climbing in behind the wheel, he began to understand, perhaps for the first time, the frustration Gilbert must have experienced after returning from the war. To feel so stifled and useless, to see no exit from an empty life where nothing seemed to go as planned—and yet, Gilbert had found a way, gathered up the broken shards and rebuilt his life with new purpose.

A bitter taste rose in Thomas's throat. Even with one leg and confined to a wheelchair, his brother continually outshone him.

Slumping forward, Thomas rested his head on the steering wheel. He despised himself for such raging self-pity. Worse, for this unfounded jealousy toward Gilbert. He must get hold of himself, and quickly. With a muted groan, he straightened and backed the car into the street. But instead of returning to the Arlington, he drove straight to the Army and Navy Hospital. After parking near the administration building, he marched inside and asked to see Chaplain Vickary. If anyone could help Thomas regain perspective, it was Sam.

"Thomas, good to see you." Waiting outside his office door, Samuel welcomed him with a firm handshake. "I was surprised when Reception notified me you were here. Is everything all right?"

"Yes . . . and no." Thomas preceded Samuel into the small office and sank into one of the chairs facing the desk. Leaning forward, he massaged the back of his neck. "I'm feeling a little crazy these days, and I guess I just needed to talk."

Samuel took the chair next to his. "What's going on, Tom?"

"Where to begin?" Lifting his gaze toward the ceiling, Thomas inhaled deeply before attempting to put his inner turmoil into words.

Long before Thomas finished, Samuel nodded in understanding. He'd known the Ballard family long enough to have observed the friction between the two brothers. Sam had also fallen in love with a woman who hadn't immediately returned his affections, and Thomas hoped he could offer advice on how to deal with these unrequited feelings for Joanna.

With a sad chuckle, Samuel shook his head. "You have it bad, don't you?"

"I don't know what to do, Sam. I've never felt so . . . so directionless in my life."

"You were happy in your work before, weren't you? You've always seemed quite competent in your profession."

"I thought I loved my job." Rising, Thomas stood before the small window and shoved his hands into his pockets. "Yes, I'm good at what I do, but now . . . since Joanna . . . I keep asking myself if there isn't something more."

"Annemarie has told me of her admiration for Joanna. She sounds like quite a spirited girl." Samuel came up beside Thomas and folded his arms. "The question you must ask yourself is, do you desire a different kind of life only because of how Joanna makes you feel, or because, deep within yourself, you sense it's time to move in a new direction?"

"That's the problem, Sam." Shoulders sagging, Thomas turned to face him. "I honestly don't know."

Shutting off the motorcycle engine, Joanna took a moment to regain control of her surging anger. Slowly, she removed her goggles and dismounted, then swiveled to face Lily, still seated in the sidecar and staring at her knees.

Joanna held out her hand. "Goggles, please."

Stiffly, Lily obeyed, then pushed up from the seat and stepped to the driveway. While Joanna stowed the goggles and pretended to check one of the tires—she wasn't yet calm enough to deal with her sister—Lily trudged to the back door and let herself in.

Alone on the driveway, Joanna set her hands on her hips and glanced skyward. She should pray—that's what good Christian girls did, right? It's what Jack did every morning and every night. She'd overheard him often enough as she passed by his bedroom door.

Well, she was just about desperate enough to give prayer another try. Nothing else seemed to help. Not with Lily. Not with Joanna's unrelenting confusion about her own life.

Fingers plowing through her tangled hair, she plopped onto the bottom step of the back porch. *What am I supposed to do, God? Haven't I tried in every possible way to do the right thing for my family?* She'd willingly—all right, not so willingly—set aside the life she'd grown to love, the people and country she'd come to care so deeply for. She'd left behind the grave of the only man who'd ever found the cracks in her iron shell of independence and worked his way into her heart.

Not the only man.

The sudden thought made her breath hitch. Overcome with conflicting and utterly bewildering emotions, Joanna lowered her head into her hands and let the tears flow. Only when she felt a hand on her shoulder did she raise her head.

"I'm sorry, Jo." Lily sat beside her on the step, her own face blotchy and streaked with tears. The faint outline of goggles appeared as pink ovals around her eyes. "Please don't stay mad at me. I know what I did was wrong, and I couldn't bear it if you hated me forever."

"Oh, Lily, how could I ever hate you?" Sniffling, Joanna pulled her sister into a hug. "More than anything, I worry about you. The thought of you repeating my mistakes—"

Lily pulled away to brush the wetness from her cheeks. She looked up at Joanna with a question in her eyes. "Have you—I mean—with a boy?"

Her sister didn't have to say the words. "No, honey, but it doesn't mean I was never tempted." She turned away with a grimace. "Believe me, I understand those feelings, more than you can imagine."

"When?" Lily's voice became tiny, pleading. "Were you my age, or was it after you got older and went away?"

Joanna swallowed and faced her sister, digging deep for the courage to be honest. "Both. When I was in high school, my life seemed so stifling. Mother's moods had become intolerable, schoolwork had become a bore, and all I could think about was getting out of Hot Springs." She smoothed a hand across a wrinkle in her skirt as the memories rushed back. "There was a boy, eighteen, who had a thing for me—a boy our parents would never have approved of. He rolled his own cigarettes and could swear like a drunken sailor. I heard he used to steal money from teachers' purses, too."

Lily's eyes widened, whether in shock or admiration, Joanna preferred not to guess. "What was his name? Is he still in Hot Springs?"

Joanna pictured the boy's mesmerizing gaze and cocky grin. "His name was Arthur Spence. I have no idea where he is now. Last I heard, he'd gone to work for his uncle in Boston."

"Did you go out with him?"

"Worse." Joanna quirked her lips. "The summer after he graduated, I ran away with him. We made it all the way to St. Louis before I came to my senses and caught the next train home."

"But if you were so close to escaping, why did you change your mind?"

Leveling a solemn gaze at her sister, Joanna stated, "Because I realized I was about to ruin my life. Arthur talked big about the future we'd have, but the only thing driving him was satisfying his appetite for pleasure. I decided, first of all, that I didn't care to provide the particular sort of satisfaction he wanted from me."

Frowning, Lily nodded knowingly.

"I also realized I wanted much more from life, and I knew it wouldn't be possible unless I stayed in school and applied myself."

A hopeless look clouded Lily's features. She toed a tuft of grass. "But school was easy for you. You always made good grades and even went to college. No matter how hard I study, I'll never be as smart as you."

"Being smart has little to do with how hard you study." With one hand, Joanna tipped Lily's chin higher. "What makes you smart is how well you listen to your head"—she tapped Lily's forehead—"and your heart"—then tapped her chest.

Lily pulled her lower lip between her teeth. "Jack calls it listening to the Holy Spirit."

"I suppose he's right." Locking her arms around her knees, Joanna inhaled deeply and stared across the lawn. Had the Holy Spirit been with her in her decisions all these years? She remembered Pastor Yarborough teaching how once someone became a Christian, the Holy Spirit came to live with the person forever, even when the Spirit's leading was ignored. How often had Joanna paid attention instead of impetuously making her own choices? How different would her life be today if she had listened?

A few moments of silence passed, and then Lily touched Joanna's arm. "You said you had those . . . *feelings* . . . after you went away, too. Did you meet someone at college, or in France?"

With a harsh attempt at a laugh, Joanna pushed up from the step and dusted off her hands. "That's a story for another day. Let's go inside and see what we can throw together for supper. As long as you're out of school for three days, you may as well make yourself useful."

Supper was a subdued affair. Joanna had taken Jack aside the moment he walked into the house, and he'd been livid over Lily's suspension. Only after Joanna explained they might finally have reached a turning point did he calm down and listen. Though she hadn't told him everything she and Lily had talked about on the back steps, it seemed enough to convince him she had things well in hand.

Before she left for the hotel two hours later, she elicited Jack's promise not to lecture Lily or punish her further, but to trust Joanna's judgment and allow their sister these three days out of school to sort things out.

By the time Joanna reported for duty at the switchboard, she felt as exhausted as if she'd climbed Hot Springs Mountain on her hands and knees with her motorcycle strapped to her back.

Lifting off her headset, Lillian Zongrone swiveled in her chair and shot Joanna a concerned frown. "Honey, are you all right?"

"Not one of my better days." Sinking into an empty chair, Joanna briefly described the latest incident with Lily, along with her hopes for positive change.

"No wonder you're in a state. At least it looks like it'll be a quiet night. A good number of guests have already checked out to head home for the Thanksgiving holiday."

Joanna sighed as Lillian rose to retrieve her sweater and handbag. "Then my only problem may be staying awake at the switchboard. I hope there's plenty of coffee."

"Just started a fresh pot." Buttoning her sweater, Lillian sidled toward the door. "Oh, speaking of change, we'll have a new boss to report to for the next couple of weeks."

Moving to the swivel chair at the switchboard, Joanna halted mid-stride. "I—I don't understand."

"It was a surprise to me, too. In all these years I never once recall Mr. Ballard taking vacation time. But he stopped in earlier to say he's getting away for a while. Starting tomorrow, in fact."

"I see." Joanna's throat ached with an emotion she couldn't name—probably the aftereffects of the day she'd had. With a purposeful sigh, she settled in and reached for the headset.

"Hard as the man works, he sure deserves a little time off. Well, I'm headed home. Have a good night, honey. See you same time tomorrow."

"Right." Hardly hearing her, Joanna did a routine perusal of the message log. "Good night, Lillian."

Left alone in the quiet room, she took a moment to probe her thoughts. Why should it concern her if Thomas left on vacation? If what Lillian said was true, he'd rightly earned a temporary escape from responsibility.

In the meantime, Joanna had responsibilities aplenty. The switchboard buzzed, signaling an outside call. "Thank you for calling the Arlington Hotel. How may I assist you?"

"Hi, Joanna, it's Thomas." He sounded shyly hesitant. "I assume Lillian told you my plans?"

She wedged a smile into her voice. "I hope you're going somewhere pleasant and warm. Winter will be upon us before we know it."

"Haven't decided on a destination yet. Just needed some time away."

His melancholy tone worried her. "Sometimes half the fun is figuring out where you're going."

"If you have any problems while I'm away, just ask Stanley at the front desk."

"I'm sure everything will be fine."

"Yes, I'm sure." A lengthy pause stretched between them. "I should let you get back to work. Take care, Joanna."

"You, too, Thomas. Enjoy your vacation."

Disconnecting the call, Joanna realized she'd be counting every minute until he returned.

13

A sharp rap on Thomas's bedroom door startled him out of his mental stupor. "Who is it?"

"It's your mother. May I come in?"

He suspected his inner sanctum was about to be breached whether he gave his permission or not. Shifting upright in the cushioned armchair by the window, he made sure his robe covered his pajamas. "Door's open. Come on in."

She stepped into the room, her mouth pinched as if she'd bitten into a lemon. One look at him and her expression turned into a full-blown scowl. "It's been over a week now, Thomas. How long do you intend to sit up here moping?"

"I'm not moping. I'm thinking." Thomas ran his palm along the six-day growth of whiskers covering his jaw. Though he retained sufficient self-respect to bathe regularly since beginning his "vacation," shaving had quickly gone by the wayside.

His mother shoved his feet off the ottoman and plopped down in front of him. "This attitude of yours has grown quite tiresome. To succumb to depression and self-pity as your brother did after the war? Honestly, Thomas, I thought more of you."

Thomas bristled. "This isn't self-pity. And anyway—"

Her last statement finally penetrated: *"I thought more of you."* The backhanded compliment stirred something inside him, and for the first time in ages his chest swelled with a dim but welcome sense of his mother's respect.

Distress etching every line of her face, she rested a hand on his pajama-clad knee. "If it isn't self-pity, then what would you call it? You come home one day announcing you're 'on vacation,' yet you haven't left the house. You hardly even show yourself downstairs for meals, and with that ridiculous beard you look like a wild and woolly mountain man. Please, Thomas, tell me what this is about."

Gazing out at the nearly leafless trees on the front lawn, Thomas clenched a fist. "Ever since Gil went off to West Point and then to fight in France, I've done my best to fill his shoes as man of the house. I've lived up to my responsibilities both at home and at the Arlington as well as I know how."

"And you've done so admirably. I couldn't be more proud."

"Do you mean it, Mother?" He studied her face, noting the worried half-smile beneath her piercing stare. "Because it's always seemed I came in second to Gilbert in your affections . . . and your esteem."

"Ridiculous! I love both my sons equally." She moved clumsily from the ottoman to the arm of Thomas's chair, where she wrapped her arms around him and held him close. "Oh, son, if I lavished more attention on Gilbert after his return, it was only because of how close we came to losing him. If anything took either of you from me, I would be devastated."

The stiff lace collar of her dress scraped like sandpaper against Thomas's ear, not to mention her ample bosom came close to smothering him, but he wouldn't complain. His mother's reassurance meant the world to him. She may have her faults, but she loved with unmatched passion.

Shifting to catch a breath, he worked an arm around her waist and tilted his head to kiss her on the cheek. "I love you, too,

Mother, and I'm sorry for being such a slug lately. I promise I'll pull myself together—even shave, if you insist."

Straightening, she patted his head as if he were a young schoolboy. "In your seclusion, you may have forgotten tomorrow is Thanksgiving. Your Uncle Bob and Aunt Betty arrive tonight, and I should have a difficult time explaining your appearance if you came down to dinner with this . . . *shrub* covering your face."

Ah, back to normal, and Thomas was glad of it. Mother's fawning attention could sometimes be harder to bear than her bossiness. He shooed her from the room before gathering up a fresh shirt, slacks, and pullover sweater, then headed to the bathroom. Maybe looking like a human being again would help him feel like one.

And when did it get to be Thanksgiving Eve? The smells wafting up from the kitchen should have clued him in—Marguerite's delicious cherry, pumpkin, and sweet potato pies, the citrusy scent of her special cranberry compote. Tomorrow morning the tempting aromas of roasting turkey, giblet gravy, and sage dressing would fill the house, along with Uncle Bob's roaring laugh as he regaled them with stories from his bottomless reservoir of family *faux pas.*

After stripping off his pajama top, Thomas stood before the bathroom sink and set out his shaving supplies. Then, glimpsing his reflection in the mirror, he decided the beard gave him a rather distinguished mien. He'd wanted to make some changes, after all, and why not start with his appearance? He could simply trim up the beard and keep it awhile, see how well he liked it over the long term. His barber could do a better job, but Thomas doubted he could get an appointment the afternoon before Thanksgiving.

He found a pair of scissors in the drawer and set to work. Soon a fine mess of short, dark bristles lined the basin. Once he'd trimmed the mustache and tamed the overgrowth of chin whiskers, he mixed up a small amount of shaving soap and neatened the areas around his nose, cheeks, and throat. With the suds rinsed away, he admired his new look.

Yes, indeed, quite distinguished. The beard lent an air of maturity and sophistication. Mother might balk at first, but she'd get used to it.

Showered and dressed, he sauntered downstairs to find Uncle Bob and Aunt Betty had arrived.

When he stepped through the parlor doors, Uncle Bob let out a guffaw and slapped his thighs. "Glory be, look at you, boy! I thought for a minute it was Captain Noah Ballard back from the grave."

Thomas's mother gasped, a look of stunned recognition widening her eyes. Then her lips trembled in a sad smile. "It's true, Thomas, and I can't believe I never realized before how much you look like your father."

His gaze flew to the family portrait hanging over the mantel— Father in uniform, Mother in her Sunday finery, Gilbert so young he had to hold Mother's knee to stand, and Thomas only a babe in his father's arms. Funny, all these years Thomas had believed Gilbert most resembled their father. Now, as he studied his father's bearded face, and picturing his own as he'd seen it in the mirror minutes ago, he realized Mother and Uncle Bob were right.

The awareness buoyed his spirits much as his mother's reassurance had earlier. He was more than Gil's kid brother or his parents' younger son. More than a weakling who couldn't pass the army's health assessment. More than a stodgy, stuck-in-a-rut hotel manager.

Each new realization brought him closer to answering the question Sam had posed in his hospital office last week. More powerfully than ever, Thomas sensed the time had come to venture in new directions. His feelings for Joanna may have ignited such thoughts, but the need for change must have been there all along for him to feel it so strongly.

Now, the crucial question became, which direction to choose?

Awake at the first fingers of dawn, Jack dressed in slacks and a warm wool sweater and started a pot of coffee brewing. It would be another hour or two before he could expect to hear his sisters moving about. Perhaps longer for Joanna since she'd worked at the Arlington last night. Jack doubted she'd given so much as a fleeting thought to today's being Thanksgiving.

So much for any hopes of a turkey dinner with all the trimmings. His first Thanksgiving home from the war, and all he could look forward to was a day off work and whatever interesting meal Joanna decided to burn beyond recognition.

He wasn't being completely fair. His sister certainly knew how to build a delicious roast beef or ham sandwich. Joanna favored the thick, crusty bread and spicy brown mustard similar to what they served in France, and one of her hearty sandwiches could carry a man for days. A Thanksgiving sandwich didn't hold the same appeal as turkey and dressing, but when Jack considered how much more pleasant life with Lily had been the last several days—all thanks to Joanna—he'd eat his sandwich and be thankful indeed.

While the coffee finished perking, Jack lit the oven to warm the batch of cinnamon rolls Mrs. Kendall had brought over last night. She'd apologized profusely that she couldn't invite Jack and his sisters for dinner, but since this year marked Annemarie's first Thanksgiving as a married woman, she had insisted on hosting the meal.

"I'm afraid with Joseph and me, along with Samuel's mother and one or two bachelor doctors Samuel invited from the hospital," Mrs. Kendall had explained, "Annemarie's little house will be bursting at the seams."

To be truthful, Jack wondered why a traditional Thanksgiving dinner had grown so important to him. It wasn't as if his mother ever made much of the holiday. A roasted chicken, mashed potatoes, perhaps a pie if she could find the energy. More often than not, and except for Dad having a day off from the accounting office, Thanksgiving had been a day like any other.

This year, though . . . this year was special. The war had ended, the country was slowly rebounding from the incomprehensible loss so many families had endured, rationing was no longer crucial, and life crept steadily toward normalcy.

Normal. Jack wondered what the word even meant for his family.

Removing the baking pan from the oven, he scooped one of the gooey cinnamon rolls onto a saucer, then grabbed a fork from the drawer and poured a mug of coffee. He carried his breakfast into the parlor, where he settled into an overstuffed chair and flicked on the reading lamp. While chewing a bite of the roll, he riffled through the basket of reading material beside the chair until he found the newspaper he'd been saving.

Folded open to the second page, the paper contained the text of President Wilson's November 5 proclamation exhorting the American people on this Thanksgiving Day to "look forward with confidence to the dawn of an era where the sacrifices of the nations will find recompense in a world at peace."

Jack had reread the proclamation almost daily since the newspaper published it. Of course, American presidents had been issuing Thanksgiving proclamations since George Washington held office. The ones Jack had seen, when he took note at all, read like thinly reworked statements from the year before. How many ways could you proclaim a national day of thanksgiving?

But Jack had only to recall where he'd been one year ago, still in France awaiting his release from duty at the end of the worst nightmare he could have imagined. He may have been spared the heat of battle, but he'd lost too many friends, or seen them dragged broken and bleeding into ambulances and rushed to the nearest field hospital.

So today, yes, he gave thanks to Almighty God that he'd come home whole—that he'd come home at all. More importantly, that he'd spend this Thanksgiving with his family, shattered though it was, and somehow they'd make the best of things.

As he laid the newspaper aside and reached for his coffee, the telephone rang. Probably Grandmother, calling to wish them a happy Thanksgiving. She'd written a few weeks ago saying once winter set in, her arthritis made it too difficult to travel, but she hoped Jack and the girls would consider visiting her in Kansas City for Christmas.

He almost answered the telephone with "Hello, Grandmother," but thought better of it at the last moment. The caller might just as easily be someone from the Arlington needing Joanna to work an extra shift at the switchboard.

"Good morning, Mr. Trapp." The lilting female voice definitely didn't belong to his grandmother. "I hope this isn't too early to call."

"Er, no." Jack tightened his grip on the earpiece. He should know the voice . . .

"I'm sorry. You probably have no idea who this is. It's Madison Maynard, Lily's teacher."

"Miss Maynard." Jack's stomach shifted. For Lily's teacher to telephone on Thanksgiving Day could only mean more trouble. Sending a panicked glance toward the upstairs landing, Jack willed Joanna to wake up and come down to deal with this.

The woman uttered a tiny laugh. "I suppose I'd better get right to the point before you think the worst."

Too late. "Perhaps you should."

"It's rather short notice, I know, but it occurred to me, knowing Lily lost her mother recently, your family might be having a difficult Thanksgiving, and . . . well, I'm not saying this very well, but if you don't have other plans . . ."

Never in all the times Jack had spoken to the woman had he ever known her to be tongue-tied. "I'm not following you, Miss Maynard."

She gave a brusque sigh. "I don't have any family in town except an ancient aunt, and this is my *very* awkward way of asking if you and your sisters would care to join us for Thanksgiving dinner at my home. I'm a Thanksgiving traditionalist and have been cooking every evening for a week, so there's more than enough food, and if you don't come, my aunt and I could be dining on leftovers well into the new year."

Mouth already watering, Jack swallowed. "It would be a shame. I mean, since you've gone to so much trouble."

"So, is it possible you could come? You and your sisters, I mean. The three of you. Together." A muted groan sounded through the telephone line, bringing a curious smile to Jack's lips.

Then a crazy thought rushed through his brain: *She's interested in me!*

A strange tingling set his nerves aflame. How long had it been since he'd given so much as a passing nod to a pretty girl? Too many other things had occupied his mind since he'd come home from France.

"I, uh . . . well, I'd have to ask . . ." Now it was his turn to stammer.

"You probably already have plans. I understand."

"No!" Jack almost shouted. "It's just my sisters aren't up yet, and—"

He felt a hand on his shoulder and whirled around to find Joanna staring at him, worry in her eyes. "Who is it? What's wrong?"

Excusing himself to Miss Maynard, he held the mouthpiece against his sweater while he hurriedly explained. "So what do you say? Shall I accept?"

Joanna skewed her lips as she studied Jack's face. Then she lifted one eyebrow in a knowing grin. "Turkey with all the trimmings served by the prettiest teacher at Hot Springs High? Say yes, Jack, and quickly, before she changes her mind!"

Dinner at Miss Maynard's wouldn't be served until two, which allowed Joanna plenty of time to bathe, wash her hair, and decide what to wear. Her frayed traveling suit was scarcely warm enough for an Arkansas winter. Never planning to extend her trip home any longer than necessary, she'd left her heavy wool coat in France as well.

Obviously, since she'd decided to remain in Hot Springs for the foreseeable future, another shopping excursion would be in order soon.

Dragging a towel across the misted-over bathroom mirror, Joanna glimpsed her own resigned expression. No longer certain exactly when she'd made up her mind to stay, she only knew it was the right thing to do. She'd shirked her family responsibilities for far too long.

Poor Jack. He'd looked beyond relieved—ecstatic, actually—since Joanna had consented to joining Miss Maynard for Thanksgiving. Now the trick would be convincing Lily, who still hadn't stirred from her bed. Joanna only wished she could sleep as soundly.

In her room, she searched through the wardrobe for what to wear. The pink dress she'd worn to the Ballard dinner party seemed almost too dressy, so she settled for her beige skirt and a blue-and-white striped blouse.

Yes, she must go shopping soon.

As she leaned over the furnace vent to dry her hair, Jack called up the stairs. "Jo, you have a telephone call. It's Thomas."

Her head shot up. Thomas should be miles away enjoying his vacation. Flipping the mass of damp hair over her shoulder, she marched down to the foyer. Jack handed her the telephone, and she could have sworn he returned the same knowing look she'd given him earlier.

Gripping the telephone, she pressed the earpiece to her ear. "Good morning, Thomas. I'm surprised to hear from you. How's the vacation?"

"I didn't exactly go anywhere," he said with an embarrassed chuckle. "Mostly I've been puttering about the house."

"And here I was picturing you lounging on a tropical isle and soaking up sunshine."

Thomas remained quiet for a moment. "I hope I've been considerably more productive."

Curious at his tone, Joanna perched on the narrow chair beside the hall table. "Vacations aren't supposed to be productive. That's the whole point."

"Then perhaps I shouldn't call it a vacation. *Sabbatical* or *retreat* would be more accurate."

"Hmm, sounds serious."

"I'll tell you about it sometime. But I actually called for a different reason." He exhaled softly. "Unfortunately, it seems I'm already too late with my invitation. Jack says you're having dinner with Lily's teacher."

"Yes. Miss Maynard." Joanna glanced at Jack, who leaned in the parlor doorway with his ankles crossed and a silly grin on his face. "*What?*" she mouthed.

He whispered back, "Just say yes."

Between Thomas's puzzling comments and her brother's strange behavior, Joanna bristled with annoyance. Glowering at Jack, she returned her attention to the call. "What were you going to ask me, Thomas?"

"I thought if you didn't have plans, the three of you might like to have dinner with my family. Marguerite puts on quite a Thanksgiving Day spread, and—don't take this the wrong way—I had a suspicion you wouldn't have done much in the way of preparations."

"And you'd be right. But, as Jack said—" Her brother stepped forward, waving his hand in her face. "One moment, Thomas.

Jack is frantically trying to tell me something." With the mouth-piece covered, she arched a brow and waited.

"I think you should accept," Jack stated.

"But you've already accepted Miss Maynard's invitation."

"She'll understand. Lily and I will go, and I'll explain you had a last-minute invitation from your"—he wiggled his brows—"boss."

Joanna scowled. "Are you sure I shouldn't be chaperoning you and the lovely Miss Maynard?"

Heaving a regretful sigh, Jack shrugged. "I'm sure Lily and Miss Maynard's elderly aunt will serve the purpose more than adequately."

Blasting out a sigh of her own, Joanna returned to the call. "Thomas, I've been informed I may be excused from the previous invitation. What time would you like me to arrive?"

"Dinner's at six, but you're welcome anytime. I can pick you up—"

"No, don't trouble yourself." Already having second thoughts, Joanna preferred the freedom to come and go as she desired. Clearly, Jack already suspected there was more to her friendship with Thomas than she would admit.

Then why this frisson of anticipation, when she did not need or want a man in her life? At least not in the way Jack insinuated. She had no room in her heart for romance.

"So may I look for you around mid-afternoon?"

Giving herself a mental shake, Joanna softly cleared her throat. "I'll be there." As an afterthought, she added, "It was kind of you to think of me. Thank your mother for allowing me to come."

Hanging up, she rose stiffly and started for the stairs. High time her little sister roused herself and dressed for dinner.

Before she reached the bottom step, Jack caught her by the elbow. "You're not mad, are you?"

"Mad? Not exactly." Joanna glanced away. "I guess I just feel manipulated."

"But you and Thomas seem to get along so well. I thought you'd enjoy the day more if . . ." He lifted one shoulder in a help-less gesture before turning away, hands rammed into his pockets. "Why do I even try?"

One hand on the banister, Joanna whipped her head around. "What's *that* supposed to mean?"

"It means I feel like I hardly know you. It's like you're here, but not really. When you first came home, I could tell you were itching to return to France, and every day when I came home from work, I half expected to find your suitcases packed and train tickets on the table."

"I would never just leave, Jack. I know what my responsibilities are."

He slanted her a doubtful glance. "Is that all Lily and I are to you—*responsibilities?*"

Her brother's accusation made her flinch. *Perhaps because it's too close to the truth?* "I admit I did resent being called home. But not because of you or Lily. This just didn't feel like my life any-more. I left . . . so much . . ." Her throat closed, and she lowered her gaze to the floor.

"I get it. Your 'real' life is back in France." Jack strode a few paces away. "If you want to return so badly, then do it. Don't let Lily and me keep you here."

"You're not listening to me." Following him across the foyer, Joanna came up beside him and touched his arm. "I've come to realize this is where I'm meant to be. It's where I *want* to be."

Jack swiveled to face her, his steely gaze sharp as a razor. "Then quit holding out on us."

14

*P*ausing on the Ballards' front porch, Joanna straightened her skirt and tidied her bun. The ride over on her motorcycle had left her not only disheveled but chilled to the bone. She should have called to say she'd changed her mind, but then she'd have to explain, and it had been hard enough trying to make Jack understand her erratic emotions.

"It's like you're here, but not really. . . . Then quit holding out on us."

Did she come across as such a fraud?

The front door opened, and Thomas stood before her. At least she thought it was Thomas beneath the facial hair. "I thought I heard your motorcycle. You look nearly frozen. Come inside and get warm by the fire."

She allowed him to take her hand but couldn't take her eyes off his chin. "You look so . . . different."

Thomas chuckled. "Different good, or different bad?"

Standing in the entry hall, she studied him as he nudged the door closed. "I think I like it. You look quite professorial." As he led her into the parlor and over to the fireplace, she said, "Surely, growing a beard isn't what you meant by having a productive vacation—excuse me, sabbatical?"

"Let's just say the beard is an unexpected corollary." Selecting an iron poker, Thomas stooped to push the logs around, and the flames leapt higher.

As Joanna let the warmth soak into her, she noticed the quiet. "Where is everyone?"

"Mother took the visiting relatives out to see Gilbert's farm. They should be back in an hour or so." He motioned toward a side table. "Marguerite set out some hors d'oeuvres to tide us over until dinner. She has hot spiced cider on the stove as well."

"Hot cider sounds wonderful."

While Thomas excused himself to call Marguerite, Joanna moved to the sofa. Thomas joined her there, and shortly Marguerite brought in two china cups and a steaming carafe.

"Now, y'all don't be burning your tongues." Marguerite winked as she poured. "There's lots better ways to keep warm."

When they were alone again, Thomas murmured, "You'll have to forgive Marguerite. She's been trying to match me up with someone since I finished high school."

Joanna balanced her cup and saucer on her knees and gazed into the shimmering amber liquid. "I'm experiencing a similar problem with my brother. He practically insisted I come here today. It's obvious he thinks—" Any lingering chills banished by embarrassment, she bit down on her lower lip.

"No need to explain." Thomas set his cup on the low table in front of them.

"Actually, there is." Joanna did the same with her cup and saucer, then shifted to face Thomas. She pulled one leg under her on the sofa and folded her hands. "As Jack so clearly pointed out to me this morning, I've been holding back."

Brows drawn together, Thomas sent her a questioning look. "In what way?"

"Jack thinks I'm only staying in town because I feel a responsibility toward him and Lily." She toyed with a dangling thread on her sweater. "And I do, naturally. But there's much more. Though I wasn't at first, now I'm glad I came home."

"Good to know." Thomas nodded thoughtfully and reached for his cider cup to take a quick sip. He glanced her way as if waiting for her to continue.

She took a deep breath. "The truth is, if my mother hadn't died and Jack hadn't written begging me to come, I'd still be in France and probably would never have returned. But since I have, I've realized how much I love my family and how much they love me." Giving a low chuckle, Joanna shook her head. "At least it seems Lily has grown to love me after all. She certainly resented me in the beginning."

"So things are better between you? No more problems at school?"

"Maybe you haven't heard—Lily was given a three-day suspension last week for sneaking out of school to see Rudy."

Thomas sucked air between his teeth. "Oh, no."

"The blessing is, this seemed to be the turning point." Joanna smiled as she recalled her conversations with Lily over the past several days. She'd been more honest with her sister than she had with anyone since Walter.

And yet Jack was right. She still held things inside, things she wasn't sure she'd ever be ready to share.

When she remained silent for several moments, Thomas covered her hand with his own. "If you keep pulling on this thread, your sweater will end up a pile of yarn on the floor."

She gasped, completely unaware she'd unraveled the edge of her sweater. Slipping the loose thread through a loop, she tied it off in a knot. "Oh, well, it's an old thing I should have thrown out ages ago." She retrieved her cup only to discover the cider had grown cold. Even so, the liquid soothed her dry throat. "You've been so patient to listen to my rambling. But it's Thanksgiving. We should be talking of cheerier subjects. Tell me more about this sabbatical of yours."

Thomas uttered a grating laugh. "What makes you think the subject of my sabbatical constitutes cheerier conversation?"

"Well, it should certainly be more interesting." Anxious to shift the focus from herself, Joanna sat forward with feigned enthusiasm. "So, Thomas, what deep issues have you been pondering? That is what a sabbatical is for, isn't it—to ponder deep subjects?"

Rising abruptly, he crossed the room to toss another log on the fire. After stirring the embers, he set aside the poker and turned to Joanna with a bemused half-smile. "I need to ponder awhile longer before I'm ready to talk about it. Besides," he said, returning to the sofa, "I don't believe you've finished the explanation you began when we first sat down."

Her thoughts had traveled such a circuitous path since then that she struggled to recall exactly what she'd started out to say.

As if sensing her confusion, Thomas offered, "Remember, about holding back?"

She nodded. She owed him the truth about why she couldn't return his feelings. Twisting the dangling sweater thread around her finger, she closed her eyes briefly before straightening to meet Thomas's probing gaze. "What I haven't told you—what I haven't even told my brother and sister yet—is that I lost someone very dear to me in the war. If he hadn't been killed, we'd be married now."

The pain, as raw as the day she'd learned of Walter's death, slashed through her. She shuddered but held back the tears.

"Joanna, I'm so sorry."

She knotted her fists, pressing them together on her lap. "Most days I'm perfectly fine . . . until I remember." With a ragged laugh, she continued, "He was such a daredevil, full of life, always seeking the next adventure."

Thomas glanced away with a sad smile. "Sounds as if you two were perfectly suited to each other."

"We were, which is why I can't seem to move on." She reached for Thomas's hand, curling her fingers around his. She lowered her voice to a pleading whisper. "Which is why I can't be more to you than a friend."

◦❧◦

Lily set up the checkers board for another game with Miss Maynard's aunt. The old woman may be half blind, but she already led by five games to Lily's two. "Your move, Mrs. Connealy."

With a cackling laugh, Mrs. Connealy started one of her red game pieces across the board. Lily slid a black disk forward and then glanced toward the kitchen, where her brother and Miss Maynard washed up the dinner dishes. Lily never imagined her teacher could giggle so girlishly.

Nor her brother look so besotted!

"Wake up, Miss Trapp. Your play." Almost deaf as well, Mrs. Connealy tended to shout. After Lily made a move, the old woman snickered and jumped two of Lily's men. "Honey, if you have any hopes of winning, you must pay closer attention to the board."

Three plays later, Lily had lost another man and crowned one of Mrs. Connealy's. The game was shaping up to be another runaway. Lily couldn't say she minded, though. Suffering a few losses at the hands of an aging checkers tyrant seemed a small price to pay for the pure pleasure of feasting on Miss Maynard's delicious Thanksgiving dinner. Turkey with cornbread stuffing, the fluffiest mashed potatoes ever, creamed asparagus, tart cranberry sauce, and three kinds of pies—truly heaven on earth!

Shortly, her opponent gloated with triumph over another win. "Had enough yet, dearie? I could keep this up all afternoon, you know." She thrust out her lower lip in an exaggerated pout. "But I do hate to make little girls cry."

"Maybe I should help with the dishes," Lily said, pushing away from the game table.

"The baby ate the fishes?" Mrs. Connealy's gnarly brows drew together. "What baby? Did you bring a baby?"

"No, I said *maybe*." Raising her voice, Lily leaned across the table. "*Maybe* I'll help with the *dishes*."

"Oh, the dishes! Yes, those belonged to my grandmother. She brought them from England after her wedding trip. Aren't they lovely?"

"Yes, lovely!" Lily's ears rang. When she looked toward the kitchen to see Jack and Mrs. Maynard coming through the door, she jumped up from her chair. "Finished already? Are you sure I can't wash, dry, put away leftovers—"

"All done." Miss Maynard cast her a knowing smile. "You're so sweet to keep Aunt Ruth entertained. She does love to play checkers." Moving beside the elderly woman, Miss Maynard rested an arm about her shoulder and spoke directly into her ear. "Aunt Ruth, how about a nap? You can lie down in my room if you like."

"Thank you, my dear. Winning does take a lot out of a body." Wagging a finger at Lily, Mrs. Connealy said, "But don't you worry, missy. An hour or two and I'll be raring to go again."

While Miss Maynard helped her aunt to the bedroom, Lily crossed to the settee and plopped down with a loud groan.

Jack joined her. For a moment or two, he simply gazed at Lily in silence, a funny smile on his face. Finally, he said, "Have I told you lately I'm proud of you?"

Heat rose in her cheeks. She stared at her hands and picked at a hangnail. "No."

"Well, I am. I can see the effort you're making to straighten up and act like the young lady you are. And today," he said, nodding toward the game table, "your attentiveness to Mrs. Connealy showed true kindness."

"She's a nice old lady." Deaf as a doorpost, but nice. A tiny grin curling her lips, Lily peered at her brother. "Couldn't help noticing your attentiveness toward my teacher."

Jack's Adam's apple shifted. He blushed beet-red. "She's nice, too."

"Who's nice?" Miss Maynard entered the parlor.

"Your—your aunt," Jack said, rising. "A sweet old lady."

"Thank you. She's special to me—practically raised me after my mother passed away." Taking a chair, Miss Maynard motioned for Jack to be seated. Then, glancing toward Lily, she continued, "I wasn't much older than you when my mother died. I still miss her terribly."

"I . . . I didn't know." Lily studied the pink rose petal pattern in the Oriental carpet.

"I still had my father, for a few more years, anyway. But a woman's influence meant so much. Though it was hard at first, I needed Aunt Ruth in ways I only came to appreciate as I grew older."

Lily immediately grasped Miss Maynard's implied message, a subtle reminder for Lily to treasure Joanna's presence in her life. And she did, more every day as she got to know her sister better. Over the past few days, Joanna had opened up even more to Lily about her own youth and how she'd struggled to cope with their mother's depression. Even after Joanna broke things off with the wild boy she'd run off with, the damage to her reputation had been done. As with Lily, the boys at school made assumptions, and only after Joanna went away to college could she put that part of her life behind her.

Would it be the same for Lily? How would she ever survive the next two years of high school?

But Joanna had said she must hold her head high. No matter if the other girls gossiped, no matter how rude the boys' insinuations, Lily must believe in herself, for actions spoke much louder than words.

The parlor had grown quiet, and Lily looked up to see Jack and Miss Maynard sharing shy glances. The sight brought a tingle to her chest, and she realized she liked the idea of her brother and her favorite teacher together. True, the relationship might carry certain advantages where Lily's discipline was concerned.

But even more important, if Jack were to marry Miss Maynard, Lily would have a new "sister"—a kindhearted woman she could trust and look up to. For she couldn't shake the growing dread that one day soon Joanna would have had enough of Hot Springs and pack her bags for France.

Thomas stood at the parlor window and gazed toward the quiet street. The furnace hadn't yet dissipated the early-morning chill seeping through the house, nor had the golden light of dawn lifted the disappointment shrouding his heart.

Yesterday he'd been so hopeful. All he'd needed was to convince Joanna he could change, become someone as open to adventure as she.

Then to be told the real reason she couldn't return his affections—he'd never have guessed her heart belonged to a dead man.

"Mister Thomas," Marguerite called from the parlor door, "you coming in to breakfast?"

"Later, perhaps." He spoke without turning from the window.

The servant's footsteps brushed across the carpet as she stepped up beside him. "The Lord don't make mistakes. Miss Joanna's come into your life for a reason, so you gotta give it time. The Good Book says, 'And let us not be weary in well-doing: for in due season we shall reap, if we faint not.'"

Amazed, as always, at Marguerite's intuitive powers, Thomas smiled down at her. "If I could be certain God intended Joanna for me, I'd wait forever." He sighed. "I'm just not sure she's getting the same message."

"Then I reckon we best turn our Bible back a few pages to Proverbs. 'The soul of the sluggard desireth, and hath nothing; But the soul of the diligent shall be made fat.' It ain't about waiting, son. It's about believing in what the Lord has put before you and then claiming it with all your might." She emphasized her words by holding up both hands and curling them into fists.

Thomas could only sigh and shake his head. "How, exactly, would you suggest I go about 'claiming' her when she has told me point-blank she isn't interested?"

Marguerite set her arms akimbo and scowled at him as if he were the stupidest man to ever walk the earth. "If I gotta explain the ways of courting a woman, then you are lost before you even get started." Nose in the air, she harrumphed and marched from the room.

Drawing a hand down his face, Thomas considered the possibility he might well be as thickheaded as Marguerite implied. She certainly had it right about one thing. He could hang around the house like a sluggard while the inertia of indecision took over, or he could pull himself together and act.

Uncle Bob's chortle resounded from the dining room, followed by Mother's and Aunt Betty's shocked gasps. Another embarrassing family story, no doubt. Hoping to stay out of Uncle Bob's line of fire, Thomas edged across the hall to the study and closed the door behind him.

A sense of quiet reverence came over him as he approached his father's desk. Thomas retained few memories of his father, but one vivid image unexpectedly filled his mind—sitting on his father's lap behind the desk and reaching up to tug on his beard. Father gave a yelp, then laughed his gentle laugh and said, "One day, my little lad, you'll be man enough to grow your own beard. And then the world had better watch out!"

Stroking his whiskery jaw, Thomas circled the desk and sank into the big leather chair. If only his father were still alive to show him how to be the man he longed to be.

He'd come to one decision, anyway. Finding some stationery in a side drawer, Thomas pulled out a sheet of paper. He swiveled the chair to face the typewriter table against the rear wall and rolled the page into the platen. A painstaking twenty minutes later, he glanced over the letter he'd typed to Mr. Upshaw, the Arlington's general manager, then uncapped a fountain pen and signed his name with a flourish. He folded the letter in thirds, slid it into an envelope, and then debated whether to deliver the letter at once, or wait until Monday when he returned to work after his two weeks off.

No, as his grandfather used to say, in for a penny, in for a pound. If Thomas intended to follow through with these changes, he may as well start now.

Tucking the envelope into his shirt pocket, he stepped across the hall to the dining room. "Good morning, all."

His mother set down her coffee cup with a clatter. "Thomas, where have you been? Marguerite served breakfast nearly an hour ago."

"I'll grab a bite in the kitchen. Just popped in to say I'm going out for a bit." Thomas nodded a greeting to his aunt and uncle. "Have a good day, everyone."

"Thomas!" His mother's strident voice halted him mid-step. "Don't think you can simply rush off after you've been a virtual hermit for days on end. Where, pray tell, are you going?"

"Hotel business," he hedged. "Don't wait lunch for me."

After a quick trip upstairs to slip on a herringbone sack coat over his sweater vest, Thomas grabbed a leftover biscuit from the kitchen counter and swept out the back door. Within minutes, he parked the yellow Jeffery in his usual spot behind the Arlington.

His pulse hammered as he wound through the corridors toward the management offices. A part of him couldn't believe he was about to go through with this, while another part felt like shouting from the rooftops.

Lord, am I doing the right thing?

Had he even considered praying about this decision first, or did he suppose God would bless his plans and ensure he didn't make a first-class fool of himself—or worse?

Pausing outside Mr. Upshaw's office, Thomas tugged the envelope from his pocket. As he steeled himself to knock on the door, a secretary emerged from her office across the hall.

"Mr. Ballard? My goodness, I almost didn't recognize you." She tilted her head and smiled. "The beard becomes you."

Thomas gave a nervous cough. "Hello, Miss Hiers."

"Aren't you on vacation? We didn't expect you back before Monday."

"I, er, needed to discuss something with Mr. Upshaw."

"I'm afraid he's out until Monday as well. He went to Chicago to spend Thanksgiving with his daughter."

"I see." Thomas hoped his sudden swell of relief wasn't obvious. He held up the envelope. "In that case, I'll just leave this on his desk."

"Oh, sure. Go on in." The secretary wiggled her fingers as she continued down the corridor, calling over her shoulder, "Enjoy the rest of your vacation."

The letter delivered, Thomas slunk out of the office and closed the door. Maybe it would be better, after all, if the boss read the letter of resignation without Thomas present. After Mr. Upshaw had a chance to digest the news, they could have a much more productive discussion about the terms of Thomas's leaving the Arlington. His letter offered two weeks' notice, which would also allow him time to determine the next phase of his plans. As for his replacement, he'd recommended Stanley Fessler. An astute staff member with nearly ten years of hotel experience, the desk clerk had the makings of a fine manager.

With a sigh, Thomas glanced toward the lobby. He'd miss the Arlington, no doubt about it. But today the opulent decor, the elegantly attired patrons, the savory aromas of rich food wafting from the dining room—every expensive thing about the hotel stood in stark contrast to Thomas's new outlook.

True, nothing he'd set in motion today might ever be enough to win Joanna's heart, but he had no choice but to keep moving forward and leave the results to God.

Then, striding down the passageway, he turned a corner and ran straight into Joanna.

"Thomas? What are you doing here?" Gripping his coat sleeves, Joanna found her balance.

He responded with an uneasy chuckle. "I could ask you the same thing."

"I traded shifts with Lillian. She wanted the day off to shop with her daughter." Standing erect, Joanna gave Thomas the once-over. He obviously hadn't dressed for work. She grinned, admiring how the herringbone coat complemented his beard. "Now you *really* look like a college professor."

He flicked his gaze to the side, a thoughtful smile turning up his lips. "Maybe I should apply for a teaching position at the University of Arkansas."

Joanna narrowed her gaze. "You almost sound serious."

"Maybe I almost am."

"Thomas . . ." Puzzling over his meaning, she drew a quick breath. "I wish I had time to wheedle an explanation from you, but I need to relieve Pamela. So unless you want me pounding on your front door later today, you'd better tag along and tell me what you're up to."

He beamed. "You'd do that?"

"Do what?"

"Pound on my front door."

The puppy-dog slant to his brows tugged at her heart. When a bellboy rounded the corner, she stepped to the side and waited until he moved out of earshot. Then, facing Thomas with a stern look, she lowered her voice. "Your friendship is important to me. If you're about to do something crazy, I want to know."

Thomas ducked his head as two maids passed by, one of them pushing a rattling housekeeping cart. As they continued on toward the service elevator, the slim brunette muttered, "Was that *our* Mr. Ballard looking so dapper? I need to get reassigned to cleaning management offices."

Stunned by a twinge of jealousy, Joanna stiffened and crossed her arms. "Busybodies."

Smirking, Thomas motioned Joanna down the passageway. "Come on, I'll walk you to the switchboard."

Nose in the air, she swept past him. The scamp had sensed her discomposure, had he? Well, she wouldn't give him the chance to press his advantage. As soon as they entered the switchboard room, Joanna cheerily took over for Pamela and sent the girl on her way. After she arranged herself in front of the board and checked the calls in progress, she swiveled to face Thomas. "All right, mister, time to level with me."

Thomas lowered himself onto the vacant chair and released a long, slow breath. "I've just tendered my resignation."

"You *what?*" The words exploded in the small room. "But you love your work. Why on earth would you quit?"

He shrugged. "Why did you leave Hot Springs? Why did you join the Signal Corps? Why did you want to stay in France?"

His questions, though spoken softly, stabbed like knives. "Don't turn this on me, Thomas. My family needed me, and I came home. Now it sounds as if *you're* the one running away."

"Not any more than you were." A faraway look in his eyes, Thomas braced his palms on his knees and sighed. "I want to do something besides sit behind a desk all day. I want to do something meaningful. Something . . . adventurous."

She glanced away as Walter's handsome face filled her mind. Her voice trembled as she replied, "Believe me when I say the adventure isn't always worth the consequences."

As Thomas gazed at her in silence, the switchboard buzzed with an incoming call. She swung around and adjusted her headset. Despite her agitation, she smoothly transferred the caller to the accounting department. She turned to find Thomas still staring at her.

"How long has it been?" he asked. "More than a year, surely. We just celebrated Armistice Day."

She didn't have to ask what he meant. "October 8, 1918. That's the day he died in the battle for Blanc Mont Ridge."

"And you've been grieving all this time?"

"I'm not grieving. I'm—" Another call came through, and Joanna steeled her voice. "Arlington Hotel. How may I help you?"

The caller asked to be connected with one of the guest rooms. Joanna's hand shook as she jabbed the plug into the jack. When she peered over her shoulder to see if Thomas had noticed, she discovered he was gone.

Just as well. His remarks had sliced too deep. A year was nothing, and yet a lifetime, and she would remain faithful to Walter's memory.

She owed him that much, and more.

15

Arriving at the hotel Monday morning, Thomas slipped into his office unnoticed. He'd seen a light under Mr. Upshaw's closed door and wondered how long it would take for the general manager to find and read Thomas's letter of resignation.

Not long, apparently. The fuming Mr. Upshaw barged into Thomas's office brandishing a wrinkled sheet of stationery. "Ballard! What is the meaning of this?"

Thomas stood, fingertips pressed into his desktop. "Good morning, Mr. Upshaw. I see you've read my letter. Everything should be self-explanatory."

"Self-explanatory, my foot!" The tall, hoary-haired man slammed the page down on the desk, scattering loose papers. "After thirty years in management, I can usually discern well in advance when an employee is looking to move on." He shook his head in disbelief. "With you? Nothing."

"I realize it's sudden, sir." Avoiding his boss's gaze, Thomas made a halfhearted attempt to straighten the papers on his desk. "I only recently realized my discontent—and not with the job or the hotel, I assure you. It's strictly personal."

Bushy white brows knitted, Mr. Upshaw collapsed into a chair. "Maybe I shouldn't be so surprised after all. A young man like you, from a family rich as Croesus—only a matter of time before you grew bored with the responsibility of a full-time job."

"Family money has nothing to do with it. As I said, I've found my work here most fulfilling. I simply feel the time has come to move in new directions."

Mr. Upshaw narrowed his gaze. "So help me, Ballard, if those *new directions* have anything to do with the Eastman or Majestic offering you a better deal—"

"Absolutely not! I wouldn't think of leaving here for one of our competitors." With an exhausted sigh, Thomas settled into his desk chair and rubbed his eyes. "I'm sorry, Mr. Upshaw, but there is nothing more I can say except to plead your acceptance of my resignation."

With a stone-faced glare, the general manager stood. "I haven't decided yet." He snatched up the letter and marched to the door. Then, hand on the knob, he turned and scowled. "As for the facial hair, make sure it's gone by tomorrow."

Thomas waited for the door to slam, then leaned back to stare at the ceiling. It wasn't as if Mr. Upshaw had a choice in the matter. At the end of two weeks, replacement or not, Thomas intended to clear out of this office and be on his way to bigger and better things.

In the meantime, he'd better continue plowing through his inbox before the mile-high stack buried him. Since his secretary had done an admirable job of handling urgent matters, his primary task involved perusing the items to bring himself up to date and then filing them away. Mindless work, to be sure.

By noon, he'd gone nearly cross-eyed and remembered why in the past he'd seldom taken off more than a few days at a time. The catch-up chore was a killer. Needing some lunch and a long walk, he strolled through the lobby and out the front doors to Central Avenue. With no particular plans, he soon found himself seated at the soda fountain counter in Sorrell's Drug Company.

"Afternoon, sir. What'll it be?"

A soda wasn't exactly lunchtime fare, but tendering his resignation had left Thomas feeling rakish. "How about a peach—no, let's make it an admiral frappé."

He'd never forget the day he'd shared one with Joanna—or her teasing words: *"Now, Thomas, sometimes you have to leave behind the familiar and try something different. A little adventure never hurt anyone."*

"Make it two, my treat."

Thomas spun around to see Joanna at his elbow. She nodded at the boy behind the counter, who gave a quick tip of his cap before busying himself preparing their sodas. As Joanna climbed onto the stool next to Thomas's, he grinned. "This is a nice surprise."

"I came in to pick up a few things, and when I saw you sitting here, I couldn't resist." Joanna arched a brow. "I noticed you weren't in church again yesterday."

"Most people thought I was still on vacation. I decided to take a lesson from Matthew 6 and spend some time praying alone. It's a great way to improve your perspective."

With a tight smile, she faced forward. "Why'd you disappear the other day at the hotel?"

Her nearness made it increasingly harder to breathe. "You were trying to work. I could tell our line of conversation had upset you."

Joanna drew a long breath through her nostrils and let it out slowly. "It's true. I still have a hard time talking about Walter."

"Walter was his name?"

Lowering her head, Joanna nodded. "Corporal Walter Garritson, 142nd Infantry."

"I'm sure he died bravely." Thomas rested an elbow on the counter, his gazed fixed on Joanna's folded hands.

With another deep sigh, Joanna straightened her shoulders and turned to Thomas with a broad smile. "You're trying the admiral frappé again?"

Apparently, they were changing the subject. "I thought I'd see if it tasted as good as I remembered."

"I hope you won't be disappointed. The second time around is rarely as wonderful as the first."

The double meaning behind her words brought a clutch to his chest. No matter what might develop between them, he would always be second in her heart to Walter.

Strained silence settled over them until their sodas arrived. Thomas put the straw to his mouth and took a careful sip, the blended flavors of tart strawberries and sweet cream tasting even more delightful than he remembered. He chuckled softly. "You were wrong, Joanna."

Sipping her own drink, she slanted him a questioning look. "About what?"

"Some things *are* better the second time around."

Her gaze darkened briefly, and something between surprise and hope warmed her expression. "Thomas . . ."

He leaned closer, catching the faint scent of strawberries as she exhaled short breaths through parted lips. He wanted to kiss her so badly it made his throat ache.

Then someone jostled him from behind, bringing him instantly aware of the bustle of lunch-hour shoppers all around. The moment lost, he sat erect. Joanna faced forward as well, fingers wrapped around the base of her soda glass. Thomas watched from the corner of his eye as she drew the straw between her lips and sipped. When she swallowed, her eyes drifted shut, and the corner of her mouth turned up ever so slightly.

Thomas smiled a secret smile of his own. Perhaps Marguerite was right. In time, and with both patience and persistence, he might find a chink in the armor surrounding Joanna's heart, and maybe . . . just maybe . . . she'd let him in.

$\mathcal{L}$♥

Joanna savored the last drops of frappé from the bottom of her soda glass. Thank goodness for the crowd in Sorrell's, or Thomas would surely have kissed her.

And she wouldn't have resisted.

Guilt eating her alive, she scooted off the stool and snatched the ticket off the counter. "Lots of errands to run yet. I'll see you around, Thomas."

"Joanna, wait." He gulped the rest of his drink and followed her to the cashier. "Where are you headed? Can I walk with you?"

"I truly doubt you'd enjoy traipsing through dress shops." She tugged a bill and some change from her wallet and handed the money to the clerk. "Anyway, don't you need to get back to work?"

He looked as if she'd just told him Christmas had been cancelled. Glancing at his watch, he mumbled, "Yeah, guess so." Then, eyes brightening, he added, "I'm so far behind, I'll probably still be at my desk when you come in for your shift later."

A prickle of anticipation shot through her, along with another dose of guilt. "Maybe I'll see you then."

They parted ways on the sidewalk, and Joanna steeled herself to complete the task she'd set out on today: to advance the quality of her wardrobe from "ancient history" to "passable."

In the first shop she entered, a middle-aged saleswoman greeted her at the door. "Good afternoon, miss. How may I assist you?"

Clad in her faded traveling skirt and the sweater with the unraveled hem, Joanna extended her arms and turned in a small circle. "Do I need to explain?"

The woman appraised her with a knowing frown. "My dear, you've come to the right place."

An hour later, and having parted with a large chunk of her earnings, she left the shop with four new dresses, a winter coat, feathered felt hat, two pairs of shoes, and directions to a charming lingerie shop around the corner. Laden with packages, she wished she'd traded vehicles with Jack and driven the Dodge today instead of her Indian.

As she strode up the sidewalk to where she'd parked the motor-cycle, she came to a window display of exquisite ceramic pieces. The sign on the door read:

Annemarie Kendall Vickary
Studio And Showroom

Joanna had been meaning to visit Annemarie's shop ever since Mrs. Kendall first mentioned it. Juggling her purchases, she gripped the knob and pushed open the door. A tiny brass bell signaled her entry, and moments later Annemarie appeared through a rear door.

"Joanna, how nice to see you!" Annemarie wiped her hands on her apron. "I've been working in the back. I'm a mess."

Glancing around the showroom, Joanna smiled her amaze-ment. "You made all these pieces yourself?"

"It's a dream come true, and all thanks to my dear husband and his mother." Annemarie shrugged out of her apron and wad-ded it up behind the counter. When she stepped around to the front, the small mound of her pregnancy became obvious.

Joanna's mouth formed an O, and one of her packages slipped from her arms.

Scooping up the white bag, Annemarie read the name printed beneath the logo. "One of my favorite dress shops. Looks as if you made quite a dent in their inventory!" She relieved Joanna of more bags and set everything on the floor by the counter.

Straightening, Joanna eased her tired shoulders. Again, her gaze fell to Annemarie's abdomen.

One hand resting at her waist, Annemarie offered a demure smile. "Yes, it's true. Sam and I are expecting."

"I'm so glad for you. And amazed your mother hasn't shouted it from the rooftops. She must be thrilled."

"She is, but she's also leery of sharing the news too soon. If Mama had her way, I'd stay home with my feet up until the baby's arrival."

Joanna wrinkled her brow. "Sounds a bit overprotective to me."

With a sigh, Annemarie studied the arrangement of a nearby display and made minute adjustments. "My mother lost a baby many years ago. I don't think you ever really get over such grief."

Joanna traced the lip of a bowl with a gentle fingertip. "How did it happen? Was there an accident, or had she . . . done something she shouldn't have?"

"Nothing like that. I was only a little girl and didn't fully understand at the time, but I do know Mama followed her doctor's instructions to the letter. She would have sacrificed anything to protect her baby."

"She must have been devastated."

Annemarie nodded. "It was close to a year before the good days outnumbered the bad."

A catch in her throat, Joanna turned away. "At least she could rest in the assurance she'd done everything she could."

"Even in the darkest days, Mama leaned on Jesus to carry her through." Annemarie touched Joanna's shoulder. "You can lean on Him, too. He's strong enough for whatever burden you're bearing."

"How did you—" Joanna swiveled to meet Annemarie's gaze.

Annemarie uttered a quiet laugh. "I'm married to a chaplain, remember? I suppose some of Sam's sensitivity has rubbed off on me." Her eyes softened. "Is it Lily? Are you feeling as if you haven't done all you could for her?"

"It's Lily. It's Jack. It's my mother." *And Walter, most of all.* "When others needed me most, I wasn't there."

"Or perhaps you were exactly where God wanted you to be. He has a surprising way of working things out according to His purposes, even when they're beyond our mortal comprehension."

Joanna paced to the window and stared out at bustling Central Avenue. Across the street, a gentleman assisted an elderly woman up the steps of the Fordyce Bathhouse. His tender concern tugged at Joanna's heart. She sighed and faced Annemarie with a weak smile. "I hope you're right, because then maybe my poor choices don't have to haunt me forever."

"I am, and they don't." Annemarie gripped Joanna's shoulders and gave them a quick shake. "Now come to the workroom and let's have a cup of tea. And bring your purchases so you can show me all the lovely things you bought."

An hour later, Joanna felt refreshed and encouraged to have laughed and chatted with a friend. Just like Véronique, Annemarie had a knack for cutting to the heart of a matter yet with a tender touch. Perhaps as they renewed their acquaintance, Joanna would find in her another kindred spirit.

"Oh, dear, look at the time!" Joanna bounced up from the chair and began stuffing her purchases back into the bags. "I need to pick up Lily from school and then help her with a history report."

Annemarie helped gather up the packages and followed Joanna to the front door. "Sam and I must have all of you over for dinner one day soon. Perhaps next Sunday after church?"

"Let me check with Jack and Lily." If her arms weren't full of packages, she'd wrap Annemarie in a hug. Instead, she beamed a smile. "I'm so glad I happened upon your shop today. It was a lovely afternoon."

$\mathscr{L}$❦

It was a horrible afternoon. After Thomas returned to the Arlington, everything went downhill. Three maids called in sick, the fire department extinguished a grease fire in the kitchen, and Lillian Zongrone spilled scalding hot coffee on her hand and rushed out to the doctor. Thomas covered the switchboard himself until he could grab Austin Lindsey from the front desk.

"Maybe Joanna could come in early," Austin suggested as he took over the headset. "I don't like leaving the new guy up front by himself."

"I'll keep an eye on him. Joanna's busy with other things today." He almost laughed to recall her morose expression at the mere mention of visiting dress shops. In his opinion, she'd look breathtakingly beautiful in a potato sack!

With the Thanksgiving holiday past, spa clientele began returning to the city for extended courses of bath treatments. By late afternoon, several taxis and depot hacks lined up under the portico to drop off travelers. Thomas darted back and forth between checking hotel guests into their rooms and making sure Austin didn't get his lines crossed too often. When eight o'clock rolled around, Thomas had just sent a bellhop upstairs with a couple's six suitcases and a steamer trunk—the last scheduled arrival of the day. Exhausted, legs aching from being on his feet most of the afternoon, he breathed a sigh of relief when Stanley Fessler arrived to take over.

Dispensing with more commentary on his beard, Thomas simply waved a hand. "It'll be gone tomorrow—Upshaw's orders."

"Well, I rather like it." Stanley clipped his name tag to his lapel before reviewing the registration book.

"By the way, there's something you should know." Thomas explained about his resignation and his recommendation that Stanley be groomed to replace him.

"Sir, I'm honored—but the Arlington won't be the same without you." Stanley's face filled with concern. "If I may ask, sir, what will you do?"

"Well, I—" Seeing Joanna approach, he froze. She most definitely was *not* wearing a potato sack! A camel's-hair coat draped over one arm, she wore a periwinkle-blue wool dress with a dropped waist. The color flattered her beautifully, and beneath the soft glow of the electric chandeliers, her neatly coiffed hair looked like spun gold.

She arched a brow. "Do tell, Thomas. What *will* you do after you depart the Arlington?"

He croaked a nervous laugh. "I, uh, I'm still deciding."

Her expression hardened. "Oh, yes, I forgot. You're planning something *adventurous*. Excuse me," she said, turning toward the switchboard room. "I'm running late for my shift."

"Joanna." His tone halted her mid-step. With a nod of apology to Stanley, he snatched Joanna's hand and led her down a hallway to an unoccupied conference room.

"Thomas, I told you," she said as he kicked the door shut behind them. "I need to get to work."

"And I need to do this." Before he lost his courage, before common sense kicked in, he lifted one hand to cradle the base of her neck. Tipping her head back, he fixed his gaze on her parted lips.

"Thomas . . ."

Slowly, tenderly, he lowered his lips upon hers, and he couldn't have stopped himself if he tried. She stiffened in shock, but as her mouth warmed beneath his, she melted against him. Her coat fell to the floor, and her arms snaked around his shoulders. A soft moan escaped her throat, and it seemed she tried to pull him closer while at the same time pushing him away. She returned his kiss with lips as sweet as ripe cherries, and her responsiveness only fed his desire.

Then, setting her hands against his chest, she lowered her head and nudged some space between them. "Stop, Thomas, please. We can't do this."

Pulse pounding, breath rasping, Thomas fought for control. *Stop*—when he'd never felt anything so incredibly amazing in his life? "You felt it, too, Joanna. I know you did."

"It doesn't matter. It can't happen." She bent to retrieve her coat. When she straightened, she wore a dispassionate smile utterly incongruent with the moment they'd just shared. "I won't deny I enjoyed the kiss. Certainly I was as curious as you about what it would be like."

"*Curious*? Is that all you can say?" Thomas plowed his fingers through the hair at his temple. He couldn't believe he'd misread her response so completely.

Keeping her eyes averted, she edged past him. "I thought I explained. My heart belongs to Walter and always will."

"You're going to let a dead man come between us."

She shuddered. "You don't understand, Thomas. I made a promise. To Walter, and to myself. I won't break it again." She swept from the room.

Again?

Stunned and confused, Thomas sank into the nearest chair. What sort of promise could a dead soldier possibly hold her to? Thomas was here, flesh and blood, ready to love her with more passion than he ever dreamed himself capable of. She could love him, too—he sensed it the moment she surrendered to the kiss. No woman could return a kiss so fervently out of mere *curiosity*.

Determination filled him—he'd *make* her explain herself, force her to let go of the past and admit her feelings for him. Storming from the room, he strode down the corridor and around the corner to the switchboard room.

Halting outside the partly open door, he took one look at her weeping form slumped over the desk and swallowed his anger. Her entire body trembled with each muffled sob, and the agony of witnessing such grief shattered his own heart into a million shards. Though he ached to wrap her in his arms and kiss away every tear, he sensed she'd never want him or anyone else to know how she wept.

Clenching his jaw, he drew a silent breath and eased the door shut until the latch caught. At the front desk, he motioned Stanley aside. "I don't think Joanna is feeling quite herself this evening. If you wouldn't mind, give her an hour or so and then suggest it's going to be a quiet night. Tell her you'll cover for her and send her home."

"Happy to, sir." Questions shone in Stanley's eyes, but like the loyal employee he was, he refrained from voicing them. "Thank you again for the recommendation. Have a good evening, sir."

Sorry, too late. "You're most welcome, Stanley. Good night."

16

After sending Lily off to school Thursday morning, Joanna started a fresh pot of coffee brewing. She'd slept even more fitfully than usual the past few nights and would need the extra caffeine to get through the day . . . and tonight at the switchboard.

Why did you have to kiss me, Thomas?

Three days later, her lips still tingled with the memory. She shouldn't have enjoyed it so much, shouldn't have responded so wantonly.

But if he kissed her again, would she respond any differently? She didn't dare imagine.

While the coffee perked, Joanna carried a basket of laundry out to the screened back porch, filled the wooden tub of the Maytag washer, and started the electric motor. The sloshing sound mesmerized her, and for several minutes she stood with eyes closed and emptied her mind of all other thoughts.

Finally the December chill penetrated her sweater and sent her inside, where she went to the stove and poured a steaming mug of coffee. Hands cradling the warm cup, she sat at the kitchen table and steeled herself to finish composing a letter to Véronique. She'd begun the letter nearly two weeks ago, but with everything distracting her since returning to Hot Springs, she hadn't found the energy or the words to describe it all to her friend. Perhaps if she could only get her thoughts on paper, she'd finally begin to make sense of things, herself.

With a groan, she pushed up from the table and went to the rolltop desk in the parlor. Opening the bottom drawer where she'd hidden Véronique's letter from Jack's prying eyes, she withdrew the envelope along with her own unfinished letter. After collecting more stationery and a fountain pen, she returned to the warmth of the kitchen and spread the pages across the table. A quick perusal of her hastily jotted paragraphs from two weeks ago left her no choice but to tear them up and begin again. She uncapped her pen and wrote in fluent French, a language almost as comfortable to her as her native English.

My dearest friend Véronique,

I should have written sooner, but readjusting to life in America has not been easy. I can't tell you how many times I almost packed my bags and purchased a ticket on the next ocean liner back to France—most especially when your letter came with the news of poor Yvette. I remember how sickly she was, how tiny and frail, but I always hoped she would grow stronger and someday know the love of a real family again.

Family—so much more important than I ever wanted to admit. You know how hard I resisted coming home. But now I'm glad I did. In these few short weeks, I've gained new appreciation and respect for how my brother has kept what's left of our family intact. He has stepped up as head of the house and shouldered the responsibilities I selfishly avoided.

So now, though I miss you terribly and wish we were still tromping the streets of Paris together, working side by side in the telephone office, and helping in the orphanages, I know I must stay where I am. I can't leave my little sister again, not when she so desperately needs the influence of a strong woman in her life.

I laugh to write those words—me, strong? How could I ever think so, when all my adult life I've fled from my obligations and disappointed the ones who loved me most?

I know, I know. You'll say I served my country well, never shirking my Signal Corps duties. But really, wasn't my service only another form of escape? Clad in my navy wool uniform—bought with my own money, no less!—and connecting calls for generals and presidents, I could pretend to be important, worthy, respected. Let someone else tend the home front, because Joanna Trapp is occupied helping the war effort!

Please don't think I'm belittling the fine women I served with, nor the value of the job itself. I'm confident what we did made a monumental difference in assuring an Allied victory, and I'm honored to be counted among the "Hello Girls" recognized by General Pershing for our loyalty and dedication.

The problem is within me—my own self-righteous pride. I couldn't even—

Joanna's fingers tightened around the pen as her throat clamped shut. After making a fool of herself Monday night at the switchboard, she refused to cry again. Though she couldn't be certain anyone had seen her break down, it seemed too coincidental that not an hour later, Stanley had suggested she leave early and catch up on her rest.

Drawing a tremulous breath, she blinked several times and then read over the words she'd just written.—*my own self-righteous pride. I couldn't even—*

Oh, how it hurt to remember! She could still hear Walter's voice in her headset that night.

"Hey, gorgeous! Can't believe how many hoops I had to jump through to get you on the line. I've got a six-hour pass, and I want to spend every possible minute with you before—well, you know as well as I do I can't say more. Can you get away, meet me in an hour?"

And what had she told him? "You mean tonight? I can't. I still have four hours left on my shift."

"Can't you get someone to cover? I really need to see you. Baby, where they're sending us . . . I've got a funny feeling."

She hadn't even wanted to think what he meant. Besides, Walter was invincible. To admit anything different would have exposed her heart to unspeakable fear. "Don't talk this way. The war is sure to end soon, and then we'll be together always."

"Jo, please. One hour. It's all arranged."

She'd been almost afraid to ask. "What, Walter? What's arranged?"

"I want us to get married tonight. Let's not wait. If I die—"

"I mean it—don't say such things!"

"No, listen. I love you, Jo. Give me tonight. Please."

She'd finally agreed to try to get away. Walter gave directions to a small hotel in the village near where Joanna was stationed and said he'd be waiting downstairs in the café. Then, as her eagle-eyed supervisor moved down the row of operators, Joanna told him a hurried goodbye and disconnected the line.

Minutes later, the switchboard lit up with a flurry of calls. Joanna lost all track of time as she and the other operators frantically connected front-line commanders or passed along coded messages. Bomber planes droned overhead. Artillery explosions thundered in the distance. Though the old barracks housing the switchboard had been fortified with sandbags, Joanna could still feel the vibrations and catch glimpses of far-off red and orange flashes through the boarded-up windows. She kept too busy to worry about any danger to herself. Even if the threat to their location had been immediate, she'd never have deserted her post. Too much depended upon connecting those red and green wires and getting the calls through.

Only after the rush had subsided did Joanna remember she'd promised to meet Walter, but by the time she found someone to cover for her and finagled a ride to the hotel, he had only a couple of hours' leave remaining.

For as long as she lived, she'd never forgive herself for squandering the last two hours she'd ever share with the man she'd pledged to love for eternity.

$\mathscr{L}$♥

Groaning, Jack massaged his eye sockets with the heels of his hands. He'd been staring at the same ledger page for a good twenty minutes, while his brain betrayed him with thoughts of the pleasant Thanksgiving he and Lily had spent with Miss Maynard.

Madison. What he wouldn't give to see her again!

But she was his sister's teacher and academic advisor. Would his growing affection for the lovely Miss Maynard create a conflict of interests?

Maybe he'd ask Joanna. She surely had more romantic experience, considering what he remembered about her high school years and running off with an older boy. Jack's face warmed as he recalled his embarrassment over the rampant rumors.

Although once Joanna had broken it off with the creep and buckled down to her schoolwork, Jack had never known her to be in a relationship since. Could she possibly have stayed celibate all the while she attended Barnard or worked as a telephone operator in New York? And then her years in France—it seemed unrealistic to believe she hadn't so much as dated during the entire time.

If she had, she certainly didn't talk about it. Had Jack been so far off base to imagine something might be developing between Joanna and Thomas?

Behind Jack's desk, the workroom door creaked open. At the unmistakable sound of Mr. Kendall's heavy steps, Jack cleared his throat and tried to look busy.

Smelling like pottery dust and smoke from the factory kiln, the large man cast Jack a meaningful glance as he thumbed through the purchase orders on the corner of the desk. "It's almost noon, lad. Seeing as how you're near stupefied from staring at numbers all morning, why don't you run out for a bite of lunch? You can swing by the depot on your way and deliver the crate we're shipping to Memphis. It's already loaded on the truck."

Usually one of the factory workers or Mr. Kendall himself drove the delivery truck, but Jack wouldn't turn up his nose at a chance to escape the office for a while. Besides, the depot was only a few short blocks from the high school. Perhaps Jack could drop by—if Miss Maynard wasn't busy, of course—and ask about Lily's recent scholastic performance. It would only be conscientious of him, right?

"I'll take care of it right away, sir." Marking his place in the ledger with a pencil, he closed the book and tidied his desk. In the workroom, he snatched his overcoat from a hook, pressed his tan fedora on his crown, and yanked open the door to the dock.

He hadn't taken three steps when Mr. Kendall's voice bellowed behind him. "Forgetting something, my boy?"

Jack halted and spun around, only to see his boss wearing a teasing grin and jangling a key ring. "You won't get too far without these. Oh, and watch your p's and q's with the pretty schoolteacher."

Wondering how the man could possibly be aware of Jack's interest in Miss Maynard, he could only reply with a shaky smile. He caught the keys Mr. Kendall tossed to him and climbed into the truck. Good thing his first stop was the depot, because he'd need every spare moment for his heart to stop pounding.

After turning the shipping crate over to the station manager and confirming it would go out on the next train to Tennessee, Jack continued to the high school. A secretary informed him Miss Maynard had a conference period and could be found in her classroom. Hat in hand, Jack made his way to the second floor.

Pausing outside the partially open door, he peered inside. Red pencil in hand and a stack of papers on her desk, Miss Maynard appeared to be alone in the room. When Jack tapped on the door frame, a welcoming smile brightened her face as she stood and motioned him to enter.

Jack sidled into the room, his gaze riveted by how her stylish pink and orange dress flattered her creamy complexion. "I hope I'm not interrupting."

"Not at all. I'm getting a head start on these test papers so I don't have so many to grade at home tonight."

"Would one of those test papers be Lily's?"

"As a matter of fact, yes." Miss Maynard returned to the desk and shuffled through the pages, then held one up for Jack to see. "An excellent score—she missed only one question."

Jack closed his eyes for a moment in silent gratitude. "I can't tell you how such news relieves my mind."

"Lily has been a different girl the last couple of weeks."

"It's mostly thanks to Joanna. I certainly can't take the credit." Mangling his hat brim, he stepped closer. "Miss Maynard, I . . . well, the truth is I didn't come by for the sole purpose of asking about Lily's progress."

Her eyes widened. "Oh?"

"Actually, I wanted to . . ." Jack swallowed and then had to peel his tongue from the roof of his mouth. "I wanted to thank you again for allowing Lily and me to join you for Thanksgiving."

"You're quite welcome." Smiling demurely, Miss Maynard dipped her chin. "But you didn't have to come all the way over to the school just to say so."

"But I wanted to. I mean—"

With a sympathetic laugh, Miss Maynard gently detached Jack's fingers from his hat brim and smoothed it with the side of her thumb. "Perhaps you should state clearly what you mean, Mr. Trapp," she began as she handed back his hat, "before you completely ruin this handsome fedora."

Maybe he should just say it—admit he found her incredibly beautiful and the kindest, most enchanting woman he'd ever met. Too nervous to meet her gaze, he stared at his hands. "I wonder, would we be committing a terrible infraction in the eyes of the school board if we were to . . ."

For a painful few seconds, all Jack heard was the sound of his own heartbeat thudding in his chest. Then the object of his affection said softly, "Are you asking to court me, Mr. Trapp?"

A grin crept across his face, but he kept his chin down. "Yes, Miss Maynard, I am."

"Then you may call on me Sunday afternoon at four o'clock. My aunt shall chaperone." She winked. "Aunt Ruth's late husband served on the school board for fourteen years, so you may be sure she'll report us if you make any improper advances."

His chest on the verge of exploding, Jack backed toward the door. "I'll be proper as a monk!"

Thomas arrived home from work Thursday evening to find his mother storming through the house and raving like a madwoman. He caught up with her as she reeled into the parlor, arms flailing.

"This is the end—the *end*! Things simply could *not* get any worse!" Spying Thomas in the doorway, she thrust a hand to her bosom. "And *you*—you are the cause of it all!"

He set his attaché on a chair while he shucked his overcoat. So much for her recent protestations of motherly pride. "What have I done now—or is it what I *haven't* done?"

"Isn't it enough you have besmirched the family name by walking away from a perfectly respectable position at the Arlington—and for no good reason, I might add?"

"I had my reasons, Mother." Although none he could easily justify to her, to himself, or anyone else. He had yet to determine where his rash decision would lead. He had, however, succumbed to pressure from his boss and rid himself of the beard. Perhaps after his two weeks were up, he'd grow it back. Crossing to an overstuffed armchair, he sank onto the seat cushion and loosened his shoelaces. "Anyway, you've known about my resignation for days. Obviously, something else has set you off."

"Something else indeed." With a dramatic sigh, she flung herself onto the sofa. "I have been spurned, Thomas. Do you hear me? *Spurned!*"

She couldn't possibly be talking about a suitor. Removing his tie, he sat back and waited for her explanation.

"It's the Hegneys, thank you for asking. They have declined my dinner invitation."

Thomas massaged his right eyebrow with his index finger. "And why, pray tell, am I to shoulder the blame?"

"Because of your relationship with the Trapp girl, of course!"

Of course. Thomas closed his eyes briefly and wondered if by chance Gilbert had a spare room at the farm and would hire him on as a stable hand. He may not know one confounded thing about horses, but Gil could certainly teach him a thing or two about reinventing himself.

Drumming his fingers on the chair arm, he willed himself to speak calmly. "What does Joanna have to do with inviting the Hegneys to dinner?"

"Absolutely everything. Fannie asked me point-blank if Miss Trapp would be in attendance, and when I said it was likely you might ask her to join us, Fannie stated she could not possibly share a meal with—and I quote—'that hypocritical termagant.'"

"Terma-*what?*"

"Termagant." Nose in the air, his mother crossed her arms. "Check the dictionary. It means a quarrelsome woman."

Fuming, Thomas clamped his teeth together. "Joanna is neither hypocritical nor quarrelsome. Where is this coming from?"

"You haven't heard? Apparently the younger Miss Trapp has followed in her elder sister's wanton footsteps. Together they have conspired to have Rudy Hegney expelled from school."

Thomas knew about Lily's suspension, but this was the first he'd heard about Rudy. If the cad had been expelled, he likely deserved it, considering what Thomas had learned from Joanna.

Then his brain ricocheted to his mother's use of the word *wanton*. Incensed, he slammed his fist on the side table, rattling the crystal teardrops trimming his mother's favorite lampshade. "Just when I think you've curbed your blue-blooded bigotry, you stagger me yet again."

"I'm *bigoted?* For speaking the truth?"

"Sounds more like idle gossip to me. You have no call to slander Joanna's character with such talk."

"What reason would the Hegneys have for making any of this up? Fannie reminded me their daughter Caroline was Joanna's classmate, and Caroline remembers quite well how Joanna ran away with an older boy one summer." Thomas's mother sniffed. "It takes little imagination to guess what transpired on the trip. And even less to surmise the younger Miss Trapp beguiled Rudy Hegney in exactly the same way."

A crushing pain filled Thomas's chest. In high school, he'd been too preoccupied trying to emerge from his older brother's shadow to pay much attention to rumors about a younger coed taking off with Gil's rascally friend Arthur Spence. Thomas never much liked Arthur—for good reason, as it turned out—and now he couldn't dislodge the sudden bitter jealousy gripping his heart to realize Joanna had been the girl.

No—he wouldn't succumb to such feelings. He loved Joanna for the woman she was today. How often had Pastor Yarborough preached on 2 Corinthians 5:17, *Wherefore if any man is in Christ, he is a new creature: the old things are passed away; behold, they are become new?* It had been true for Gilbert, it must be true for Joanna, and Thomas would make it true for himself.

He shoved to his feet and stood over his mother. "I'm sorry, but I cannot continue living under the same roof with a woman who not only puts stock in hearsay but habitually disparages anyone who doesn't meet her impossible standards."

Her head jerked backward, and her eyes became saucers. "Wh-what are you saying?"

"I'm saying—" Thomas exhaled sharply, suddenly unsure exactly what his intentions were. After living his entire life in a fine house with money and servants, did he have the courage to move out on his own? Gilbert may have done so successfully, but Gilbert had always been the favored one.

Angry at himself once more for entertaining such begrudging thoughts, Thomas turned aside. He shoved his hands into his pockets and heaved a tired sigh. "All I know is that things can't continue as they are. I'm falling in love with Joanna Trapp, and I intend to do everything in my power to become the sort of man she could love in return, even if the day never comes."

As he trudged upstairs to pack a bag, the last sounds he heard were his mother's whimpers and her confused cry, "Thomas, don't leave like this! If I upset you, I'm sorry!"

If? If she lived to be a thousand, would she ever understand? Would she ever change?

Thomas doubted it, which was exactly why he had to get out now, before her poisonous judgments destroyed any chance he might have for lasting happiness.

17

Strolling along Central Avenue, best friend at her side and their arms laden with shopping bags, Lily felt free for the first time in weeks. Things had been going well both at home and at school, if she didn't count the nasty glares from Rudy's friends. Why should they blame her for his expulsion, when it was his own fault? Seemed Lily wasn't the only girl he'd been putting the moves on. How could she ever have been so gullible?

"Oh, look!" Abby plucked at Lily's coat sleeve then pointed in a shop window. "Isn't it adorable?"

Glimpsing the purple ceramic piggy bank, Lily chuckled and bumped Abby's shoulder. "It's purple and it's a pig. What's not to like?"

Turning to Lily, Abby grew sober and dipped her chin. "Not so long ago I didn't think you liked me anymore."

"It wasn't you," Lily said with a regretful sigh. "I didn't much like myself, and I guess I thought hurting someone else would make me feel better. Only it turned out the person I hurt most was myself."

"Well, it's in the past, and all is forgiven." Laughter bubbled up from Abby's chest. "Today we're back to being best friends *and* getting an early start on our Christmas shopping!"

Lily blinked back a tear before Abby could notice. "Joanna should be waiting for us at Sorrell's by now. How about I treat my best friend to a soda?" She jiggled her purse. "I *think* I might have enough money left."

"I *love* Sorrell's sodas! There's a new flavor I've been dying to try."

As they started down the sidewalk, Lily made a mental note to return later on her own and purchase the piggy bank for Abby's Christmas gift.

Chatting and giggling with her friend, Lily only gradually became aware of male voices behind them. Then a throaty laugh sent chills up her spine. She glanced over her shoulder to see two of Rudy's friends marching in step with her and Abby.

One of them, a boy named Dennis, caught her eye and grinned. "Going our way, ladies?"

Lily halted and faced him, glad her wool muffler concealed the rapidly pulsing vein in her neck. "I don't know, Dennis. But tell us where you're headed and we'll be sure to turn in the opposite direction."

His gaze turned icy. "Hmm, guess it's true what Rudy says—you're as uppity as your big sister." He sidled closer and lowered his voice. "And as free with your affections, too, so we're told. Admit it—you were only playing coy with Bill and me. If we'd been anywhere but church then, I bet you'd have shown us a little of what Rudy's been getting."

Teeth clenched, hands trembling, Lily glared over her bundle of shopping bags. "Rudy hasn't been getting *anything*—"

"Don't, Lily." Abby gripped her arm. "They're not worth it. Let's just go."

"Yeah, run along, *little girls*." Bill snickered. "Come on, Dennis. Rudy'll be waiting at the movie theater."

After the boys strode past, Lily blew out a tremulous breath. She hoped her legs wouldn't turn to limp noodles before she and

Abby made it to Sorrell's. How had Joanna ever survived her last years at high school with everyone believing the worst about her?

With effort, she got her feet moving again, only to be caught up short when Abby stepped in front of her. With a pointed stare, she said, "What were they talking about, Lily? What happened at church?"

Stalling, Lily chewed her lip. "Remember when I was accused of trying to steal from the offering plate?"

Abby's eyes widened. "Those boys were there?"

Lily nodded. "Jack and Joanna were taking forever visiting with everyone after the service, and I saw Bill and Dennis giving me leering looks, so I ducked through a side door into the corridor, hoping they wouldn't notice. But they did, and—" She shuddered at the memory of their hands all over her. "When they tried to . . . touch me . . . I ran into the pastor's office and locked the door."

"Oh, Lily. Why didn't you tell me sooner? Have you told *anyone?*"

"I was too ashamed. Nobody would have believed me anyway. At least, I didn't think so then."

"Now you have to tell. Miss Maynard can make sure—"

"It's too late." Mouth firm, Lily glanced in the direction the boys had gone. "I just need to concentrate on the future and try to be a better person." She met Abby's gaze with a shy smile. "And as long as I have you for my best friend, I know it's possible."

The minute Joanna spotted Lily and Abby making their way through the drugstore, she sensed something amiss. She returned the current issue of *The Atlantic Monthly* to the periodicals display and strode down the aisle to meet her sister.

"Hi, Joanna." Lily's smile seemed forced. "I promised to buy Abby a soda. Do we have time?"

"I was thinking about having one, myself. Hello, Abby." Joanna led the way to the soda fountain and helped the girls set their shopping bags on the floor. "Have you had a nice afternoon?"

"It was . . . okay." Lily climbed onto a stool. On Lily's other side, Abby whispered something in her ear, and Lily nodded solemnly. She turned pleading eyes to Joanna. "Don't ask now, okay? But later, when we get home, I need to tell you something important."

"All right." Despite her growing concern, Joanna willed herself to be patient. She waved the counter attendant over to take their orders.

While they waited for their sodas, Joanna invited the girls to show her a few of their purchases. The distraction of oohing and aahing over their matching new blouses, Lily's jaunty beret, and Abby's purple-and-pink-striped winter scarf alleviated the tension, at least temporarily.

As they sipped their drinks, Joanna happened to glance toward the front of the store and noticed Thomas perusing the aisles. Her stomach did a tiny somersault. She hadn't seen him since Monday evening and their untimely kiss. Since then, she'd intentionally avoided every possibility of seeing him, even going so far as to use a different entrance at the Arlington.

One glimpse, though, and she already missed the handsome beard he'd sported over Thanksgiving. As he studied the label on a container of shaving soap, he absently rubbed his clean-shaven jaw as if he, too, regretted the change.

When he turned in her direction, she hurriedly looked away and tugged up the collar of her coat. Maybe he wouldn't notice her. Taking three long sips from her straw, she emptied her soda glass with a sputter. "Almost done, girls? We should get going."

Lily stirred the froth in the bottom of her glass. "Can we have another minute? Abby isn't finished yet."

"I guess—"

"Hello, Joanna."

Swallowing hard, she swiveled to face Thomas and delved deep for a semblance of a smile. "Nice day for shopping, isn't it? Finding everything you're looking for?"

"Not everything." His smoky gaze was fraught with meaning. "I hope you've been well."

"Very. And you?"

He grimaced and glanced away. "I've been better."

Joanna winced. She turned and patted Lily's shoulder. "Finish your sodas. I need to talk to Thomas for a few minutes."

Climbing down from the stool, she motioned Thomas farther along an adjoining aisle. Looking up at him with all the courage she could muster, she murmured, "I feel terrible that I've hurt you. I wish I could—"

"Don't apologize. It's my fault for looking for something that wasn't there." He cradled her hand in his. "Are we still friends?"

"Of course. Always." With a shaky half-smile she slid her hand free and nodded toward the soda counter. "I should go. The girls are waiting."

"Right." Thomas edged backward. "Uh, by the way, if you should need to reach me at home—I mean, since I'm still officially your boss for another week—don't call my mother's house. I've moved out."

Joanna's chin jerked up. "Moved out? Why?"

"It's a long story. Suffice it to say Mother and I don't see things the same way anymore." He shrugged tiredly. "If we ever did."

Tilting her head, Joanna studied his expression. "I hope I'm not to blame."

He hesitated just long enough to convince her otherwise. "It's been coming for a long time."

"What is it you're not telling me?"

"Nothing. It's nothing." Hands stuffed in his coat pockets, Thomas toed a seam in the tile floor. "Your sister's waiting. I'll see you around."

As Joanna watched him march purposefully toward the front of the store, a coldness seeped into her bones. Lost in thought, she startled when Lily nudged her arm.

"Was that Mr. Ballard? He looked upset."

Joanna sighed. "I know."

Stepping in front of her, Lily said, "So do you, Jo. What's wrong?"

Touched to know her little sister would even notice, Joanna smiled and brushed one of Lily's floppy curls off her face. The time for evading the truth had passed. "I'll tell you when we get home."

Lily's brows met in the center as she cast her sister a knowing frown. "Guess we both have some explaining to do later."

"Let's take Abby home and then find a quiet place to talk."

Twenty minutes later, Joanna rolled the Dodge to a stop in the driveway. She helped Lily gather her packages and carry them inside, where they found Jack prowling through the pantry and tossing canned goods onto the kitchen table.

"Taking inventory?" Joanna asked with a smirk.

"Thought I'd get supper started." Jack hefted a can of peas. "There's leftover ham in the icebox. I could warm it, or we could make sandwiches."

"Warm, please. You can set it in the oven on low heat. Lily and I have some talking to do."

Striking a match, Jack opened the oven door and lit the gas burner. "Girl talk, I presume?"

Joanna turned to her sister with a questioning glance. Lily chewed her lip for a moment, then shrugged and nodded. "Let's call it *family* talk," Joanna told Jack. "You're welcome to join us—but on one condition."

His face lit up in a mixture of surprise and curiosity. "Okay, what is it?"

"No judging. Whatever we share, we support each other one hundred percent."

Jack nodded his agreement. While he went to the icebox for the ham, Joanna found a small baking dish. After setting the ham in the oven, Jack followed his sisters into the parlor. Joanna motioned for Lily to take the end of the settee nearest Jack's easy chair and then sat next to her, one arm resting along the back.

"Do you want to go first, or shall I?" Joanna asked softly.

"Let me." Fingers laced tightly on her lap, Lily stared at her hands as she confessed what had happened four weeks ago at church. Tears cascaded down her cheeks long before she finished. "You believe me, don't you? I'd never steal anything. I was only trying to get away."

Her own throat aching with the tears she held back, Joanna glanced over at Jack. Fists knotted and teeth clenched, he looked ready to punch someone in the face. All Joanna could think of were the countless times she'd fended off unwanted attention from eager schoolboys, especially after Arthur Spence and the St. Louis episode. To protect her little brother from the rumors of her presumed promiscuity, she'd never let on to her family or anyone else about what happened in dark hallways or behind buildings. If Jack had been a few years older and several inches taller, he'd surely have fought for her honor. At least her discretion had spared him black eyes and a broken nose.

In the silence, she reached for her sister's hand. "Of course we believe you. I'm only sorry you didn't trust us enough to tell us sooner."

Lily swiped at her wet cheeks. "Me, too." With a relieved sigh, she squeezed Joanna's hand. "Your turn."

Joanna blinked, almost forgetting she'd promised to explain her conversation with Thomas at the drugstore . . . and so much more. "Oh, my, where to begin?"

"There's something else?" Jack's forehead wrinkled.

Memories propelled Joanna off the settee and across the room. Hugging herself, she spun around and faced her brother and sister. "If things had turned out differently—" She stopped herself.

"No, if I hadn't been so cruelly selfish, I would be Mrs. Walter Garritson."

Lily's eyes flew open. "You were going to get married?"

"He was a corporal, killed in the battle of Blanc Mont Ridge only weeks before the Armistice." Joanna concentrated on the facts to avoid giving grief a foothold. "I met him not long after I arrived in France, and we became engaged a few months later. Before his division went north, he asked me to meet him. He'd arranged for us to be married the same night, but the switchboard got busy and I couldn't get there soon enough. And when I did"—she swallowed to keep from choking as unshed tears slid down the back of her throat—"I told him I wouldn't marry him."

"But why?" Lily scooted to the edge of the settee cushion. "Weren't you in love?"

"I loved him desperately!" Unexplained anger surged, and Joanna couldn't mute the pain in her voice. "But one of us had to act responsibly. This was wartime, and we were serving our country. What right did we have to put personal feelings over patriotic commitment?"

Jack and Lily shared bewildered looks. Mouth firm, Jack rose and slowly crossed to where Joanna stood. "What I'm hearing in your voice isn't patriotism, Jo. It's guilt."

An early-morning December chill permeated the farmhouse. Shivering, Thomas tightened the sash on his flannel robe and slid his feet into cozy wool slippers. As he stepped into the upstairs hallway, he heard rustling sounds from the kitchen. The door to Gilbert and Mary's room remained closed, so it must be Mrs. Frederick up and about.

He found the gray-haired German housekeeper tending something on the stove. "Smells good. What's cooking?"

"*Ach*, good morning, Thomas. I hope you like sausages and potato pancakes. I'll start the eggs as soon as Gilbert and Mary come down." Anyone else might have thought it odd she'd use their first names, but Mrs. Frederick had watched Thomas and Gilbert grow up with her own children. More than a house-keeper, she was a family friend and Gilbert's partner in running the farm. She nodded toward the back burner. "Coffee is ready. Help yourself."

He fetched a mug from the cupboard. "This makes three mornings in a row you've cooked up a storm. Do my brother and his wife eat like this every day?"

"Oh, no. Usually we have a simple breakfast of oatmeal or cold cuts and sliced bread. But I know you're accustomed to finer fare."

A subtle dig at his formerly privileged life, no doubt. He'd have to find a place of his own soon and learn to fend for himself—something he realized he didn't particularly look forward to. The cooking part, at least. "No need to go to so much trouble on my account. Oatmeal or cold cuts would have been fine."

The thump of crutches on the stairway announced Gilbert had started down. Stubborn as he was, Gil had refused Mrs. Frederick's offer to exchange her first-floor quarters for his upstairs bedroom. When he'd first come home from the hospital after his accident, he'd slept on a cot in an alcove off the kitchen. But as soon as enough strength returned, he'd mastered the use of crutches for maneuvering about the house and to get himself up and down the staircase.

Gilbert worked his way into the kitchen. "Up early again, Tommy-boy? Thought you might sleep in on a Sunday morning."

"Too much on my mind." Thomas carried his coffee mug to the table and pulled out a chair.

"Here is your coffee, Gilbert." Mrs. Frederick brought him a cup while he eased into a chair.

Setting his crutches against the wall, Gilbert smiled his thanks. With a grimace, he massaged the stump of his amputated leg. "Got a few things on my mind, too," he said with a meaningful glance at Thomas. He pulled an envelope from the pocket of his robe and slid it across the table. "This came yesterday. Take a look."

Curious, Thomas read the return address and Washington, D.C., postmark. "From Dr. Russ?" Only a few months ago, army surgeon Donald Russ, formerly stationed at the Hot Springs Army and Navy Hospital, had married Mary's widowed mother. Now the couple resided in D.C. "Looks like a personal letter. Are you sure I should be reading this?"

"I'll give you the short version. Donald's been working extensively with amputees at Walter Reed. He thinks he's come up with a procedure to let me wear a prosthesis again."

"Terrific. Are you going to do it?"

"I'm seriously considering it." Gilbert's jaw muscles flexed. "Only thing is, it'll mean more surgery and another lengthy recovery. And I'll have to go to Walter Reed. They don't have the necessary facilities here."

Mrs. Frederick brought over steaming plates of eggs, sausage, and potato pancakes. "I think you should go. What do you have to lose but your wheelchair?"

"I agree." Thomas reached for the salt and pepper. "What does Mary think?"

"She wants whatever I want. But she used up all her leave taking care of me. There's no way Mrs. Daley would authorize another month or two off so she could accompany me to D.C., and Mary loves nursing too much to leave the Corps."

Thomas savored a forkful of peppered scrambled eggs. "How soon would you go?"

"Donald said he'd work me in whenever I can get there." Lips turned down in a wistful expression, Gilbert gazed out the window toward the barn and paddocks. "Sure would be easier tending my horses if I could get around on two legs again. Problem is, I don't think I'm up to traveling so far unassisted."

"Then let me go with you," Thomas blurted. "One more week at the Arlington, and I'm free as a bird."

Gilbert glanced up hopefully. "Are you sure?"

"You name the date and I'll buy the train tickets. Let's see, today's the seventh, so anytime after the twelfth—" Thomas drew a quick breath. "Except it puts us awfully close to Christmas. Are you sure you don't want to wait until after the first of the year?"

"Indeed he doesn't." Mary marched into the kitchen and rested her hands on her husband's shoulders. Shimmering red curls danced down her back. "The sooner you go," she said, gracing Gilbert's temple with a kiss, "the sooner you'll be home and striding about like I know you're itching to do."

With a groan, Gilbert reached up to pat her hand. "You're assuming the procedure will be successful. Donald's letter was clear—there are no guarantees."

"No, but he's the finest army surgeon I've ever worked with, and if he can't fix you up, no one can."

"But Christmas without you . . ."

Mary went to the stove for coffee. "I'm certain I can twist Mrs. Daley's arm to give me a few days off to visit you and Mum and Donald for the holidays." Sashaying over to the table, she winked. "I've become quite Mrs. Daley's favorite, you know. Shorthanded as they were, she was beyond grateful when I transferred back from Walter Reed."

Thomas chuckled under his breath. Not even a year ago, Gilbert's romantic overtures had almost gotten Mary booted from the Army Nurse Corps. Then late last summer, things between Mary and Gilbert had gone awry, and Mary requested a change of duty stations. Donald Russ had pulled some strings so she could join him and her mother in D.C. If not for Gilbert's encounter with a runaway horse, she might still be there today and the two of them would never have married.

Funny how one twist of fate could completely turn things around.

No, not funny at all. And not fate, either. How did the verse from Romans go? *And we know that to them that love God all things work together for good, even to them that are called according to his purpose.*

No question about it, God Himself had brought Mary and Gilbert together, and faith had carried them through the hard times.

Mrs. Frederick handed Mary a plate of food as she took the chair next to Gilbert's, and Thomas couldn't suppress a twinge of envy at the tender looks they shared. Dear God, how he longed to experience such closeness with Joanna! Surely the Lord wouldn't bring her into Thomas's life without also having a plan to heal her grief and allow her to fall in love again.

"Thomas, are you sure you don't mind . . ." Mary's voice trailed off when he met her gaze. She leaned forward, stretching one hand across the table. "Oh, my, you look so sad all of a sudden. What's wrong?"

Poking at his potato pancake, he edged the corners of his mouth into a smile. "Just sitting here appreciating how much in love the two of you are."

Gilbert arched one eyebrow in a knowing smirk. "If you get a move on, you can make it to church before a certain young lady arrives."

Thomas shifted uncomfortably. "I thought I'd go with you and Mary to Sam's chapel service at the hospital."

"Playing the avoidance game, are we?" Gilbert finished his last bite of sausage before sharing a loving look with his wife. "While it's true absence can make the heart grow fonder, it's also true that faint heart never won fair lady."

The old feelings of inferiority curdled in Thomas's belly. "I don't share your courage under fire, brother. Remember, I was the one sitting safely behind a desk while you were over in France fighting a war and getting your leg blown off."

An uncomfortable silence descended before Gilbert politely asked the ladies if they would mind stepping out of the room. When the kitchen door swung shut behind them, Gilbert pushed his empty plate aside and rested one clenched fist on the table.

Thomas could tell he was in for a lecture. "I spoke out of line, Gil. I'm sorry."

"When are you going to get over this, Tommy? We may have served in different ways, but we each did our part. Your responsibility was taking care of Mother and keeping things running on the home front. Be glad you never saw a blood-drenched battlefield." Gilbert's eyes darkened. "Believe me, I wish I never had."

"I said I'm sorry." Thomas rose and carried his plate to the sink. He lowered his head and a curse slipped out. "I'd give anything if I could have traded places with you. Not because I wanted the glory, but to spare you everything you've endured."

A sad laugh escaped Gilbert's throat. "The picture becomes clear. You'd have left *me* at home to deal with our dear sainted mother. Sorry, little brother, but that's one duty I didn't mind escaping in the least."

Thomas returned to the table with the coffeepot and refilled both their mugs. "What are we going to do with her, Gil? The whole reason I moved out was because she maligned Joanna one too many times."

"Yeah, Mary's had a rough go of it, too. Face it, Tommy, no woman will ever be good enough for Evelyn Ballard's sons."

"Mary certainly held her own at Thanksgiving." Thomas recalled how she'd calmly rebuffed their mother's not-so-subtle gibes about Mary's returning to work at the hospital.

Gilbert sipped his coffee. "From what I know of Joanna, she can hold her own as well."

"No argument there." With the pungent aroma of coffee filling his nostrils, Thomas rested his folded arms on the table and stared out at Gilbert's winter-brown backyard and barren trees. "But I'm beginning to doubt she'll ever be willing to try."

18

$\mathcal{P}$leading a headache and far too little sleep after her shift at the Arlington, Joanna stayed home from church Sunday morning. What little sleep she'd managed in the wee hours before dawn had brought confusing dreams. In one, she'd chased after Walter as he marched off to battle, rifle slung over his shoulder and his "tin pan" helmet set firmly on his head. The images paraded across her mind's eye as she sat in the quiet kitchen, hands wrapped around a mug of coffee growing colder by the minute.

Her feet mired in thick ooze, she fought to reach him. When at last she drew near enough, she closed her fingers around the sleeve of his olive-drab uniform. "Don't go, Walter! Don't leave me!"

He paused and turned, his rakish smile almost mocking. "It's too late, Jo. We had our chance, and now it's gone."

"I couldn't marry you—don't you understand? It would have been tempting fate."

Walter laughed, but his eyes held disappointment. "Never in a million years thought my girl would turn superstitious. And where did it get us? I'm still dead."

"No, Walter! No!" She fell to her knees in the mud. "Please stay! I'll be true to you always, I promise!"

"It's too late, baby . . . too late . . ." Walter slowly slipped from her grasp, his boyish face and tawny curls obscured by the smoke and flames of a raging battle.

Then the smoke cleared, and Thomas walked toward her. He held out his hand, beckoning her to climb up out of the mire and come with him.

"I can't. I made a promise." The mud crackled and groaned, sucking her deeper.

Thomas's eyes became disbelieving slits. "You're going to let a dead man come between us."

"I promised I'd never love anyone but Walter. I promised to live my life for him."

"You call this living?" Slowly, Thomas shook his head, while the mud closed around her throat until she could scarcely breathe—

"Joanna!" Jack stood over her, a worried look clouding his face. "What are you doing? The telephone's ringing off the hook."

Startled, she pushed up from the kitchen table, cold coffee splashing over the rim of her cup. "I didn't hear it. I'll—"

"Lily went to answer." He gripped her shoulder. "Are you okay?"

"Fine, fine. I was lost in thought." Joanna smoothed her uncombed hair away from her face. "You're home from church already? Let me get lunch started."

"I'll take care of it. Maybe you should go back to bed."

"No!" She sucked in a tiny breath, embarrassed by the vehemence of her protest, but she wouldn't risk more unnerving dreams. "It's past noon. I should have been dressed hours ago."

Lily peeked around the doorframe from the entry hall. "Jack, it's for you." She grinned. "Miss Maynard."

Joanna couldn't miss her brother's rapid switch from concern to bright-eyed anticipation. He exited the kitchen in three long strides, then nudged Lily through the door and closed it between them. Through the wall came undistinguishable murmurs as he spoke with Miss Maynard.

Lily rolled her eyes. "I think our brother is falling in love."

"I'm glad for him." Pulling herself together, Joanna went to the icebox and brought out the package of sliced corned beef she'd picked up yesterday at the butcher shop. "If you'll get the bread and start making sandwiches, I'll run upstairs and get dressed."

"Jo, wait." Lily caught her wrist. "Someone asked about you at church this morning."

Joanna pressed her lips together. "Thomas?"

"Um, no." With a curious smile, Lily stated, "It was Mrs. Ballard."

"What did she say?"

"She was acting kind of strange. Not all uppity like she usually is. She asked me to give you a message for Thomas. She said to tell him"—Lily closed her eyes as if drawing upon memory—"she's sorry for what she said about you and didn't mean a word of it, just a fit of temper or something, and would he please forgive her and come home."

Joanna's stomach tensed. So she'd been right all along. She was the reason Thomas had moved out. If there was one thing she didn't need more of, it was guilt, and she refused to be responsible for breaking up a family. Brushing past Lily, she set her hand to the hallway door. "You and Jack start lunch without me. I'll be out for a while this afternoon. It's best I take care of this issue with Mrs. Ballard in person."

Within the hour, she'd bathed, dressed, and tamed her unruly hair into some semblance of a bun. By the time she returned downstairs, Jack had settled into his easy chair with a magazine, while Lily sat at the rolltop desk taking notes from a reference book.

Jack looked up. "Lily says you're going out. Aren't you having lunch?"

"I'll get something later." Joanna found her coat in the hall closet and stood in the doorway as she pulled it on. "Mind if I take the Dodge?"

"Sure, but I'll need it back by four." Face reddening, Jack grinned over the top of his magazine. "Madison and I have plans this afternoon."

"She's a lovely lady. I'm glad you asked her out."

Jack cleared his throat, then mumbled into his magazine page so she almost didn't hear. "Actually, she asked me."

Lily snickered but didn't look up from her schoolwork.

Joanna nodded without commenting as she buttoned her coat.

"Surrounded by independent women, that's what I am." Harrumphing, Jack scooted deeper into the chair cushions. "Definitely take the car, Jo. It's blustery outside."

She had half a mind to assert her independence by climbing on the Indian instead, but when an icy north wind snatched at her coattails, she capitulated. Besides the risk of freezing her ears off, it wouldn't do to arrive at Mrs. Ballard's looking like she'd been swept across town by a tornado.

Even so, after she parked the Dodge in the Ballards' driveway, the wind took full advantage as she made her way up the porch steps. By the time she rang the bell, her coif had been whipped into a mass of tangles.

Marguerite answered the door. "Why, hello, Miss Trapp. Come on in out of the cold." Her smile faltered as Joanna stepped inside. "You know Mister Thomas isn't here? He's moved out to Mister Gilbert's farm."

"Yes. I mean, no, I didn't realize he was staying with his brother." Joanna hugged her purse to her chest. "However, I came to see Mrs. Ballard. Is she at home?"

"Just this minute. She's gone up to change from her church clothes." Marguerite took Joanna's coat and then showed her into the parlor. "Make yourself comfortable. I'll tell Miz Ballard you're here."

There would be nothing comfortable about this visit. While Joanna waited, she tidied her bun and wandered about the room, taking in the masterful oil paintings gracing the walls along with several family portraits in gilt or silver frames.

One in particular caught her eye, a photograph of Mrs. Ballard seated regally between her two sons. Gilbert stood at her right, proud and tall in his lieutenant's uniform, while Thomas, on the left and attired in a three-piece dark suit, wore a half-smile Joanna could only describe as strained. While Gilbert and Mrs. Ballard looked straight into the camera, Thomas appeared to gaze into the distance.

What were you thinking then, Thomas? Was he already missing his brother, perhaps dreading the burden of staying behind? Only since returning home herself had Joanna come to appreciate how much courage such a commitment required. After leaving Hot Springs, her life had been all about new experiences and adventure. Even her whirlwind romance with Walter had taken on a surreal quality—so far from home and responsible to no one but themselves and the army they served.

Was any of it real—their love, their dreams, the promises they'd made? Certainly her grief was real. Nothing false could possibly hurt so terribly or so long.

"You're going to let a dead man come between us." Thomas's words the afternoon he'd kissed her so passionately in an Arlington conference room, repeated in last night's dream.

The headache she'd tried all day to ignore returned with a vengeance. Edging into the foyer, she found the closet where Marguerite had hung her coat. Moments later, she slipped out the front door and drove away.

"Delicious, Annemarie." Using his fork tines, Thomas collected the remaining crumbs of pineapple upside-down cake. He refused to miss so much as a morsel.

"Marriage has forced me to become *slightly* more adept in the kitchen." Giving her husband a wink, Annemarie reached for Thomas's empty plate. "Care for another piece?"

With a hearty chuckle, he waved his hand. "After the huge breakfast Mrs. Frederick served this morning, and then your scrumptious Sunday dinner, three dessert servings are plenty!"

"Then why don't you gentlemen retire to the parlor. Mary and I will take care of the dishes."

"Nonsense." Samuel rose and began collecting plates. "You cooked. The least we *gentlemen* can do is clean up."

"I agree." Thomas pushed back his chair. "I don't have much experience, but it's high time I learned."

Gilbert rolled his wheelchair away from the table. "Come on, Tommy. I'm not much use at the sink for washing, but I'll teach you everything I know about drying and stacking."

Mary shook her finger at her husband. "Just don't you be breaking one of Annemarie's lovely china plates."

He seized her hand and drew her fingers to his lips for a kiss. "Are you ever going to let me forget I broke your favorite teapot?"

"Only when you buy me another. I've had my eye on a pretty one in Annemarie's shop window."

Annemarie's lilting laughter echoed as she hooked her arm through Mary's and led her toward the parlor. "I've already put it aside for you."

Smirking at his brother, Thomas gathered an armful of empty water glasses. "Bet that'll cost you a pretty penny."

"Worth every cent." Gilbert spread a napkin across his lap and piled it full of used silverware. "Don't let on, but I sort of dropped her old, chipped teapot on purpose. Otherwise, I'd never have convinced her to let me buy her another."

Samuel held the swinging door to the kitchen as Thomas and Gilbert passed through. "Amazing what tricks we've learned as 'old married men,' isn't it?"

Coats off and sleeves rolled up, the three men set to work washing dishes and putting the kitchen in order. As the only bachelor among them, Thomas silently enjoyed the friendly teasing between Gil and Sam. The jokes they shared about married life were sometimes beyond his understanding, but he took mental notes anyway, because he hoped one day to join in.

As entertaining as Samuel and Gilbert were together, Thomas also couldn't help his amazement at the deep friendship between the two men—not to mention their wives. He could only chalk it up to the miraculous changes God had wrought in Gilbert's life, combined with an abundant capacity for forgiveness in all of them.

"So you're going through with it," Samuel said as he set a stack of plates in the cupboard. Gilbert had just shared more details about the letter from Dr. Russ. "I'm glad for you, Gil. I'll pray the procedure is a complete success."

"Whatever happens, I have to try." Gilbert tossed the wet dishtowel at Samuel. "Lord knows I can't be any worse off than I am now."

"The Lord knows indeed." Samuel caught the towel, twisted it three times, then gave Gilbert a playful snap on the arm. "He also knows you're a woefully impatient fellow who doesn't take anything sitting down."

Brow raised in mock disdain, Gilbert glared. "Are you belittling my handicap?"

"Wouldn't dream of it. I have no doubt you can roll your chair much faster than I can run away."

"All right, you two." Grinning, Thomas stepped between them. "Before this comes to fisticuffs—or broken dishes—I suggest we wrap things up in here and see what your lovely wives are up to."

Both men's faces instantly brightened. Gilbert spun his wheelchair around and led the way through the dining room to the parlor. "Wouldn't dare leave them alone too long," he called over his shoulder. "No telling what sinister plots against us they've already dreamed up."

"So right," Sam agreed, trotting after him. "Annemarie already has a chore list for me a mile long. I'll be painting rooms and trimming shrubbery from now until the baby's born."

Thomas brought up the rear, never fully able to hold his envy at bay. He'd enjoyed accompanying Gilbert and Mary to Samuel's inspiring chapel service, and Sunday dinner with the Vickarys had been delightful. Now, he wished he'd driven his own automobile so he could politely take his leave. This double exposure to wedded bliss had begun to wear on him.

With the excuse of needing to stretch his legs and walk off those three slices of pineapple upside-down cake, Thomas fetched his overcoat from the hall closet, looped a wool scarf around his neck, and tugged on his leather gloves. Tapping his fedora firmly onto his head, he stepped off the front porch into a biting north wind. Certainly not ideal conditions for a Sunday constitutional, but he felt the need to be alone with his thoughts.

Five more days and he'd be done with the Arlington. This fact alone deserved some serious pondering. He tamped down the nagging panic that never failed to erupt when he dwelt too long on his decision to resign. Everyone else clearly thought he'd lost his mind, and maybe he had.

Maybe this trip with Gil would help him find himself. Panic shifted to anticipation as he pictured them on the train to D.C., spending time together like they used to before adulthood pushed them in different directions, bringing changes and responsibilities neither of them ever expected.

"Thank you, Miss Hiers. And here's the status report Mr. Upshaw requested on Stanley Fessler's training. The transition into his new responsibilities should go without a hitch." Thomas exchanged folders with his boss's prim secretary and then checked his watch. Another hour and he could call it a day.

Then two more days and he'd say goodbye to the Arlington and pack his bags for D.C. He'd picked up the train tickets on his lunch hour today. By this time Saturday he and Gil would be halfway to Nashville.

Someone rapped on his door. Without taking his attention from a conference room reservation form, he called, "It's open. Come in."

"Hello, son."

His head jerked up. "Mother."

Moving farther into the room, she absently stroked the foxtail boa attached to her coat. "Since you have made no effort to communicate with me, I realized I must come to you." She glanced at one of the guest chairs. "May I sit?"

Putting aside his paperwork, he signaled her to take a chair. "You know perfectly well why I haven't been in touch. Is there any reason to assume things have changed?"

"Didn't Miss Trapp say anything to you?"

"About what? I haven't seen her in several days."

"I didn't realize." His mother plucked nervously at a coat button. "I sent word to her of my regret over anything I may have said to disparage her."

"You . . . sent word." Thomas laced his fingers atop his desk. "What exactly does that mean?"

She explained about giving the message to Lily in church last Sunday, and then told him Joanna had come by the house in the afternoon. "I have no idea why she didn't stay. It was quite rude, if you ask—" Straightening abruptly, she cleared her throat. "I mean I probably kept her waiting too long. It was my fault entirely."

Thomas blinked. His *mother* had accepted the blame?

"Well, anyway . . . I did try." She shifted and inclined her head. "However, the main reason I have come is the concern that you would leave town without so much as telling me goodbye."

"Then you've spoken with Gil."

"He and Mary came to the house yesterday to share their news about this procedure he intends to have." Sniffling, she rummaged in her purse for a handkerchief. "Please tell me you would have come to see me before you left."

"Mother . . ." Resolve weakening, Thomas circled the desk and took the chair next to hers. In truth, his driving thought had been to quietly put as much distance between himself and his overbearing mother as possible.

And now he sounded unsettlingly like Joanna. Was Thomas now running away from his family obligations just as she had implied? No, he was only being a good brother, doing what he could to help Gilbert. Besides, his mother would be fine. She had Marguerite, Hank, and Zachary to see to her every need, not to mention her bevy of society friends.

She dabbed her eyes and peered at him hopefully. "Will you be home for Christmas, at least?"

"I seriously doubt it. Gil's series of procedures is expected to take several weeks if not months."

"Then I shall be"—her voice broke—"all alone."

He wanted to say it was her own fault. He wanted to make her see how she'd driven both her sons from her home with her domineering and judgmental ways. But the woman he saw before him bore none of those qualities. Evelyn Ballard looked as hopeless and beaten down as he'd ever seen her.

Drawing a shaky breath, Thomas reached for her hand and willed kindness into his tone. "Your boys will always love you, Mother, but neither Gil nor I can be held responsible for your happiness. You must allow us to lead our own lives, as you must live yours."

She nodded as if she understood, but Thomas had the feeling she didn't understand at all. She pushed tiredly to her feet. "You are obviously quite busy. I shan't take any more of your time."

Thomas followed her to the door. "Come to the depot Saturday morning and see us off. Gil would like it, too. And you can keep Mary company. She'll need the support."

His mother paused and looked at him, eyebrows bunched. She started to speak, only to snap her mouth closed in a puzzled frown. Then, head erect, she glided out the door and disappeared around the next corner.

Had anything he'd said gotten through? A sharp breath exploding from his lungs, Thomas marched back to his desk and tried to pick up where he'd left off.

Too bad his brain wouldn't cooperate.

19

For a full week now, Joanna had stumbled through her days and caught only fragments of sleep each night. She tried not to let fatigue affect her work, but as the frequency of misdirected calls increased, complaints had started to filter in.

Though she hadn't seen anything of Thomas since the Saturday they ran into each other at Sorrell's, it still felt strange to report to work Friday night and find Stanley Fessler waiting for her, and not as the desk clerk but as her boss. He said he'd only come by to make sure Joanna knew how to reach him at home should she encounter any problems the front desk couldn't handle. However, he also subtly suggested she consider taking a few days off if the job was proving too stressful.

"It isn't the job, Stanley." She braced a shoulder against the doorframe to the switchboard room. "I'll do better, I promise."

Eyes filled with kindness, Stanley shrugged. "Just let me know if there's any way I can help." He nodded toward Lillian, seated at the switchboard. "Good night, ladies."

As Joanna took over the desk and headset, Lillian refilled her coffee cup and then poured one for Joanna. "Looks like you could use a little caffeine tonight."

Joanna gave a weak laugh. "Are the bags under my eyes so obvious?"

"Honey, they're hanging almost to your knees. Aren't you getting any sleep?"

"Not enough to matter." She hiked a brow. "And what are you still doing here, especially drinking coffee this late?"

"Nothing to go home to tonight. My husband had some business up in Fayetteville and won't be home until Monday." Lillian eased her back. "So I was thinking. About what Stanley said, if you need a few days off . . ."

"Oh, no, not you, too." Joanna swiveled toward the switchboard to avoid her friend's pointed stare.

"Just offering." Taking the vacant chair, Lillian sipped her coffee while Joanna responded to a call. When Joanna was free again, Lillian casually stated, "I guess you heard Thomas is leaving for D.C. in the morning."

Joanna swallowed her surprise. "No, I hadn't heard."

"Thomas mentioned it when he made the rounds telling everyone goodbye this afternoon." Lillian explained about Thomas accompanying Gilbert for his surgical procedure. Then she sighed meaningfully. "Yes, it's a real shame you missed him earlier. No telling how long he'll be gone."

Ignoring a twinge of dismay, Joanna twirled a pencil between her fingers. "Surely he wouldn't have to stay throughout Gilbert's recovery."

"Sure sounded like he planned to. I mean, what's he got waiting for him here? Not counting his dear mother, naturally."

Another call came through, and Joanna focused on connecting the plug to the correct jack. When she finished, she caught Lillian watching her with a crooked smile. Joanna inhaled deeply. "I can tell you want to say something else, so spit it out."

"I just thought . . . if by chance you wanted to see Thomas before he leaves in the morning, I could cover for you."

For a split second, Joanna considered accepting Lillian's offer. Then common sense prevailed. It was already half past eight, and Joanna had no idea how to find the Ballard farm. Besides, considering how cool she'd been recently, what could she possibly say?

"Don't go, Thomas. I've been an utter fool. Can't we start over?"

Maybe she had been a fool—her dreams of late certainly seemed to be telling her as much. And Véronique had written again, chiding Joanna for not answering her letter but also hoping Joanna's silence meant she'd begun to rebuild her life.

Had Joanna put off completing the letter she'd started weeks ago because subconsciously she'd begun cutting ties with her life in France? with Walter?

It is time, you know, Véronique's letter stated. *There must be many handsome young men in your city who would crawl over hot coals to merit one of your kisses. Is there not one who has caught your eye, one whose tender devotion has the power to banish grief from your heart?*

"He's a good man, Joanna." Lillian's quietly spoken words returned her thoughts to the present. "Don't let him get away."

Jack sensed the tense excitement in Madison's grip as they stepped off the elevator onto the observation platform. "Don't be afraid. The tower is solid steel and perfectly safe."

"Perhaps, but we're so high!" Madison's nervous laughter caught on the December breeze whipping across the mountain.

Jack still couldn't believe the lovely high school teacher had never been to the top of Hot Springs Mountain Tower. "Just look at this view! See what you've been missing all your life?"

"Hot Springs is equally lovely when I'm *not* viewing it from this height."

When she trembled, it seemed like the perfect excuse to tuck her safely beneath his arm. "There. Better?"

Her cheeks reddened, whether from the chilly air or from Jack's nearness, he wouldn't guess. He only knew how much he enjoyed holding her close. If this weren't only their second date, he'd steal a quick kiss . . . or a longer one.

As other tourists arrived on the upper deck, Jack led Madison farther along the rail. By the time they'd circled the platform, her teeth were chattering from the cold. Shielding her from the wind, he said, "Let's go down and get warm."

She smiled her gratitude and snuggled closer as they waited for the elevator car. After they began their descent, Jack reluctantly slid his arm from her shoulder. A thrill shot through him when she didn't immediately move away.

Reaching the bottom, they disembarked and strode quickly to Jack's automobile. "Where to?" he asked as he started the motor. The afternoon was still young, and he hoped she wouldn't ask to be taken home quite yet.

Madison rubbed her gloved hands together. "I'd love some hot chocolate. How about the new café on Park Avenue? I believe it's open on Sunday afternoons."

"Great idea." Jack steered the Dodge down the winding mountain road. Following the curve onto Park, they passed the imposing Majestic Hotel and minutes later arrived at the café.

After helping Madison off with her coat, Jack seated her at a small table near the front windows, then took the chair across from her. A waiter soon delivered hot chocolate and two large oatmeal cookies.

"Just what I needed to warm up." Fingers wrapped around her cup, Madison smiled over the rim. "Perhaps you'll take me back to the tower next spring when the dogwoods are in bloom."

Jack's pulse thrummed at the suggestion they'd still be together come springtime. "It would be my pleasure."

Eventually the conversation drifted to Lily. "She's come so far in so short a time," Madison said. "I'm proud of her."

"Joanna and I are, too." Jack broke off a piece of cookie and chewed thoughtfully. He'd told Madison about Lily's encounter with the boys while out shopping, and how the incident led her to admit what really happened at church a few weeks ago. "I only hope she won't be adversely affected by the gossip."

"Lily's tough. And brave."

"Like her sister." Only Joanna hadn't seemed quite so tough and brave lately, and Jack couldn't help worrying about her. Was her restlessness a sign she would return to France?

"It's clear Lily looks up to her older sister. I hope to get to know Joanna better." Madison's eyes brightened. "Do you suppose she'd consider speaking at a school assembly about her service with the Army Signal Corps?"

Jack couldn't imagine she would. "She's been awfully tired lately. You know she works nights at the Arlington."

Madison nodded and nibbled her cookie. "Those late hours must make it difficult to enjoy a satisfying social life."

"Social life—*Joanna?*" Jack snorted.

"Certainly she has a friend or two. And what about church?"

Jack thought back to this morning, the second Sunday in a row he couldn't persuade Joanna to attend worship with him and Lily. More than simple fatigue seemed at play here. Jack wished he were better equipped to understand what went on in his sister's head—or Lily's either, for that matter. Women!

He studied Madison across the table. Without thinking, he blurted out, "Have you ever been in love before?"

A rosy blush crept up her cheeks. She dabbed her lips with a napkin and softly cleared her throat. "I—well—perhaps once, a long time ago. At least, I thought it was love."

"Sorry, I didn't mean to pry." Embarrassed, Jack slid his fingers through his hair and tried again. "What I'm asking is, once a relationship ends, how long should it take to get over it?"

"I'm sure it depends upon the situation." Madison's eyes narrowed. "Are you asking for yourself . . . or someone else?"

"It's Joanna. She got engaged in France. Then her fiancé was killed in battle. It's been over a year."

Gaze softening, Madison sighed. "And she's still mourning?"

"I think the grief is holding her back from letting anyone else into her life."

"What a shame. I wouldn't wish such loneliness on anyone."

Madison's hand rested upon the table, and Jack couldn't resist reaching for it. Cradling her delicate fingertips, he admired each gently curved pink nail. "Have you been lonely, Madison?"

She glanced up shyly and smiled. "Once . . . but not anymore."

Thomas stood next to Gilbert's hospital bed as Dr. Russ performed a preliminary examination. One hand on his brother's shoulder, he gave a reassuring squeeze. "Don't worry. God's in control, and He'll work things out for the best."

Gilbert nodded, his smile tense. "If a new leg isn't part of His plan, all it means is I'll be going home to Mary even sooner."

Dr. Russ spread the sheet over Gilbert's legs and looked up with a grin. "Don't count on it, Gil. I foresee two or three surgeries in your future followed by extensive physical therapy. *And* a new prosthesis."

"Yes!" Thomas clasped his brother's hand in a victory salute. "What did I tell you?"

Moisture filled Gilbert's eyes. "I don't know what to say, Donald. 'Thank you' doesn't seem enough. Especially after . . ."

"Not another word." Dr. Russ shot Gilbert a quick smile as he jotted notes on a chart. It hadn't been so long ago that the two men had been at odds. While still pursuing Annemarie, Gilbert had resented the doctor's loyalty to Samuel Vickary. Only as Gilbert found his way back to God and began building a life with Mary had he released his bitterness and sought to make amends.

"When will you get started?" Thomas asked.

Dr. Russ consulted his notes. "My first surgical opening is Wednesday morning. It'll give you a couple more days to rest up from your travels."

Gilbert groaned. "So I'm supposed to lie around in this bed until then? I'll go stark raving mad with anticipation."

"All right, all right." Dr. Russ laughed. "If you promise not to overtire yourself, I'll release you temporarily. But I want you back in this bed no later than 1600 hours tomorrow."

"Will do!" Gilbert maneuvered himself to the edge of the bed. "Push my chair over here, Thomas. Let's go see some sights."

Within the hour, Thomas had arranged a taxicab tour of Washington, D.C. Both men rode in awed silence as their driver took them past the White House, the United States Capitol, the Lincoln Memorial still under construction, and finally, the Washington Monument.

Thomas breathed out an appreciative sigh. "Never thought I'd actually see all this in person."

"Neither did I." Gilbert leaned forward for a last glimpse of the white marble tower overlooking the Potomac. The top was almost obscured by snowflakes swirling in the air. "Someday I'll be back, and I'll climb all the way to the top."

"I'll take the elevator," Thomas said with a chuckle. "Even with two good legs, you couldn't persuade me to take the stairs."

The taxi driver grinned over his shoulder, teeth gleaming in his dark face. "I tried it once. They about had to haul me out on a stretcher! Most wiped out I've been since boot camp training."

Gilbert sobered. "You served in the war?"

"Proud member of the 369th Infantry Regiment, better known as the Harlem Hellfighters."

"Then you must have fought at the Marne. I lost my leg there."

"Yes, sir, me and my three best friends. Only two of us came back." The driver glanced at Thomas. "You serve, too?"

Resisting the familiar sense of unworthiness, Thomas swallowed. "No, I—"

"My brother had important responsibilities at home," Gilbert interjected. "Our widowed mother would have been left completely alone if we'd both gone off to war."

Thomas cast his brother a grateful glance. Gil's statement might be a slight exaggeration, but it soothed the ache in Thomas's soul nonetheless.

Since Gilbert didn't need to return to the hospital until tomorrow, they checked into a hotel room and then dined in the hotel restaurant. After dinner, they found comfortable chairs in the lounge and enjoyed the warmth of a roaring fire.

Feeling mellow, Thomas slid lower in his chair. "What you said today . . . it meant a lot."

Gilbert yawned and stretched. "What did I say?"

"You know—what you told the taxi driver about my not going off to war."

"It's true. I rested easier knowing you were looking after Mother while I was in France." Gilbert rested a clenched fist on the arm of Thomas's chair. "Then after I came home, you shouldered the burden of keeping Mother sane through my period of 'conduct unbecoming.' For that, you deserve a medal."

Thomas harrumphed. "Not entirely sure I succeeded."

"Be patient with her, Tommy. It can't have been easy raising two sons after Father was killed."

"Marguerite raised us. All Mother cared about was maintaining her position in society."

"I know it seems like it." Shifting, Gilbert adjusted a cushion behind his back. "But think about it. Wealth and prestige are all Mother has ever known, and she's an expert at using those assets to her own advantage—and ours. By keeping up her social standing, she made sure you and I always had the best opportunities."

Thomas couldn't deny his mother's connections had carried a great deal of weight when he applied for the management position at the Arlington. "So you're saying I should appreciate her more?"

"I'm saying she's the only mother we've got and maybe we both need to be more forgiving."

"I don't know if I can." Thomas's eyes stung from the haze of cigarette smoke floating above them. Even months after giving up his Camels, sometimes the craving for tobacco grew almost as fierce as Gil's former addiction to morphine. "You're stronger than I am, in so many ways. So is your capacity for forgiveness. You and Mary both, after how Mother treated her."

"Mary's taught me a lot. Her faith . . . her patience . . ." Gilbert gazed into the fire. "She saved my life."

Thomas studied his brother's solemn profile. "I'm glad you and Mary are so happy together."

Gilbert smiled and nodded, then sank deeper into the chair cushion and closed his eyes. "I'm beat. Wake me when it's time to go up to bed, will you?"

"Right." His own thoughts still in turmoil, Thomas knew sleep would be hours in coming.

A hot drink might help. He stepped into the restaurant and ordered a cup of cocoa, then carried it back to the fireplace and sat down to the music of Gilbert's snuffling snores. In the yellow and orange flames licking the chimney, he imagined he saw Joanna's snapping eyes and messy, flowing waves. He checked his watch. She'd be arriving for work about now. Maybe sharing a few minutes of coffee and conversation with Lillian.

Do you ever think of me, Joanna? Do you ever miss me, ever wonder what might have happened if you'd given us a chance?

He sipped his cocoa, a pleasant warmth spreading through his chest. If he couldn't hope for happiness with Joanna, maybe he'd stay in D.C. after Gil went home. Or maybe he'd explore Atlanta, or Boston, or Chicago. He could even head west to San Francisco. If anywhere in these great United States offered adventure and escape, it was California.

So what if he was running away? He had nothing in Hot Springs to return to.

20

As Christmas approached, Joanna noticed a definite change in the Arlington Hotel clientele. Those who came to Hot Springs for the baths and local attractions were returning home for the holidays. A few travelers coming to town to visit relatives had made reservations, but even so, many rooms remained unoccupied. With less activity at the switchboard, especially overnight, Joanna found herself twiddling her thumbs and looking for other ways to occupy the hours.

Other than imagining how different things would be if she hadn't pushed Thomas away.

In church on Sunday, Pastor Yarborough included Gilbert Ballard in the prayers, then later announced Gilbert had come through his first surgery with promising results. After the service, a crowd gathered around Evelyn Ballard to learn more and to extend their good wishes.

To Joanna's eye, Mrs. Ballard looked pale and haggard. If anyone could recognize when someone had gone without sleep for long, it was Joanna.

Mrs. Kendall came up beside Joanna in the aisle. "She doesn't look well, does she?"

"It must be hard having both her sons so far away. I'm sure she's worried."

"I hope that's all it is." Mrs. Kendall's shoulders heaved in a doubtful sigh. "Evelyn's been known to have heart trouble from time to time."

Joanna watched Mrs. Ballard slowly make her way toward the front doors. "Surely she's being treated by her doctor."

"She is, of course." Mrs. Kendall cast Joanna a meaningful glance. "But certain types of heart trouble can't be cured by medicine."

Guilt welled in Joanna's chest. "You're speaking of my mother now."

Her neighbor answered with a flattened smile. "I know you had a hard time of it, but so did she. Don't think for a moment your mother chose to be the way she was."

Nodding slowly, Joanna let Mrs. Kendall's words sink in. Somehow, she must learn to forgive the woman she'd failed so horribly to understand.

Jack and Mr. Kendall joined them, Lily trailing behind. "Ready to head home, Jo?" Jack tweaked one of her stray locks. "You look like you could use a nap before you go to work tonight."

Thankful for the interruption, Joanna forced a shaky laugh. "Are you kidding? Lately, I *always* look like I could use a nap."

Saying goodbye to the Kendalls, they greeted the pastor on their way out and then climbed into the Dodge. At home a few minutes later, Joanna checked the pot roast she'd set in the oven before leaving for church. The aroma filled the kitchen.

Jack sniffed appreciatively and rubbed his growling stomach. "Must say, Jo, your cooking skills have come a long way since you first came home."

"Practice makes perfect, right?" She hung the potholder on a hook and reached into a cupboard for plates. "Lily, will you set out the silverware and napkins?"

Lily started to open the drawer and then hesitated. "How about we eat in the dining room? I could get out one of Mama's tablecloths, and we could use the good china and silver."

Joanna couldn't recall the last time she'd taken a meal at their dining room table, much less using her mother's Spode wedding china.

Then the exact day and occasion came rushing back to her—Saturday, September 6, 1913, Jack's eighteenth birthday. For his sake alone, Joanna had returned home from college for the weekend to help him celebrate. Only what should have been a day of celebration came on the heels of catastrophe. One day prior, a fire had raged through nearly sixty city blocks of Hot Springs' business district. Caught in the path of the fire, the utility plant and water system failed. Stores and factories went up in flames, and thousands were left homeless. Just beginning his senior year, Jack had been devastated to learn the high school building, barely five years old, had been destroyed, along with so many other familiar landmarks.

But Mama seemed oblivious, determined to carry on with Jack's birthday festivities despite having neither electricity nor running water. Joanna remembered sitting at the table and seething at her mother's indifference to how upset Jack was. Several of his friends were among those affected, and he wanted to be out there helping them.

He looked at her now, his thoughts clearly mirroring hers. "She was sick, Jo. She couldn't help herself."

Lily turned to her brother. "What are you talking about?"

"Let's just eat in the kitchen like we always do, all right?" Joanna plopped the stack of plates onto the table. "Jack, get a trivet so I can bring out the pot roast."

As she turned to the stove, Jack stopped her, his tone low and determined. "Lily wants to eat in the dining room. I think we should."

Joanna's meager attempts at forgiveness faltered. "Why? So we can all be reminded how utterly insensitive our mother was?"

"Now who's being insensitive?" Jack nodded toward Lily. "You think you're doing her any favors by nursing your resentment?"

"I'm trying as hard as I can to work through it." Joanna snatched the potholders and yanked open the oven door. The blast of heat made her cringe.

"Well, you're not trying hard enough." The clatter of plates and the slamming of a cupboard door told her Jack had put the everyday dishes away. "Go on, Lily. Set the dining room table. We'll be right there."

"No," Lily burst out. "Not until you tell me what you're fighting about. Is it Mama? Because I'm not a baby. I know what she was like—better than either of you. I was the one left at home with her, remember?"

Joanna's shoulders sagged. "You're right, Lily, and I'm sorry." She turned to her brother. "You're right, too, Jack. I have been storing up resentment—for years now. And taking it out on the people I care about."

"Not so unlike Mother, don't you think?" Jack drew her into a hug, his chin digging into the top of her head. Extending one arm toward Lily, he included her in his embrace. "We may never understand why Mother grappled so long with sadness, but we must accept it was an illness of the mind and that she never meant to hurt us. We have to forgive her—not only for her sake, but for our own. Whatever happened in the past, whatever mistakes our parents made, it's over. We're new creations in Christ, remember? With God's help, we can make a better future for ourselves."

Joanna had never admired her brother more. The three of them clung to each other, and Joanna took strength from the love flowing between them. She gave Jack a squeeze before wriggling free. Giving Lily's ear a gentle pinch, she sent her to the dining room. "Pick out the prettiest linens and dishes. Today we'll have Sunday dinner in style."

As Joanna finished getting dinner on the table, she recalled Mrs. Kendall's words in church earlier: *"Certain types of heart trouble can't be cured by medicine."* Mama's "heart trouble" had proved incurable by any means, dragging her deeper and deeper into a pit of despair. Even when she'd tried to fight it, as she had the day of Jack's birthday dinner, everything came out wrong.

And Joanna hadn't helped. Hadn't shown the least compassion for her mother's inner turmoil. Instead, she'd grown more and more self-absorbed and quarrelsome, until the chasm between them had grown too wide to bridge.

On her way to the dining room with a basket of rolls and a crock of butter, Joanna paused in the hallway, a prayer rising up within her. *Dear God, give me the strength to forgive, just as I need to be forgiven, because my heart needs healing, too. Please don't let it be too late to find the cure.*

"Thanks, Mrs. Russ." Thomas accepted a cup of eggnog from Mary's mother. "Bad enough you've put up with me as a houseguest for nearly two weeks. Now I feel like I'm imposing on your family Christmas."

"Nonsense. You're family, too, and we're delighted you're here, especially since you can't be celebrating at home." The petite woman offered him a sad smile and continued in her lilting Irish accent. "A shame our dear Gilbert must spend Christmas Eve in the hospital."

"He had a good day, though, Mum." Mary carried her eggnog to the settee. "Much less pain, he said."

Dr. Russ stirred the fireplace logs and tossed in another. Sparks shot up the chimney. "How much longer will you stay, Thomas? Gilbert could be here a long while yet."

"I'm in no hurry. I'll stay as long as I can be of any help to Gil."

"Not much you can do—but don't think we're trying to get rid of you," the doctor added with a laugh. "Just understand Gilbert will have to heal between surgeries, and then it'll be a lengthy period of rehabilitation before he can try a prosthesis."

"Donald is right, Thomas," Mary said. "Grateful as I am you were able to make the trip with Gilbert, neither of us expects you to put your own life on hold indefinitely."

Thomas strode over to the buffet and selected a gingerbread cookie. He studied the swirls of green and white frosting. "I don't think of it that way at all, Mary. I'm glad I can be here for Gil."

"Still, I can't help feeling sorry for your dear mum." Mrs. Russ patted him on the shoulder as she crossed to the settee. "She must be missing her boys something fierce. Have you written or telephoned?"

Fighting pangs of conscience, Thomas carried his cookie and eggnog to a side chair and eased onto the cushion. "Gil's been writing, I think. He's also telephoned a couple of times."

"You should call her tonight and wish her a Merry Christmas. Use Donald's telephone in the study."

"Maybe later . . ." Avoiding Mrs. Russ's persuasive smile, Thomas took a sip of eggnog while his gaze drifted toward the six-foot-tall spruce filling one corner of the room. Silver and gold ornaments shimmered in the glow of newfangled colored electric lights strung through the branches. A benevolently smiling angel with a porcelain face and lacy wings adorned the treetop.

Thomas stifled a sigh. Maybe he did miss home . . . a little. Boyhood memories flooded him—waking his brother before sunup on Christmas morning and sneaking down to see what Saint Nicholas had brought. Marguerite's Christmas feast of roast turkey, oyster dressing, and candied yams. Watching the skies for any sign of snow and a chance to bring out their sleds. Unfortunately, snowfall in central Arkansas was a rarity, perhaps only two or three times a season, and even then, it might not last more than a day or two.

He wondered if Joanna liked snow. She must have seen plenty while living in New York. Did it snow much in Paris?

Mary rose abruptly, her sudden movement drawing Thomas out of thoughts he should never have indulged in. Covering a yawn, Mary strode to the front windows and gazed into the night sky. "I hope I can stay awake for the candlelight service. What time should we leave?"

Dr. Russ checked his watch. "Ten-thirty should be soon enough. You'll join us, won't you, Thomas?"

He drained his eggnog, then stared into the empty cup. "The truth is I'm not much in the mood for Christmas."

Turning from the window, Mary cast him a worried frown. "All the more reason you should come with us. The carols and readings, a thousand candles all alight as we sing 'Silent Night'—there'll be Christmas spirit to fill you in abundance."

"I'd just put a damper on your experience. I'll be fine here by myself." Thomas went to the buffet to pour himself more eggnog—not because he cared for more, but to evade his hosts' concerned glances.

After a few more minutes of stilted conversation, Thomas found an opportunity to excuse himself and slipped away to the guest room. A short time later, as he lay stretched out on the bed, he heard Mary and her family depart for church. Feeling restless, he wandered through the quiet townhouse. In the kitchen, he found Mrs. Russ's cookies on a covered tray and helped himself to another, washing it down with a glass of milk.

On his way to the parlor, he passed Dr. Russ's study. The door stood ajar, and rays from a streetlamp cut a silver swath across the floor. Glimpsing the telephone on the corner of the desk, Thomas sucked air between his teeth. *Call your mother,* the blasted machine seemed to shout. Or was it the voice of his conscience?

He didn't want to admit the impulse might be a prompting from God Himself. He knew well the commandment to honor one's father and mother, the first commandment with a promise—

that thy days may be long in the land which Jehovah thy God giveth thee.

But how did you honor a parent who continually disappointed you? A parent who felt entitled to sit in judgment of everyone else while refusing to examine her own faults?

Call your mother.

Thomas groaned. Whatever the source, the voice wasn't going away. He checked the time. It should be around 10 p.m. back home. If Mother hadn't gone to bed already, she might be leaving soon for the Ouachita Fellowship Christmas Eve worship.

All right, he'd make the call. Even if no one answered, he could at least go to bed tonight knowing he'd done the honorable thing. Leaving the lights off in the study, he sat in Dr. Russ's chair and lifted the telephone earpiece. "Long distance, please. Hot Springs, Arkansas." He gave the operator his mother's number.

After five rings, Marguerite answered. "Oh, Thomas, I'm glad it's you." Agitation filled her tone. "Your mama ordered me not to call you, but she didn't say one word about what I could and couldn't say if you called here."

Thomas sat forward, an uneasy tingle at the base of his neck. "Marguerite, what are you talking about?"

"She's been doing poorly for several days—her heart, you know. She was sitting in the dining room at breakfast this morning, not eating a bite and holding her chest like she had indigestion real bad, and then she just keeled right over."

"She had a heart attack?" Fear clutched Thomas's throat. "Where is she now?"

"Dr. Lessman put her in the hospital. Oh, Lordy, Mister Thomas, your mama should not be alone at a time like this. Please, please, won't you come home?"

The visit to Grandmother's in Kansas City ended all too quickly, but neither Joanna nor Jack could afford extra time off work. The train pulled into the depot shortly after six on the Friday after Christmas, giving Joanna barely enough time to freshen up, grab a quick bite of supper, and hurry over to the Arlington.

"How was your trip?" Lillian asked as Joanna hung up her coat and purse.

"It was good to see my grandmother again. I didn't realize how much I've missed her." Joanna poured herself some coffee. "Did you have a nice Christmas?"

"All the kids were in town. We had a grand time." Rising, Lillian handed the headset to Joanna. "Should be another quiet night."

"Good. I brought the needlepoint pattern my grandmother gave me. Maybe if I stare at it long enough, I'll actually figure it out."

Lillian's light laughter filled the room. "Somehow I can't picture you doing needlepoint."

"Neither can I." Joanna rolled her eyes. "But Grandmother wants to see the finished product next time she visits, so if I don't want to disappoint her, I'd better get busy."

"Come early tomorrow evening, and I'll help you. Who knows?" Lillian added with a wink. "You might find you actually enjoy doing needlepoint. It can be relaxing, you know."

Relaxing—just what Joanna needed these days. Or at least something to occupy her thoughts other than missing Thomas more and more each day. It still surprised her to find herself thinking of him as often as she did . . . and of Walter less and less.

A shiver of remorse coursed through her. She covered it with a weak smile as she bade Lillian good night. "Just be prepared to help me undo all my messy stitches tomorrow."

"Oh, you'll do better than you think. Take care, honey. Good night."

Joanna's shift began with three calls in a row requesting room service, then four outside calls asking for the reservations desk and a couple of room-to-room calls. Finally things tapered off and she worked up the courage to pull the needlepoint canvas from her bag. The stenciled design depicted a doe and her fawn beside a waterfall and surrounded by pine trees and wildflowers. Joanna wondered how she'd ever do the scene justice.

By midnight, and after several false starts, she'd stitched three tufts of grass and one daisy. The petals weren't exactly uniform, but at least to the casual observer it looked somewhat like an actual flower.

"Nice work."

Joanna's head shot up, her heart racing. "Thomas! I thought you were in D.C."

"Got back a few hours ago." Wearing a rumpled overcoat and an edgy frown, he appeared at loose ends.

Not taking her eyes from him, she stuffed the needlework into her bag. "You look exhausted. Why aren't you home in bed? I mean, at the farm, or . . . wherever you're staying now."

Slicking a hand through disheveled hair, he released a humorless laugh. "I knew you'd be here, and I couldn't think where else to go."

Sudden dread filled her. "Oh, Thomas, is it Gilbert? Did something happen?"

He looked at her in confusion. "Gil? He's fine." He laughed again. "Yeah, I guess you wouldn't have heard. Mother's had a heart attack."

Without thinking, she tugged off the headset and went to him, wrapping him in a comforting hug. His coat smelled of stale cigarette smoke, combined with the faintest hint of spicy aftershave. "Thomas, I'm so sorry. Is she—"

"No. No, she's been admitted to St. Joseph's Infirmary. Dr. Lessman says she'll recover." Hesitantly at first, his arms crept around her, and he settled his chin on her shoulder. "I haven't even seen her yet. I know it makes me an awful son, but I just can't face her."

"You're not an awful son." No more so than she'd been an awful daughter. "Here, sit down and let me get you some coffee. Looks like you could use it."

For a moment she didn't think he'd ever let go of her, and for a moment she wished he wouldn't. Then he nodded slowly and broke away. While Joanna poured coffee, he sank into the chair. "If she'd died, I could never have forgiven myself."

"But she didn't. You said she's going to be fine." Joanna handed him the mug. "Careful, it's hot."

He smiled his thanks. While he sipped the steamy brew, Joanna resumed her position at the switchboard. After a few minutes, his breaths sounded less ragged. With a deep sigh, he set the coffee mug on a shelf and spread his hands on his thighs. "I had no right to burden you with this, but I knew you'd understand."

"I'm glad you came." She reached across the space between them to take his hands. "Because now I can offer you the same advice I refused to heed." *Oh, God, so many missed opportunities!* "You still have time to resolve things with your mother—or at least to try. Don't risk living with regrets. Believe me, they'll eat you alive."

Slowly his eyes met hers. "I'm sorry you didn't get to say goodbye to your mother—or your dad."

Joanna slid her hands from his and straightened. "Oh, I told them goodbye, all right. Just not in the way I should have." She picked up her headset and held it in her lap, twisting the cord around her fingers. "The thing is, we never get to say a last goodbye. No matter our good intentions, things are always left unsaid . . . or else we carry the memory of all the words we wish we'd never spoken."

"Are you speaking of your parents now, or Walter?"

She smiled sadly. "All of them."

The switchboard buzzed, and Joanna turned away to answer. The interruption pulled her back from the painful past, a place she'd visited all too often lately and was glad to escape. After connecting the caller with the front desk, she tugged off the headset, rose, and stood over Thomas. Gripping the lapels of his overcoat, she urged him to his feet, then aimed him toward the door. "It's late. Get some sleep. Things will look better in the morning."

He stopped just short of the door and turned slowly to face her, his gaze searching hers. He lifted one hand to caress her cheek, his thumb tracing the outline of her mouth, and she trembled beneath his touch. Her lips parted, her eyelids drifted closed. She ached to feel the warm press of his lips on hers.

Then his hand fell away, and when she blinked in surprise, she saw only his retreating back as he trudged through the lobby toward the exit.

Longing filled her, a need so intense it rocked her to the core. She wanted to rush after him, to take him in her arms and demand from him the kiss he'd denied.

Oh, Lord, what's happening to me?

Oh, Lord, it would be a long, long night.

21

It felt strange to sleep in his own bed again, in his own room in the house where he'd lived all his life. Only three weeks ago, Thomas had vowed never to set foot in this house again.

Except he hadn't slept. How could he, between worrying about his mother and reliving the kiss he *hadn't* shared with Joanna. She'd wanted the kiss, he could tell by the way she shuddered when he grazed her mouth with his thumb, the way she leaned toward him, a longing in her heavy-lidded eyes.

Then why hadn't he followed through? Why deny them both what clearly they both wanted?

Because the next time he kissed her, he had to be certain the memory of another man no longer stood between them.

And for the first time since she'd told him about Walter, Thomas dared to hope that day might come.

Trekking downstairs to the kitchen, he found Marguerite tending a skillet of scrambled eggs. A platter piled with crisp bacon sat on the counter.

"Morning, Mister Thomas. Breakfast will be ready in two shakes of a lamb's tail."

Thomas scuffed across the tile floor in his bedroom slippers. "I hope you're not expecting me to eat all this."

The housekeeper gave an embarrassed chuckle. "Can't seem to stop cooking like you and Mister Gilbert are still growing boys and eating us out of house and home. Don't worry. I'll put aside the leftovers for cold bacon sandwiches later."

Thomas helped himself to a cup of coffee and leaned against the counter while Marguerite dished up the eggs. "Don't bother with the dining room. Sit with me at the kitchen table."

She looked at him askance. "You know Miz Ballard wouldn't approve."

"Mrs. Ballard is not here to voice her disapproval." Thomas motioned Marguerite to the table with the platters of food, then took two plates from the cupboard.

"Now, Mister Thomas, you know good and well I can't eat with you."

"Why not?" After setting down the plates and his coffee, he gathered silverware and napkins. "Have you had breakfast yet?"

"No, sir." Marguerite gripped the back of a chair, her gaze darting uneasily. "I always eat with Hank and Zachary after I serve the family."

"Then let's all have breakfast together." Thomas went to the cupboard for two more place settings. "Where are they? I'll call for them."

"Hank went down to check on the furnace fuel, and Zachary's working in the garage. Said the Peerless was running a little rough yesterday."

Just then, Hank stepped through the cellar door. Seeing Thomas, he faltered. "Mister Thomas, everything okay?"

"We're about to have breakfast, Hank. Would you run out to the garage and call Zachary in?"

Marguerite shared a bewildered look with her husband, then shrugged and waved him to the back door. Narrowing her gaze at Thomas, she muttered, "We are gonna catch all kinds of you-know-what when your mama finds out about this."

Thomas had already made up his mind on the issue. Lying awake most of the night, he'd had plenty of time to think—and not just about Joanna. "Things are about to change around here, Marguerite. For one thing, Mother is likely to be in the hospital for some time. For another, when she is well enough to come home, it will still be some time before she's up to running the household again. Therefore, it falls to me. Now, sit down, please, and let's eat before these eggs get any colder."

A few minutes later, Hank and Zachary joined them, the men looking as confused and uncomfortable as Marguerite. They appeared even more dumbfounded when Thomas rose to serve them all more coffee. He secretly enjoyed their discomfiture. In some strange way it reenergized him, as if by changing this one small way of doing things, he could somehow alter the direction of his entire future—and even more profoundly than handing in his resignation at the Arlington.

For fear of frightening poor Marguerite into apoplexy, he decided to forego helping with the kitchen cleanup. Instead, he went upstairs to shower and dress, then steeled himself for a trip to the hospital. Joanna was right—whether his mother survived another year or another decade, he couldn't risk living with the regret of not clearing the air.

"Hello, Mother."

"Thomas?" Her eyelids fluttered. Her long, silver hair lay in a messy braid across one shoulder. She shifted her head on the pillow, making a choking sound in her throat as she extended her hand toward him. "My son . . ."

He strode across the slick floor and pressed her hand between both of his. Her fingers felt limp and cold and small. Struck by her vulnerability, he couldn't find his voice.

Her eyes welled. "I didn't think you'd come."

"Of course, I came. As soon as I learned you were ill, I caught the first available train." Thomas pursed his lips. "You should have let Marguerite notify me at once."

She pulled up the corner of the sheet to dab her cheeks. "Why, when I know how much you hate me?"

"I don't hate you, Mother." Sinking onto the edge of the bed, Thomas brushed back a stray lock of her hair. "We don't have to talk about it now. You need to concentrate on getting well."

Her chest rose and fell with a quavering sigh, and she rolled her head away. "Perhaps it would be better if I had died. Then you and Gilbert would both be rid of me and so much happier—"

"Stop!" Thomas gave her wrist a firm shake. "Never in my life have I known Evelyn Carnahan Ballard to succumb to self-pity. Self-righteousness, yes. Self-absorbed snobbery, absolutely. But never blatant self-pity. And I won't stand for it now."

"Oh, Thomas, my son—" Her voice broke on a sob, and she reached up with her free hand to touch his cheek. "I have failed and disappointed you so miserably. Can you ever forgive me?"

Thomas closed his eyes, looking deep within himself for the answer that still eluded him. He wanted to forgive her—he knew God commanded him to—but he didn't yet know if he had the strength. He cast her a determined stare. "I'm working on forgiveness, but I need something from you in return."

His mother glanced up at him, a silent question in her eyes.

"I need you to grant me the freedom to live my own life. I need you to respect my decisions, even if you don't agree with them. And when you don't agree, especially where my romantic interests are concerned, I need you to refrain from interfering in any way whatsoever."

Biting her lip, his mother nodded. "I'll promise anything, if only you'll come home."

"It's not good enough." Thomas drew a tired breath. "I'm a grown man, Mother. I want a home of my own someday, with a wife and children." He chuckled softly and tweaked her chin. "You do want grandchildren, don't you?"

A frail smile brightened her ashen face. "I long for grandchildren." Then she sniffled and blinked back more tears. "If only I might live long enough to enjoy them."

Rather than indulge her worries—and his own—Thomas opted for practicality. First on his list was to track down Dr. Lessman and learn more about his mother's condition. "Why don't you get some rest, Mother? I have a few things I need to take care of, but I'll be back later."

Exiting the room, he found their family physician poring over a chart at the nurses' station.

Dr. Lessman looked up as Thomas approached. "I was just about to check on your mother."

"Before you do, might I have a word?"

"Certainly." The crusty physician wasn't much for small talk, giving only brusque answers to Thomas's questions. Using the term *coronary thrombosis*, he stated Thomas's mother had suffered a relatively mild incident. With plenty of rest and a healthy diet, she could expect a gradual but steady recovery.

Rubbing perspiring hands on his pants legs, Thomas inhaled a cautious breath. "So . . . death isn't imminent?"

"Not by a long shot." Chuckling, Dr. Lessman thumped Thomas on the back. "I suspect your mother will be around to annoy you for several years to come."

As the doctor marched down the corridor, Thomas sank onto a nearby bench, head in his hands. He'd never expected to feel such relief to know his mother wasn't dying. But would she be true to her word? Or was she too set in her ways to change?

Then, as he lifted his head, his gaze fell upon a painting of Jesus, arms outstretched and a smile of promise on His face. Across the bottom of the painting were the words, *Behold, I make all things new.*

All through the Sunday-morning prelude, Joanna kept glancing over her shoulder in hopes she'd see Thomas. As the congregation rose for the opening hymn, he slipped into the sanctuary. He started to take his seat in the Ballards' usual pew, but when Joanna caught his eye, he hesitated. With an uncertain smile, he continued up the aisle and paused at the end of Joanna's pew.

He nudged Jack's arm. "Room for one more?"

A half-smile curling his lips, Jack shifted his gaze from Thomas to Joanna. She nodded, a flutter in her chest. As Jack and Lily edged further along the pew, Joanna crossed in front of them so she could stand next to Thomas on the aisle. Sharing her hymnal, she pointed to the verse they sang. Thomas's strong tenor sent a shiver up her spine, her own voice sounding feeble in comparison.

When the hymn ended and they sat down, Joanna whispered, "How is your mother?"

"Weak, but recovering. The doctor is optimistic."

"I'm glad." Joanna resisted the impulse to take his hand.

He surprised her by taking hers. Warmth spread through her chest as she faced forward and tried to concentrate on Pastor Yarborough's epistle lesson. She vaguely heard him announce Galatians, and something about not growing weary in doing good.

She *was* "doing good," wasn't she? Maybe she'd rebelled at first about coming home to help raise Lily. But as the weeks passed, her assurance had only increased that she'd done the right thing, both for herself and for her family.

And the longer she stayed, the less she thought about Walter. Maybe this was God's doing as well. Maybe He'd needed her to get away from France and the constant reminders of war so her broken heart could finally, fully heal.

After the service, she invited Thomas to come over for lunch. "It won't be anything fancy. We usually have sandwiches."

Jack spoke up. "But you won't leave hungry, I guarantee. Joanna makes the best sandwiches I've ever eaten."

Joanna beamed beneath her brother's praise. "We have dessert, too. Lily baked a marble cake yesterday."

"Then how can I refuse?" Thomas helped her on with her coat, then offered his arm as they proceeded down the aisle. He had to stop often to answer questions about both his mother and Gilbert. By the time they made it out to the parking area, an edginess had crept into his responses.

Waving Jack and Lily on, Joanna walked with Thomas over to his automobile. She peered up at him with a worried gaze. "Are you all right?"

He glanced toward the church building. "Usually, it's Mother getting all the attention. Strange to have everyone focused on me." Exhaling slowly, he looked deeply into Joanna's eyes. "There's only one person on this earth whose attention I crave."

Fire rose in her cheeks. She couldn't make her throat work to form a response—not when she could barely breathe. *Then why,* she wanted to ask—*why didn't you kiss me the other night when you had the chance?*

All around them, parishioners climbed into their cars and drove away. From the corner of her eye, Joanna glimpsed Jack and Lily approaching in the Dodge. Jack slowed and shot Joanna a questioning look through the windscreen. *See you at home?* he mouthed. With a brusque nod, she motioned him on.

Finally, only Joanna and Thomas were left in the parking area. Thomas hunched his shoulders against a chilling gust of wind. "Guess we should get going."

Neither of them moved.

Joanna ached to crush Thomas in her arms and wrest from him the kiss he refused to give, yet fear held her back. She'd never have shown such restraint with Walter. Though their courtship remained chaste, everything else about their romance had been impulsive and uninhibited. Maybe they'd both sensed how transitory those stolen moments were, while the war raged and the odds of beating death grew worse with every passing day.

With Thomas, though, Joanna wanted permanence. She wanted to rest in the knowledge that he'd always come home to her, every single day until they were old and gray and sitting in rocking chairs on a sunny front porch.

Smiling curiously, Thomas touched her cheek. "What are you thinking?"

She felt the heat of his touch even through the soft leather of his lambskin glove, and still she shivered. "It isn't important." She forced a light laugh. "You're right, we should go. Jack and Lily will wonder what happened to—"

His mouth came down upon hers with such urgency that she stumbled backwards, only to be caught by his hand at her waist. Her whole body trembled as she tasted the sweet, cinnamony warmth of his lips, and she moaned in delicious agony. Eyelids fluttering, she scooped her arms around him and clung with all her might, because if either of them let go, she'd melt clean away.

The kiss crescendoed like a beautifully played symphony, until slowly, tenderly, Thomas's mouth softened over hers with a languorous but insistent pressure. She moaned again as a measure of strength returned to her limbs. Their foreheads touching, Thomas cradled her head in his hands as their lips drifted apart and they both fought to steady their breathing. Each exhale rose like a puff of smoke in the chilly air, but Joanna felt only a placid warmth . . . and delight such as she'd never known.

"I'm in love with you, Joanna." Thomas's voice grew husky with desire. "I can't endure this torture one more day, so tell me honestly, is there any chance for us at all?"

Throat constricted, pulse hammering, Joanna could only nod.

Looking skyward, Thomas breathed out one long, grateful sigh. He pulled her close to drop a kiss on her forehead and then guided her toward the passenger door of his yellow car. "Then let's get out of here now, or I can't be held responsible for my actions."

They didn't speak on the drive home. Joanna kept her gaze averted, pretending to watch the passing scenery while secretly reliving the kiss. Her lips felt pleasantly bruised—would Jack or Lily notice? She could feel the pins slipping from her bun as well. One look at her and they'd surely guess something more than casual conversation had transpired after they'd left Joanna and Thomas in the parking lot.

She stole a glance at Thomas, and her heart flip-flopped. Could she be falling in love again? *Lord, help me get it right this time.*

Lily hoped Joanna and Thomas didn't notice her watching them over lunch, but how could she stop herself? Something had changed about her sister since she'd come home from France. In the past few weeks, Joanna seemed quieter, more serious and thoughtful. And somehow, Lily believed this was the real Joanna. No longer hiding behind the mask of a daring, self-sufficient woman of the world, she now revealed a softer side.

She looked like a woman who'd fallen in love.

At least, considering what Lily imagined about romantic love. What Rudy and the other boys wanted from her certainly didn't qualify. Recalling their groping hands and leering grins, she struggled to swallow a bite of roast beef sandwich. When the bread stuck to the roof of her mouth like wet cardboard, she tried to force it down with a gulp of water.

"Lily? Are you all right?" Joanna peered across the table with a concerned frown.

Only able to nod, Lily covered her mouth with a napkin. After another sip of water, she cleared her throat and found her voice. "May I be excused? Abby's coming over soon, and I need to straighten my room."

"But you've barely touched your lunch."

"Let her go," Jack said with a smirk. "Her room's a mess, as usual."

Picking up her plate, Lily scooted her chair away from the table. "I'm not hungry anyway. I'll wrap this up and have it later."

Joanna didn't look at all reassured, but Lily kept a smile in place as she covered her sandwich and set it in the icebox. Slipping from the kitchen, she hurried upstairs to change out of her church dress, make her bed, and pick up some of the clutter. Abby wouldn't care, of course, but busyness helped rid Lily's mind of the ugly memories never too far from her thoughts.

Someday she'd ask Joanna how long it had taken after she'd run away with Arthur Spence before others stopped treating her as if she wore a scarlet A on her chest. Unfair how the males involved generally managed to sidestep the blame and humiliation. Thanks to the Hegneys' school board connections, Rudy was already back in class, but did self-loathing ever keep him and his cohorts awake at night?

Lily seriously doubted it.

Abby arrived shortly, and the girls sat cross-legged on Lily's bed to page through the latest Sears, Roebuck and Co. catalogue.

"Oh, here's the dress I want for Easter!" Abby pointed to a drop-waist lavender frock with a frilly lace collar and puffy sleeves. "A white straw boater with trailing purple ribbons would be perfect with it."

"Mmm." Lily's gaze skimmed the page, but her thoughts kept wandering.

"All right, Lillian Matilda Trapp, why so preoccupied? It isn't like you to turn your nose up at the Sears catalogue."

Lily straightened her stockinged legs and dangled them off the edge of the bed. "Do you ever wonder what it'll feel like to fall in love?"

"All the time." With a dreamy sigh, Abby flipped the catalogue closed and moved it aside. "Honestly, though, I can't imagine falling for any of the boys in our class. They're all so"—she wrinkled her nose—"immature."

"The upperclassmen aren't much better." Lily quirked her lips. "I think I'll wait until I go off to college to fall in love. A new place, new friends—it has to be better than Hot Springs High."

"You're starting to sound like your big sister."

"Would it be so bad? Except . . . now Joanna's falling for a guy right here in the town where she grew up."

"I saw Mr. Ballard when Joanna answered the door. He's so handsome and distinguished-looking. Smart, too." Abby flopped onto her stomach and rested her chin in her hands. "Maybe we just need to wait for those infantile jerks at school to outgrow their stupidity."

"We'll be old and gray by then, and I don't intend to wait so long." Lily reached across Abby for the catalogue and paged through to the menswear section. "In the meantime, it doesn't hurt to dream."

Rolling onto her back, Abby pulled a pillow under her head and then laced her fingers atop her abdomen. "You were telling me the other day about Joanna running away with a boy. Are you sure they didn't . . . you know?"

Lily glared. "I'm positive. Joanna promised me she's never been with any boy."

"But she's so much older and more experienced. She was in France with all those soldiers, for heaven's sake—even engaged to one. Don't you think she was tempted, at least once?"

"Pastor Yarborough says temptation is only a sin if you give in to it." Lily certainly hoped it was true, because she couldn't deny the secret sensations Rudy's attentions once evoked.

Staring unseeing at the catalogue page, Lily imagined her sister with the Spence boy, and then with her doughboy fiancé in France. Did temptation feel different when you were in love? Would it be easier to resist—or even harder?

22

You have to go. *I* have to go." Joanna nuzzled Thomas's neck as they stood next to his car behind the Arlington. If only they weren't separated by layers of coats, gloves, and mufflers.

Groaning, Thomas drew her closer. "You shouldn't have to work on New Year's Eve. How will I kiss you at midnight?"

"If you were still my boss, you could give me the night off. But since you're not . . ." Her lips teased his with a fluttery kiss, and she relished how their contact made him tremble.

"Joanna . . ." The urgency in his raspy whisper sent shivers down her limbs. He gripped her shoulders and gently pushed her away. "You're right. I need to leave, and you need to go in to work. Otherwise, I'll be tempted to whisk you away for our own private New Year's celebration."

She straightened the wool scarf tucked beneath his chin, a practical activity for the sole purpose of preventing herself from leaving with him right now and forgetting all about the night shift at the Arlington switchboard. Being with Thomas awakened feelings within her she hadn't experienced since—

No, she couldn't even say *since Walter*. This was different in so many ways. This time, love felt real, honest, pure. Uncontaminated by war, unconstrained by duty.

Catching one of her hands as she fiddled with his coat collar, Thomas tugged off her wool glove and pressed his lips to her palm. The moist warmth made her catch her breath, and he chuckled softly. "I warned you. Stay a moment longer and I won't be able to let you go."

"All right, all right." She snatched back her glove and edged out of reach as she slipped it on. "When you pick me up at three—if you're still awake—I'll give you a New Year's kiss you'll never forget."

Thomas's eyes darkened. "Do you promise?"

Pulling her lower lip between her teeth, Joanna gave a quick nod before hurrying inside. Her heart pounded frantically at the desirous thoughts racing through her head. Before relieving Lillian, she ducked into the ladies' lounge to make sure she didn't look as brazenly lovesick as she felt. If common sense hadn't deserted her after a movie matinee followed by an early dinner at the Emerald Club, she'd have insisted Thomas take her home so she could drive her own automobile to work. Truly, she was playing with fire to have him return when her shift ended. They'd both be tired and sleepy, their resistance down, and who knew where their passions might lead?

Standing before the ladies' room mirror, Joanna smoothed her hair into place and inhaled several deep, slow breaths. A minute or two more, and the high color began to fade from her cheeks. At least she could lay partial blame to having just come in from the cold. Satisfied no one would be the wiser about how she'd spent the last twenty minutes in the parking area, she hurried to the switchboard room.

"Good evening, Lillian," she said as she slipped out of her coat and gloves. "How's your day been?"

"Hectic! You'll be in for some fun tonight, I'm afraid." The switchboard buzzed, and Lillian turned her attention to the call. "Yes, ma'am, the Lucy family party is being hosted in the second-floor parlor. Would you like me to connect you?"

While Lillian concluded the call, Joanna hung up her things and then perused the message log. "Lots of parties at the hotel tonight."

"It's like this every New Year's Eve." Lillian rose and passed Joanna the headset. "I doubt you'll get much needlepoint done."

Joanna shrugged. "Just as well, since I forgot and left it at home." She looked up at Lillian with a sheepish grin. "I was . . . rather preoccupied."

"With a certain young man, I imagine." Lillian wiggled her brows. "How is Thomas these days? Any plans to return to D.C. while his brother's there?"

"If his mother continues to improve, he'll go back next week for a few days. Mary had to come home and return to work at the hospital, and Thomas hates for Gilbert to be alone while he heals from these surgeries."

Lillian gathered up her coat and handbag. "Is Mrs. Ballard still at St. Joseph's?"

"She may be released by the weekend. Thomas has already engaged a private nurse." Another call came through, and Joanna excused herself to answer. By the time she finished, Lillian was on her way out the door. Joanna barely had a moment to say goodbye before the switchboard buzzed again.

At this rate, it would either be a short night, or an extremely long one.

*

Leaving the Arlington, Thomas struggled to keep his mind on his driving. These last few days with Joanna had been amazing. She hadn't spoken the words yet—*I love you*—but the kisses they'd shared said plenty. Thomas dared to believe she'd moved past her grief and guilt over Walter and was ready to let Thomas into her heart.

At St. Joseph's Infirmary, he stopped at the nurses' station for an update on his mother's condition.

A middle-aged nurse adjusted wire-rimmed glasses as she paged through a chart. "Dr. Lessman is quite pleased with Mrs. Ballard's continued progress. He wants to know the status of your home nursing arrangements."

"The private nurse I've hired is available beginning Sunday."

"Excellent." The nurse made a notation on the chart. "I believe your mother is still awake. She hoped you'd come by."

Thomas thanked the nurse and continued to his mother's room. Muted strains from a Beethoven symphony met him as he tapped on the door. "Mother?"

"Come in, Thomas." Her voice definitely sounded stronger.

Sidling into the room, he took note of the myriad bouquets decorating the dresser and windowsill. The music emanated from a Victrola in the corner. "Where'd this come from?"

"I had Marguerite send it over with Hank." His mother's bosom rose and fell in a dramatic sigh. "Do you have any idea how tedious it is to lie in a hospital bed day after miserable day?"

Yes, Mother was almost her old self again. Hiding a smirk, Thomas shrugged out of his overcoat and moved a chair closer to the bed. "You'll be happy to know Dr. Lessman will be releasing you soon."

"So he told me." She pursed her lips. "However, with Marguerite, Mary, and you looking after me, why do you feel the need to hire some stranger?"

"First of all, Marguerite has her hands full managing the housework and cooking. Second, you know Mary has returned to the hospital full-time. She doesn't need to be burdened—" Poor choice of words. Thomas cleared his throat. "I mean, between her job and seeing to the farm in Gil's absence, she has plenty to think about already."

Thomas's mother gave an understanding nod. "And you, naturally, will be otherwise occupied courting your young lady." She quirked a brow. "And possibly looking for other employment?"

Avoiding his mother's eyes, Thomas braced his elbows on his knees and laced his fingers together. "I have yet to decide on a course of action."

"I have acquaintances at the Eastman, should you—"

"Please, Mother. I need you to trust me to find my own way."

She fell silent for a few moments, then spoke quietly, "Of course, son. I won't interfere."

Straightening, he cast her a dubious glance. "Are you sure you're not having a relapse? Maybe I should send for Dr. Lessman at once."

Her scowl assured him this was indeed the Evelyn Ballard he knew so well—or thought he did. "I'm trying, Thomas. But you know the old saying. It isn't easy to teach an old dog new tricks." She patted the mattress. "Now pull your chair closer and tell me how this romance of yours is proceeding."

At the reference to Joanna, Thomas's pulse stammered. An image rose in his mind of her pouty, just-kissed lips as she waved goodbye in the Arlington parking area earlier. He swallowed. "It's . . . proceeding."

"Well? Is there a wedding in the foreseeable future?"

Thomas lifted one hand. "Let's not get ahead of ourselves." As if he hadn't fantasized about taking Joanna as his bride—and the sooner, the better! Spending so much time lately with Gilbert and Mary had only heightened his longing to experience marital bliss for himself.

And spending time with Joanna only deepened his conviction that she was the woman he wanted to spend the rest of his life with.

"Humph. Only the other day you were promising me grandchildren."

Stifling a laugh, Thomas gave his head a quick shake. "Mother dear, you are a case. As I recall, I said if you ever wanted grandchildren, you'd have to give me the freedom to live my own life—which *doesn't* include rushing me to the altar before either I or my bride-to-be is ready."

Her eyes widened. "So marriage *is* in the picture!"

Thomas thrust up from the chair. "I think I'd better leave right now before you get yourself any more worked up over something I haven't even spoken of with Joanna."

"But you're thinking about it!" The playful twinkle in her eye kept Thomas from completely losing his good humor.

He smoothed a gray curl from his mother's forehead and leaned in to kiss her cheek. "If and when the lovely Miss Trapp consents to be my wife, you shall be the first to know. Now stop planning my wedding and get some rest."

"Happy New Year, son. I love you."

Her words stopped him at the door. He turned with a smile. "I love you, too, Mother. Happy New Year."

On his way out to the car, he checked the time—only a little past nine. Still hours to go before Joanna's shift ended. Already he missed her so fiercely it made his chest ache. How was he to pass the time until he could hold her close again and taste her sweet, warm lips?

He climbed in behind the wheel and sat in the darkened car while he debated what to do with himself until three a.m.

And dreamed about how he'd usher in the New Year with Joanna once he picked her up after her shift.

It took only moments of observing the direction of his thoughts to realize exactly what he must do. With a reluctant sigh, he started the motor and steered the car toward home. Entering the study, he went straight for the telephone.

Three rings later, Lily Trapp answered.

"Hello, Lily. This is Thomas Ballard. Is Jack at home?"

"Yes, but he's entertaining company this evening." A girlish giggle sounded through the telephone. "I'm chaperoning him and Miss Maynard. We're playing charades."

Thomas should have expected Jack to have New Year's Eve plans. "If you wouldn't mind interrupting, I promise this will only take a moment."

Lily excused herself, and shortly afterward, Jack came on the line. "What can I do for you, Thomas?"

Stomach curdling with sudden awkwardness, Thomas swallowed. "I hate to trouble you, but can you pick up Joanna when her shift ends?"

Jack hesitated. "Joanna said you were bringing her home."

"I'd planned to, but—" What he wouldn't give for a tall glass of water to soothe his dry-as-dust throat. "Speaking man-to-man, Jack, I think you can guess why my picking your sister up at three a.m. on New Year's morning is a *very* bad idea."

✐❧

When Nora, the part-time operator, arrived to take over the switchboard, Joanna wanted to fall on her knees and kiss the woman's feet. "It's been the craziest night ever! I didn't think the New Year's revelers would ever slow down."

Nora laughed tiredly. Dark circles under her eyes suggested she'd stayed up later than usual to see in the New Year. "If it was anything like last year, half the callers were three sheets to the wind."

"At least half—and even with Prohibition in effect. Unbelievable." Rising to stretch, Joanna passed the headset to Nora.

"Don't kid yourself. There's plenty of illegal booze to be had if people know where to look. Temptation is everywhere."

Joanna offered a tight smile. She knew exactly where tempta-tion lay at this moment—not twenty feet past the Arlington's rear exit in a shiny yellow Jeffery Touring Car. "At least things have quieted down for now. Hopefully everyone's finally gone to bed."

As if to mock her, the switchboard buzzed. Nora rolled her eyes as she poked a plug into a jack. "Happy New Year from the Arlington Hotel. How may I direct your call?"

Quietly gathering her things, Joanna waved goodbye and slipped out. On her way through the hotel, she slid her arms into her coat sleeves and pulled on her gloves, energy returning as she imagined Thomas waiting for her outside. As adventurous and spontaneous as he'd proven himself lately, she couldn't even guess what surprises he'd dreamed up to continue their celebration.

Reaching the door, she froze. *Oh, you foolish girl.* Why hadn't she tried to reach Thomas at home while she had the chance and simply explained her apprehensions about what might happen if they spent any more time alone together?

Then another thought slammed into her. What if Thomas believed what so many others had thought true of her since high school? He must have known about her fling with Arthur Spence, and he knew she'd once been engaged. Perhaps he fully expected their kisses would lead to something more.

Perhaps he expected it tonight.

Well, she would quickly disabuse him of such notions. Though disappointments and loss had strained her faith, she still believed in obeying God's word and fully intended to remain pure until she gave herself to the man she married. Not even the fiery passion she'd shared with Walter had been enough to tempt her off the path.

In the dimly lit corridor, she rested her forehead against the door. *Dear Father, I've made a lot of mistakes. Don't let Thomas be only one more.*

Steeling herself to insist he drive her straight home, she stepped outside into the frigid night.

Then, seeing Jack parked near the door in the Dodge, she laughed out loud. She strode to the car and pulled open the passenger door. "I should probably ask why you're here instead of Thomas, but at the moment I'm too relieved to care."

Jack greeted her with a yawn. "Good thing I love my sister so much. Last time I hauled myself out of bed this early was to catch the next transport home from France."

As Jack exited the parking lot onto a side street, Joanna snuggled deeper into the upholstery. "I am curious, though," she began sleepily. "Was this Thomas's idea, or yours?"

"One hundred percent Thomas's. He telephoned sounding terrified about the possibility of besmirching your honor." Jack glanced her way with a knowing grin. "The guy's crazy for you, in case you didn't know it."

A happy smile curled Joanna's lips. "Thanks for coming for me, Jack. It's nice both the men in my life care so much about protecting me."

When Jack parked in the driveway at home, she somehow managed to stumble up to her room, change into her nightgown, and fall into bed. She didn't remember another thing until chimes from the grandfather clock in the parlor penetrated her consciousness. Lying there blinking the sleep out of her eyes, she counted eleven bongs. No wonder the room was so bright!

Had she really slept so soundly and so long? Joanna couldn't recall waking up this rested in ages.

Her bedroom door creaked open, and Lily peeked in.

"It's okay. I'm awake." Joanna elbowed her pillows against the headboard and pulled herself upright, then tucked the covers around her chest to stay warm a little longer.

Lily scurried across the floor and climbed onto the foot of the bed. "I thought you'd never wake up. I've been dying to tell you about our brother and Miss Maynard!"

The catlike grin on her sister's face said more than words. "Let me guess. They've decided to marry at once and run away to Tahiti."

"Don't be silly!" Gasping, Lily leaned forward and lowered her voice. "But they *did* kiss at midnight. Oh, you should have seen them, Jo! It was so dreamy the way Jack took her hands and smiled into her eyes. And when Miss Maynard looked up at him all soft and dewy-eyed . . ." Lily hugged herself and sighed. "I can't wait to grow up and fall in love."

"You'll meet the right boy someday, I promise." Joanna patted the space beside her. When Lily scooted closer, she snuggled her under her arm. "When you do fall in love, I hope he'll be every bit the honorable man your brother is."

"Jack is a good brother." Lily rested her head against Joanna's shoulder. "I wish I'd been a better sister instead of causing him so much trouble."

"I could have done better, too—for both you and Jack. I thank God every day for giving me another chance to be the sister both of you deserve."

"I'm so glad you came home." Lily took Joanna's hand and wove their fingers together. They passed several moments in pleasant silence before Lily asked timidly, "You're not going back, are you? To France, I mean."

It saddened Joanna to realize Lily still worried about being abandoned again. Yet whose fault was it? Joanna couldn't deny how only weeks ago, she couldn't wait to return to Paris—her work at the telephone office with Véronique, their volunteer service at the orphanage. Her intention from the outset had been to stay in Hot Springs only long enough to make sure Lily straightened out her life. If things fell completely apart, France would always be her escape.

But things were definitely *not* falling apart. Not only had she reconnected with her brother and sister, growing closer with them than she'd imagined possible, now she found herself falling in love with a wonderful, caring man. How could she ever return to Paris now?

"Joanna, why are you crying?" Lily's forehead creased as she shifted to face Joanna. "Please don't say it's because you're going to leave us soon."

Only then noticing the wetness sliding down her cheeks, Joanna gave a sniffly chuckle. "No, honey, I'm not going anywhere." She dabbed at her tears with the edge of the sheet. "But I'll always treasure my life in France—the friends I made there, the experiences we shared."

Lily offered a sad smile. "And Walter?"

"I'll always remember Walter." Joanna spread her left hand and pictured the "engagement ring" he'd given her. Not a real ring, but a circle woven from the raveled threads of his uniform.

"This way you'll always have me with you, even when I'm out there fighting the Germans. And when this blasted war is over, I'll buy you the best, brightest, most beautiful diamond ring you ever saw!"

A few months after Walter was killed, Joanna had realized the threads were wearing thin. Rather than risk losing the ring entirely, she'd removed it from her finger and wrapped it in the embroidered silk handkerchief Walter had given her for her birthday. The packet now lay tucked away in her dresser drawer for safekeeping.

"I'm sorry I made you cry," Lily said.

"It's all right. Sometimes tears are healing."

"And now you're falling in love with Thomas." Lily curled her legs beneath her. "Do you suppose you'll marry him someday?"

Joanna started to say it was far too soon to think about marriage, but then she realized she couldn't imagine anything more wonderful than to become Mrs. Thomas Ballard. With Walter, though they'd dreamed about a future together, planned how they'd spend their lives after the war ended, Joanna could never fully give herself over to the anticipation, not when the next bullet or artillery shell might have her sweetheart's name on it.

"Only God knows what the future holds." Giving Lily's arm a pat, Joanna shoved the covers aside and sat up. "I've wasted too many years living life on my own terms. It's well past time I turn the reins over to the Lord and let Him decide what happens next."

23

Thomas straightened the quilt across his mother's legs, then made sure her favorite magazines were in easy reach on the bedside table. "Marguerite will bring your lunch shortly. Anything else you need before I see to some household business?"

His mother gazed up at him with puppy-dog eyes. "*Must* you leave me all alone? Stay a bit longer and keep me company."

"You're supposed to be resting." Wagging his finger, Thomas edged toward the door. "I'll come up after you've had lunch and a nap. Dr. Lessman doesn't want you overdoing your first few days at home."

No one had perfected the pout like Evelyn Ballard. Refusing to be hornswoggled, Thomas ignored his mother's melodramatic sigh and pulled the door closed as he stepped into the hall. Whooshing out a relieved sigh of his own, he started downstairs.

Marguerite met him at the foot of the steps, lunch tray in hand. "Your mama behaving herself?"

"For now." Thomas caught the aroma of homemade chicken noodle soup and fresh-baked yeast rolls. A bowl of tapioca pudding with raisins sat on the corner of the tray. "Remember, easy on the salty foods. Rich desserts as well. Dr. Lessman thinks Mother's health would improve if she could lose a little weight."

Making a disgusted noise in her throat, Marguerite pursed her lips. "These fancy doctors and their newfangled ideas. What's wrong with having a little meat on your bones?"

Thomas patted Marguerite's forearm. "Ours not to reason why . . ."

"Uh-huh. Follow orders and don't ask questions. I know my place, Mister Thomas."

Her subservient tone rankled. Thomas fixed her with an accusing glare. "Don't talk this way, Marguerite. You know how much you mean to this family. Anytime you have questions or thoughts about how things should be done around here, I fully expect you to speak your mind."

Slowly she shook her head, bemusement bringing a twinkle to her eyes. "Now, Mister Thomas, you know I never hesitated a day in my life to speak my mind. But it sure is good to know somebody might actually listen for a change."

He chuckled. "Better take Mother her lunch before the soup gets cold, or you'll be getting an earful from her."

"Won't mind a bit, if it means she's on the mend." Marguerite winked and started up the stairs.

As Thomas continued to the study, his mind raced with everything he needed to handle between now and his return to D.C. When Mary had stopped by after work yesterday, she brought news that Dr. Russ had scheduled Gilbert's next procedure for a week from Friday, this surgery expected to be even more excruciating than the first. Knowing Gilbert's fear of succumbing to morphine addiction again, Mary worried he'd resist taking needed pain medication and hoped Thomas's presence would reassure him.

At least Thomas could make the trip knowing he left his mother in good hands. Nancy Gray, the private nurse, had proven herself quite reliable since joining the staff last weekend. And despite her grumbling, Marguerite doted on Thomas's mother and would probably spoil her beyond redemption. Mary promised to check in often as well.

The hard part would be leaving Joanna, just when their romance had begun to blossom with the promise of a future together. They'd laughed often the past few days over their New Year's silliness, each concerned their attraction might lead them down unsafe paths. Since then, Thomas had been careful to court Joanna only in more public situations. No more kisses in the dark or late-night rendezvous.

While he sorted through the mail and organized monthly bills for payment, voices from the hallway drifted through the door. Sounded like Mrs. Gray had just returned from the pharmacy with the prescription Dr. Lessman ordered.

A few minutes later, the doorbell rang, and Marguerite's footsteps sounded in the foyer. "How-do, Miz Hegney. Come have a seat in the parlor while I see if Miz Ballard feels up to company."

So Fannie Hegney had decided to pay a call. Thomas hadn't forgotten the tantrum his mother had thrown over the Hegneys' refusal of her dinner invitation last month, all because of their aversion toward Joanna. What was the word they'd used—*termagant*? He had a notion to step into the parlor and give the woman a piece of his mind, after which he'd show her the door and inform her she wasn't welcome to return.

Except then he'd have to answer to Mother, and he certainly wouldn't risk causing her blood pressure to rise.

More footsteps, then Marguerite's voice again. "Miz Ballard said to come on up. I'll show you to her room."

Thomas wished he'd had the foresight to close the study door. Maybe if he switched off the desk lamp and sat quietly, Mrs. Hegney would pass by without noticing him.

He'd barely reached for the pull chain when she halted at the door and peered inside. "Thomas, I didn't realize you were at home."

"How are you, Mrs. Hegney?" Thomas hoped he sounded reasonably polite.

"Quite well, thank you." She hesitated, her mouth curving downward in a concerned frown. Motioning for Marguerite to give her a moment, she strode into the study. "Thomas, I don't have to remind you how long our families have been friends, so you must know how highly I think of you."

"You're very kind." Maybe if he looked busy enough with the bills, she'd leave him in peace. "I know Mother will be glad to see you. Enjoy your visit."

"I'm sure I will. But first . . ." When the woman perched on one of the chairs in front of the desk, the hairs on the back of Thomas's neck rose. "Our daughter Caroline and her husband came to visit over Christmas, and naturally we reminisced about her school days."

"Naturally." Thomas forced an interested smile.

"You do remember I mentioned Caroline and your . . . *friend* Miss Trapp went to school together."

Laying aside his fountain pen, Thomas laced his fingers together. "I remember."

Mrs. Hegney inhaled deeply, while giving inordinate attention to smoothing a wrinkle from her skirt. "Perhaps I shouldn't even bring this up."

"But now that you have . . ." Thomas's jaw ached with the effort to maintain a neutral expression.

She cleared her throat. "I know I've been rather harsh in my opinion of Miss Trapp, and I do try to be fair-minded. So I asked Caroline what more she recalled from their acquaintance."

Thomas waited. He had no doubt the busybody was about to impart some unpleasant gossip he'd just as soon not hear.

"The girls weren't close friends, as you can imagine, being from different social strata. But Caroline did remember quite well the unpleasantness surrounding Miss Trapp's . . . How shall I put this?"

I'd rather you didn't put it any way at all. "Call it what you want, it's in the past. I think we should leave it there."

Mrs. Hegney pursed her lips. "I know you would like to believe only the best of Miss Trapp. We all would, I assure you. I'm afraid this relates to your brother's horrible accident last fall with the bees and the runaway horses. Your mother confided in me that everyone believed Gilbert's old school chum Arthur Spence was responsible."

Totally confused now, Thomas gave his head a quick shake. "Yes, Gil suspected Arthur, but they never found any proof."

Mrs. Hegney waved a hand as if none of it mattered. "The thing is, Caroline remembered it was the Spence boy Miss Trapp ran off to St. Louis with."

"This isn't news to me. But as I keep saying, it's irrelevant."

"One can only hope." The woman glanced downward. "However, since Arthur has been seen about town lately, well . . . one can't help but wonder."

Arthur Spence was in town? The man had some nerve! The last Thomas had heard, Spence had slunk back to Boston and his uncle's factory. He must have returned to Hot Springs to spend the holidays with his parents.

Thomas massaged the bridge of his nose. Well-intentioned or not, Fannie Hegney—like so many of his mother's cronies—was an insatiable scandalmonger. No doubt before she left this afternoon, she intended to use Joanna's connection with Arthur Spence to poison his mother's mind against Joanna all over again. What was it with people who claimed to be forgiven children of God and yet refused to allow others to leave their sins behind?

Fingertips whitening as he pressed them into the desktop, Thomas rose. "I believe Marguerite is waiting to take you upstairs to see Mother. As I'm sure you wouldn't want to cause her any distress, I'd appreciate it if you would refrain from bringing up the subject of Arthur Spence."

"Of course." Mrs. Hegney stood and edged toward the foyer. Worry creased her brow. "Thomas, you do understand—"

"Good day, Mrs. Hegney." Thomas ushered her out and thrust the door closed behind her.

⚜

"Joanna?" The male voice behind her sounded hesitant. "Joanna Trapp?"

Standing before the display case in Kittelberger's Bakery, she sucked in a quick breath without turning around. *Dear Lord, please don't let it be him.*

Maybe she could pretend she hadn't heard—or let him believe he'd mistaken her for someone else. She nodded toward the proprietor. "Two of your whole-grain harvest loaves, please."

"Thick-sliced as usual, Miss Trapp?"

She flinched. He *would* call her by name. "Yes, thank you."

"I thought it was you." Keeping his voice low, Arthur Spence stepped up beside her, his features shaded by a wide-brimmed fedora. Even behind his hesitant grin, his charm shone through. "I'd recognize your messy blonde hair anywhere."

Joanna gave him a tight-lipped smile while self-consciously smoothing her bun. "I didn't know you were still in Hot Springs."

"I came back to, uh, take care of a few things." He glanced around uneasily. "You're the one I never expected to see around these parts again. What brought you home?"

"Family matters." She handed Mr. Kittelberger some cash as he passed her purchase across the counter. "Well, have a good visit."

"Please don't rush off, Jo." Arthur blocked the quick exit she'd hoped for. "Running into you is—well, it seems more than a coincidence. Could we go somewhere and catch up?"

"Sorry, but I have several more errands to run. It's a busy day."

"Joanna." Arthur's tone turned insistent, and for a heady moment she felt the pull of his sensuality—a trait he'd owned in abundance as a teen and clearly had honed to perfection.

"Arthur, please." She hugged her sack of bread as if it could protect her from his allure. "I wish you nothing but the best. However, I have no intention of resurrecting the past."

"Me, neither. These days I'm all about changing the future." His gaze shifted anxiously before he pinned Joanna with a beseeching half-smile. "Just a few minutes, Jo. I need to believe someone in this town will still give me the time of day."

His strange remark piqued her curiosity. There was a time when his smooth tongue and boyish good looks could have compelled her to follow him anywhere—which she had, all the way to St. Louis. Now, as she stood inches from the all-grown-up boy she once rapturously called her knight in shining armor, the boy she'd thought would rescue her from her oppressive home life and the ever-increasing difficulties with her mother, it galled her how quickly those old feelings came rushing back.

But these weren't so much feelings as memories, and she did know the difference. She would *not* be taken in by him again. "Arthur, I have to go. Goodbye."

Without giving him a chance to stop her, she rushed past him and out to the street. Tossing the bread sack into the sidecar with the groceries she'd picked up earlier, she climbed onto the Indian and sped away.

By the time she arrived home, the wind had whipped her hair into a tangled mess. Her cheeks and ears stung from the cold, but with school dismissing in less than half an hour, she had no time to warm up, much less comb the snarls from her hair, before rushing to the high school to pick up Lily. The best she could do was put away the groceries and then tuck her hair into the stocking cap she should have had sense enough to don before venturing out the first time.

Parked on Oak Street across from the high school, Joanna shivered and tugged her coat collar higher. Though she'd arrived with only five minutes to spare, it seemed forever before the doors opened and students flooded down the steps. Finally, she glimpsed

Lily weaving through the crowd along with Abby. Heads together, laughing at some shared joke, the girls looked happy and carefree.

Joanna smiled to herself. Lily had only just begun to find her way again before the Christmas break. Apparently, everything remained on track and school was going well.

Moments later, Rudy Hegney emerged from the building. When he jogged passed Lily, the unconcerned glance she tossed his way reassured Joanna even more. Lily may not realize it, but she was stronger than Joanna ever was. *Dear God, let her always be as innocent and goodhearted as she is today.*

After telling Abby goodbye at her mother's car, Lily trotted across the street. "I hoped you'd come for me on the motorcycle." She tossed her books into the sidecar and then took the goggles Joanna handed her. "I finished all my homework already. How about we go to the church parking lot and you can teach me how to drive this thing?"

"I think not!" Joanna tugged her own goggles down over her eyes and waited for Lily to settle into her seat. "Sorry, my dear, but I need to get home and change. I'm going to Thomas's for dinner."

"I should have known. You two are inseparable these days." Lily's shoulders rose and fell with an exaggerated sigh. "Won't be long before I'll have to decide which newlyweds I'm going to live with—Mr. and Mrs. Jack Trapp, or Mr. and Mrs. Thomas Ballard."

Rolling her eyes, Joanna started the motor and hoped it would drown out any further commentary on Trapp family romances.

This time after returning home, Joanna wasted no time hurrying upstairs and drawing a hot, sudsy bath. She should wash her hair, but it would take too long to dry, so while the tub filled, she pressed Lily into service brushing out the tangles—and with no shortage of yelps and grimaces.

"Before I get my own motorcycle," Lily mused as she worked at a snarl, "I'm going to cut my hair in a bob."

Joanna winced as the brush tore through another knot. "Why are you so certain you want a motorcycle? They're not ladylike, you know."

"Maybe not, but they sure are fun! Anyway, the world is changing. Women can do or be anything they want. Now that women can vote, maybe someday there'll even be a woman in the White House."

Unable to suppress a grin at her sister's optimism, Joanna reached for the brush. "Give it to me, before you rip every last strand from my head." Pinning her hair up for her bath, she eyed Lily in the mirror. "It makes me proud to know you have such high aspirations." She turned with a sad smile and cupped Lily's face between her palms. "Just promise me—and yourself—you will never base your self-worth on anything but who God says you are. Not even to win a man's heart."

Lily furrowed her brow. "Is that what you did, Jo? Is it why you're so worried about me?"

Joanna pictured Arthur as she'd seen him in the bakery, his smile as suave as she remembered. She pictured Walter, dapper in his olive-drab uniform and gazing at her with eyes as deep and dark as the ocean. She pictured Thomas, sincerity and trust as much a part of him as his chiseled cheekbones and raven hair. Looking earnestly into her sister's eyes, she said, "I worry because I know what it is to desperately want to be loved and accepted for who you are—to want it so badly you'd sacrifice almost anything. But when you find the man who'd willingly sacrifice himself for you, you'll know you've found your true love."

"Like you have with Thomas?"

"Yes. Like Thomas." Before the conversation grew any more maudlin, Joanna whirled Lily around and shooed her out the door. "Now give me some privacy for my bath, or I'll never be ready in time."

L

The New Year had barely begun, but business at the pottery factory had Jack racing along faster than Howdy Wilcox's Peugeot at the 1919 Indianapolis 500. As if keeping up with orders and invoicing weren't enough, Jack's front-office position had him fielding more and more job applications from returning soldiers who hadn't yet found work. He hated having to turn them away, but in the months following the armistice, Mr. Kendall had hired all the staff the factory could support and still pay their salaries.

Pulling into the driveway at home, Jack sat in the car for a few minutes, forehead resting on the steering wheel. He needed to shift his mental gears before dealing with the two effervescent females he lived with. Over the winter, the changes in both Lily and Joanna had been remarkable. No longer the sullen, sour-faced girl with a chip on her shoulder, Lily had blossomed into a vibrant young woman.

And Joanna—no longer flaunting her independence or threatening to bolt back to France at the first sign of trouble, she'd settled into the role of "big sister" and forged a bond with Lily that sometimes left Jack feeling out in the cold.

Which he was right now, and getting colder by the minute. Bustling from the car, he slammed the door and hurried into the house. Reluctant to shrug off his overcoat too quickly, he filled the teakettle and set it on the stove to boil, and in the meantime glanced around to see if Joanna had started supper.

Apparently not, since the oven was cold and no enticing aromas greeted his nostrils.

"Joanna! Lily! Anybody home?" He unbuttoned his coat on his way through the foyer.

"You don't have to yell," Lily called from the parlor. Jack spied her curled on the sofa with a book on her lap. "Jo's upstairs getting dressed. She's having dinner with Thomas before she goes to work."

Jack's shoulders slumped. He massaged his growling stomach. "What are *we* supposed to eat?"

"Don't be such a grump. Jo shopped today. As soon as I finish this chapter, I'll fry us a couple of pork chops and warm up a can of green beans."

"Yum," Jack said without feeling.

As he shed his overcoat and hung it in the hall closet, Joanna came bouncing down the stairs. Wearing what appeared to be another new frock, she looked a lot more dressed up than she usually did for working the Arlington switchboard. "Did Lily tell you I'm going over to Thomas's?"

"Just did."

Joanna tugged her wool coat from the closet. "Sorry to rush out and leave you two to fend for yourselves, but the afternoon got away from me." A dark look came into her eyes as she fumbled to work her arms into the sleeves.

Jack helped her on with the coat. "Something wrong?"

"Nothing important." She gave her head a quick shake and reached for her handbag. "You don't mind if I take the Dodge, do you? I was zipping around all day on the Indian and nearly froze my ears off."

The brightness in her tone rang false, and for the first time in a long time, Jack had the sinking feeling his sister might desert them again. "What aren't you telling me, Jo?"

She pursed her lips as if trying to decide whether to answer. Drawing a slow breath through her nose, she squared her shoulders. "I ran into an old acquaintance this afternoon. It brought back unpleasant memories I've been trying to shake ever since."

Jack followed her through the kitchen. "Who was it? Can I help?"

Reaching the back door, she set one hand on the knob, then turned and smiled tiredly. "Thank you, little brother, but the past is best left in the past."

As the door closed behind Joanna, Lily stepped into the kitchen. "You noticed, too," she stated. "Jo's seemed kind of melancholy all afternoon."

"She mentioned running into someone earlier. Any idea who?"

"She didn't say anything to me." Lily went to the icebox and brought out a package wrapped in butcher paper. "But the mood she's in . . ." Gnawing on a thumbnail, she cast Jack a worried frown. "What if it was Arthur?"

Jack slanted a brow. "Who's Arthur?"

"You know. Arthur Spence. The boy from high school." Lily spread open the butcher paper and selected two thick-cut pork chops from the package.

Jack had heard the name, all right, but never from Joanna's lips—at least not in connection with her St. Louis fiasco. Maybe because of Jack's age at the time—more likely because of Joanna's shame and embarrassment—he'd never learned the details.

Apparently, since returning home, Joanna had confided in Lily.

Pivoting on his heel, he massaged the back of his neck. It sickened him to think a man with Arthur Spence's shady reputation might also be the boy who'd beguiled Joanna and tainted her reputation as well.

If Spence was back in town, it could only be bad news. Jack may not have been old enough, wise enough, or big enough to defend his sister's honor all those years ago, but he certainly could now. Let Arthur Spence cross paths with any of Jack's family again, and he'd be sorry.

24

*J*oanna yawned and stretched. Ten minutes more and Pamela Clement should be strolling in to take over the switchboard. Joanna dreaded the frigid trek to her car, but at least she had a warm bed to look forward to—and the hope of a few precious hours of sleep before dragging herself out of bed to see Lily off to school.

These days, she'd been sleeping both better and worse. Better, because she felt more settled about life, family, and faith than she had in a long time. Worse, because sometimes she'd lie awake for hours thinking about Thomas and imagining their future together.

"Wake up, sleepyhead. Time to go home." Pamela's chipper tone stirred Joanna from her lethargy.

"Thank goodness! It's one thing when the calls keep you jumping, and quite another to pray the telephone will ring just so you won't fall asleep on the job."

"Slow night, huh?" Pamela pulled off her mittens and scarf, tossing them onto a chair as she unbuttoned her coat.

"By one a.m. everyone must have been snug in their beds." Joanna lifted off the headset and pushed away from the switchboard. "Which is where I'll soon be."

"Not before you tell me the latest about you and Thomas. Didn't you have another date last night?"

"Just dinner at his house. He's staying close to home since his mother's out of the hospital."

Pamela took Joanna's place at the switchboard. "How is Mrs. Ballard?"

"Better." Smiling thoughtfully, Joanna tipped her head. "Mellower. Thomas took me upstairs to say hello, and she was actually civil to me."

"Maybe nearly dying scared some sense into her."

"We'll see how long it lasts." Joanna winked as she reached for her coat and handbag. "See you same time tomorrow."

Occupied with buttoning her coat and dredging her gloves from deep within a pocket, Joanna nearly ran into someone idling in the corridor. "Oh, excuse me—" She gasped. "Arthur?"

"Hi, Joanna." Arthur Spence leaned against the wall with his overcoat splayed open, hands stuffed casually into his pants pockets. "Thought you'd never come along."

Confused and apprehensive, Joanna edged toward the opposite wall. "How did you even know to find me here?"

"Like I said before, running into you at the bakery seemed like fate, so I asked around and found out you worked the night shift. Please don't be mad. I had to take the chance."

"I thought I made it perfectly clear. I'm *not* interested in revisiting the past."

"Don't shut me out, Jo." Arthur turned up the charm with his twinkling blue eyes, a pleading smile curling his lips. He reached for her hand. "We had something once. You believed in me. We believed in each other."

At his touch, she dropped the glove she held. Her hand slid into his with sickening familiarity, and feelings long suppressed but never forgotten rippled through her abdomen. She tried to wrench her hand away, but he held on tight, an eerie intensity filling his gaze.

"I need you, Jo. Please . . ."

"Don't do this, Arthur. What we had is over, and the only thing I feel now is regret. We were only kids—misguided kids about to make the biggest mistake of our lives. If I hadn't come to my senses—"

"Yeah, you were always the sensible one." Arthur shook his head, one finger tracing the outline of her chin. When she shivered, he clenched his jaw and inched backward. "I'm not handling this well. I need to explain."

"Yes, please do explain why you insist on insinuating yourself into my life *now*, of all times."

Collapsing against the wall, Arthur palmed his eye sockets while he heaved a jagged breath. When he faced Joanna again, all traces of bravado had vanished. Instead, he looked tired, broken, distraught. "I've made some lousy choices. I gotta find a way to fix things."

She eyed him warily. "What are you talking about?"

"I got involved with—" Voices at the other end of the corridor distracted him. Taking Joanna by the shoulders, he shifted her around, giving his back to the intruders.

The motion threw Joanna off balance, and she groped for Arthur's arms to keep herself upright. The voices behind him faded, and once again they were alone, yet he didn't release his hold. With her face just inches from his, she felt the heat of his breath against her cheek. His deep blue eyes bored into hers, and she sensed his desperation . . . then his desire.

His mouth lowered tenderly upon hers, stunning her so completely that her knees buckled. She shoved her arms upward and pushed against his shoulders, but the action only seemed to encourage him. He groped beneath her coat, his hand like a firebrand against her back as the kiss grew more demanding. She clawed at his lapels, hardly able to breathe as she fought to break away. Nauseated and angry, she resisted until she couldn't fight any longer. As the kiss subsided, only the strength of his arms kept her from sliding down the wall.

When a tear slid down her cheek, he captured the wetness with one finger. "Aw, Jo, I'm sorry. I never meant—"

"Of course you did," she responded huskily. "It's what you wanted ever since you saw me in Kittelberger's."

"No, you're wrong! It's just, being so close to you, I couldn't help myself—"

"You never could." Joanna made a feeble attempt to straighten her clothes. "I'm sorry for you, Arthur. You're still the lecherous, manipulative, self-centered kid you were in high school."

Releasing a moan, he planted one palm on the wall beside her head. "I'm trying to change, Jo. You gotta believe me."

"Yes, I can see how hard you're trying." Her tone dripped sarcasm. "After you've just manhandled me—not to mention those awful rumors you once spread about me—why should I believe a word you say?"

"You shouldn't. But I'm asking you to, anyway. Help me, Jo. Be the one person in my life who doesn't judge and condemn me based on past mistakes."

The urgency in his tone touched something deep in Joanna's heart. Didn't she want the same for herself—to leave her mistakes behind and be accepted for the person she was today? Taking a long, slow breath, she stated, "All right, you have my attention. What exactly do you want from me, Arthur?"

"If all I can have is your friendship, I'll settle for it." Timidly, he reached up to touch her cheek, and she glimpsed the anxious hope in his eyes. "I've been trying to tell you, Jo, I'm in serious trouble. Just let me talk to you."

Heaving a resigned sigh, she nodded. "Not here, though. Come to my house and we can talk in the kitchen. But you'll have to leave before Jack and Lily wake up."

L♥

Thomas had seen enough. More than enough. Stomach in knots, he slipped around the corner and out the rear door of the Arlington.

What a fool he'd been! No wonder Joanna had insisted he no longer see her home after the night shift. And he'd thought her so chaste and honorable, protecting them both from temptation.

Obviously, she'd been saving herself for another kind of temptation. Thomas's mother, Fannie Hegney, and everyone else who'd tried to warn him about Joanna's loose ways had been absolutely right.

He leaned against the fender of his car and sucked in cold, noisy breaths. While his heart hardened in his chest like a chunk of glacial ice, his shuttered eyelids burned with the vision of Joanna melting into the arms of Arthur Spence. Kissing him, caressing him, gazing up at him with the fiery passion of long-lost lovers reunited.

God, why? Why let him fall in love with a woman who'd never be his? He'd risked everything for Joanna's love, even walked away from his career in hopes of becoming the adventure-seeking, free-spirited man she could fall for.

The kind of man Arthur Spence was and always would be.

So much for believing Joanna had changed and was ready to settle down. Maybe she'd been using Thomas all along, first to get a job, then for the pretense of respectability. If a man like Thomas Ballard courted her—someone from among Hot Springs' elite—how could anyone doubt her good character?

Blast it all, why hadn't he listened to the warnings? He'd have saved himself all this heartache.

Climbing into the Jeffery, he yanked the door closed and gave the steering wheel a hard whack before starting the motor. If Prohibition hadn't closed all the saloons, he'd have stopped for a drink—or four or five—and drowned his sorrows. He couldn't even resort to Mother's stash of brandy in the liquor cabinet, thanks to Marguerite's purging of all things alcoholic from the house.

So it was home to the bed he'd so eagerly crawled out of an hour ago, still thinking happy thoughts about the dinner and conversation he'd shared with Joanna the evening before. Even their short visit with Mother had gone well, and after Joanna left for work, Thomas realized how desperate he was never to be parted from her. His return to D.C. to be with Gilbert still lay on the horizon, and he got to thinking if Joanna would marry him right away, she could give notice at the Arlington and accompany him on the trip. The situation with Lily seemed to be under control—surely Jack could handle things on his own for a few weeks. His plan seemed so perfect, so right . . .

Until the moment he'd seen the woman he adored in the arms of her erstwhile lover.

Slipping soundlessly upstairs to his room, he stripped off his tie and dress shirt, then kicked off his shoes and flopped onto the mattress. He knew he wouldn't sleep, not with the images scalding his brain. Not with the unshed tears clogging his throat.

Finally, the gray light of dawn filtered through his bedroom curtains. Groaning, he heaved himself out of bed and padded to the bathroom. One look in the mirror destroyed any illusions he could hide his misery from his mother or the household help. Disheveled hair, purple blotches under red-rimmed eyes—maybe he could claim he was coming down with something.

Only then Mother would worry and Marguerite would fuss. He splashed his face with cold water, then ran a comb through his hair and decided he looked marginally better. He'd shaved at two o'clock in the morning, just so he could kiss Joanna without scratching her delicate skin when she joyfully accepted his proposal.

Returning to his room, he donned a clean shirt and slipped on his shoes. Ready or not, he had responsibilities. Life marched on, even with a broken heart.

Marguerite met him at the top of the stairs. Narrowing her gaze, she reached up to pinch his chin between her thumb and forefinger. "If I didn't know better, I'd think you been out carousin' all night at some speakeasy." She sniffed his breath as if to convince herself. "All right, Mister Thomas, I can see something's wrong, so you best 'fess up right now before I drag it out of you."

The unbearable reality of his situation drilled through his abdomen. He couldn't stifle a grimace. "If I tell you, will you promise to keep it from Mother for the time being? She doesn't need anything upsetting her."

Marguerite set her arms akimbo. "Ain't nobody gonna be more upset than me if you don't tell me what's going on."

"It's over," he forced through clenched teeth. "Joanna and I are through."

"You can't mean it!"

"It's true. I completely misjudged her. She isn't the right woman for me." Thomas started downstairs.

"Oh, no, you don't!" Seizing his arm, Marguerite jerked him around. "I've seen with my own eyes how happy Miss Joanna made you. You better have a real good reason for letting her go."

"Rest assured I do." Once more, the image of Joanna in Arthur Spence's embrace blazed through Thomas's mind. In as few words as possible, and making sure his voice didn't carry farther than the two of them, he told Marguerite what he'd seen.

She pressed a hand to her mouth. "Oh, Lawdy! I don't want to believe it!"

"How can I can deny what was right before my eyes?" Shoulders drooping, Thomas drew a shaky breath. "All things considered, I think it best if I return to D.C. as soon as possible. Between you and Mrs. Gray, Mother is in good hands, so I'll be of more use to Gil than I am here."

"Maybe you shouldn't rush off too soon. You and Miss Joanna could try to work things out."

"I don't see how, when it's perfectly clear she was only using me." He steeled his spine. "Some people never change."

✑❤

People could change, and Arthur Spence was living proof.

After seeing him out the back door, Joanna returned to the kitchen table and the cup of coffee she'd allowed to grow cold while he spoke. He'd begun by confessing his involvement with bootleggers and his futile attempts to convince Thomas's brother to join him. Only after he learned of Gilbert's accident—which Arthur swore he had nothing directly to do with—did he realize how dangerous a business he'd gotten himself into. He'd high-tailed it back to Boston hoping to put the past behind him, only to find himself cornered by a guilty conscience.

"When I heard from my parents that Gil could have been killed, I was sick," Arthur had explained as they sat together in the quiet kitchen. "It's taken me much longer than it should have to come home and face my part in this, but now I'm scared to come clean with Gil and his family. What if they don't believe me? What if they press charges? I want to make amends, Jo, but if it means going to jail—"

She'd tried to reassure him neither Gilbert nor Thomas was vindictive, explaining a surgeon had recently begun procedures with the potential to restore Gilbert's mobility. "But whether the Ballards or the police believe you or not, what matters most is getting yourself right with God. He has already forgiven you, and He will give you the strength to face whatever your future holds."

She'd spoken those words to encourage Arthur, but also because she needed so badly to believe them for herself. Alone now, she lowered her head and wrapped her fingers around the cold coffee cup while praying a silent prayer for her own forgiveness. Had she done enough to atone for her lack of compassion for her mother, then deserting her family? Would she ever be able to make up for turning Walter away when he needed her most?

"Jo?"

She looked up to see Lily standing over her and coaxed her lips into a smile. "Up already? Let me get breakfast started."

Lily adjusted the sash of her plaid flannel robe. "You look awful. Have you even gone to bed?"

"I . . . I had some thinking to do." Not a lie. Joanna pushed away from the table and lit the burner under the coffeepot. It would be strong enough to stand a spoon in by now, so she added a little water.

"Then go get some sleep. Jack and I can fend for ourselves." Lily brought the oatmeal from the pantry.

Jack appeared in the doorway, dressed for work in all but his coat and tie. "What's this about fending? You're not going to make me cook again, are you?"

"Jo hasn't been to bed yet. I'll fix oatmeal, if you'll make toast."

Joanna felt her brother's eyes on her as she poured her cold coffee down the drain. "I'll get some sleep later. Sit down, Jack."

Relieved when he didn't argue, Joanna helped Lily finish making breakfast, though she ate little herself. When Lily went upstairs to dress for school, Jack cornered Joanna at the sink.

"Lily mentioned something yesterday," he began tentatively. "You never told me Arthur Spence was the boy you ran away with."

Surprised he'd bring up Arthur's name, Joanna nearly dropped the bowl she was about to rinse. "It wasn't a secret." She coughed a harsh laugh. "Half the school knew."

"Guess I wasn't paying attention."

"You were a kid. I didn't expect you to."

Jack poured coffee, took a sip, then made a face. While stirring in cream and a big spoonful of sugar, he shot Joanna a sideways glance. "You'd tell me if Spence is bothering you again, right?"

She leaned her hip against the counter. No sense hiding the truth. "I've seen him, yes. It was upsetting, but I'm convinced he's trying to straighten himself out." She wouldn't say more. It was Arthur's place to reveal his connections with whoever caused Gilbert's accident.

"I trust your judgment, but . . ." Jack fixed her with a worried frown. "Promise me you'll be careful. I'm not your *little* brother anymore. If you need me, I'll be there for you."

Touched by Jack's concern, Joanna drew him into a hug, not for the first time noticing the solid feel of his muscled arms. It was comforting to know she had the love of not one but two strong, dependable men who'd do anything to protect her.

Thinking of Thomas, she smiled. They'd had such a lovely dinner together—so lovely that she'd been reluctant to leave for the hotel. Thomas clearly hadn't wanted her to go, and right up until the moment he saw her to her car, she had the strangest sense he wanted to ask her something but couldn't quite find the words.

Maybe this morning he would. As soon as she'd shooed Jack and Lily out the door, she went to the telephone and rang up Thomas's number. Fatigued as she was, she longed to hear his voice before she crawled under the covers.

The telephone rang several times before Marguerite answered. Stifling a yawn, Joanna asked for Thomas.

"He, um . . . he's tied up right now. Real busy. Can't talk." The housekeeper sounded unusually edgy.

"I hope Mrs. Ballard isn't worse."

"No, Miz Ballard is doing real well." A scratchy noise sounded in Joanna's ear. Marguerite cleared her throat loudly. "I gotta go, Miss Joanna. I'll tell Mister Thomas you rang."

The phone went dead.

L♥

Marguerite seared Thomas with a glare as she hung up the study extension. "Don't you *ever* ask me to lie for you again!"

"You didn't lie. I *am* busy. Very." Thomas thumbed through the stack of mail he'd been sorting.

"Yeah, adding to your stamp collection. I've seen grass growing that looked busier than you."

So this was what he got for encouraging the staff to speak their minds. Taking a moment to compose himself, Thomas folded his hands atop the desk. "I appreciate your concern, but there's no going back." His voice faltered, and he stared at his hands. "Anyway, I . . . I don't even know what I'd say to her."

"How about, 'What exactly's gotten into you, missy? Why'd you want to throw away the good thing we had?' You could try that for starters."

Torn between laughing and crying, Thomas only shook his head. Tiredly, he pushed up from the desk. "I'll be out for a bit. I need to go to the depot and purchase my ticket to D.C."

Marguerite blocked his exit from the study. "No need to be in a hurry, is there? Mister Gilbert's in no rush for you to get back, and anyways, your mama will be glad to have you around awhile longer."

"I thought I'd leave Monday morning. It will give me time to make sure everything is in order here. I have an appointment with Martin Greenslade later to arrange for him to handle Mother's financial affairs until further notice."

"Sounds like you don't plan on comin' home anytime soon." The housekeeper thrust out her lower lip.

Thomas closed his eyes briefly. "My plans are indefinite at best."

"Humph. Seems to me if you'd made your plans a little more *definite* weeks ago, you might have kept your sweetheart from straying."

"Marguerite—" Thomas stifled an angry retort. Was it his fault Joanna couldn't curb her more *adventurous* impulses? She was the one who for so long had held back from a deeper relationship. And now he knew why. A woman like Joanna could never be satisfied with dull, boring, stick-in-the-mud Thomas Ballard.

Mustering every last ounce of politeness, he gave a curt nod and excused himself. If not for the need to be close at hand for his mother, he'd spend the remaining time before his departure at Gilbert's farm. At least out there, he wouldn't have to listen to Marguerite's harangues—although once Mary found out, she might be equally vocal with her opinions.

Might as well face it—he was surrounded by plainspoken women.

Unfortunately, the one woman whose honesty he most needed had proven false.

25

$\mathcal{T}$homas was avoiding her—Joanna had no doubt.

She hadn't seen or spoken to him since their dinner last Tuesday, and every time she telephoned his house, one of the staff informed her he was "out" or "unavailable."

She'd served in the Signal Corps long enough to recognize code words when she heard them. Thomas's message couldn't be clearer: *It's over. Don't call me again.*

But why? What had she done? Things had gone so well over dinner that evening.

Joanna couldn't help remembering the voices she'd heard while Arthur had her cornered in the Arlington corridor. What if someone had noticed them—worse, seen Arthur's kiss? If word had gotten back to Thomas, it would explain his sudden coolness toward her.

All the more reason she must find a way to speak to him and explain.

Except she'd promised Arthur she wouldn't say anything until he'd had a chance to come clean on his own—which he'd better do soon, or Joanna would have to take matters into her own hands.

At the least, she could telephone Arthur and insist he tell her where things stood. It was just after 10 p.m. and the switchboard remained quiet for now, so after making sure no one from the front desk listened in, she rang up the Spence house.

"I wish you hadn't called me at home," Arthur rasped. "My parents won't be happy to know I've seen you again."

Joanna bristled, her tone equally hushed. "How do you think *my* family would react to knowing you practically forced yourself on me the other night?"

He exhaled sharply. "I told you, I'm sorry. If I could take back the moment, I would."

"The thing is, I'm afraid someone may have seen us and told Thomas. He won't accept my calls."

Arthur cursed under his breath. "The last thing I wanted was to ruin things for you."

"Then you need to contact him yourself and explain. Putting this off isn't going to make it any easier."

"What am I supposed to do—simply march up to the Ballards' front door and ask to be invited in for tea?"

"I see your point." Trying to think, Joanna massaged her temple. "Tomorrow's Sunday. Thomas usually attends worship at Ouachita Fellowship. He can't easily ignore you there."

Arthur remained silent for a moment, then released a rueful laugh. "Clever girl. What better place to make confession than in church?" He paused before asking hopefully, "Will you be there?"

She'd debated the question herself. If Thomas refused her telephone calls at home, seeing him at church could turn even more awkward. What if he didn't accept Arthur's explanation and apology? What if he didn't believe her account of what happened in the Arlington corridor? What if he believed she had given herself to Arthur all those years ago in St. Louis as the high school rumors claimed? And Thomas must secretly doubt she could possibly have returned from France and her engagement to Walter with her virtue intact. Was it any wonder he'd assume the worst of her now?

Then into her thoughts came the first line of the psalm Pastor Yarborough read in church last Sunday: *In thee, O Jehovah, do I take refuge; Let me never be put to shame: Deliver me in thy righteousness.*

A loving, forgiving God would not allow the shame of her youth to destroy her chance for happiness now. Somehow she'd make Thomas understand.

"Yes, Arthur, I will be at church in the morning. We'll talk to Thomas together."

A stuttering sigh sounded through the telephone line. "You honestly think he'll listen?"

"He's a good man. I know he will."

Drawing a chair next to his mother's bed, Thomas clicked his tongue. "You've barely touched your breakfast. If you want to get your strength back, you need to eat."

She wrinkled her nose. "Marguerite's farina is so bland. What's wrong with biscuits, buttered eggs, and sausage patties?"

"You heard Dr. Lessman's advice. Rich foods are not what's best for you." Thomas unfolded the newspaper he'd carried in with him. "Shall I read to you while you eat?"

A grimace accompanied his mother's next bite. She glanced at the bedside clock, then feigned a gasp. "Dear me, look at the time! You must leave immediately, or you'll be late for church."

"Trying to get rid of me?" Crossing his legs, Thomas flapped the newspaper pages and pretended to be engrossed in an article. "Since Mrs. Gray has the morning off, I thought I'd stay home and keep an eye on you."

"Marguerite is perfectly capable," his mother said with a sniff.

He peered over the paper to watch her dip the tip of her spoon in the bowl. Another grimace followed. He ignored it and continued reading.

"I haven't heard you mention your sweetheart lately," his mother said lightly. "I would hate to think you are sacrificing time with Miss Trapp on my account."

"Nothing of the sort. We've both been . . . busy." Doing what, he'd rather not imagine.

"Darling." Thomas's mother reached across the space between them and pushed down the newspaper. "Go to church. Have a lovely lunch with your young lady. I shall be perfectly fine here until you return. Besides," she added with a mischievous gleam in her eye, "since I can't go to church myself, how else am I to keep up with the latest gossip?"

The last thing Thomas wanted was to risk running into Joanna at church. But if he admitted as much to his mother, he'd have to explain why, and then he'd never outlive the I-told-you-so's. Mother might pretend, for his sake, to have accepted Joanna, but Evelyn Ballard would also be the first to celebrate the end of the relationship—especially if Fannie Hegney ever revealed what she knew.

Thomas certainly wasn't celebrating. However, he owed it to himself, if not Joanna, to let her know exactly how badly she'd hurt him. Church may not be the ideal venue for such a confrontation. On the other hand, it might be the best setting to assure neither of them said or did anything they'd later regret.

"All right, since you're so insistent, I'll go to church." Shoving up from the chair, Thomas refolded the newspaper and tossed it onto the seat. With a wry glance, he added under his breath, "I just hope you appreciate the gossip I bring home today."

He purposely took his time getting ready. No sense arriving any earlier than necessary. If he had to face Joanna, he'd rather do so after an hour of Scripture readings, preaching, and prayer.

Enough mistakes had been made. He didn't need to add to them by failing to put God first.

Even if Joanna seemed intent on breaking every commandment along with his heart.

Arriving at church, however, he wasn't prepared to find her shivering under the portico and looking as beautiful as ever.

"Hello, Thomas." Joanna smiled up at him, though her eyes shimmered with profound sadness. "I almost decided you weren't coming."

He tried to keep his expression passive. Hearing organ music and singing coming through the closed doors, he gave his watch a pointed glance. "Excuse me, I'm late for worship."

"Thomas." Her hand came down upon his arm. "Five minutes. It's all I ask."

So much for preparing himself with prayer. A quick one would have to do. *Lord, help.*

Steeling himself, he faced her squarely. "I can't imagine what you have to say to me. In fact, I'm surprised to see you here at all."

"Here? You mean at church?" Joanna lifted her chin. "I thought this was a place for forgiven sinners."

Bitterness boiled up inside him. "Then you admit you've sinned."

"Haven't we all?" Her expression softened, then became pleading. "Whatever you think you know about me, believe I love you. I never wanted to, never planned to, but there it is. And though I have no right to ask, I need you to trust me one more time."

The music swelled, then ceased. Pastor Yarborough's firm voice resounded in the opening prayer.

Thomas looked longingly toward the closed doors. "And why would I trust you now?"

Footsteps sounded on the steps behind him. "Because she's telling the truth."

Thomas swung around, sucking in a breath as he came face-to-face with Arthur Spence. Pulse hammering, he balled his fists. "You!"

"Just listen, Thomas. Let me get this off my chest. Then, if you're so inclined, you can haul me to the police station and press charges."

"I should anyway, after what you did to my brother."

"It wasn't me. I mean—" Arthur's face contorted. He clawed the back of his neck. "I made a terrible mistake. Lots of them, in fact."

As Arthur poured out his story of how he'd gotten involved with the bootleggers, then tried to rope Gilbert into partnering with him, Thomas seethed. All because of Arthur, Thomas's brother had nearly died, and now faced even more surgeries along with excruciating physical therapy just to regain some semblance of a normal life.

Then, unbelievably, Arthur swore he'd had nothing to do with the vandalism at Gilbert's farm—setting the horses loose, upending the beehives—retaliation for Gil's refusal to let Arthur and his cohorts set up their stills in the backwoods of his property.

"When I found out what they'd done, I went crazy with guilt." Arthur's lips quavered. "Gil was my friend. I never wanted to see him hurt."

Thomas ground his teeth together. "So you just ran back to Boston with your tail between your legs?"

"I was scared. I knew no one would believe me, and I didn't want to go to jail."

Chest aching, Thomas turned away. How was he supposed to take this all in? More importantly, why should he believe anything this man said?

"There's one more thing," Arthur stated. "You have to know there's nothing between Joanna and me. Whatever anyone might have seen, whatever you may have heard—"

"Don't." Shooting a glance first at Arthur, then at Joanna, Thomas shook his head. "I can't listen to another word. I don't know what to think anymore."

"Thomas—" A sob caught in Joanna's throat. She stretched out her hand to him.

Palms raised, he edged down the church steps. "Not now. I need some time."

✒

He didn't want to go home, and he most certainly wouldn't return to church. If anyone could help Thomas make sense of what he'd just been told, it was Samuel Vickary.

Chapel services at the Army and Navy Hospital were just ending as Thomas made his way through the building. He lingered in the hallway until the last of the patients and visitors had left the chapel.

"Got a minute, Padre?"

Samuel turned from extinguishing the altar candles. "Thomas! Always have time for you. What brings you by?"

Before his legs collapsed, Thomas sank into the nearest pew. "Maybe you'd better sit down, too. This could take a lot longer than a minute."

In fact, it took more like twenty minutes by the time Thomas relayed what Arthur had admitted, then confessed his doubts about Joanna's faithfulness.

A thoughtful look in his eye, Samuel straightened a hymnal in the pew rack. "So you believe Arthur, but not Joanna?"

"Yes—no—" Thomas groaned and palmed his forehead. "I just don't know anymore."

Removing the narrow white stole he wore while leading worship, Samuel methodically folded it and laid it beside him. "Here's the bottom line: Whether they're guilty or innocent, whether they're telling the truth or not, God doesn't give us permission to pick and choose whom we'll forgive."

"So you're saying I should simply forgive and forget? I shouldn't even care whether the woman I love is having an affair with another man—the man who, intentionally or not, bears some responsibility for the pain my brother is suffering right now?"

Samuel crossed his arms. "Did you come here for spiritual guidance, or for my blessing to sit in judgment?"

"Not fair, Sam. I'm just trying to sort things out."

"If anyone isn't being fair, it's you. If I heard you correctly, you grudgingly listened to Arthur's admission, but never gave Joanna a chance to explain what happened between them."

"What's to explain? I know what I saw." Unable to purge the image from his thoughts, Thomas slouched lower in the pew.

"Or what you *think* you saw. You said yourself the light was dim. And could you hear anything they said?"

"No, but . . . she obviously feels something for him. Why else would she be so concerned about clearing his name?"

Samuel sighed as he rose to his feet. "Perhaps if you asked *her* the question . . ."

"I know, I know." Thomas stood and followed Sam out of the pew, then paused in the aisle. "I'm leaving in the morning for D.C. Maybe if I let things cool for a while, we'd all be better off."

"Better off without the woman you love?" Samuel fixed Thomas with a solemn gaze. "Leave without clearing the air with Joanna and you'll be making the biggest mistake of your life."

When Joanna didn't join them at worship, Lily knew something was wrong. Joanna had told Lily and Jack she needed to wait out front for a friend, but then she never appeared. All through the service, Lily kept glancing over her shoulder hoping to see her sister coming down the aisle.

Even after worship, Joanna was nowhere to be found. Had she left with the friend she'd been waiting for? Lily fervently hoped the "friend" was Thomas, because he hadn't been in church either. For days now, Lily had suspected trouble between them, and she hated seeing her sister so sad.

"She'll turn up," Jack said as they strode to the car. "Bet she's home making lunch."

"Probably so." Lily doubted she sounded any more confident than her brother.

Opening the driver's-side door, Jack paused and reached for something on the seat. "Here we go. Jo left us a note."

Lily breathed out a quick sigh of relief. "What's it say?"

"'Need some time away. Don't worry about me. Love, Jo.'" Which each word he read, Jack's tone grew more hesitant.

Lily's throat closed. "She's leaving us again."

"We don't know for sure." Jack tucked her under his arm. "Anyway, she promised she wouldn't. She loves us too much."

A gust of wintry air nipped at Lily's wet cheeks. "When she first came home, I didn't want her here. But she's been more of a mother to me than Mama ever was. I don't know what I'd do without her."

"Same here, kiddo. So we've both got to stop worrying and have a little faith." Jack nudged her around to the passenger side. "Let's go home. She's probably already there waiting for us."

Drying her eyes, Lily obeyed, but it would take all the faith she could muster to believe Joanna hadn't packed her things and booked passage on the next ship back to France.

26

$\mathcal{T}$hank you for listening, Mrs. Kendall." Legs curled beneath her on her neighbor's sofa, Joanna dabbed her cheeks with a damp handkerchief. "You've always been such a sweet, caring friend."

Seated beside Joanna, Mrs. Kendall lowered her head. "Perhaps if I'd been a better friend to your mother years ago, things might be different today."

"Or if I'd been a better daughter . . ."

"Now, now, let's both stop wallowing in what-ifs. The Lord works *everything* together for the good of His children." Mrs. Kendall patted Joanna's arm. "So you can count on the Lord working things out for you and Thomas. Arthur Spence, too, bless his tortured soul. It's a blessing and a mercy he wants to straighten himself out."

Joanna sighed and glanced toward the front windows. An hour ago she'd seen the Dodge pull into the driveway across the street. Her cryptic note, combined with her absence from worship, must have raised all sorts questions for Lily and Jack. She only hoped she hadn't worried them too much. Lily may be doing better both in school and at home, but the girl's confidence remained fragile.

Rising, she straightened her skirt. "I've bent your ear long enough. I should get home."

"I'm here anytime, dear." Mrs. Kendall followed her to the door, giving her a warm embrace before helping her on with her coat. "My prayers will be flying toward heaven on your behalf, rest assured."

Coat collar turned up against the wind, Joanna smiled over her shoulder as she marched down the porch steps. Entering the kitchen at home, she'd barely shut the door when Lily shrieked her name and barreled in from the parlor. Lily tackled her in a frantic bear hug, nearly taking both of them to the floor before Joanna found her footing.

"Honey, honey, it's okay!" Joanna smoothed her sister's curls.

"I was so scared! I was afraid you'd gone back to France." Tears rolled down Lily's cheeks and soaked into Joanna's shoulder.

The depth of her sister's affection brought fresh tears to Joanna's eyes. She glimpsed Jack in the doorway and cast him a regretful smile.

Jack leaned against the doorjamb and crossed his arms. "Want to tell us where you've been?"

She would, if she could ever untangle herself from Lily. Planting a kiss on the girl's forehead, Joanna managed to step far enough out of reach to shed her coat. "I'll explain, I promise."

She didn't particularly want to rehash everything she'd just confided in Mrs. Kendall, but her brother and sister deserved to know. She only hoped Jack wouldn't fly off the handle when she brought up Arthur's name.

He controlled himself—just barely—as they sat around the kitchen table sipping hot cocoa while Joanna revealed what had happened over the past few days.

"If he's so intent on professing his innocence," Jack wanted to know, "why didn't he come forward right after Gilbert's accident? He might have helped the police nail the real culprits."

"He didn't think anyone would believe him." Joanna shot her brother an accusing frown. "Admit it. You wouldn't have. Anyway," she went on, stirring her cocoa, "according to Arthur, our police force isn't exactly above reproach. They've been known to turn a blind eye toward the bootleggers."

"How awful," Lily said. She scooted her chair closer and linked her arm through Joanna's, looking up wistfully. "But Thomas will believe *you*, won't he? Doesn't he know how much you love him?"

"I thought he did."

"I know Thomas," Jack insisted. "He'll come around."

Joanna wasn't so sure. Staring into space, she heaved a shaky breath as memories assaulted her. Arthur . . . Walter . . . Thomas. Each time, she'd thought herself truly in love. With Arthur, it had been youthful infatuation, followed by a rude awakening to his baser impulses. With Walter, their love became a fortress in the midst of war's death and destruction. But if Walter had survived, once the battlefields had emptied and the thrill of adventure gone, would their love have faded like a distant echo?

Now Thomas, a man of peace and quiet strength. He'd lured her back down to earth, taught her once again how to appreciate home and family and ordinary things. His love, his steadiness, his permanence—how could she go on without him?

"Oh, Jo." Lily pressed her cheek against Joanna's shoulder. "It'll be all right. Please don't cry."

Only then did she become aware of the tears dripping off her chin. Sniffling, she reached for one of the gingham napkins stacked at the end of the table and mopped her face. She smiled at her brother and sister with a watery gaze. "As long as I have both of you, I know I'll be fine."

"Don't pretend with me, son. I'm your mother. I know when my boys are unhappy."

Pacing in front of his mother's boudoir chair, Thomas avoided her penetrating gaze. After his confrontation with Joanna and

Arthur, he'd driven around for an hour, then returned home and slunk inside through the rear door hoping no one would notice.

Naturally, Marguerite read him like an open book. Though her self-preservation instincts kept her from probing too deeply, she'd done the next-best thing to force the truth from Thomas's lips—sent him upstairs with a tray of tea and sandwiches to share with his eagle-eyed mother.

And Evelyn Ballard wasn't about to give up. "You say you didn't attend church services after all. You haven't eaten a bite of Marguerite's lunch—though I can't blame you, insipid as her meals are these days. Now you're wearing a path in my imported Persian rug. You haven't moped this much since before your ill-fated decision to submit your resignation at the Arlington."

Cursing under his breath, Thomas sank onto the chair across from his mother. "Why is it, just when you think everything's going along swimmingly, something always comes along to knock the wind out of your sails?"

Mother cocked a brow. "I do believe that's a mixed metaphor, son. Didn't Mrs. Lawson teach you better?"

Thomas ignored the reference to his former high school English teacher, along with his mother's assessment of his grammar. He sat straighter. "You'll drag it out of me sooner or later—or else Marguerite will let it slip. So you may as well know. Joanna is out of my life."

"*What?*" She thrust a hand to her bosom. "Oh, Thomas, now what have you done?"

He looked at her agape. "What have *I* done?"

"Well, of course this must be your fault." While he struggled to catch up with her reasoning, she continued on. "Miss Trapp is a woman who knows her own mind, a woman with a strong work ethic and forward-looking ideals. I can't imagine she'd tolerate a man who'd walk away from a lucrative and fulfilling career and become complacent living off the largesse of his wealthy mother. And close your mouth, Thomas. You look like an imbecile."

"I'm not complac—" He bit down on the words, two fingers jammed against his temple. Who was this woman, and what had she done with his real mother?

Lips pursed, she fiddled with her lap robe. "And now I suppose you are going through with your plans to rush off to Washington tomorrow while leaving all this unsettled."

"There's nothing to settle." If only he believed as much. For the time being, at least, he'd continue to keep Arthur Spence's admission to himself. Once he got to D.C., he'd break the news to Gilbert and let him decide what, if anything, should be done with the information. Ultimately, the right to withhold or bestow forgiveness lay with Gil, but knowing how much his brother's faith had grown in the past year, Thomas imagined he'd be all too willing to extend grace.

So why can't you? You didn't even let Joanna explain.

But how could he, when every time he closed his eyes, he saw her locked in Arthur Spence's embrace? Why should he, when she'd let another man's lips claim hers so passionately?

Pulse throbbing, stomach churning, Thomas thrust up from the chair. He gave his mother a perfunctory kiss on the cheek. "I need to pack. I'll check on you later."

For the first time since Thomas resigned from the Arlington, Joanna felt relief she couldn't expect to see him there. Only the love of her brother and sister had gotten her through the rest of Sunday afternoon. They'd finally given up trying to convince her to drive over to the Ballard house and make Thomas listen to her. He was right—they both needed time.

Exhausted as she was from the emotional toll, having to report for work at the switchboard was a welcome distraction. For most of the evening and late into the night, enough calls came through to keep her mind off other things. During the quiet moments, she simply closed her eyes and silently repeated the Scripture Mrs. Kendall had reminded her of: *And we know that to them that love God all things work together for good, even to them that are called according to his purpose.*

Just when it seemed the last of the late-night carousers had crawled off to bed, the switchboard buzzed again. Joanna glanced at her watch as she reached for the plug—2:25 a.m. "Arlington Hotel. How may I direct your call?"

"Is . . . is this Miss Trapp?"

The voice was eerily familiar, yet completely out of context. "Yes, may I help you?"

"Joanna, dear, it's Evelyn Ballard."

Joanna's breath caught in her throat—first from surprise, then from anxious concern. "Are you all right? Is Thomas all right?"

The woman sighed audibly. "I'm afraid everything has all gone quite *wrong*. I'm sorry to bother you at this time of night, but I've been tossing and turning for hours trying to think of some way to fix things. I beg you, don't break Thomas's heart. You *must* give him another chance."

Joanna pinched the bridge of her nose. "I don't understand." Actually, she wasn't sure Mrs. Ballard understood. Slowly she asked, "What exactly has Thomas told you?"

"Not nearly enough, sadly. He said it's over between you." Her tone became shrill with urgency. "I know my son has his faults, but whatever he's done, surely you can forgive him and take him back. He needs—"

"Wait, you're asking *me* to take *him* back? He's the one who shut *me* out."

Mrs. Ballard grew silent, then gave a haughty sniff. "Why, that boy! If I weren't a recovering invalid, I'd thrash some sense into his backside."

In spite of herself, Joanna had to stifle a laugh, and it came out more like a whimper. "Oh, Mrs. Ballard, you don't know the whole story, do you?" Aware of the woman's health condition,

Joanna spoke carefully. "The truth is, Thomas saw me with . . . with an old boyfriend and wrongly assumed we still had feelings for each other. I tried to explain, but he wouldn't listen."

An unladylike snort sounded in Joanna's ear. "Isn't it just like a man? Well, then, you must simply *make* him listen."

"Perhaps in time—"

"But there *isn't* time! Don't you understand, my dear? Thomas has moved up his departure for Washington. His train leaves in only a few hours, and I'm afraid once he's away from here, he'll decide he has no reason to return—*unless you give him one!*"

Her troubles with Thomas aside, Joanna had to wonder what had come over Evelyn Ballard. "I must say I'm confused. I thought you'd be glad if Thomas and I stopped seeing each other."

"What a monstrous hypocrite you must think me to be!" Mrs. Ballard clicked her tongue. Her voice became more subdued. "I have committed many wrongs over the years, most of them to do with my sons' happiness. It took coming face-to-face with my own mortality to make me realize there is more to life than status and wealth." She chuckled softly. "Though wealth certainly has its advantages."

"I daresay." Joanna swallowed her growing surprise.

"What I'm trying to say is I'm through interposing my bias upon my sons' affairs of the heart. I raised them to be honorable men fully capable of making wise decisions in all areas of life. How can I not trust them to bestow their love upon equally honorable women?"

Joanna felt there must be a compliment in there somewhere. She brushed away a tear. "Thank you, Mrs. Ballard. But if Thomas has made up his mind to leave Hot Springs, what makes you think I can convince him to stay?"

"Because I know he loves you with all his heart. Be waiting at the station when he arrives. Don't let him go without a fight."

Thomas may as well have caught an earlier train, considering how little sleep he'd gotten. All night long, he'd wrestled with his conscience over leaving without telling Joanna his plans—worse, without giving her the chance to explain what happened in the Arlington corridor with Arthur Spence. It didn't seem to matter that he'd never known her to lie to him before. He simply couldn't reconcile the woman in Arthur's arms with the woman he was once so determined would be his wife.

Driving the Peerless, Zachary brought him to the depot an hour before his 7:40 a.m. departure. A crisp January breeze whipped at his coattails as he stepped to the curb and waited for Zachary to lift his valise from the floorboard. Giving the chauffeur a farewell nod, Thomas trudged inside the building. At the window, he handed the stationmaster his ticket.

The white-haired man in the visored cap studied the paper. "Sorry, Mr. Ballard. This ticket's no longer valid."

"What? But it's bought and paid for." Thomas had no time for such nonsense. He plopped a clenched fist onto the counter. "What's the problem?"

Someone came up behind him, speaking into his left ear. "I'm the problem."

At the sound of Joanna's voice, Thomas's heart plummeted to his toes. He turned with pained slowness, while his mind raced to form a response.

He had none. Instead, he found himself drowning in the depths of determined brown eyes. Her messy, straw-colored hair tumbled about her shoulders, and beneath her wool coat she wore the same travel-worn beige suit she'd had on the first time he saw her in church last fall. A small suitcase rested at her feet.

Somehow, he managed to swallow past the tightness in his throat. "Going somewhere?"

"I've heard D.C. is pretty this time of year. If you like snow."

"Joanna . . ."

Her mouth quirked into a provocative grin. "Aren't you the least bit curious why your ticket isn't valid?"

His gaze shifted toward the ceiling, and he held back an irritated sigh. "I'm sure you're about to tell me."

"Because I just paid a small fortune to book our seats together. There's only so far you can go on a train to avoid me, and I figure by the time we get to Washington, I'll have had plenty of time to make you believe how deeply I adore you."

He should tell her straight out what a ridiculous and utterly hopeless plan this was. He should return to the stationmaster and insist he honor Thomas's original ticket. He should—

He should forget his stupid, selfish pride and thank the Lord above for sending a stubborn, forthright, adventure-loving woman like Joanna into his life.

"Aw, Jo . . ." He cradled her face between his palms, his gaze drifting to her softly parted lips. Was that a self-satisfied smile creeping up the corners of her mouth? Well, he'd simply have to kiss it away.

When their lips met, a shiver coursed through her body, and she melted against him. He tasted the salty wetness of her tears and pulled away, stroking aside an errant lock of her hair. "My darling, why are you crying?"

"For all the memories. The ones we've made already, and the ones we'll make after you marry me in D.C."

"Marry you—" Laughter bubbled up in Thomas's chest, and suddenly nothing else mattered except kissing her again and again and again. He didn't pause for breath until the third blast of the train whistle.

"We're going to miss our train," Joanna murmured against his cheek.

With one last kiss, he tucked her beneath his arm and guided her onboard. After they found their seats and settled in, he shifted to gaze at her with disbelieving eyes. "You'd marry me, even when I'm jobless with no idea what the future holds?"

"I've been thinking a lot about our future." She lifted an eyebrow. "I think it's time for some new adventures."

The train car lurched forward, along with Thomas's heart. "What exactly did you have in mind?"

Joanna's smile turned wistful as she squeezed his hand. "I thought perhaps with your business sense and my connections in France, we could start a foundation for war orphans."

Warmth spread through his chest, along with a growing sense of rightness and purpose. Whatever the future held, he couldn't imagine facing a moment of it without Joanna, and he couldn't wait to discover what new adventures lay ahead.

A Note from the Author

Our family's first taste of Hot Springs, Arkansas, was in the early '80s, an unplanned side trip at the conclusion of a summer sightseeing vacation. Not long afterward, my husband and I succumbed to the sales pitch for a timeshare condo on Lake Hamilton, and though at first we questioned our sanity, we've since had no regrets. We now enjoy a restful Hot Springs getaway almost every year.

Hot Springs is both a modern city and a step back in time. The earliest arrivals were probably Native American tribes, who used the invigorating thermal waters as part of religious ceremonies and health treatments. As word of the water's supposed medicinal properties spread, more and more visitors flocked to the area. By the mid-1800s, bathhouses began cropping up all along the foot of Hot Springs Mountain and became what is known today as Bathhouse Row. Called the "World's Greatest Health Sanitarium" in the 1917 edition of *Cutter's Official Guide to Hot Springs, Arkansas*, the city has thrived on its enduring reputation as a health resort.

Several books have been written about the history of Hot Springs, many of which you'll find in gift shops along Central Avenue. I was also delighted to discover the wealth of material amassed by the Garland County Historical Society, and I remain deeply indebted to the GCHS staff and volunteers for their research assistance. The early chapters of *Leo and Verne: The Spa's Heyday*, by GCHS volunteer Orval E. Allbritton (Garland County Historical Society, 2003) provided some of the local color for my novels, including the supposedly true story of the elephants drinking beer outside Jack Goodine's saloon in *Whisper Goodbye*.

GCHS also supplied me with city maps from the era, along with articles and photographs detailing the Hot Springs Army and Navy Hospital, which opened to patients in 1887 and featured prominently in *When the Clouds Roll By* and *Whisper Goodbye*. Several of the original buildings still remain, although in 1933, the Swiss chalet-style administration building was replaced by a more modern brick-and-steel hospital in the Spanish Revival style. In 1960, the military turned the facility over to the state of Arkansas. The imposing structure, now the Hot Springs Rehabilitation Center, continues to dominate the mountainside overlooking Reserve Avenue.

A key setting in all three novels, especially *Every Tear a Memory*, is the Arlington Hotel. Visitors to downtown Hot Springs today can't miss the regal yellow structure at the corner of Central and Fountain. Built in 1924, the current building is actually the third Arlington Hotel. The second Arlington, and the one described in my novels, was a 300-room Spanish Renaissance structure situated across the street on property that today is a small city park. The hotel was destroyed by fire in 1923. Other hotels mentioned in the books, including the Eastman and Majestic, were also real places. Though abandoned, the Majestic still stands at the corner of Whittington and Park. The Eastman, which was taken over by the military to provide bed space for returning wounded from WWII, was demolished shortly after the war.

Another historic landmark is the high school, and I'm especially grateful to GCHS volunteer Renee Lucy for providing me with so many helpful details. Located on Oak Street, the first senior high school burned in 1913 and was rebuilt the following year in the Late Gothic Revival style. Still in existence, the impressive red-brick facility served Hot Springs students (including President Bill Clinton, who graduated in 1964) until 2006. From 1917 until the late 1920s, high school football games were played in the infield of the Oaklawn Park horseracing track.

In researching the novels in this series, I also learned far more about World War I than I ever recalled from my high school history classes. The personal stories recounted in *Doughboy War*, edited by James H. Hallas (Stackpole Books, 2009), were both inspiring and humbling in their descriptions of battles, life in the trenches, shell shock, crippling physical wounds, and so much more. In the words of Civil War General William Tecumseh Sherman, and quoted by army surgeon Donald Russ in *When the Clouds Roll By,* "War is hell."

From *American Women in World War I: They Also Served,* by Lettie Gavin (University Press of Colorado, 1997), I gleaned many details about the Army Signal Corps and the women who served. These stories about the "Hello Girls" provided the background for Joanna Trapp's character. After General Pershing declared the French telephone system "atrocious," he asked the War Department to send over 100 French-speaking telephone operators to staff the Army switchboards. Each recruit was expected to purchase her own uniform, consisting of a dark blue wool jacket and matching skirt plus shoes, boots, hat, raincoat, overcoat, and undergarments (specifically, black sateen bloomers in case the wind should blow their skirts up), at a total cost of up to $500.

These brave women often served in dilapidated barracks where they could hear the roar of planes flying low overhead, see flashes of artillery fire in the distance, and feel the thunderous explosions. Even with danger imminent, the operators valiantly stayed at their posts, connecting fighting units with their commanders until ordered to leave. Therefore, it came as a bitter surprise to learn after the war that the army considered them civilians and ineligible for military benefits. A sixty-year battle with the U.S. government ensued, until finally the women were approved for veteran's status under the G.I. Bill Improvement Act of 1977. By then, there was only a handful of the 223 "Hello Girls" still alive.

Finally, for the avid historians who may have picked up my book, if you find any errors, please accept my apologies. I made every attempt to remain true to historical facts as I found them, but undoubtedly some mistakes slipped through. With certain elusive details, sometimes I had to rely on my writer's imagination. Above all, I wanted to tell a good story, and I hope I've succeeded. Thank you for going along for the ride.

Discussion Questions

1. Why do you think it was important for Joanna to visit the battle site where her sweetheart was killed? What are your thoughts about the modern term "closure"?

2. Describe Joanna in your own words. What do you admire about her? What are her weaknesses? Do you empathize in any way?

3. Joanna clearly resists returning home to Hot Springs, yet she feels an obligation to her brother and sister. Describe a time when you made a difficult choice to do the right thing. What was your strongest motivation—love, or duty?

4. What were your first thoughts when Lily is caught in the pastor's office after church? Why do you think she is "acting out" this way? Would you say your teen years were harder or easier than what Lily is going through?

5. Thomas struggles with feelings of inferiority because he was not medically fit to join his brother to fight in the war. For those who are not called to fight for their country, do you believe there is any less honor in serving on the home front? Why or why not?

6. Gilbert has come a long way since he returned from the war a wounded and bitter man. Do you believe God really can bring about such dramatic changes in a person? Have you experienced anything similar in yourself or someone close to you?

7. What is a reasonable length of time for grieving the loss of a loved one—or can we put time limits on grief? What kinds of circumstances can either shorten or lengthen the grieving process? Where do Joanna's experiences lie on the spectrum, and how would you comfort or counsel someone like her?

8. Compare Joanna's love of adventure with Thomas's need for stability and routine. Is it really possible to grow a lasting relationship between two people with such divergent personalities? What changes do you observe in each of them as the story progresses? Do you see these changes as positive or negative?

9. Describe the growth you see in Lily over the course of the book. What events helped or hindered her relationship with Joanna? Have you ever had a friend like Abby to stand by you through the rough patches while also holding you accountable?

10. Evelyn Ballard's heart attack seems to come as a wakeup call. Is her transformation from opinionated society snob to understanding and accepting mother believable? Has a health scare or other traumatic experience changed you or someone you know for the better?

11. Depression and mental illness were not nearly so well understood in the early twentieth century. Do you feel Joanna grew in compassion and understanding toward her mother as the story progressed? Have you or has someone close to you ever struggled with depression? What helped? What didn't?

12. Up until the end, Thomas isn't sure what he'll do with himself after resigning from the Arlington. How do you see Joanna's idea of establishing a foundation for war orphans as both an "adventure" and the meaningful work Thomas thrives on? What ups and downs do you envision in their future together?

Want to learn more about author
Myra Johnson and check out other great
Fiction from Abingdon Press?

Check out
www.AbingdonPress.com
to read interviews with your favorite authors, find tips
for starting a reading group, and stay posted on what
new titles are on the horizon. It's a place to connect
with other fiction readers or post a
comment about this book.

Be sure to visit Myra online!

www.myrajohnson.com
www.facebook.com/MyraJohnsonAuthor
www.seekerville.net

We hope you enjoyed *Every Tear a Memory*. If you missed *When the Clouds Roll By*, the first book in Myra's Till We Meet Again series, here's a sample from chapter one.

1

Hot Springs, Arkansas
November 11, 1918

If perfection existed this side of heaven, Annemarie Kendall had just achieved it.

A thrill dancing up her spine, she rotated the tall, tear-drop-shaped vase and examined it inch by beautiful inch. When she wasn't busy keeping books for the family pottery business or putting together Red Cross comfort kits for the boys serving in France, she found immense satisfaction in creating her own works of ceramic artistry.

Certainly not her father's preferred use of her time, as he'd told her often enough, but Annemarie aspired to more than utilitarian bowls, urns, and butter churns—the mainstay of Kendall Pottery. Someday . . . someday . . . visitors who came to Hot Springs for the baths would also take home a one-of-a-kind piece of her ceramic art as a lasting reminder of their stay in this scenic and charming city.

For the past few months, Annemarie had been experimenting with a crystalline glazing method, striving for the perfect blend of ingredients, timing, and technique. With this vase, she'd achieved her vision—a design reminiscent of a Ouachita mountain sunrise, the view she'd awakened to nearly every morning of her life here in Hot Springs.

Her smile widened, her cheeks warming with the glow of victory. Her ears hummed with imagined celebratory cheers—

Except the cheering wasn't coming from inside her head. Beyond the workroom walls, the sound grew louder, the eruption of excitement drawing Annemarie's attention from the vase she so tenderly cradled.

Suddenly the door from the adjoining factory slammed open. The vase slammed against the stone floor.

"Annemarie!" Her father blew into the room like a late-season tornado. "Annie-girl, have you heard the news?"

A thousand shimmering shards scattered at her feet, Annemarie barely comprehended his words. She stood frozen and held her breath—along with the shriek that begged for release.

One . . . two . . . three . . . four . . .

With a stubborn lift of her shoulders, she turned to face her father. What news could possibly have Papa—and the entire factory, so it seemed—in such a state of jubilation?

Unless . . .

"It's over, Annie-girl! The war is over!" Papa lunged toward her, his work boots grinding the pottery fragments to powder. He scooped her into his beefy arms and twirled her around the shop.

"What? *What* did you say?" Annemarie's heart slammed against her breastbone. She pounded her fists upon her father's thick shoulders until he released her. "Papa, is it true?"

"You heard me, girl! Kaiser Wilhelm has abdicated. They've signed the armistice. Our boys will be home before you know it!"

Head spinning, Annemarie stumbled backward and braced herself against a worktable. Tears choked her. She pressed the back of her fist against her mouth. Dear God, so much suffering, so many lives lost. How she'd prayed for this day—the Great War over at last! "Oh, Papa. Praise God!"

"Praise Him indeed!" Papa enfolded her in his arms, with gentleness and care this time, and let her sob into his grimy muslin shirt that smelled of sweat and smoke and clay. "There, there,

Annie-girl, you're not the only lass weeping tears of joy this day. The Lord willing, Gilbert could be home by Christmas!"

Annemarie straightened and sniffed away her tears. Finding a handkerchief in her apron pocket, she dabbed at her cheeks with a trembling hand. "I almost forgot. A letter came this morning. I haven't even had a chance to open it."

"A letter from your sweetheart and you *forgot?*" Papa clucked his tongue.

Her happy smile faded. It pained her to admit the letters she'd so looked forward to this past year now evoked more distress than delight. She wrung her hands and swallowed the bitter lump of guilt. "I . . . I was working at the wheel when Morris delivered the mail. He said there was a letter from Gilbert, but my hands were covered with clay, and . . ."

Papa's disgruntled sigh spoke louder than words. His gaze slid to the pottery fragments littering the floor before he skewered Annemarie with a disapproving glare. If Papa weren't so anxious to learn the latest word from Gilbert, she'd surely be in for yet another lecture concerning the "abominable waste of time and money" spent upon her "art."

He was right, though. She had no business concerning herself with anything so frivolous when brave soldiers lay wounded or dying on the Western Front. She prayed the Lord's forgiveness for her selfishness.

"Well, go on, now. Get the letter and let's hear what our Gilbert has to say." Papa pushed the factory door closed and then plopped onto a stool and propped one elbow on the worktable.

Her face burning with remorse, Annemarie tucked in her chin and strode through another door to the front office. Sorting through the mail on her cluttered desk, she retrieved Gilbert's letter and hurried back to the workroom, careful to sidestep the broken vase. She would not mourn over pottery shards, not when Gilbert—her dear Gilbert, the boy she'd loved since childhood— would soon be in her arms again.

Letter in hand, she scooted a stool close to her father's. She slid a stubby, clay-stained fingernail under the envelope flap and tugged out the single page. The thin, cream-colored sheet crackled beneath her fingers as she unfolded the letter. As usual, the censors had already done their damage. Though as an officer Gilbert was particularly careful to avoid specifics, smudged ink and the occasional blacked-out word interrupted his spidery scrawl.

Smoothing the wrinkled page, Annemarie cleared her throat. "Shall I read it aloud?"

"Oh, no, no." Papa chuckled and waved a hand. "I'm sure it's full of personal stuff between you and your sweetheart. Just tell me the important parts—how he's mending, when he expects to ship home."

Annemarie stifled another frisson of worry. Wanting to shield both her family and Gilbert's from further concern, she hadn't shared how utterly *impersonal* Gilbert's latest letters had become—a coolness that had nothing to do with concerns over censorship. The letters he'd written as a West Point cadet, and even during the early months of his deployment to France, had been filled with declarations of love, how he strove every day not only to honor his father's memory but also to do both Annemarie and his country proud. It wasn't long, however, before the tone of his letters had darkened. While she knew he did his best to protect her from the ugliness of war, clearly he had been changed by it.

Then in August, word had arrived that Gilbert had been wounded. An artillery explosion had taken his left leg and shattered his left arm from wrist to shoulder. He'd nearly lost an eye and for eight days had feared permanent deafness. His first letters after evacuation to a French field hospital, dictated to the chaplain on duty, were terse and factual, which she'd attributed to the fact that Gilbert chose not to share too personally through a stranger.

Yet when he'd recovered enough to take up pen and paper himself, Annemarie could no longer deny the truth that lay beneath his deceptively courteous words. Her dear Gilbert, once bold and ambitious, full of life and love and great plans for their future, now seemed dispirited, desolate, defeated. Annemarie couldn't begin to fathom the horrors he'd endured, but surely with time he would recover both physically and emotionally. She prayed night and day for his healing—as well as for the strength within herself to stand strong at Gilbert's side as the wife he would need in the months and years ahead.

Slowly, determinedly, Annemarie perused the letter, dated Sunday, October 6. *"Still in the hospital . . . constant headache but some vision returning to my left eye. . . . They say I'm one of the lucky ones—if you can call it that. So many wounded, so many dead and dying. More every day. Will this blasted war never end?"*

Annemarie's heart broke to realize Gilbert had penned these somber words only weeks before the armistice. With trembling fingers, she brushed away a tear. Her father reached across the space between them and patted her knee as she silently read on. *"Waiting for the next transport home—possibly December. Don't know where I'll end up yet. Probably a military hospital somewhere like _____."*

The name was obliterated, but wherever it was, Annemarie would find a way to get there as soon as possible. She looked up with a hopeful smile. "He's getting better, Papa. He may be home next month! He says—"

The jangle of the telephone interrupted her. Papa hefted his bulk off the stool and hurried to the front office to answer. "Kendall Pottery Works, Joseph Kendall speaking."

Within seconds, Annemarie discerned the caller was Evelyn Ballard, Gilbert's mother, and it sounded as if she'd received a letter as well. Annemarie rushed into the office and hovered at her father's elbow, waiting to hear what news Mrs. Ballard's letter contained.

"Of course, we're as thrilled as you, Evelyn," Papa was saying. "What a homecoming that boy will have! Here, I'll let you speak directly with Annemarie."

A dark tress had worked loose from Annemarie's bun, and she tried in vain to tuck it back into place. The arrogant Evelyn Ballard, with all her wealth and sophistication, never failed to intimidate Annemarie. She could feel the woman's critical eye upon her even through the telephone line. Hesitantly, she accepted the earpiece from her father. "Good morning, Mrs. Ballard. It's wonderful news, isn't it?"

"Oh, my dear, it's simply the best! I've already made some calls, and thanks to my late husband's military connections, I've arranged for Gilbert to continue his recuperation at the Army and Navy Hospital right here in Hot Springs. We'll be able to visit him every day until he's discharged."

"Really? I'm so glad!" Annemarie drew her lower lip between her teeth. "How . . . how did he sound to you?"

Mrs. Ballard released a long and pain-filled sigh. "Oh, my dear, our poor lad has suffered so much. Of course, he is unhappy about his current state of disability and naturally concerned about the prospect of a lengthy recovery. But we cannot give up hope. We must encourage him in every way possible and keep him constantly in our prayers."

Fresh tears sprang into Annemarie's eyes. "Always."

"And once he's home and we set the wedding plans in motion, I'm sure it will lift his spirits even more."

Annemarie squeezed her eyes shut. "Perhaps we shouldn't rush him in that regard. He'll have so many adjustments to make."

"Yes, but keeping his mind occupied with happy anticipation of your nuptials will be the best medicine, I'm positive." Voices in the background drew Mrs. Ballard's attention for a moment. She came back on the line to say, "Sorry, I must ring off for now. But I'll have you and your mother over for luncheon soon, and we can start making plans!"

"Yes, well . . ." No use arguing with the woman—truly a force to be reckoned with. If Mrs. Ballard had been a general, the Allies would have won the war in a single day. Annemarie said good-bye and set the earpiece on the hook.

She pivoted toward the workroom, only to find her father had returned to the factory. Beyond the open door, she could hear his booming voice instructing the pottery workers to finish their current tasks and then take the rest of the day off in celebration of the armistice.

Annemarie's current task, unfortunately, was sweeping up the remnants of her shattered vase. She found a broom and dustpan and with each stroke sang a little song in her head: *My Gilbert is coming home soon!*

With a new lightness in her step, she made quick work of depositing the broken pottery in the waste bin.

Yes, perhaps it was time to put this dream to rest once and for all, because when Gilbert returned to Hot Springs, everything about her life was sure to change.